TWENTY FOUR THOUSAND

TWENTY FOUR THOUSAND

ALAN DENT

I wanted the moments of my life to follow one another
in orderly fashion, like those of a life remembered.
You might as well try to catch time by the tail.
Sartre.

Tangle with the Prince of Peace and you'll get a knife
in your back.
Orton.

PENNILESS PRESS PUBLICATIONS
www.pennilesspress.co.uk/books

Published by

Penniless Press Publications 2018

ISBN 978-1-913144-33-3

Cover: The Painter's Mother II – Lucie Freud

PREVIOUSLY PUBLISHED IN THE
ENTIRELY AVOIDABLE INSANITY SERIES

For my parents

Connie and Wilf

TOAST AND HONEY

Nearly two million were unemployed. Elsie Lang watched the Prime Minister hand over the keys of council houses to tenants on a London estate. She was alone with her anxiety. Her son hadn't come home from work. He hadn't warned her and she had food ready to heat, but he may have had to stay late and maybe had to go straight to a meeting or to join friends. She wished he was there so she could unload her agony. He was a great comfort to her because his essential principles were identical to her own. The disappointment she experienced in his renunciation of religion, which she blamed on the influence of *fancy ideas he got from books*, and his acceptance of the changed sexual mores (she knew virtually nothing about his intimate life but enough to be aware he wasn't a virgin), didn't diminish the pride and confidence she had in him as an enemy of injustice. If he were here, he would agree with her. He would have good arguments. He could reassure her. Her sense that the world she'd seen born, and believed in fervently, was being destroyed would be diminished. A coarser, harsher, more cruel, more vulgar, less compassionate, more fearful and unhappy culture was rising from the miasma of economic crisis, like some ghoul from primeval slime in a horror film.

She'd heard Labour was well ahead in the polls. Andy had said Thatcher would be a one-term Prime Minister because unemployment and recession would drag her down. If it was only five years, that wouldn't be so bad; and Andy had argued Michael Foot should take over as Labour leader, push its policies to the left, above all democratise the workplace, starting with the public sector. There was hope in that. Yet five years was a long time. She was fifty-eight. By the time another Labour government was elected she would be retired, living on a small pension, spending as much time as she could with her grandchildren and hoping for a new world of equality and peace for their well-being.

Perhaps Andy was right. He was educated. All the same, her instincts told her different. Something was changing. It was similar to 1945. Churchill, the country's hero, the great leader without whom, many said, Britain wouldn't have prevailed, couldn't turn the river of sentiment in his direction. She recalled his speeches, warning that a Labour government would mimic the Soviet Union, and she despised him. She knew little about Soviet history. As a young woman she'd felt great sympathy for what she believed was their effort to overcome inequality and their sacrifice in the war had been heroic and decisive. When the truth about Stalin came to light, she was horrified. From that moment, she extinguished her positive feeling for the regime. She'd always deplored its lack of democracy, but to discover its leader was nothing more than a brute and bully who treated other people as means to the end of his self-aggrandizement, made her hate him as much as she loathed glib Tories who spoke of the poor as if they were to blame for their poverty.

Something was changing. It was odd how the collective mood could sway like a tall poplar in a persistent wind. Argument seemed to make little difference. It wasn't so much the arguments of Attlee and Bevan which won the post-war election, it was a mood. She knew it herself. Surely everyone did. Her emotional condition would change without her knowing why. She would wake up in the morning feeling joyful and whatever she did that day felt light and pleasurable; then she would get out of bed a few days later feeling weary and at odds and she could find nothing in her day which didn't make her want to cry.

No matter how hard she tried to explain it to herself, her orientation remained. It was hers, but it was beyond her control. There was something like that going on in the political mood. It was a tide, but who could say where its moon was? Andy was a thinker. He read books and had clever ideas; but she knew. There was a sinister mood abroad and she feared it would take hold.

Britain was in recession, people couldn't find work. She knew how that could lead to the search for scapegoats and easy answers. She'd listened to her dad talk about the rise of Hitler. His much-repeated phrase still rang in her ears:

" 'E's climbin' to power on't backs o't th'unemployed."

She'd heard, in the thirties, people from her own streets, the hard-pressed communities of Talbot Road, Hartington Road, Good Street, Marsh Lane; people who earned enough just to get by in their two-up two-downs and who fed their children bread and dripping on the day before pay day, say the depression was all the fault of the Jews.

"'Ow many Jews are there in Preston?" she'd retorted.

She'd heard them spout what they'd culled from Mosley: the Jews controlled international finance; they were sly and greedy. They were in cahoots with the Reds. The country needed a strong leader who would put them in their place and make Britain a great power once more.

Elsie had an instinctive revulsion from *strong leaders* and *great powers*. She knew what they meant: the secret police at your door in the early hours and exploitation of poor countries by the rich enforced by guns and bombs.

When Churchill won in 1951, she was saddened. For a time she feared what had been achieved would be dismantled. Above all she was worried for the NHS. It soon became clear the Tories had no mandate to overturn Attlee's quiet revolution. After all, Labour had won more votes. In three elections they'd out-polled the Tories. Elsie felt it was a pity Attlee had sought an increased majority. Though Labour had an advantage of only a few seats, she felt it would have been wiser not to take the risk. All the same, not even Churchill dared to cut the guy ropes of the welfare tent and when MacMillan came to power it was clear the Tories had to accept that socialism had created the most popular institution in the land.

Now, on her television screen, a woman she perceived as vindictive, vengeful, snobbish, sunk in her self-glorifying ideology was selling off homes which had given people security and the chance of a steady, responsible life. She owned her home. It was a good house in a nice area. How much was it worth? Probably twenty-five or thirty thousand. She was a property owner surrounded by property owners. She knew why they voted Tory. She was glad she'd never lived in a council house and she would have liked to see a society where everyone could own their home. She knew it provided a sense of responsibility, but she knew also that when your income was small, it was a burden. She'd heard the Tory argument that Labour politicians were hypocrites, men and women who, many of them, owned more than one house: dogs in the manger; but that was a manipulation. The fact, a fact she had lived close to in the years of poverty when her parents could barely feed their children, was that without council houses, millions would have been homeless and the estates, though often unimaginative, sparse in amenities and blighted by the foolishness of herding families on low incomes, beset by the problems that engendered, were better than the jerry-built back-to-backs people were living in when she was at school.

Council houses were an emergency measure. The emergency was long. It was the emergency of inequality, of poverty which could shred people's hope and crush their morale more resolutely than drink, drugs or debauchery. She wasn't a hypocrite. She wouldn't have denied anyone the pleasant home she enjoyed; but she knew if her parents hadn't been exceptional people who on a minimal income knew how to establish a strict hierarchy of priorities and scrimped as they grafted to ensure their house, small and modest though it was, belonged to them, she might have needed a council house to protect her from the gutter.

Thatcher was smiling and intoning in that artificial enunciation which gave away her hollowness as she passed on the keys to a delighted couple. In that action, Elsie saw the collapse of the moderating influence which recognised the privilege, circumstance, aggression or sheer luck which elevated a few, could not be allowed to rule unchecked. Into her head came the image of people sleeping on the streets, of young adults still occupying the bedroom in their parents' house, of unscrupulous private landlords squeezing people into damp, dangerous insanitary flats and houses at strangling rents. It was bound to happen. The smile on Thatcher's face was the measure of her ignorance. She was an educated woman, but she was stupid in her instincts.

Elsie's mortification at what was happening politically intensified her loneliness. She felt her mind couldn't tolerate the invasion of overwhelming hurt. She wanted to rush out of the house and find someone to talk to, but who was there? Once, she had lived with neighbours who were of her kind and who were available. In the old days in Talbot Road, when she was a girl, and even after her marriage, there was always someone at their front door, or pegging out washing in the backs, or pushing a baby in a pram, who would share five minutes; and in those brief conversations, with Maggie Nightingale or one of the other congenial, working-class, Labour-voting folk, her mind was settled. The exchange of a few words deploring the actions in Kenya or celebrating free health care was like a drug which found its way infallibly to those centres in her brain which sparked her anxiety and low mood. Ten minutes a day could make the difference between calm and near-panic.

Who could she talk to now? None of her neighbours agreed with her. When the steelworkers had been on strike, she'd hoped for a victory which would gird the sense that working people had to be treated with dignity, but if the issue cropped up during a chat in the butcher's or over a hedge, all she heard was disdain for strikers and the claim they were traitors, lazy, over-paid, and in need of being taught a lesson. She lived in a nice house, but she had no friends. Property had brought her loneliness and she wished she was still in Talbot Road where she would surely find an easy, sympathetic ear.

When she went to bed, exhausted as always after her shift in the training kitchen and dreading the morning when she would have to force herself to her feet at six, be at her station for seven, sweat and strain in the heat till four and pad home weary in body and mind, sure there was something wrong with her and frustrated the doctor couldn't discover it, Andy wasn't in. She fell asleep quickly and dreamed of war. Thatcher, a twelve-inch cigar in her mouth, was riding in a tank declaring: "We'll fight them in Talbot Road." There was a blackout. She was in a bomb shelter. Her mother had her arm round her. Everyone was singing "There'll be bluebirds over…" Bert appeared in his RAF uniform, his big charming smile illuminating his young face. Anthony Eden was coming down the steps from an aeroplane, waving a slip of paper, declaring: "Peace in our time." There was a knock at the front door. She opened to Jack Jones who asked her if she would join the strike. Mau Mau came charging down Woodland Grove, spears in their hands. Soldiers appeared from nowhere and shot them to pieces. Patrick Jenkin was on the news. He announced the closure of the NHS.

She was awoken by the heavy closing of the front door. The disturbing images quickly ebbed from her mind. She looked at her alarm clock. Twenty-past eleven. That was late, and Andy had work in the morning.

Mary McIllwaine watched the same news broadcast as her mother and deplored as thoroughly the folly of ideological conviction driving out objectivity. At thirty-two she'd been living for five years in the four-bedroomed detached house Ted had built. Opposite was the field belonging to the farm in Back Lane so when she looked out of her living-room window or opened those in the front bedrooms to let the day in, she had a great sense of space, of not being hemmed in which, from time to time, made her think with a mixture of nostalgia and regret of the cramped, hard, concrete and brick of her first little home in Talbot Road. The village contained no more than a thousand. She got on with her neighbours as easily as a butterfly lands on a flower and knew virtually everyone well enough to ask about their children, their problems with the roof, their ageing parents, their trip to America, their recent spell in hospital, their new job. She helped with the Brownies, was on the church's fund-raising committee and one of the chief organisers of the annual village fair. Popular and praised because of her modest selflessness, everyone knew she could be turned to in a crisis or difficulty, as they recognised after a brief spell in her company that her mind was as clear of ulterior motives as the arctic of trees.

She disliked Mrs Thatcher with the kind of instinctive intensity with which she'd loathed Mr Kane. Just as she'd sensed something malicious in his character, behind his brisk, efficient manner, his smart dress, his tight demeanour and apparently beneficent smile, so she intuited a nastiness in Thatcher, an intent to raise herself by doing others down, the kind of purblind lack of awareness of the injury her words and actions caused typical of the vulgar, bullying girls she'd known at school and kept her distance from. She recoiled from what was being done politically, but she didn't experience the loneliness, anxiety and near-panic which seized her mother.

Her second son was twenty-seven months old. Patrick was at the village school round the corner. Her days were a blissful routine. Ted set off for work early and alone with her two boys she relished getting Patrick into his smart uniform and holding his hand while she pushed the toddler in his pushchair to the school gate where she chatted with the other mothers. She had the day's tasks worked out in her head and knew her timetable. She glanced at the clock and if she was five minutes behind in setting the house straight, hurried to meet her own imposed standard. When she brought Patrick home, she had a snack ready and within ten minutes of Ted coming through the door, the evening meal was on the table and the four of them sitting in the dining area which overlooked the garden, as Ted teased his eldest about school, and Luke banged his plastic cup as he uttered a stream of garbled sounds which were his contribution to the conversation.

"Yes," Mary would say, turning to him her eyes big and her smile wide, "that's right. You know, don't you? Yes, you do. You're a good boy, aren't you? Yes, that's right, little chap."

She had her responsibilities and she rose to them. There was no gap between what she wanted to do and what she was doing and therefore no opportunity for that condition given the generic term *stress* and which invariably means someone is having to struggle, *contre-coeur*, against what is forced on them. Not even Ted's remarks as they sat on the sofa side by side watching the news, the children in bed, the house in order, the kitchen as tidy as an accountant's desk, could trouble her essential contentment.

"Why shouldn't they buy their 'ouses?"

"Because they're getting them cheap and they're needed."

"Aye, but everyone wants to own their 'ome. Good for her, I say."

"I agree. Everyone who wants to should have the chance to own their home, but not by selling off what's been built to help people who can't get a start."

"We've done all right."

"I know, but not everyone is in the same position."

"I'm just a working man. If you work 'ard you can do it. We 'ad to save and I worked like a donkey to build this."

"Very good, but there are two million on the dole. It can happen to anyone."

" 'Asn't 'appened to me."

"You've been lucky."

"I've made my own luck."

"I'm not saying you haven't. You've worked hard, I know, but some people work hard and still get nowhere."

"Why should that 'old back them as do?"

"It's not a matter of holding people back, it's about helping people when they're in difficulty."

"That'll make 'em lazy, if they get summat for nowt."

"I don't agree. Look at my grandad. He wasn't lazy. He worked hard and he was frugal, but he was on the dole for years in the thirties."

"This in't thirties, luv. Folk don't get sent t't'workhouse. Eh, like Elsie thinks. Clogs and bread and drippin'. Them days is gone."

"Life's still hard for a lot of people. Think what it'd be like if you didn't have a job. How would we manage?"

"You'd 'ave to tek in washin' or go on't streets, luv. Eh?" he said nudging her and laughing.

"I wouldn't dream of either. Stop that, you fool. You know what it's like. There are people in Skem and Wigan who've lost their jobs since she came to power. It's no joke and it can happen to anyone."

"Not 'er," he said pointing to the screen.

"No, that's the problem. It's the people at the bottom who get punished."

"Aye, but where would we be bar't them at top? Them's the ones who know 'ow to run things."

"Maybe, but they don't run them well just because they're at the top, and anyway it's the work we all do that makes the wealth, so we should all benefit."

"We ? Eh, what work 'ave you done today, luv? Ironed a shirt and washed a plate and bin t't'shop? Eh, luv? I've bin on a roof all day maulin' wi' timber," he was nudging and laughing as he teased her.

She didn't mind. She liked that the day was winding down and he was creating a light- hearted mood before bedtime as a prelude to intimacy; but there was a hard grain of seriousness in the balm of his raillery: he did believe her life was easy, that looking after a house and children wasn't real work. He did set his own effort above hers and assume that sawing roof joists, hauling them up, nailing them in place, climbing the ladder twenty times in an afternoon was by definition real work which made a contribution to the country's wealth, while what she did was ineffectual and peripheral.

It offended her, superficially, that her work wasn't properly valued, but it couldn't trip her ankles because she was so sure in her feelings. It wasn't merely Ted who accepted without thinking the diminished value of the domestic; it was society's assumption. It annoyed her when she heard politicians, vicars, priests, bishops, lauding family values. It was sentimental and dishonest. By making raising her children her first priority she was denied an income, except for the trivial child benefit. Ted gave her enough for the shopping and to pay the bills, but she always had to ask. Putting the electricity bill in front of him in the kitchen and waiting two or three days for him to give her the cash was a small humiliation, a dependence she felt she shouldn't have to suffer. If she wanted to spend on herself, she either had to save from what the State gave her, or put her case to Ted. A new pair of shoes inevitably brought the usually teasing: did she know how many nails he had to hammer in to earn that much? He never denied her, but the simple fact of having to ask, like a beggar, was an irritation.

Ted made her an offer: if she wanted a bit of pocket money, she could clean the car every week. She rebelled at first, but reflecting on how little time it would cost and calculating what her frugality could make of the few quid, she relented, for a while. She would be polishing the bonnet when Ted would come out in his stocking feet, a little cigar in her fingers:

"Hey, you've missed a bit 'ere, luv. That's fifty pence docked from your pay," and he would laugh in that somewhat childish, slightly sniggering way he'd learned through his father's daily jossing with his mother and the mockery of boys who didn't fit in at school.

Mary set the money aside and bought herself an occasional skirt or cardigan, but more often she spent the savings on the children. After six months, sitting during a rare pause with a cup of tea and a biscuit, she reviewed what the arrangement had brought her. She was annoyed with herself for having accepted, and more with Ted for having offered. She was his wife not his employee. This was a partnership; but she knew he didn't see it as she did. He was adjusted to society's systems and had a curious sensitivity about his work and what he earned from it. While she'd been a conscientious employee, she'd never imagined her essential sense of self depended on what she took home at the end of the month. She thought the idea ridiculous. A job was just a matter of a contract. The employer paid the money and she did the work. There was no test of her intrinsic worth involved. She was too secure in her sense of self to permit such a notion to take hold; but she knew Ted defined himself in terms of his work and wage. As he had to build roofs and fix window-frames for his money, she should have to work too; and as he was the wage-earner, he was in a position to pay, so she must accept the power of money, just as he had to, every day, as he planed timber in his garage, climbed ladders, hung doors and cut floorboards.

She couldn't hide her disappointment from herself. She loved her husband. Had she been working and he at home with the children, she would have given him enough of her salary to be independent. She wouldn't have wanted him to have to ask. She knew he loved her, but his love didn't extend beyond society's stupidities. It was stupid to define yourself by money, to imagine that what you were worth to an employer defined your worth as a human being. All human beings were of equal worth. The rest was mere convenience. Yet, here, in her marriage, in the most intimate relation of her life, a contingent economic arrangement intruded and diminished the idealism of love.

As she went to run her cup under the tap, glancing at the clock and inwardly assessing the progress of her day, she thought of her brother. He was far-gone in his rejection of the current arrangements. She couldn't follow him. She was moderately annoyed that Ted didn't see there was no place for calculation in love, but it didn't make her rage against the system like Andy did. She wondered how he was getting on in his new job. He would probably visit less now, which she regretted. He had a good relationship with Patrick and she would like the same for Luke. She heard the child rouse from his nap and went to the stairs.

"Okay, Luke, mummy's coming, little one," as she went up her mood cleared and lightened and seeing the little boy standing in his cot his eyes heavy with sleep filled her with joy.

At that moment, Andy Lang was sitting in the staff-room whipping through a set of second-year exercise books. They were a good group, clever and hard-working and he had a good, let's-have-some-fun rapport with them. On the other hand, he'd been allotted 2Z, the low-ability group in the same year which had been taught by four French specialists in the previous year. One had a nervous breakdown, two resigned and the fourth was asked to move on. The pupils were convinced they were unteachable. One of them, Roger Baker, an unruly, intrusive, disturbed boy who had been in detention every week since his first day, declared loudly as Andy was bringing the class to order in his second week:

"We got four teachers sacked last year and we'll get you sacked too," at which twenty of the thirty boys began to jeer and bang on the desks.

They were just kids. Their behaviour hardly caused a ripple in Andy's mind, but he had to be cautious of the response of his superiors. He'd quickly appreciated their conformism. While he had come into teaching because he needed a job and to be near his dad for the time being and was subversive in his orientation, seeing the system as one of control, having read John Holt, Piaget, Ivan Illich; his colleagues were for the most part categorical agreeers, who treated the education system as if it were a natural phenomenon, as if children in rows, in uniforms, and learning divided into subjects as if reality were composed of discreet, unconnected realities were as inevitable as mountains or clouds.

Already he'd had an awkward conversation with his Second in Department, a gangling, loud, immature, narcissistic Germanist who had displayed prominently on his classroom wall: *Das Gymnasium muss bleiben*. On the Friday lunchtime of the first week, the eight new teachers had gone to the *Black Bull* in Longton and while Andy ate his cherry pie, Mike Chambers had enunciated loudly, his mouth full of lemon meringue, his view that discipline wasn't tight enough: only that morning he'd seen a boy crossing the quad with his tie askew and his top button undone.

"Well," said Andy, "being strangled by a tie is hardly a *sine qua non* of intellectual accomplishment."

"That's not the point," said Chambers and turned to the others for support. "Eh? Is it? Discipline. That's what kids need. They like it. Eh? I've always been a strict teacher."

"Have you read *The Rainbow*?" said Andy.

"Eh?"

"D.H.Lawrence. Ursula Brangwen becomes a teacher. Lawrence makes a nice remark about the hard-bitten, cynical teacher who she has to learn from. He says he could *inflict* learning on children. Sixty of them at a time. Yes, we don't believe in that any more and in a century from now, people will look back on what we do in dismay."

"I don't think so," said Chambers, raising his chin. "I don't hold with these trendy ideas. Traditional methods, that's what I'm for."

Though he was ridiculous, Andy didn't dislike Chambers. He applied his customary easy-going, tolerant judgement. The man had been brought up in a Tory family, educated at *Queen Elizabeth's Grammar* in Blackburn where snobbery was as much a part of the curriculum as maths; and he was no intellectual. He was merely one of that tribe of duteous, diligent mediocrities who work like steam engines to pass their exams, read a hundred books to secure a degree and imagine that by so doing they are on the same level as Tolstoy. The flimsy structure of his selfhood couldn't bear the weight of exaggerated importance loaded onto it. He was constantly trying to reinforce his failing sense of identity.

Andy and he were complete opposites. While Chambers thought himself an exceptional person because he understood the verb second rule, Andy thought himself just a bloke who knew French. He knew how to use the imperfect subjunctive but he had no idea how to lay bricks, wire a house, decoke an engine or fit a catheter. Everyone had their forte. Everyone had their skill. Why pump yourself up ? Do what you do and get on with people.

2Z was the kind of class a probationer teacher shouldn't be given. Don Crawley, the Head of Modern Languages, who'd been in the school for quarter of a century, had said to his colleague, Alma Mayor, when they were thinking about the distribution of classes the previous June:

"Post-grad student, is he? Well, let's see how he gets on with this lot."

Alma, recoiling from the vindictiveness, drew on her long cigarette as she tottered on her stilettos, smoothed her black, pencil-line skirt and said:

"Do you think you really should, Don?"

"Why not? Straight out of college, he should have the answers. We'll see what Roger Baker and John Rivers make of him. Mincemeat I should expect," and his face broke into that little boy's grin which disturbed her and made her compliant for fear of offending him.

Andy had soon realised he was going to have trouble. The class's books were full of work but when he asked questions relating to it, they looked blank. He kept behind one day a quiet boy who tried to get on with things.

"All this stuff in your book, Tom, do you understand it?"

"No, sir."

"Why's that, Tom?"

"We just copied it out, sir."

"Yeah? Where from?"

"The board, sir."

"The board. Tell me about that."

"Well, Mr Rifkind, he just wrote it all on the board and we had to copy it out."

"Every lesson?"

"Yes, sir."

"And did he explain it to you?"

"No, sir."

"Did you do anything else?"

"No, sir."

"Did he speak to you in French or play tapes of French?"

"No, sir."

"Did he get you to speak in French?"

"No, sir."

"Okay, thanks, Tom. Good lad."

Andy went to Crawley.

"There's a problem with 2Z, Don. They have all this work in their books, but they simply copied it from the board. They've been taught nothing. They've made no progress."

"Well," said Crawley, rising on his toes and grinning in the nervous way which made Andy want to rebuke or mock him, "what does it matter? They're thick anyway," and he walked away with his brisk stride, his rubber soles squeaking on the floor, his bald head thrown back as if he was a schoolyard fighter who had just floored an opponent.

Not long before Christmas, Andy was visited by a County Adviser. It was the routine inspection of a probationary teacher; but his bad luck was he came to see him teach 2Z. As the pupils filed in noisily and the tall, pot-bellied bureaucrat, his gold-framed glasses sliding down his nose stood at the back of the room, Roger Baker shouted:

"Are you going to hit me today, sir?"

Throughout the lesson he and John Rivers, a big, heavy-limbed, lugubrious bully of a boy whose family ran a farm in Longton, and whose father was reputed to be a brute, called out, stood up, threw bits of rubber, refused to work and became the nexus from which dendrites of disruption spread through the room. The adviser questioned Andy about the work in their books. He explained. He pointed up the bad behaviour, Andy told him they'd been badly served the previous year. He said he was unhappy with the lesson and would have to make a second visit.

Andy was called in by Lawrence Palfrey, the acting Head; a tall, wiry, man who taught Geography, and who seemed to experience life as a constant test of his worth. He marched along the corridors and paths as if the devil was behind him with a whip and in his strenuous effort to appear utterly efficient and in control, to assert by movement, expression and intonation that between his performance and what was demand of him, there was not space for a passing breath, Andy believed he saw the desperate need of a man haunted by alienation to convince himself his mind wasn't divided against itself.

His beloved activity was scrambling over glaciers and following perilous mountain paths, wrapping himself in a survival blanket and huddling down against the wind and the snow in a tent not big enough to fit his six feet two length. For two weeks every summer he pitted himself against rock, ice, snow and the elements, living off dried food which engendered either concrete constipation or its opposite and returned to civilization with a sense of superiority over his coddled, heated, well-fed, comfortable countrymen (women he consigned to a different category) which made him stride his little village of Knott End (God's own country) as if he were Marco Polo himself.

His conception of education was essentially punitive, in keeping with the ethos of the minor public school where he'd been subjected to a regime of cold showers, bullying by prefects, and masters who wielded the cane with as much relish as the sarcasm which made first formers shrink and shrivel in humiliation. He would reinforce his constantly expressed disdain for the incorrigible ignorance and laziness of pupils by giving his fourth years an outline map of Africa and ten minutes to fill in all countries. The inability of fifteen-year-old boys to pinpoint Gabon, Lesotho or Tunisia was all the proof he needed of their wayward neglect of learning, the terminal decline of standards, the spread of a culture of yobism and the perilous threat to all it meant to be British.

Nor was his view of his colleagues much more benign. Having achieved a First from Durham and an MA with distinction from London, he viewed with horror applications from teachers with a derisory 2:2, or even, heaven help us, a Third; was appalled at the rapid disappearance of the requirement for an O Level in Latin to access university courses in Humanities and considered the second-chance doctrine of admitting mature students, a reward for failure and fecklessness.

The last-minute nature of Andy's appointment meant he hadn't been involved, didn't read his application form, didn't know his background, but had picked up that he had done post-grad work and was suspected of being something of an intellectual. He made a barely conscious assumption that he must have secured a First to have progressed and was moderately impressed by Andy's quiet, self-contained demeanour. There'd been an incident a few weeks earlier when a knock on his door preceded Andy's head appearing. Furious that a member of staff dare open his door without invitation, he pulled himself to his full height behind his desk, creased his craggy face into its most disapproving frown only to see Andy produce his lever arch file, packed with essential documents.

"You left this in the gents. It looked important so I thought I'd better bring it over. Sorry to intrude, I was just going to pop it on your desk if you weren't here."

Faced with the evidence of impossible inefficiency, Palfrey relaxed, smiled and held out his big, browned, hairy hand to receive the incriminating item.

"Thank you, That's good of you. I wonder how I managed to forget that? Someone must have distracted me."

Andy was tempted to joke that maybe his desperate need for the urinal had temporarily suspended his attention, but thought better of it.

"That's okay.," he said, turned and left.

21

Palfrey worried that the probationer might tell the tale. If it got around that he'd left important documents in the gents, that anyone could have picked up the file and read confidential letters, his reputation for nailed-to-the-floor punctiliousness would suffer. He spent a few days in preternatural attentiveness: if people knew, someone would make a stray comment. That nothing was said tilted him to the conclusion that Andy had said nothing, a discretion Palfrey considered greatly to his credit.

"Crisis," said Palfrey. "The adviser wants a second visit."

"Yes," said Andy, "it was unfortunate he came to see 2Z."

"All classes have to be up to scratch."

"Of course, but I did mention to Don Crawley that things weren't right with that group."

"What did he say?"

Andy blenched from repeating Crawley's judgement. The last thing he wanted was to get anyone else in trouble. All the same, he felt he'd been badly served.

"Not much. The class did have an unfortunate time last year."

"Can't be helped," said Palfrey who seemed to believe the crisper and blunter his utterances, the more reality would bend to them. "Got to get things right for the next visit."

"Perhaps if he came to see a better group."

"Good idea. Can't force him, of course. They look at what they like. Who else have you got?" and the acting Head stood up and crossed to the timetable on his wall, a great oblong of squares each one containing a pin whose five-pence-piece sized head was marked with the designation of a class, 2P1 or 4M3 or 1G2.

"Well," said Andy, "3F1 are very good. Bright and hard-working."

"Yes," said Palfrey studying the line of pins indicating Andy's classes, "who's in there?"

"Michael Greatrix, John Collini, Matthew Henderson...."

"Ah, yes. That might be just the trick. Leave it with me, I'll see what I can do. But make sure everything's tip-top. He complained 2Z's books weren't marked."

"That's last year's work."

"Maybe, but it looks bad."

"Sure."

The second visit brought a thoroughly different result: the class behaved impeccably, the work got done, the books were in good order and Andy was deemed competent.

"Seems he was assessing the class not my teaching," Andy said to Gerry Beckett, the young art teacher who began on the same day.

"Mmm. Things went all right for me. The adviser was very pleased on her first visit."

It didn't take long for his out-of-place status to be brought home to Andy. Some of the antediluvian staff, people who'd been there years before it was forced to relinquish its grammar- school exclusivity, openly used the word "nigger" in the staffroom and Don Crawley had whispered conspiratorially as Andy was heading along the language corridor for his first meeting with his fifth form:

"Watch out for the one who's *different*."

There was a West Indian among the thirty white, middle-class boys.

Nor was anyone, pupil or staff, acknowledged to be homosexual. The cheering openness of university life where the Gay Liberation movement was active, some lecturers known to be homosexual or lesbian and prejudice seen as petty-minded, feeble and retrograde, was absent. It was impossible that in a school of nine hundred where seven hundred and fifty were boys there were no homosexuals. Yet officially, that was so.

Girls had been admitted to sixth-form two years earlier, in spite of a rearguard action in which Crawley and half a dozen established masters argued they would be a distraction, the boys would be more interested in them then their work, standards would decline, it would be the end of the school's long tradition of excellence.

Their arrival, however, hit the Head of Modern Languages like the shock of adolescence hits a twelve-year-old.

He lived with his mother in the house where he'd grown up in a little town in West Lancashire. His quick mind and talent for language was spotted by his first teachers at the Church of England primary school five hundred yards from his front door. As soon as his parents realised they had a child with brains, they moved in on him in one of those parental pincer movements which superficially look like concern for the child's best interests but are in fact a vicarious desire for glory. They kept him at his books, bought a piano, paid for lessons and listened to him progress easily, restricted the time he was allowed to play out and, above all, kept him away from the common children, the sons and daughters of manual workers who showed none of his capacity for school work and were obviously destined for the factory, the building site, the shop counter and the filing-room.

One of only two boys in his cohort to pass the eleven-plus, introduced in his final year at primary school, he moved on to the boys' grammar with its Latin motto (Dum spiro spero), masters in gowns, vigorous caning for the slightest misdemeanour, enforced hymns and prayers in assembly every morning, fun-destroying quantities of homework and not a female in sight apart from the dinner ladies and cleaners. When his hormones went haywire, he experienced his burgeoning sexuality as something remote from everyday life. Unable to make any connection between the raw ferocity of the impulses which arrived like storm clouds on a sunny day and the girls or women he knew – neighbours, relatives, shop keepers, those he spoke to at church - his attitude to sex became inevitably furtive and sentimental. The idea of any girl or woman he knew engaging in what he understood of the gross activity necessary to produce babies seemed impossible.

Diligent, fearful, nervous, compliant, he passed through seven years of grammar school without a single punishment, sat the A Levels whose inception coincided with his upper sixth year and achieving four distinctions, went on to King's College, Cambridge where, for another three years, he was exempted from female company. A year's national service after graduating with a First in French only reinforced the sense that women who did it, who descended to the baseness of grunting, sweating, conjoining must exist in some other realm, and what could that be but prostitution? The rational, intellectual recognition that the millions of people who constituted British society must all have been conceived in the manner biology dictated, made no difference to his emotional orientation.

Inevitably, when he looked for work, the idea of teaching in an all girls' or co-educational school was as unpalatable as the idea of educating negroes. Luck favoured him. He saw the advert, applied and was taken on because of his background, his degree and his submissive demeanour. He was very proud, as was his mother (his father, a clerk in an insurance office, had died of a heart attack while he was at university). There were forty applicants. Jobs in all-boys grammar schools, in leafy, quasi-rural locations in the mid-fifties were highly desirable. His timetable was light, the boys biddable, clever and terri-fied into conformity. The pay was good. He bought his first car and took his mother for a run through the Trough of Bowland on Sunday afternoons, stopping for a cream tea in Scorton.

For twenty-two years he hid from the fact of gender in this male en-clave where the curious practices of some of the housemasters and the rumours of unspeakable acts performed on aghast first-years on the far rugby field by lower-sixth bullies were smothered in order to protect the school's extraordinary reputation. Closer to fifty than for-ty he was a virgin. He'd seen the images in girlie magazines and even, on occasion, heart-stopping photographs of practices he'd nev-er imagined, black and white reproductions of women obliging four men at once with their mouths, hands and what lay between their legs. He'd suffered the torment of unbidden erections he didn't know what to do with, but he had the refuge of school where a class of thir-ty fourteen-year-old boys was a better antidote than bromide and where he could convert his erotic energy into sarcasm, violence and humiliation.

And he had his mother who still ensured he polished his shoes in the morning and sang heartily in church on Sunday.

The first time he stood in a classroom containing girls, he was over-come with the horror that his trousers might start to bulge. They were sixteen, charming, fair-skinned, mostly fully developed. He watched their bottoms bob along the corridor. He cast furtive glances at their breasts as they worked on a translation; and he couldn't quell the odd idea that their multiple attractions were meant for him. His life took on a new meaning. He woke every morning thinking of Rachel Pen-rose or Jane Jackson or Yvette Baxter, was as full of nervous expec-tation as thirteen-year-old who has been smiled at coyly for the first time by a girl who is already a woman, and found, as never before, a motivation to diligence other than agreement with authority, desire to do well in tests or repression of unruly instincts. He drove to school for the girls. He marked books for them. He attended staff meeting for them. He completed reports for them. He set end of year exams for them. He sat through tedious parents' evening for them. He cleaned his shoes for them. He brushed his teeth for them. He combed his hair for them. He bought new suits for them. He knotted his tie for them.

In his sixth-form classes he was as jumpy as an expectant father. He rose on his toes rubbed his palms together, smiled and giggled like a little boy unsure of himself among adults. The bitter sarcasm he employed with the boys for two decades, the cuffs round the ear with his hand or a book, the famous event which had entered the school's folklore when he'd chased around the room an unfortunate fifth-former who had difficulty knowing when to use the perfect tense, banging him on the crown with his copy of Longman's Audio Visual French Book 4 and shouting with glee, "J'ai frappé Fletcher", were set aside when girls were in the room.

He spoke to them like a mother to a three year-old.

"You see, there, Rachel," he'd say leaning over the girl to run his stubby, hairy finger beneath a line of her work, "you've made a little mistake." And he would giggle as if to excuse himself for daring to correct her. "L'heure où je fais mes devoirs, not que. Que is the relative pronoun, you see, and refers to an object."

The girl would lift her head and turn to him and in her expression he read her incomprehension. He jigged a little, smiled as if at a child who has just been sick on the best tablecloth, giggled:

"It's a bit hard, isn't it. Never mind. I'll explain it to the class."

It occurred to him he could make the offer of one-to-one sessions at lunchtimes. One or two girls took him up and he sat beside them for half an hour, his heart beating like a central heating pump, his demeanour solicitous and his lips pressed tight, his eyelashes fluttering like those of a shaky teenager on her first date. The grammar which had once been his defence against the incursion of dangerous sentiments, meant nothing. He was transported by delicate hands, slim wrists, piping voices, hair curled over little ears, soft cheeks, bulging blouses, thick thighs, slim ankles, pink lips, long lashes, white necks, blue eyes, brown eyes, green eyes.

Never before had he been alone with girls. Now, he had the perfect excuse. He lay in bed, his mother in the neighbouring room, thinking of the next day when he would sit next to Helen Grey for half an hour, her sunny, blonde hair no more than few inches away. Oh, how he wanted to stroke that hair, kiss those lips, lay his hand on those thighs. The inevitable tension ensued which he had to endure without intervention for fear his mother might hear.

Inevitably, there emerged a gold-digger.

Andy had to attend an after-school meeting about graded tests in a venue on the other side of town. Alma Mayor, also required to be present, gave him a lift in her orange MGB GT. On the way home, she mentioned Diane Clayton.

"Oh, he's already bought her a car."

"You're joking."

"No, and her parents are in on it."

"Doesn't he realize?"

"No. Some of the older members of staff have spoken to him. Jim Hunter who he's quite close to. They go walking in the Lakes. He's told him he's making a fool of himself, but he can't see it."

"A car," said Andy, shaking his head.

"And a baby grand."

"What?"

"Yes, a thousand pounds he paid for that."

"God," said Andy, "is he having sex with her?"

"Oh no, nothing like that. He thinks she's going to marry him."

"How do you know all this?"

"I'm his confidante. I'm worn out with it. Every day he comes to me with his tales of joy or woe. He was in tears in the stock room yesterday at eight in the morning."

"Have you spoken to the Head?"

"Of course. Old Wellington didn't want to know and Lawrence Palfrey says it's a personal matter."

"Hardly."

"I know."

"She's a nasty piece of work."

"Yes, and her parents are no better. He paid for them to go on a Mediterranean cruise."

"Worse and worse."

"I shall have to resign if it goes on much longer. It's driving me insane."

"That's not right." said Andy. "Have you spoken to your union?"

"Yes. Dave Dover has had a word with him, but it went in one ear and out the other."

"But if it's impacting on you, the union should intervene."

"I suppose so, but Dave has a senior position, he doesn't want to tarnish the school's reputation."

Alma offered to take Andy to his door but he insisted she drive home: it was a short walk from there to his mother's. She lived close to Hurst Grange park where he'd played football as a boy, ridden his bike with Duddy, Blackie, John Kenny and Marek, watched *Hill Rovers* on a Saturday afternoon, walked hand in hand with Maggie Swift and later, during his time at F.E.D., had a late-night, intoxicated encounter with Marilyn Boulting, who he'd met in *The Fleece* and the pubs in town, after which he'd never seen her again.

Alma's house was in a quite cul-de-sac, detached and impressive with a big garden at the front and a double garage whose doors were open. She turned to him as she switched off the engine.

"Do you want to come in ?"

From the corner of his eye he was aware of a slight parting of her knees. Her eyes, through her glasses whose frames were elaborately undulating were fixed on his. Her red, painted lips were smiling gently. She was the other side of forty, had piled up, back-combed hair, was always heavily made-up and perfumed, wore chunky, ostentatious rings on both hands, tall, thin heels, tight skirts, blouses unbuttoned to her cleavage which hugged her breasts.

"No, I'd better shoot home. I've a meeting to get to at half seven. Thanks."

"That's okay. See you tomorrow."

He walked home along Cop Lane his heavy briefcase in his right hand. Alma's husband, he understood, was an engineer of some kind, who often worked away. They a daughter who was being educated privately at Westholme School, Blackburn. Surely she would have been home. Surely the invitation was innocent.

It was no longer possible for Bert Lang to walk to the newsagent for his *Evening Telegraph*. He had to manoeuvre himself into his Lada (he despised it as a poor piece of engineering but had bought it because it was cheap and he was worried about how long his money might last) drive the quarter of a mile, park up as close as possible, haul himself painfully out, hobble in to the little shop run by a friendly Asian and reverse the process to get home. There wasn't much in the paper. Was it worth the effort? He liked to keep in touch. There would be the odd story concerning someone he knew. He wanted to know what decisions were being made by the council. He took a marginal interest in the fortunes of Blackburn Rovers, out of nostalgia for the days he'd run his lungs hot for Fulwood Amateurs and the couple of times he'd been on the same pitch as Tom Finney.

Getting to the paper shop and back each day was proof there was still life in him; but not much.

It occurred to him now, that when you are healthy, death seems impossible. Intellectually, you know you are mortal, but emotionally you feel as if you will last for ever. That little *as if* made life possible. If we weren't able to neglect the petty limits of our life, if we were conscious every minute of how short our lives are and how restricted what we can achieve, we would collapse into hopelessness. Nature has wired us for illusion, and without it, we couldn't get through the day. He remembered how, when Andy was a little boy, he would find him crying in bed, and when he asked him what was wrong, the child would say he was afraid of dying. Then he would reassure him with gentle, fatherly words:

"Oh, now, don't worry about that. You'll live to be a hundred," and he would wipe the tears from his cheeks, stroke his forehead and sit with him till he went to sleep.

The boy's anxiety had puzzled him. Why should a child of four be thinking about death? He was sure it was something to do with Elsie. Her anxiety could hardly ever be calmed and her religious fervour set the value of earthly life at nothing compared to the life to come. Bert wondered what such influences might do to a child's mentality. He would have kept religion at bay and allowed his children to make up their own minds once they were grown and he wished his wife could have hidden her fretfulness, smiled, relaxed and given her children fun.

But now he was dying.

It was no longer an intellectual notion without emotional traction. He might not be alive in twenty-four hours. Death was in his limbs and organs. It was slowly establishing its regime of nothingness. Even when his thigh had been impossibly painful, he'd felt fully alive. Death wasn't in his leg. He had a deficit, but he felt no less inserted in life than when he was twenty-one and would run a mile for the joy of it. Now, he was no longer fully alive. His body was giving up. He thought of his grandfather, the feckless, violent drunkard who had lived into his eighties, become slow and tired but had died quickly, passing from life into oblivion in a few days. He was lucky. The luckiest were those who went to bed and didn't wake up, who knew nothing of the cell by cell colonisation which was his fate.

What he feared wasn't death. In a way, he wished it would take him. To have it over within the next hour, half hour, ten minutes might be best. What was left of his life, after all? He was terrified of incapacity, of being unable to move, to make a cup of tea, to shave, to get to the bathroom, of becoming a prisoner in a body which no longer functioned but to be fully mentally aware.

Let death come quick, he said to himself. Yet when he arrived home with his paper, he rebelled. No. He was still alive. He could read, he could make a sandwich, he could get in the shower, he could listen to the radio and to music, he could watch the television, he could clean his shoes and iron a shirt, he could hoover the carpet, drive the car and twice a week he went to the day centre where he was given a meal, had people to talk to, played whist or dominoes and felt, still, connected to his fellow human beings.

Had he been told, even a year earlier, that the great excitement of his life would be to sit at a table with half a dozen, old, infirm men and women, some unable to feed or dress themselves, and play games he'd never liked for two hours, he would have snorted with scorn. Yet now, the day-centre was his salvation. The women (they were all women) who served him macaroni cheese, or vegetable curry or lentil soup with crusty bread or chilli bean casserole were as precious to him as anyone had ever been. They were volunteers. His gratitude was elevated into love. They were angels. They were heroines. They gave their time and energy for him, though they had no connection to him. Eating his rice pudding he reflected on his working life. ICI, *The Minotaur*, Ken Wickham, what lay behind the effort was money.

Yet these women didn't earn a penny. They earned something more valuable. He wished he'd done what they were doing.

The day-centre reinforced his socialism. When he heard Thatcher speaking of people standing on their own two feet, shifting for themselves and the need to roll back social provision, he experienced it as an attack on himself. He was born in poverty, grew in poverty and was now facing the end of his life in helpless need. He never smoked, he gave up drink in his early twenties, he was a vegetarian, he'd always worked. He wasn't in need through any fault of volition or action. In all likelihood, he was a victim of his genes. That woman was ignorant and callous. Something was missing from her mentality. She reminded him of Ken Wickham whose self-elevating optimism concealed an ingrained inability to empathise. His life was orientated to making money because money was a mirror. In the extensive power of great wealth he saw the extent of his selfhood. Yet the truth was he was inwardly shrunken and regressed. The horrifying vision of a society, a world, a species in the grip of the same delusion almost made him cry.

The phone rang. It was his son.

To hear his voice reignited positive feeling. The little boy he'd been, his sister's treasure, the four-year-old in his Preston North End kit smiling crookedly for the camera, the brown-armed, all-day-in-the-garden, summer boy, heedless and charming, was alive in his mind. To listen to Andy's voice was to be returned to the early fifties, to the days when his marriage was, if not happy, at least steady, to Woodland Grove where he belonged and his children loved him.

The job was going well. He was going to cycle over on Saturday.

He arrived at eleven.

"Do you want to put your bike in the garage?" said Bert, standing at the door, supporting himself on his walking stick.

"No," said Andy, flattening his hair which had been lifted and styled into Stan Laurel disorder by the wind, "your neighbours aren't thieves, are they."

"Well, you never know who might pass by."

"It'll be okay."

It was a red-framed, drop-handlebars tourer, new-looking and smart. Bert assumed it must be expensive.

"No, a bargain. It's not a lightweight frame and Shimano brakes or anything. It's as heavy as a tank. I got it in the sale at Ribble Cycles. I could do with something less like a hunk of lead for climbing Bird-ie Brow, but it gets me round."

In the bungalow, Bert suggested a brew.

"Sit down, dad. I'll make it."

"Thanks.. You know where everything is?"

"Yeah, yeah. Do you want something to eat ?"

"I wouldn't mind a slice of toast."

"Let me guess, with honey."

"You're a mind-reader."

To be called dad was something. It wasn't merely the word with all its connotations of responsibility, care, and inviolable relationship; it was Andy's tone of voice. How long was it since he'd heard Mary say it with that intonation of absolute trust which had surprised and pleased him when she and Andy were children. He could barely re-member Sylvia having used it. She must have. She was chattering away before he was expelled from his petty paradise.

He wished his son could stay. If he could be here every day for whatever remained of his life, the unbearable loneliness of facing extinction without anything but connections of convenience would be eased.

"There you are, dad."

"Thanks."

Andy sat opposite him in the leopard skin armchair. He was dressed in black cords, still held at the ankles by cycle clips, and a blue shirt. He looked vital and healthy. His cheeks glowed from the effort of his ride, the long push up to Hoghton and the speeding along the lanes to Feniscowles. Bert took his first bite of the warm toast, the fat of the margarine and the sugar of the honey lighting up his mouth with that sensation of familiarity and homeliness he had always found in sim-ple things. He was alive. He was with his son who had decades ahead of him. His life had been worth something. He knew it had.

OWZAT

A new Headmaster was appointed and took up tenure after the October half-term. The governors, whose response to the school having to become comprehensive ranged from regret to purple outrage, wanted someone who would represent what the school had been. What it was to become, they dreaded, and in that half-conscious way people proceed when their dearest illusions have been shattered, hoped that by resisting the inevitable they could return to what had gone forever. They found the perfect candidate in Merrick Cooper. Educated at Westminster and Balliol, son of a civil servant in the Treasury, he had tried his luck in the City, found its rapaciousness uncongenial and having absorbed a modicum of the Age of Aquarius, let-it-all-hang-out, aren't-the-Beatles-wonderful, Carnaby Street and the Isle-of-White festival atmosphere of the sixties, felt the public sector might offer him a career which would chime with his moderately liberal and respectably Church of England mentality.

He was in his early twenties when Harold Wilson won his first victory. Socialism was an affront too far but in the educated lilt of Roy Jenkins, the urbane intellectualism of Tony Crosland, the reassuring, avuncular, old-fashioned ways of Jim Callaghan, the obviously middle-of-the road instincts of Peter Shore, he detected a social-democratic drift which would hold back the unruly tendencies of the more intemperate Trade Union leaders and achieve that balance he favoured which would deliver a civilised capitalism in which the pursuit of great wealth could sit comfortably with decent provision for all.

In the light of his family's eschatology, the decision to work in the public sector was radical, and the choice of teaching, reckless. By September 1967, when he took up his first post at an ex-grammar in the South-West, his father despaired of the education system. The grammar-secondary arrangement had been reassuring and in keeping with his typically upper-middle-class, one-nation Toryism which conceived of the nation as irrevocably divided between the intellectually and morally limited, who must be given an education of some kind, and the astute, energetic and morally discerning minority, who obviously must be educated separately and directed towards responsible careers. The State education system was now a refuge for the disillusioned, the trendy, the radical. That his son's ambition was to rise to a headship as quickly as sharp-elbowed decency would allow didn't temper his disappointment.

Young Cooper felt himself independent and subversive. He could have taken a job in a comfortable private school. He might have ended up at Eton, Ampleforth or The Dragon's; he was rejecting the neurotic fears of his father, the belief that the lower-classes are incorrigibly corrupt and must be ruled, the conviction that Abraham Lincoln had been almost right: democracy ought to be rule of the people, by their better for their betters.

All the same, contact with pupils who might have come from outer space, children whose parents worked on building sites, in shops, in factories, on farms, who drove buses or cleaned floors, provoked a desire to revert to type. There weren't many of them in his first school. Eighty percent of the intake was solidly middle-class or above, but the comprehensive system made contact with at least a few of those people who until then he had known about only in theory, inevitable. There was balm in Gilead however. Some of the pupils from poorer households, even amongst those who responded to French as if it was an eccentricity imposed on them by an inimical system, were biddable, polite and charming. He wouldn't have wanted them to play with any children he might produce, but he felt he was doing god's work in educating the sons and daughters of hewers of earth and drawers of water.

All his colleagues were, of course, products of grammar or private schools. They were appropriately middle-class, except for one. Alex Edmondson was a cockney who made no attempt to modify his accent, a mistake Cooper felt he would regret. He was the school's sole member of the NUT, the rest of the staff preferring the NAS which advertised itself as "the career teachers' union" or one of the lesser organizations which resolutely refused to be known as unions and outlawed strike action as an outrage engaged in by miners, dockers and lorry drivers. To add to his folly, he was a Labour Party activist who had stood and been trounced in a local council election. He unapologetically expressed his support for the legalisation of abortion and homosexuality and deplored the American action in Vietnam which he called " a symptom of the USA's imperialist hangover".

Cooper stayed out of his way. A man who didn't know how to conceal his opinions in an obviously right-of-centre, Church of England school, was doomed. Cooper perceived no contradiction between his belief that he was a democrat and his recognition that it was politic not to disagree with your superiors at work. When he discovered Edmondson had been on a blacklist and had needed the support of his M.P. to get his name removed and find a job, he recoiled. He couldn't believe a man would be placed on a blacklist without reason, not in good old Britain.

He got on moderately well with his colleagues, but friendships could get in the way of promotion. He wanted to rise rapidly. His deviation into the City had cost him a few years. Having started teaching at twenty-six and calculating it might take at least a decade to achieve a headship, he was anxious that if anything tripped him, he might be forty and still not in charge of a school. There were opportunities. His Head of Department was fifty-eight, one of the Deputies, fifty-six. Within weeks of starting, he was in the Head's study, offering to take on whatever responsibilities might be appropriate and explaining that he understood he might have to fulfil them for some time without an increase in pay.

When, in the staffroom, he heard Edmondson excoriate what he called, "the pervading culture of sycophancy in teaching", he knew he was an enemy.

He was a competent if dull teacher who employed boredom as a means of discipline. Determined to have nothing to do with physical punishment, he won the respect of most of the pupils for his restraint and patience. The Head of Department retired. He took his place. Two years later the Deputy Head stepped down. He had proved himself. He advanced. His contact with pupils was reduced to eight periods a week, a relief he greatly welcomed. He had an office. He could shut his door and forget there were children in the place. He dealt with paper, figures, regulations, which were much more congenial than people.

The next eight years were fallow. The final climb to the peak proved the hardest. He'd hoped four or five years as a Deputy should be enough. He would be a Head by thirty-five; but his applications brought no interviews. It was the first time he'd experienced setback. The negative experience of the City hadn't been denial: he had made the decision. Now, he was being rejected. It forced him to examine himself. He ran through his mind, over and over the positive characteristics of his CV: pubic school education, Oxford, rapid promotion, devout Anglicanism. What was making Heads turn him down?

One morning in his office, the sun streaming through the picture window, his desk neat at nine thirty and little to burden him for the day, he was contemplating taking it easy, staying clear of the rough and tumble of the school day, being invisible at break and lunch time, when out of nowhere a painful thought seized his mind.

His background was an albatross.

He was applying for jobs in comprehensive schools. It was obvious they were the future. He didn't want to peel off into the tiny private sector where he could spend a quarter of a century of ease in an institution which excluded all but the wealthy and the intelligent. His Christianity and his liberalism impelled him to the huge public sector where more than ninety per cent of children were educated and where he could make a difference; to be involved in that great enterprise of democratic education, in schools where all were admitted and the local authority was empowered by the votes of the common folk, was to travel in the direction of social peace and cohesion. Yet it struck him with a fierce blow that shrunk his heart and made him sit behind his desk, that his privileged upbringing might work against him. Perhaps he was viewed as too rarefied for the cut and thrust of schools which welcomed the children of executives and shelf-fillers. The injustice made him livid. He went for a walk round the corridors and grounds to calm down.

The rest of the day was spent thinking through his strategy. Henceforth he would apply not to the better comprehensives as he'd done so far, but to those with a tradition in keeping with his pedigree: C of E ex-grammars, preferably with at least pretentions to public school status.

The problem proved their rarity. He tried for one in Cambridgeshire, made the interview but wasn't appointed. That the job went to a woman he judged a few years younger with a degree from Durham, wrankled. He sent in applications for two more and wasn't interviewed. When the job in the north was advertised in the TES, he discussed it with his wife.

"But do we really want to live there?" she said.

"It's not in the town," he responded. "It's quasi rural and the intake is predominantly middle-class."

He was helped by the small pool of candidates. The school had advertised at Easter, interviewed four and turned them down. It had been agreed the best was to let Palfrey take over as Acting Head for a year; but the County began to question whether, if he could relinquish his role as Deputy and the school run efficiently, the school wasn't over-managed. The governors changed their minds, advertised in late September, received only four applications, interviewed two and chose Cooper as their best chance of resisting what they saw as the onward march of Bolshevism.

After his appointment, he wrote to John Wellington. It was a public school tradition that new Heads corresponded with old. He expected to keep up a steady letter writing over the coming two decades. He would preserve Wellington's missives as his would be preserved. They might be discovered decades, nay, centuries hence. Headteachers were, in a modest way, important people. The history of a school was marked by the tenures of its Heads. The staff came and went. They were invisible to and unheard by posterity.

In his reply, Wellington mentioned the odd fact that his first and last appointments had been to Modern Languages: Rob Hesketh in 1964 and Andy Lang in his final weeks. Hesketh, he observed, was eccentric, a drunk, but entirely reliable: a good conservative, a disciplinarian and one of the staff who had fought hardest against comprehensive status. Lang on the other hand needed to be watched. He suspected he harboured radical tendencies and espoused trendy ideas.

Cooper filed the letter in the bureau at home with a little snigger. Wellington was old school. Lang, he was sure, was no threat; but in that way the opinions of others work on our minds in ways we aren't conscious of, subtly or not so subtly altering our behaviour, a worm of doubt worked its way into Cooper's assumptions and one morning, during his first term, finding a class of boys passing through the passage between the staff-room and the work-room when they should have been in class as Lang emerged from one of the doors, he turned on him and rebuked him sharply:

"What are these boys doing here at this time?"

"I've no idea. It's not my class."

Realising at once his spiked tone had been unfair, Cooper's shoulders dropped a little, he turned away, but couldn't bring himself to apologise: a Headteacher did not apologise to a probationer under any circumstances. He walked smartly to his study, closed the door and illuminated the red Engaged light. It wasn't Lang's class. He wasn't responsible. Yet perhaps John Wellington was right. Yes, Lang was someone to be watched. He was there, after all. He could have made sure the boys went by quietly. He could have stopped them and asked them why they were there. He'd been right to send a shot across his bows. He looked at the clock. Twenty minutes to break. He locked his door and walked the fifteen yards to the door of School House, the four-bedroom perk of the job.

"You're early," said Caroline. "The coffee isn't ready yet."

"Yes, quiet morning. It's only a few minutes to the bell."

She checked her watch.

"More than quarter of an hour, Merrick."

"I'll have my coffee in the lounge. Where's the *Guardian*?"

"On the table by your chair."

Her husband went somewhat morosely through the heavy, oak door to sit by the fire she'd set at nine. She went to the kitchen to prepare the cafetière wondering what had troubled him.

Andy Lang didn't forget Cooper's unwarranted upbraiding any more than the push in the back he received one morning from Dr Coleridge, the Deputy in charge of exams and curriculum development. He was leaving the work-room with a textbook in his hands, looking at the open pages when Coleridge, in a hurry to get to the door, put his right palm between his shoulders and shoved him out of the way. Andy was tempted to follow him up to his office and confront him:

"What makes you think you have the right to lay a hand on me?"

but he thought better of it. The man was immature, he hadn't intended it maliciously, he was a fool; better let it pass and play it down.

He responded in the same way to Rob Hesketh. A few weeks in to the first term, the tall, giraffe-legged, curly-headed dipsomaniac and chain smoker who arrived at school with an impressive black briefcase which when he opened it in the staff-room turned out to be full of boxes of eggs laid by the chickens on his smallholding, asked him if he could help out at a fund-raising barbecue on Friday evening. The last thing Andy intended for the end of the week was to be stuck on a muddy farm, up a lane, serving ketchup-drenched sausages in rolls and burnt burgers to fourteen and fifteen year-olds, but the funds were for the trip to the Loire Valley Hesketh ran every year. He found himself pulling pints. The make-shift bar was a line of un-even trestle tables, sinking in a sticky mixture of mud and cow dung, the pumps unreliably fixed and connected to the metal barrels he constantly jammed his toes against. The rule, enunciated by the al-ready sozzled Hesketh at the start of the evening, was that only sixth-formers should be served alcohol, but as the place filled, the young-sters crowded and clamoured, Andy spotted lads from his fourth and fifth year groups walking away with brimming plastic pints. If a lad he recognised asked, he shook his head, but he wasn't familiar enough with the pupils to be sure who were sixth-formers.

He was about to hand over a cold, flat-headed pint when Hesketh barged into him, sent the drink splashing across the trestle and grab-bing his upper right arm tightly said angrily into his ear:

"Don't serve drinks to fourth years, Andy."

He yanked his arm free and for a second was on the verge of pushing the tall, heavy-chinned, bespectacled drunkard in the chest with all his force, to watch him stagger and topple backwards into the slime, but turned away, struggled through the crowd, pupils hailing him, smiling, shouting in his ear, friendly, raucous and out of control, to leave by the inevitable five-barred gate and walk the dark, winding lane to Longton where he picked up a bus to town.

The steady stride, the dark, being alone, gave him time and inclina-tion for reflection. There was gathered malice behind Hesketh's ac-tion. He was aware of an inimical attitude amongst the older staff: it had got about that he was a Labour Party activist. For some of the part-of-the-furniture staff, like Keith Bird, the ramrod-backed, Bible-obedient Head of Physics and Third Year, voting Labour was tanta-mount to crime. It was irrevocably associated with the lower orders and their ingrained lack of responsibility, their fecklessness, laziness and greed. Educated privately, raised in an Anglican, Tory-voting family where his accountant father insisted on impeccable table manners, regular bedtimes and dutiful prayers, he had imbibed as a child the notion that poverty is the result of individual failure; that no one was denied property, advancement and status except by their own shortcomings and that it was god's will that those who knew how to behave should rule over those who didn't. That miners and factory workers, who should be grateful to their betters for their jobs, had the temerity to strike for more money when they wasted what they were paid in the pub and the bookmakers, was infallible proof of the perfidiousness of the working-class. They were workers because that was in the nature of god's order of things. He gave men free will and they chose to be irresponsible. That the Labour Party pandered to their childish selfishness was unforgivable. That a rabble-rousing loud-mouth like Bevan should ever have held government office, nothing less than treason.

Was it paranoia to imagine these members of the old guard talked to one another, that between them there was a tacit agreement that he was an interloper, an invader, a virus who should be expelled from the body of the school as soon as possible?

Rob Hesketh too was a fundamentalist Tory. He had pretentions to wheeler-dealing. After graduating he'd launched into business. Scrap metal was rumoured to be lucrative but he quickly found himself dealing with unsavoury characters and when the police arrived at his door one evening to question him about a ton of lead he'd received, he shut down his little enterprise and ran to the asylum of teaching in a C of E grammar. His view of business was romantic. It was do-what-you-like-so-long-as-the-pound-notes-flow-in. The idea of complying with regulations, of having to submit detailed accounts, of being unable to do deals in the pub, in the gents while urinating, the notion that business wasn't like drinking, a matter of self-abandonment and unfettered indulgence, led to him rely on teaching for his essential income while dabbling in whatever money-turning schemes he could on the side.

A talented linguist with an impeccable command of Latin and French who had taught himself Spanish to be able to offer it as an extra to the sixth-formers, the idea of steady, responsible work for modest remuneration made him squirm as much as the notion of tee-totalism. The pleasure and pride in learning language and teaching it well left him empty. There had to be more to life. He read the business pages. He was impressed by the stories of men like Andrew Carnegie. Money attracted him as much as booze. To be a millionaire, a multi-millionaire was to extend the range of your being, just as when you were drunk, the borders of your selfhood dissolved.

It was good to leave the darkness; the black trees that loomed over the hedges; the muddy, tractor-familiar road visible only a few feet ahead. As he emerged into the light of the village, by the side of *The*

Golden Ball where he'd drunk with Matt Ross, Blackie, Carol, Duddy and others, the red double-decker was sweeping round the bend a hundred yards from the stop. He sprinted with his arm outstretched, jumped onto the platform, paid his fare and was glad to sit in the light and be bumped and rocked towards the town.

He was here only because of his dad. Where would he be otherwise? Perpignan in all likelihood. The thought made him laugh.: what distance was there between Rob's chaotic barbecue on a damp Friday on a farm reeking of cow dung among the Tory-voting thank-god-we-don't-live-in-the-town-and-have-pakis-for-neighbours   parents and friends of the school, and the university of Perpignan where, at this very moment, he might be strolling by the sea in the subtle evening air or sitting with a *pastis* and a *grand crème* on the terrace of a city café.

He wouldn't be here long. He would diligently look for jobs elsewhere. A year, two at the most. It would become an amusing interlude and a rich source of funny stories, but it would have no hold on him, this reactionary place with its throwback snobbery, its dark secrets and its joke-shop professionalism.

He was tempted to ride into Preston and have drink in the *Fox and Grapes* or the *Exchange*, but he jumped off in Penwortham and nipped into the *Fleece*. There was usually someone he knew, but he was surprised to find John Rutherford playing darts in the little snug. Slim, bearded, dressed in his customary faded jeans, his smile was a reminder of the carefree days when they sat at the back of class six and John took the newts from the glass tank and explained their behaviour while they were supposed to be writing a composition or solving maths problems.

"All right, John ? Can I buy you one?"

"Yeah. I won't say no. Bitter."

A Phd under his belt, John was now working at the National History Museum and enjoying London life. He was amused to discover Andy was now teaching at his old school.

"That's a funny circle, isn't it?" he said as he threw for double tops.

"I guess so."

Andy was surprised by his embarrassment. He wanted to tell his old friend that he'd come home because of his dad's illness, that he was living at his mother's and visiting his dad in Blackburn, that his father probably wouldn't live much longer and then he'd be away, but it felt apologetic and excuse-making. Better to let John think he'd come to start his teaching career here because it was convenient.

Inevitably, they talked of the old times as if they were ageing men, as if most of their lives wasn't still before them. Duddy, who John had become very friendly with, was now a prison officer in Northern Ireland.

"You're joking."

"No, sleeps with a revolver under his pillow."

"What made him go there?"

"Love," said John, pulling his darts from the board, "well, sex probably." He laughed. "He got involved with a girl from Belfast. Led him by the nose, or a more intimate part of his anatomy to tell the truth." He laughed again in that free, gentle way Andy had always appreciated. "She went back home so he followed. Needed a job and that's what he landed."

They ran through the destinies of their former classmates and pals. Andy explained that Stu Archer was married and living in Nottingham with a charming, pretty wife who taught French. Stu's grandparents had bought them a house.

"Outright?" said John.

"Yeah, ten thousand. Nice place. Modern and big enough for a family. They have two kids."

"God," said John, "better get moving," and he laughed once more.

They were joined by a couple of blokes Andy had known in passing, both at school with John, one now a maths teacher and the other working in insurance. The four of them paired up for twice round and two tops. At a certain point, the maths teacher mentioned Alan Madison.

"How is Maddy?" said Andy. "I haven't seen him for years."

A wary look appeared in the mathematician's eye.

"He's okay. Four kids."

"Four. He's doing well."

"Yeah," said the other lifting his straight glass of yellow bitter. "Wife's had a bit of a problem though."

"Oh, sorry to hear that."

"Not been too good."

"Is she getting better?"

"I think so. Maybe." He turned to Andy and looked him in the eye. "Breakdown, as far as I know. Difficult things, aren't they?"

"Sure. I'm sorry to hear that. I really am."

At ten, Andy shook John's hand.

"Will you be around for a while?"

"No, I'm back to London tomorrow. Just had a couple of days to come up and see my folks."

"They okay?"

"Not bad. My dad has the usual design fault. Prostate," he laughed in his beard.

"Well, good to see you, John. Hope I'll see you soon."

His mother had gone to bed. He locked up, made a cup of tea and sat in front of the television trying to be interested in the news. Duddy, his roguish, always-ready-for-a-laugh mate who had saved him from a smashed head and probably death, was caught up in the horrible events of Northern Ireland. He was a Brit. A prison officer. A legitimate target for the republican para-militaries. He had the curious feeling that part of him was in Northern Ireland too. Something of himself was under threat because Duddy was part of him. How odd it was, the way a self was made. It was a kaleidoscope assembled from all a person's significant contacts. Duddy was part of him, so was Matt Ross, and Blackie and Wheels and Carol and Janice Eaves and Rob Green and Sue Border and Mike Richards and even Alan Madison who'd he'd known only in passing. Duddy was in danger. He had to sleep with a weapon. He wished he could get to him, to persuade him away from peril. He'd loved him after all.

The thought shocked him. Had he loved Duddy and all his other good mates? Yes, he had. Not in any sexual sense, but with the love that is recognition of commonalty. He had depended on him and Duddy had been a good mate. Without him, and his other mates, how would he have come through, how would he have grown, how would he have been who he was?

And Maddy's wife had had a breakdown, with four kids to look after. How could things have gone so wrong? Maddy was such a let-life-throw-at-me-what-it-likes lad, untroubled, able to find himself on a football pitch or a cricket square, as remote from depression as Novisibirsk from Newcastle. Danger and unhappiness had befallen lads he'd hoped would come through life unscathed, who he'd assumed would be happy. It filled him with a sense of dread and made him review his own life. What had happened? He wasn't where he'd intended to be. What was to say the future wouldn't be the same, that he wouldn't arrive at some unsought-for destination that would be a burden?

His mother was always away to work before him. Often, they didn't exchange a word in the morning. She was out of the door while he was making toast. Saturday morning was no exception to her up-before-the-birds routine. Andy roused at eight and out of his hypno-pompic fuzziness as the hallucinatory images melted like ice in a kettle, his brain brought into focus that he'd promised to ride over and see his dad. It was a while since he'd cycled to Mary's. He wished he'd chosen that.

"Are you going to your dad's today?" said his mother as he settled on the sofa with his brew.

"Yes, I'll go this morning for an hour or so."

"How is he anyway?"

There was wariness in her question. Andy detected no concern for her ex-husband's welfare. Her interest was more nosiness. How to answer was a conundrum because the plain response was he was dying. Andy was surprised he was still alive. He hadn't realised a body could come so near to death and yet linger, like a rock balanced on a cliff edge which can tilt for years before a tiny pressure makes it fall. He'd made his decision because he thought he might be dead in weeks, months at the most. What should he say to his mother? Would it shock and upset her if he announced the unpolished fact? Or would she be glad? The horrible thought crept into his mind, like a spider appearing through a crack in the floorboards, that she wanted to hear he was about to expire, that it would rid her of a burden.

"Not so good. He can barely walk and he's lost a lot of weight but they can't get to the bottom of it."

"Well, he always did…." she began, but Andy didn't hear what followed. He'd perfected, over the years, the technique of shutting out those negative iterations he knew so well and which helped no one, least of all her.

"Look at the time," he interrupted, "I'd better get a shift on or the traffic'll be deadly."

He was quickly out of the house on the perilous bike which made her fear for his safety. He'd always been adventurous on two wheels. She remembered the bike she'd bought him when he was twelve, after Bert had left. A *BSA Golden Fifty*. He'd chosen it from the shop in Market Street because of the gears. Something she didn't understand. He was out on it in all weathers and she'd assumed he went to call for his pals, rode the mile to Howick or the few miles to Deepdale where his friend Jeff Wheeler lived; but one day during a summer holiday he'd gone out with David Thomas. A couple of days later she'd met his mother as she was trudging from the shops. She'd told her they'd ridden to Dunsop Bridge; on the way back, at five, tight between the lines of creeping vehicles approaching Penwortham Hill, David had fallen off and bumped himself against a car.

"Great 'Eavens," said Elsie, "was he all right?"

The boy was fine apart from bruised confidence.

Elsie walked the hundred yards home with her heavy bags determined to berate her son for his irresponsibility, but when he came in from tennis, sun-and-fresh-air healthy and sat at the table to devour his corned beef hash and six slices of bread and butter, she fixed him with a hard, objective stare. Something in his careless freedom at that moment stopped her. He was a natural lad, not like Robert Jones, or many of the kids she considered artificial and cramped by being forced into the mould their parents had chosen for them. A tenderness of maternal love for his unaffected ways spread through her. She withdrew to the kitchen and never mentioned the ride through Bowland.

She liked that he was independent. Yet she feared. Let him go, she said to herself, let him ride and enjoy himself. Let him be free and natural and grow happy.

That Bert was dying troubled her, not so much because she pitied him his suffering, nor because his death would be a loss to her and she would have to grieve. She'd lost him long ago and her grieving was done; but because she didn't know how to respond. Part of her rejoiced and her delight in the idea of his death made her flee from her own mind. It couldn't be right to be glad of anyone's demise. She hadn't exulted when she'd heard of Hitler's grisly end in his bunker. It was pitiful. She hadn't celebrated the disappearance of Stalin, though she loathed him as monster who had betrayed a high ideal. Death, even of the most corrupt, blood-stained, vile, malicious, manipulative, self-serving, purblind, benighted, tyrannical person the earth had ever borne, was sad.

In her rapid, appalled flight from her own despicable response, she arrived at a sentimental destination. What she couldn't genuinely feel for Bert, she worked up factitiously. She convinced herself she must feel his loss as poignantly as that of her mother or father. He had been her husband. She had given birth to his children. The heat of pity, regret and sadness she generated was for herself. It was a performance in which she concealed from herself the terrible truth that her husband of sixteen years was dying and she was glad.

Like in many people, disappointment and bitterness had engendered unacknowledged murderous impulses. She believed herself incapable of them, as do millions of respectable men and women who never glimpse the vicious impulses which bubble beneath the surface of their assumed reasonableness. The ease with which the human mind moves to destructive impulses towards those who are a source of frustration or jealousy or regret or denial would come as a shock to commonplace self-complacency but ensures the buoyant sales of spatchcock paperbacks telling of stabbings, shootings, strangulations, dismemberments; the acceptable outlet for unacceptable motivations.

The house empty, a terrible lonely, weariness seeped into Elsie's mind. Her day would follow its usual routine: she would catch the bus to town, shop in Marks and Spencer and the market, come home laden her back aching from the effort. No doubt, as ever, she would fall asleep on the sofa after her lunchtime sandwich and cup of tea. Later, she would start to prepare a meal for herself and her son. They would eat together and he would thank her, then go upstairs, get himself ready and go out.

Wherever he was going would involve alcohol, which offended her Methodist strictures. She liked to think she was proud of her tee-totalism but she didn't know that being imposed rather than chosen, it easily became a source of anxiety and lack of confidence. Her child's mind had absorbed the prohibition and never grown to an independence that could question it. Being an absolute for her, it shook the flimsy structure of her selfhood when it collided with the relaxed attitude she thought shouldn't exist; the source of the exaggeration with which she defended her self-denial and condemned the indulgence of others. Never having tasted alcohol, she didn't recognise the difference between a drinker like her son who sat with a pint only for the company, and the alcoholic whose slavery was as imposed and absolute as her own.

What time would Andy be home? Once he was out of the house, he followed his own timetable. He might be back for no more than an hour or two before he left. He was a grown man. Yet she couldn't let go of the idea that he was her little boy. The curious notion lingered in the hinterland of her mind that her children could be her friends. She didn't know that her failure to establish adult relations, that her dependence on Bert during her marriage for a life which broke out of the defended cave of family, that her take-pity-on-me-withdrawal were a denial of a fundamental need and that a need denied will not disappear but merely reinvent itself in a perverse form.

She would spend the evening alone. She thought of Mary and Sylvia. Her elder daughter had two children and was pregnant and Sylvia's first was due in June. She ought to be at the centre of this joy. Had her mother been in danger of spending a Saturday evening alone, she would have visited. She would have insisted Bert and the children go too. Why did her own children abandon her to loneliness? It was a mere five miles to Sylvia's house and no more than twenty to Mary's. They had cars. How easy it would be for them to slip over and brighten her evening. She couldn't understand why they didn't. If only Patrick and his little brother could be here. They should be with their grandma. How would they feel, as they grew, if they knew she was lonely to the point of despair?

Yet it never occurred to her, in this condition, to take responsibility, make friends, invite people, to find those kind of contacts Bert was so good at and which struck her as superficial and unfulfilling.

As she'd expected, Andy appeared and disappeared like a hard-won idea.

She relied on the television for company; nodded off a nine; roused at ten, made her hot milk and went to bed in the room whose only comfort was the soft mattress and the warm eiderdown.

She dreamed of Bert tormented in the flames of hell. Andy rode in on his bicycle, crashed into a car and got up laughing. She was knocking on Mary's door. The lights were on but no one answered. She was at a dinner dance with Bert, dressed in a silk, low-cut dress, one man after another asked her to dance and whispered what he shouldn't in her ear. The television screen went blank.

The next day Andy told her he was applying for a flat in *The Maltings*, a somewhat barrack-like structure built as part of the ambitious plans for Lancashire New Town; one of those grandiose schemes elaborated in the minds of town-planners, politicians, bureaucrats and business people, without any serious involvement by the people, which trips up over the flowing robes it has dressed itself in, leaving behind half-built developments and fully broken hopes. There was a waiting list. The flats were small but the rent was modest and it would be fine for him.

"Rent is dead money. You're better off buying."

"I know, but for the time being. And I don't know how long I'm going to be here anyway."

As ever, her feelings were divided. He should be independent, but he should be with her. Why wasn't he married, settled and living round the corner where she could visit every day? The world had changed and she didn't understand how or why.

By the time he was allocated a flat, he'd bought himself an *old banger*. The day he got the keys, before he'd moved in even a book, he took her, in the evening, to have a look. Waiting outside, the engine running, he wondered what was delaying her. She appeared with a shopping bag, locked the door and running down the path, tripped over the half-circle, little metal riser that stopped the long-removed gate from swinging onto the pavement. She went down heavily on one knee. He switched off the engine and went to help her. Her tights were torn and the blood trickling down to her flat, black shoe.

"Come on in," he said, "I'll put a plaster on it."

"No. I'm all right. I'll be all right."

"But look. It's bleeding. You shouldn't have run. There's no hurry. It'll only take a minute to patch it up."

He knew her refusal was embarrassment and pride. He was enormously sorry for her. Why did she feel the need to run? Why had she brought a bag full of cleaning equipment? He wanted it to be a pleasant moment, to show her where he was going to live, to make her feel she was welcome there; but some awful need to be forever working, as if an eternal supervisor was at her back, about to upbraid her if she dared a moment of relaxation, had destroyed the mood.

When they entered the little, first-floor place: a kitchen without a window and a bathroom the same; a small lounge and an eight by six bedroom; without taking off her coat and with the blood still oozing, she took disinfectant, bath cleaner, kitchen cleaner from her bag and began to wipe rub and polish while he stood by. He went into the lounge and looked out over the parked cars. Hadn't it always been so, that he'd sought simple, gentle, tender, warm moments with his mother and her fierce need to be always on the *qui vive* had got in the way?

"Well, what do you think?" he said when she'd done.

"I don't know who was 'ere before," she said, "but they didn't keep their cupboards clean."

Gerry Beckett had a flat on the floor above. It became Andy's habit to give him a lift in the morning.

"You get me up early," said Gerry, yawning as they trotted down the stairs.

"Think of the work you can get done before the kids arrive," said Andy, "keeps your evenings free."

Gerry was congenial enough, being young, liberal and a probationer, but one morning, making conversation, Andy mentioned a radio interview he'd heard with David Hockney.

"Oh, him," said Gerry.

"Not one of your favourites, eh?"

"I don't like the way he's cornered the market. I'm a much better painter than he is."

Andy glanced at his passenger to see if his expression conveyed irony, but he was serious. He could never see his colleague and neighbour in the same way after. Did he really think he was more talented than Hockney? Maybe he was. Perhaps he was an overlooked genius. After all, Andy thought himself a better writer than some lauded figures. He despised the rise of on-the-make performance poetry. The *Six Gallery* reading and the effort to blow the dust off poetry were genuine, but already the movement was in decline and was turning into an asinine mix of Billy Smart's and *Top of The Pops*. He'd seen Adrian Mitchell read a few times and liked him. His early work was good on the page and his somewhat childish antics in performance didn't rob his work of seriousness and depth. In Ian McMillan, on the other hand, Andy spotted a posterity-denier for whom literature was a mirror and his kind of cheap-laughs, look-at-me-everybody poetry he thought less achieved than his own.

Perhaps he was as deluded as Gerry, if the art teacher was madly wrong about his ability.

He made a point of wandering over to the art room for a chat at the end of the day now and again to see if he could get a look at some of Gerry's work. He showed him a ceramic container in the shape of a shell with a neat lid. It was perfectly serviceable, but not great art, or even much art at all. Some time later, it turned out that a young Chemistry teacher who was living in a one of four, modern, cramped houses built in a block, so that each was not much more than a converted lift-shaft, had asked Gerry if he could brighten the place with a mural. Andy showed interest and was invited. Mark Hiscock, nervy, chain-smoking, thin and compulsively voluble, sat on the brown leather sofa in the tiny living-room while Andy inspected the ludicrous, twining, pale green fronds Gerry had added to the walls.

"Pretty good, eh?" said Mark.

"Yeah, yeah," said Andy. "You're happy with it, are you."

"I think so," said Mark, drawing on his cigarette and nodding as if he was a connoisseur. "Gives the place a more organic feel, don't you think?"

"Sure," said Andy. "Organic, Yeah."

Gerry, who appeared normal in every other way, was obviously in the grip of a delusion whose extent was reinforced when Andy stuck a Picasso print to his wall.

"Picasso," said Gerry, "if ever anyone was over-rated. I can paint much better than he could."

When someone we like, in the ordinary way of social intercourse, reveals some hidden madness, it shocks us and makes us question our affections. Andy would have liked to put his arm round Gerry's shoulders and say: "You're a nice bloke, people get on with you, you don't scratch people where they're sore. There's no need to try to pass yourself off as a genius." He tried to forget Gerry's stuck-to-the-ceiling view of himself, but found, whenever he was in his company, he was always trying to see through to the source of his delusion. Little by little he grasped that Gerry had a need to push people away: what better means than to declare yourself a genius? What, though, was the source of his need? Perhaps he'd had overbearing parents who had never permitted him to develop autonomy. Whatever it was, this little craziness at the centre of Gerry's mind was much more than a peripheral quirk.

It made Andy wonder about himself. He was struggling away to make himself a writer. Dozens of poems had been rejected by magazines which published work he thought jejune and superficial. He was thirty and had managed nothing more than three poems in print, in the university magazine. He questioned, time and again, whether he was embarked on a false path. Was he as deluded as Gerry? Did he have a minute talent unworthy of recognition? Yet his resolve to silence the typewriter never came to anything. He was nagged to try like a compulsive gambler is whipped to place the next bet, sure that this time his luck will change. He was reassured by comparing himself to Gerry: he would never have declared himself a better writer than Tolstoy or Jane Austen or Gunter Grass or Flaubert or Joyce. The idea was demented. He was merely convinced he could write well enough to be published: he had something to say. There was a literature in his head he'd never read and the demand to realize it wouldn't give him peace.

He discovered the District Librarian was a published poet and wrote to him. Perhaps getting together with other writers would bring some relief; maybe he could learn something; maybe, more cynically, it was a matter of contacts. Tom Lemon replied and suggested a meeting in *The Black Horse* where they could arrange with the landlord to colonize one of the little rooms. He knew a few others who might come along.

They gathered on a Wednesday evening. Tom Lemon, a tall, well-built Liverpudlian, educated at Oxford, turned out to be pleasant, easy-going, supportive and generous. He was married with two young boys and set up in a big house in comfortable St Annes. The other four were Claire Southworth, a fifty-year-old English teacher at the Polytechnic; Will Joiner, a long-haired, heavy-smoking and drinking jack-of-all-trades from Wycoller, who lived by whatever work he could find and whatever he could wangle from the State, was competent with his hands, and had come to poetry through *On The Road*, Bob Dylan, cannabis and the notion there was some deep affinity between self-abandonment and writing; Paul McCaffrey, who shared his city of origin with Lemon, had a petty, hated, administrative job with the council from which he took too many days sick and was anxious to escape, lived in near squalor in a rented house in a poor part of the town and longed to find a way to make a living from his fascination with books and film; and Mike Flowers, a thin, high-voiced, stiff, nineteen year-old friend of McCaffrey who had escaped his oppressive, conservative, Sussex family, come north because of the Mersey Poets, hoped to settle in Liverpool, but landed instead in Preston, where he claimed benefits, stayed in bed most of the day, scribbled poetry and dreamed of being discovered and emulating Brian Patten.

The landlord was happy to receive them because Wednesday nights were usually quiet. Six people hidden away in the room to the left of the main door, reading poetry and drinking steadily was just the kind of trade he liked. They resolved a format: people should pass out copies, read their poem and be willing to listen to the criticism, praise and suggestions of the group. Tom, Will, Paul and Andy and Claire had brought copies. Will went first. He read a forty-line poem about travels in Morocco, Algiers, Tunisia:

I was a free man in Tunis,

smoking Afghan black

and lusting after beautiful African girls…

The response was generally positive. Andy wanted to take issue with the poem's conclusion that the poet was *a slave in London*. The idea seemed preposterously romantic. He wanted to say, "Well, if you fell ill, would you have a free hospital bed in Morocco? And when you get old, is there a pension?" But the feeling in the room was indulgent and he was reluctant, on this first occasion, to introduce a tone of hard-headed criticism.

Will, who had downed five pints, asked Andy as they left if he wanted a lift. Restrained by newness, Andy didn't want to mock him: "A lift? You're sozzled. Do you think I have a death wish? Sober up before you get in your car or it may be the last time you do."

"No, that's okay. It's a short walk."

"Why walk when you can ride, man?" said the other, brushing aside his long hair and laughing in his spade-under-sand-and-cement way.

Andy wasn't sure this coterie was what he needed, but it was all there was. Claire had read a poem obviously derived from Lawrence's *Snake*, with a refrain about *the voices of my education*. Nobody seemed to spot the origin, unless like him they resisted the brutality of exposure. Paul read a piece about Nelson Mandela which ended on a what's-it-to-do-with-me note which suggested a mind on the edge of despair. Tom's poem, well-structured, measured and redolent of his balanced, beneficent personality, was an ironic take on a father's shrinking from having lost his temper with his child. The comments on his own piece had been friendly but he was disappointed that they weren't more astute. In his head was an idealised critic, well-read, objective, precise, articulate and fair. He knew his work was weak, but he didn't know how to gird it, or if he could. What he craved was the dispassionate, penetrating advice of a high literary mind. Were these people, Tom excepted, more interested in their egos than in literature?

All the same, it was something. It was contact of almost the right kind. Who could say where it might lead?

During his interview with John Wellington, Andy had mildly expressed the wish to teach at least as much English as French, and the sour-faced boss had said he'd speak to Jim Hunter. Something should be possible; but his timetable was entirely French. Andy had also assumed he'd get his fair share of sixth-form teaching, but Don Crawley had given him none. The thirty-two periods a week were shared by him and Alma Mayor. Mike Chambers had mentioned it.

"Yeah, " said Andy, "I think we know why?"

"Eh?"

"Well, he has a soft spot for the girls, doesn't he?"

"Soft spot? He's soft in the head," said his subordinate spooning lemon meringue into his mouth in that slightly obscene way he had, as if every mouthful might be his last.

"I'm going to ask him to ensure I get some next year."

"Good. I'll speak to him too. It's not right."

Andy judged the best was to let Chambers put the argument first. He got nowhere and suggested a visit to the Head might be necessary. Cooper wasn't an easy man to see. Already the pupils had nick-named him Lord Lucan. He avoided being around when they arrived, didn't do a break or lunch duty and though he was, at least for the first term, on the bus duty rota, failed to turn up. He went home every lunchtime and was often early to leave and late to return, and more than once, when Andy had needed to speak to him about a union matter, having taken on the role of NUT rep in his first fortnight, was reported by the office to be *working at home*. It wasn't unusual for a knock on his door to bring alive the red OCCUPIED light.

It was the last period of the afternoon. His voice called "Come in." He was behind his desk which sat at an angle so he was almost square to the view of the lawn, the flowering cherry and the hedge of his private garden from the picture window. He looked up from his papers and smiled; one of those official smiles which have nothing about them of a true smile of friendship or gladness.

"Sit down, Andrew."

To the complaint, Cooper replied brusquely:

"I don't tell my heads of department how to run their departments. I suppose Don Crawley must have his reasons."

Shocked by what he saw as a renunciation of responsibility, Andy was silenced because what he wanted to say in response to this out-of-hand dismissal of his perceived reasonable request was too disruptive. He sat, still and intent as Cooper sat back in his chair and swayed from side to side as if he'd resolved the question with the wisdom of Solomon. His heart beat heavily. Had he spoken, his words would have been aggressive and bitter:

"You do know about Diane Clayton? You are aware that your head of department is having his pockets picked by a cynical girl he is infatuated with? You must know he is in tears in the stock room before school some mornings and his heaping his pathetic, adolescent torments onto Alma Mayor is driving her to contemplating resignation? You surely know she isn't the only one he's slobbering over? Are you telling me this is professional? Are you suggesting I have to see my chances squeezed so he can live out his repressed fantasies? You say he must have his reasons, have you no idea what they are?"

He left the study angry, disappointed but calm. He wouldn't stay in this place. He would put it behind him quickly. There was something twisted and regressive at the heart of the institution. He should never have accepted the job, but he would be away as soon as he could.

The weeks passed quickly. His days were busy. He'd joined the Labour Party when he returned to Preston and been elected secretary of his branch, delegate to the constituency, to the district party, to the county party and now was being pestered to take over as constituency secretary. He was at meetings four nights a week. The terms evaporated and the long summer days soon arrived when, the external and internal exams over, things relaxed, pupils were taken on trips by their form tutors, Rob Hesketh set up the tents on the rugby field in preparation for his departure to the Loire valley with fifty boys, the glorious six-week break beckoned like an attentive lover, there were fewer books to mark, the upper sixth and fifth form disappeared, and the clunk of a corker against willow was heard from the front field.

One Tuesday morning, Andy was left with seven second years, those who had turned down the offer of a trip to Alton Towers. They were quiet, polite boys who'd brought cards and chess sets. He sat at the front reading Anatole France while they got on with their games.

"Sir," one of them said after twenty minutes, "can we go out and watch the cricket?"

Wary of betraying his ignorance, having no idea what cricket they meant, he said:

"Well, I'm not sure that's allowed."

"We did it last year, sir."

"Did you?"

"Yes, sir. Mr Bird took us out, sir."

"Well, if Mr Bird thinks it's okay, maybe it is."

Andy wondered why there had been no announcement. Were these boys taking him for a mug?

"I'll tell you what. As it's a nice day, we'll go and have a look. If there are other classes out there, then I'll have a word and see if we can stay too. But if we can't, we can't. Do you understand?"

"Yes, sir."

"You must follow me, nice and quiet, and if I say we come back to the classroom, we come straight back. No fuss."

"Yes, sir."

"Okay. Leave your bags here and come for them when the bell goes."

On the front field, surrounded by tall sycamores, elms and oaks, smelling of newly-cut grass, caressed by the not-yet-fierce morning sun, boys who had discarded their black blazers were lying, sitting, crouching, in groups of ten, twenty or thirty around the cricket square where Tim Heath, Head of History and gifted batsman and Chris Bickerstaffe, Head of P.E. and competent all-rounder were opening for the staff against the sixth-form, facing the aggressive bowling of Craig Jackson who played for the county and whose bouncers, googlies and full-tosses terrified the older, short-sighted and slow teachers recruited for the annual ritual.

Andy spotted Keith Jackson, a young, sympathetic English teacher, on a plastic chair in the middle of a huddle of thirty white-shirted, tie-askew boys.

"Come on," he said to his seven, "let's go and see if we can join Mr Jackson."

The dark-haired, slim English teacher, his right knee hooked over his left, squinted as he looked up at Andy.

"Hello, Mr Lang. Come to enjoy the cricket as much as I do?"

"I guess so, " Andy laughed. "I was just wondering what the protocol is. Can I bring these boys out?"

"The protocol is no protocol. It's left to our discretion and as you see, discretion being the better part of a good skive, everybody's out."

"I see. I'll find a spot for them then."

"Leave them here. They don't look too psychopathic."

"Are you sure?"

"Of course. Why should two of us be bored to death watching old men with bad backs trying to recapture a glory they never enjoyed? Sit down here boys," he called to the youngsters. "Go to the staff-room and have a cup of tea for me, if you like."

"Would you like me to bring one out to you?"

"No, just had one, but if you've got something that will keep me awake for the next hour, I'll have it."

"What if you do half an hour and I take over."

"No, I'll be fine. You go and relax a bit."

"Okay. Thanks for that. I'll return the favour some time."

"I'll take you up on it. Expect a pile of illegible essays to mark."

"See you later," laughed Andy.

In the staff-room he settled with a brew and *The Guardian*. The door flew open as if a battalion was about to enter. Mike Chambers stopped dead. His lips curled into an unpleasant sneer.

"Not teaching?"

"No. I had the remnants of 2F1, seven of them. Keith Jackson is looking after them on the front field."

"The front field?"

"Yes, the cricket."

Chambers pulled himself erect.

"This place is chaos," he uttered, "absolute chaos," and he strode away on his long, thin legs and splay feet, trying to look brisk, powerful and athletic but appearing merely silly, petulant and pretentious.

Andy thought no more of it till the Friday morning staff-meeting when Cooper announced:

"For future reference, if you are left with pupils to supervise when others are out on a trip, should it be no more than seven second years, you must stay with them. It's not acceptable to let them wander the site unsupervised."

He wondered if he should confront Chambers. Wander the site unsupervised? The miserable sneak. What had he said to Cooper? He knew if he challenged him he wouldn't be able to keep his temper. He would tell him what he thought of him. Let it go, he said to himself. Let it go. I'll be out of this place in no time.

DECISION

For some months, Elsie Lang had settled into the comfortable assumption Mrs Thatcher was doomed. The opinion polls were against her. Jobs were evaporating. What worried her was division in the Labour Party. The creation of the SDP had riled her. She despised Williams, Owen, Rogers and Jenkins as opportunists who had made their names and careers in the Labour Party and were now intent on destroying it because they couldn't get their own way. Her sympathy was with Michael Foot who she saw as a man of principle surrounded by morally dubious chancers. Her instinct was unity. There had to be room for many shades of opinion, but the watchword must be solidarity to keep the Tories out of power. That the *Gang of Four* had betrayed that essential need filled her with disdain. She was horrified when she discovered some of the MPs who defected to the SDP voted for Foot as they left in the belief he would be a disaster. That was wicked. If they wanted to leave the Party, they had the freedom to do so; but to seek to inflict maximum damage on an organisation they wanted to flee, was behaviour from the gutter. They should have held their heads high, resigned and left with dignity.

She was pleased when Foot became leader and believed that in spite of the vile media campaign against him, his principle would win through. The slander that he'd worn a donkey jacket at the cenotaph struck her as typical of the cynical, mean, narrow-minded, cheap, ignorant, lying way the papers operated. It wasn't a donkey jacket, but even if it had been, so what? Couldn't a man in a donkey jacket be sincere in his regret for lives lost in war? She would have more trust in Michael Foot if he turned up at the cenotaph in his pyjamas than in Thatcher in gold braid and diamonds.

The outbreak of the Falklands War threw her assumption into the dustbin. She sensed at once the mood of jingoism she feared and despised. During the war, she'd admired the way people pulled together and sacrificed to prevail; but at the same time she'd been aware of a malicious undercurrent. It was reminiscent of Mosley and the ugly blackshirts: arrogant, regressed, purblind, self-justifying, inward, intolerant, prejudiced and vicious. She knew people who operated the black market and celebrated war as an opportunity. She heard those who argued for punishment of Germany when the war was over. She knew that war can send people insane and she was anxious.

Andy was on an exchange visit to France. She wished she could unburden her weight of pain on him. Of her children, he was the one who replicated most accurately her father's principled radicalism. She couldn't have talked to Mary or Sylvia about what was going on in the world in the same way. It wasn't at the centre of their thinking; but Andy thought about it insistently and intently.

The war was ridiculous. John Nott had sent the signal that Britain was no longer serious about defending its South Atlantic possessions. She agreed with the withdrawal of *HMS Endurance*, not because she wanted to save money and shift it to nuclear submarines like Nott, but because she viewed British possession of islands thousands of miles away, seized by violence more than two hundred years ago as morally outrageous. What was seized by violence, she believed, should be relinquished. It was ludicrous that islands a few hundred miles off the coast of Patagonia should belong to Britain, as if the Isle of Man should belong to Argentina.

Where her attitude softened was to the residents. The islands were their home. If they wanted to stay, they should be permitted to. Some arrangement should be made. They should be allowed to stay and have British citizenship, but the islands should belong to the mainland.

The last thing necessary was war. She listened to the reports and the debates. It was obvious Galtieri was trying to divert attention from his country's appalling economic failure. He was a typical tin-pot dictator. He wouldn't last, and whatever pressure was needed could be exerted through the United Nations and international sanctions. No, Thatcher wasn't sending a task force because it was the only or even a rational response, but because she wanted to emulate her hero Churchill; she wanted to be the great war leader, the saviour of her nation.

When the troops returned to adulation and she saw naked-breasted girls on the television beneath a banner bearing the slogan, *Get Your Tits Out For The Boys*, she knew her society had tipped into collective madness.

If an unnecessary skirmish thousands of miles from our shores to regain control of territory we took by piracy could raise this inauthentic sense of national greatness, people were morally and psychologically at a very low pitch. She knew it was true. Inauthenticity was everywhere. People were buying gadgets, clothes, cars, foreign holidays, to compensate for the dreadful lack of community. The riots in Brixton, Toxteth, Manchester and Leeds were the other face of the coin of breakdown and heartbreak. She was living in a heartbroken society and heartbroken people clutch at inadequate resources.

She knew herself a heartbroken woman, not only in her personal life, but because the vision of a society of cooperation in equality where the quality of your human relations mattered more than the quantity of your possessions, had collapsed. She laid most of the blame on the *Gang of Four*. The united Labour voice which could offer people hope had been silenced by their selfishness. People could put up with a lot if they had hope, but hope had to be for something more than a food mixer, a new vacuum, a new car, two cars, a fortnight on the Costa Brava, a colour television in the kitchen. That was mere aspiration. She heard the word used during a television debate. A society of aspiration. Oh, she knew what that meant: keeping up with the Jonses and the contagion of snobbery; measuring yourself by the value of your house, your car, your holiday, your fridge, your three-piece-suite. It was a doctrine of despair. It was the recognition that your relations with your fellow human being had broken down and in their place you chose to relate to things.

The things were a mirror. By valuing them you were trying to boost yourself, to see yourself as better than the next woman; and why did people need to do that? Only because they were unhappy, because they were heartbroken. Constantly comparing yourself to others was the short route to misery, even for those who could view themselves as superior. In Thatcher's phoney enunciation, for example, she heard the sound of unhappiness. Why would a happy person need to present themselves as something they weren't? She was the arch phantom, the unreal person, the person with no centre. They called her *The Iron Lady* but in truth she was *The Meringue Woman*. A meringue is hard on its surface but beneath there is nothing sustaining. Mere whipped sugar. That was Thatcher, an empty confection. Her cruelty was like the substance of a meringue: it promised you satisfaction but it was gone in a minute of unsatisfying thrill and all it gave you was weight gain and toothache.

She was cruel because her own feelings were dead. She couldn't understand the hurtfulness of her politics because she was defended against feeling. What she offered people was money, possessions, stuff, because she couldn't offer them the hope of friendly, generous, principled but easy-going, love-your-neighbour-as-yourself relations. What she believed in was power and Elsie knew love and power were sworn enemies.

What was going to happen to her society if this continued, if people turned inwards and used their possessions against one another? At the heart of it was hatred and violence, the wish to do others down. That was the truth about aspiration. It was god bless me and my wife, my son John and his wife, us four, no more. It was a kind of murder. Murdering people in their hearts. Killing their sense of self. Diminishing them. Climbing over them and trampling them underfoot to elevate yourself, in flight from your dreadful inner emptiness and heartbreak.

She was nearing sixty. Soon she would retire from the training kitchen. The work wearied her. When she thought of retirement, she thought of her grandchildren. How she would like to live close to Mary or Sylvia. How, in fact, she would like to live with them. Sylvia's daughter Louisa was approaching her first birthday. If Elsie were to move to Leyland, she could see her every day. She would have to talk to Sylvia. She would suggest it. She wouldn't turn her down. She could sell up. The house was worth maybe thirty thousand. She could buy a bungalow for twenty and feel well off. Yes, that's what she would do.

"Well," said Andy, "this is a nice house. You know the neighbours. It's handy for town."

"I can't afford th'upkeep," she said. "There's always summat. Suppose roof goes. What'll I do then?"

"We'll help you out."

"Eh?"

"Ted's a joiner. Barry could fix a broken jet engine with a hammer a pair of pliers and a box of screws. I can't do anything, but I'll help out with the cost. I'll pay your gas and electricity, if you like."

"You will not," she said, her upper body stiffening. "No, it's too big for me. I need summat smaller. As I get on, even cleanin'll be too much."

"We'll do it. I can pop in most days. Sylvia's only five miles away. Anyway, you're still active. You don't need to worry yet."

Andy had called in on his way home from work. She'd made him a welcome cup of tea and delivered the inevitable thick slice of the fruit cake she loved to bake and he loved to eat. He stayed for half an hour, tucked his trousers into his socks and climbed on his bike. In August he'd moved into a little house off Broadgate, by the Ribble; a two-bedroomed terrace with a tiny front garden and a back yard. She was glad because she felt the mortgage was a tether. He was more likely to stay. He was no more than a mile from her front door, and even if she shifted to Leyland, he'd be less than five miles away. The idea of him married and adding to her store of adoring grandchildren, she'd set aside. In that kick of fatalism which characterised her mentality, she assumed he would die a bachelor.

Alone, the evening ahead of her, without conversation or a presence, only the prospect of her lonely bed, and tomorrow another day to fill and no urgent demand on her, she sank into that mood of retrospective regret in which her mind, suffused with thoughts of the lost, happy days of her childhood and adolescence, detached itself from reality and her silent accusation against the world that had let her down became a comfort, a companion, her refuge.

She retired at the time Andy moved into his house. The longed-for relief from work delivered her to the shores of exclusion. She cleaned, she baked, she decorated. She caught the bus to town, she went to the local shops, hoping she would bump into someone; but time and again she came home not having seen a soul she knew. Her one surety was church. She caught the bus at two minutes past ten every Sunday. Before and after the service there were people to chat to. She began to make friends with Molly Parkinson and Ethel Hardman. Molly was her age and blind. She lived in a modified bungalow in Ashton and was almost independent. Her daughter, who had married a surveyor and moved to Canterbury, telephoned every day and came up regularly. Ethel was a widow whose grown-up children were both in London. A physically big, bulky woman whose size intimidated the petite Elsie, she was brusque and decisive, and though an ingrained Labour voter, having grown up in the terraced streets off New Hall Lane and felt the sharp, humiliating pinch of poverty, often expressed exasperating opinions.

"Too many Pakis in this town," she'd blurt as the three of them sat in the underground church café.

"Now that's not a Christian attitude, Ethel," Elsie would retort.

"Well, they aren't Christians, are they? They should be in their own countries."

"Eee, Ethel, should we? We had an empire, We ruled half the globe. They have a right to be here because we colonised their countries and made them British citizens. Chickens come home to roost, Ethel. Anyway, I like 'em. They're nice, hard-workin' folk, and they look after one another."

Molly remained aloof from these disputes, having no political opinions or prejudices. A quiet, timid woman, she was grateful for any company but her conversation was limited to responses and her range bounded by trivialities.

Though in these liaisons Elsie found nothing of the edifying excitement of the friendships of her girlhood, though they left her disappointed and wondering if it was worth cultivating them, she adhered to that intractable law of the human mind which makes the least congenial friend infinitely preferable to loneliness.

She worked as a volunteer in the café. Twice a week she baked scones and, unable to carry all of them at one go, made two trips by bus to deliver them, before doing her two hours behind the counter, serving, wiping, washing up. Compared to her job in the training kitchen, it was easy. She loved it. She was useful. She spoke to people. She was relied on. All the same, what nagged at her was her desire to be close to her family.

What Andy had said played on her mind. Perhaps it would be possible: if Ted and Barry were willing. She could stay. His offer to help with her bills touched her. He was a good lad. She could rely on him. Yet the impulse to move close to Sylvia, to be embedded, to see her grand-daughter every day, overwhelmed the rational recognition of her current advantages. Sylvia, the youngest child she had tried to bind to her like a sapling to the thick post without which the wind will force it over, had escaped; but if she lived a few hundred yards away, she could re-establish the dependency. She had to move.

"She wants to move to Leyland," Sylvia said to Barry.

"Yeah, why not?" he replied, settling on the sofa with a beer.

"I'm not sure I want her so close."

"It'll be all right," he said. "She wants to help out. That's fine. A hands-on grandma."

Barry was always easy-going. If she'd said her mother wanted to move in, he'd have shrugged his shoulders and been cheerful. His resolutely practical mind treated every problem in the same way: there was no difference between finding a route for the wiring in a house without chiselling into the newly-decorated plaster and resolving the neurotic conflicts of family entanglements. She was glad of it. Yet at the same time, she wasn't so sure her mother's plan would work out well. It would be good to have her on hand to help with Louisa and as they intended not to wait too long for a second, she could be a great help when there were two little ones; but five miles wasn't impossible yet was far enough to mean she wasn't intrusive. Sylvia was aware of how hard she'd had to push to break away. From the grand perspective of a twenty-three-year-old, she could look back on her teenage dreams of escape to America and understand they were the necessary fantasy of a trammelled girl.

Marriage and motherhood had liberated her. She was a woman in her own right. She had her home, her husband, her child. Barry earned enough from scrambling under floorboards and in attics, hammering at bricks with a lump hammer to fit back-boxes, for her to stay at home till Louisa and whatever children followed reached school age. She felt she'd escaped. She loved her mother intensely but at the same time regretted how she'd tried to cling to her at just the time she should have been pushing her away, lifting her into the autonomy which is impossible without distance.

"I think she'd be better staying put," said Andy when he visited one Saturday.

"Well, it's up to her."

"It is, but what I suggested was Ted and Barry could do the maintenance. I'll put up some money and help her with her bills. That's what she's worried about. Big costs for repairs and not being able to keep the place in good nick and clean and tidy."

"I know. Well, Barry would agree."

"Yeah, and Mary would bring Ted into line."

"We can only suggest it. You know what she's like. Once she's made up her mind…."

"I know, but I know too she makes bad decisions sometimes."

He wanted to say their mother moving to Leyland was a restraint. Supposing she and Barry wanted to move. Why should they feel the need to stay in Leyland? And her mother couldn't follow them everywhere. He wanted to argue that Sylvia should say that to her, make it clear that they might be in Leyland for no more than year or two, so she was better staying in Penwortham; but he resisted because it was too big a demand on his sister.

"Leave her to it, Andy. It will be helpful, after all, to have her nearby while my kids are small."

"Kids?" he said.

"I'm not sticking at one."

"Is a second imminent?"

"No."

"Oh, what a disappointment."

"You'll just have to be patient, won't you?"

Andy made three of four more assaults on his mother's resolution. When the old gas-heater-and-wringer washing machine she'd adhered to like a fanatic to his faith finally coughed, choked and died, he bought her a new one. He suggested an automatic but she wouldn't hear of it; a twin-tub would do. He paid for a carpet fitter to renew the hall and stairs. When she found rot in the pantry window, he turned up with tools, chipped out the flaking wood, filled the gaps, sanded, primed, undercoated and glossed.

"I spoke to Sylvia," he said as he washed his hands in the kitchen. "Barry will help out with repairs. He can do anything. And if I mention it to Mary, she'll twist Ted's arm."

"They're not reliable," she said. "I can't be waitin' months if summat needs doin'."

"Well, I'll always see it's done. I'll pay somebody."

Nothing availed. Elsie did the tour of estate agents, booked appointments, shook her head, started again. Barry went with her to assess the state of repair. She found a two-bedroomed bungalow in St Anne's Road, on an estate just outside the little town. It had a garden back and front and fields beyond the rear fence. Barry found damp in the bathroom, pulled up the carpet, discovered a small leak which had rotted the boards. He could fix it. She asked for a reduction of five hundred. The seller agreed. To expedite matters, she put her house on the market for twenty-four thousand. The first young couple to visit offered the asking price. She was in her new place by Easter.

"Twenty-four grand," said Andy to Sylvia.

"I know."

"She could've got thirty."

"You know what she's like."

He was convinced it was a bad decision. From the first, he didn't like her bungalow. It was adequate, but one of those 1960s buildings, cheaply put up by spec companies, with hollow doors, two-inch skirting boards, low ceilings, no features to give them character or individuality. Nor did he like the estate, which felt cramped and temporary compared to Woodland Grove. She had a five-mile bus ride to church, her lifeline. Evening events became a problem because she was nervous of coming home alone in the dark. When Andy bought a second-hand *Marina*, he offered to take her and pick her up, but she refused.

He had an ominous feeling she was going to regret her decision.

"What's her address?" said his dad.

Andy had nipped over one rainy Sunday lunchtime.

"It's St Anne's Road."

"What number?" said Bert, picking up a pen.

He was dying and he knew it. How long could he last? His life was pain and incapacity. That he managed to remain independent amazed his son. While he was out at the day-centre the previous Wednesday, someone had broken in through the bathroom window. The opening light was smashed. They'd stolen what money was around but no more. Bert believed he must have disturbed them. Some hero, Andy reflected, knowing his dad lived alone and was disabled had taken his chance. What a low, despicable way to behave. He would starve before he would steal from a vulnerable, old person. He nailed boards over the window to secure it till the joiner could come.

"Mmm. I've forgotten," he said. "I'll look it up and let you know."

His dad wanted to get in touch with his mother. He could understand. He was about to leave the earth. She'd been his wife for sixteen years. She was the mother of three of his children. He wanted to say goodbye to her; but Andy knew she would rebuff him. Even now, even though her ex-husband was frail, weak, shrunken, sunken-cheeked, barely able to walk, she would not relent. He knew his dad wanted a reconciliation before death, but he knew she would hurt him. It was better not to try.

Bert looked at his son, his pen poised over his address book. He knew he was lying.

He closed the oblong, red, gold embossed cover and put the biro aside. He was irritated and wanted to challenge Andy, but what was the point? Perhaps he was right: a reunion with Elsie wouldn't be the forgiving, gentle, I'm-dying-let's-put-our-conflicts-behind-us encounter he imagined. If she was as haughty, brittle and rejecting as ever, it would harm his feelings and in his condition, that might seriously injure his physical condition. He would have to die without seeing her.

The idea appalled and amused him.

"I'll make a cup of tea," he said about to hobble to the kitchen.

"No, sit down. I'll do it."

He dropped into the armchair by the window. How lovely the world was. Even this ordinary scene. How miraculous that humanity, from the resources provided by an earth which existed for billions of years before our evolution began, could make this civilization, these comfortable, heated houses with carpets, armchairs, sofas, beds, wardrobes, electrical wiring, copper piping, wallpaper, paint, lights, televisions, radios, telephones. The proximity of death made life sweeter, more charming, more delicious and beautiful than he could have imagined.

He had wasted his life.

It hit him with the weight and velocity of a train, yet left him curiously light-hearted. The world was inexhaustibly interesting and thrilling. He watched the trees in the garden opposite sway in the light breeze. Why had he never bothered to find out about winds and trees? What was it about the branches which made them able to bend? Why didn't they snap? What force would it take to snap them? A car went by and turned right. What a miracle. How much work and ingenuity had it taken to make such a thing possible; and we took it for granted. Not until, like him, life was about to be taken from you, did you truly realize what arrogance and folly it was to take anything for granted. If he could be young again, if he could be Andy's age, he wouldn't waste a minute. He would treasure life in all its manifestations. He would abuse nothing, neglect nothing. Given his time again, how different his life would be.

He thought of Laura Bruzzese. Would he see her again? Would she come to his funeral? Would she even know he was dead? Would most people he'd known? There would be the usual notice in the paper, but who would see that? In all likelihood, there would be no more than a dozen to see him into the flames. He couldn't even be sure that Mary and Sylvia would be there. He wished everyone he'd known who was still alive would come to visit him, even the likes of Ken Wickham. He couldn't despise him anymore. He couldn't despise anyone. There was no room in his feelings for negativity. He was clinging to life and life was a remarkable miracle. That human beings responded to it with hatred, greed, aggression, war was too stupid to think of. We should cherish and nurture life and never do any harm.

How different his life could have been. He shouldn't have made Laura pregnant. It was the act of a rash and blithe young man. Perhaps he shouldn't have married Elsie. Yet he didn't regret it utterly. The dalliance with Laura had scuppered him. He and Elsie could have stayed together. There were difficulties, but he could have brought up his children, grown old with his wife. Yes, it could have been a good marriage.

If only he'd known when he was fifteen or eighteen or twenty or twenty-five, how to treat life with the attentive, loving delicacy he now felt. He was born into poverty and neglect. He was sent to fight in a war he had nothing to do with. Huge social forces were manipulated to bring great armies into the arena of destruction and carnage. It was madness. War was madness. There was no need for it. It was no more inevitable than the punch in the face the drunk delivers over some petty disagreement in the pub. It was insanity and it could always be avoided. War was always an expression of greed, ignorance, the desire for power and the denial of human unity; and he, as a mere boy of seventeen had been thrown into it by madmen who had lost touch with life.

A blackbird landed on the lawn, a female, her feathers rich black, her beak yellow. She paused. Her head twitched from side to side before she pecked at the grass. How lovely. If only people could learn to see the miraculous wonder of simply being alive, set aside their mad pursuit of money, fame and power; if only he'd known a world where people knew how to be happy.

He was alive. If this was the last day of his life, if it was the last few hours, he was determined to relish the extraordinary fact of existence. He loved life. Merely to sit here and to be able to see was delightful. He could see. He could hear. He could move. To think he'd once been able to run.

Andy brought him his tea and a little plate of wholemeal toast and honey. He could smell the warm bread. He tasted the mixture of butter and honey. He was alive. He was eating. He was with his son. Life was wonderful, but what negligence and ignorance humanity treated it with.

Watching someone die is quite different from their sudden disappearance. One day, his grandad was in his room, as normal. The next morning he was zipped into a green, canvas bag and removed by the undertaker. It was terrible. He hadn't said goodbye. He'd seen his grandad virtually every day of his life. He had spent hours in his room watching the television and doing headstands on his bed. He'd loved the taciturn old man whose conversation was seldom more than three sentences. He was gone.

Being amongst youngsters was a relief. The pupils were full of life, brimming with chatter, energy and eagerness, though not always to learn. Andy found being in their presence a great pleasure. He enjoyed their noise in the corridors, their raucous games at break and lunchtime, even their mischief in the classroom. They were alive.

"Sit down, Martin, what do you think this is, Donnybrook Fair?"

A great roar of laughter went up from the class. He relished the banter. The idea of having children under strict control appalled him. They were young, they should be full of cheek and chutzpah.

"That's a good one, sir. Donnybrook Fair. Where'd you find that, sir?"

"I read a book now and again, Billy. Do you know what a book is? There are hundreds over there in the library. Stick your nose in one sometime."

It was all taken in good heart. The pupils liked the humour. He was one of those teachers children don't fear. Inevitably, in a regime built on mild terror, grounded in a military model where control and obedience were more important than picking up skills or knowledge, some pupils mistook his generosity for weakness. Teachers were supposed to be tough. They were meant to be strict. You were meant to be afraid. Mr Hesketh inflicted his number 13 slipper with pent up venom, chalking the inverted number on the sole and leaving its rectified imprint on the boys' backsides; and he was erratic: one day he'd let you get away with talking, the next you would be at his desk, bent double as his thick arm pulled back to its maximum height and whipped through the air to deliver one, two, three or four which made you cry.

Mr Chambers was a bully whose demeanour was a threat. He didn't use the slipper but he could make your insides melt by the way he talked to you. He would stand over you, push his face close to yours, berate you, imply you were letting him down, tell you how hard he was working on your behalf, say he was going to bring your parents in, till you felt sick and began to tremble.

Imaginative pupils recognised Mr Lang was confident enough to set this aside. He neither hit nor humiliated. He joked, cajoled, negotiated and seemed to understand that school was boring and to enliven it with a bit of gentle subversion made it more bearable. Others didn't know how to take him and seeing him simply as a weak link went wild and had to be reined in. All the same, the worst you were likely to get from Mr Lang was lines. He was sparing even with detentions.

At Easter, shortly before he'd left on the exchange to Carvin in north-east France, he'd put in an application for a second-in-department post at Morecambe High School. He could go back to Lancaster. There were still people around he knew. He knocked on

Cooper's door three or four times but he was either not there or the engaged sign lit up. In his insouciant way, he assumed if a request for a reference arrived during the holiday, Cooper would respond and speak to him at the start of term.

He called him in during the first week.

"It's customary when you apply for a job to ask your Headteacher for a reference," he began, stiff, haughty, public-school, addressing him as if he was a bumpkin who failed to comprehend a simple protocol.

"Well, I did knock on your door a few times."

Cooper bridled a little. His torso stiffened. He looked down at the papers on his desk as if he needed to remind himself of something.

"Yes," he said looking up, an artificial little smile on his lips, "I thought that might be the case."

Andy nodded and smiled in response.

"The school did take up your references."

Andy would have been delighted to hear that had it not been for Cooper's intonation making it clear something negative was to follow.

"I'm afraid I had to include a reservation," he paused.

Too dismayed to say anything, Andy sat still and silent.

"A second-in-department post is not a sinecure…"

Dismay turned to outrage but Andy made no response or movement.

"You don't have enough experience to take on such a responsibility. You can't take it on and not fulfil it conscientiously. You need to wait a while before you apply for promotion…"

Andy was asking himself whether he had a folded piece of foolscap in his inside pocket, as he often did. He could slip it out and scribble his resignation, lay it on the desk and walk out. Maybe it would be better to wait. Go straight to the staff-room and slip it in Cooper's pigeon-hole. He went on listening but he wasn't attentive to what the Head was saying. He was examining his posture, his tone of voice, his facial expression.

When he'd finished, Cooper asked him if he wished to say anything.

"Yes, did you mention the letter of commendation from the exam board?"

"The what?"

"Last September the C.S.E. board wrote congratulating me on the conduct and marking of the C.S.E. orals. I wondered if you'd mentioned that in the reference."

"I don't recall seeing the letter."

"Oh yes, you passed it to Don Crawley and he gave it to me."

"You may be right, but I don't remember it."

The interview over, Andy went for a walk round the site to calm down. "I thought that might be the case." The liar. He was piqued. He felt his authority had been snubbed. He'd taken revenge for what he felt was an absence of deference. The fault lay with him, entirely. Had he been available, Andy would have asked for his support. Five terms into teaching and the pusillanimity of a still-to-grow-up public schoolboy, touchy about his status, expecting behaviour that was the equivalent of touching the forelock from fully grown men and women, had put a barrier before him. He was leaving. He would write his letter of resignation as soon as he got his hands on paper.

What he didn't know and never would was that after a brief conversation in the staff-room with Chambers, who'd asked him whether he'd got the Head's support for his application, and Andy had answered:

"No, knocked on his door a couple of times but he must have been asleep. I'll see him when I get back from France,"

Chambers had gone to Copper and said:

"I know, Headmaster, that Andy Lang hasn't told you this, but he's applying for a job."

"Is he ? Where?"

"Morecambe High School. Second in department. I've told him he should ask you for a reference but he says he can't be bothered."

"Oh, does he? Well, thank you for that, Michael."

Nor would he ever know that Chambers, who had worked for seven years before securing a second-in-department post, was jealous and resentful: why should Andy Lang, whose easy-going ways in the classroom made Chambers anxious and angry, be promoted after only six terms? Andy's instinct was not to betray people to authority. He would have gone to the police if he knew someone guilty of rape or bank robbery but getting people in trouble at work over trivial matters was the behaviour of a cockroach. He was slow to learn most people took a very different view.

In the staff-room, he was lapelled by Don Crawley who wanted to ask him if he would write the internal exams for his classes. The rest of the day was busy. He had to rush his tea and get to a Labour Party meeting by seven. When it finished at ten, seven of them adjourned to *The Continental*.

Not long after he'd arrived in Avenham Branch, reports having come their way from South Fylde, and no one else being willing, the members asked him if he'd take over as secretary. He'd established solid, warm, little friendships with a core of members. They went out to the pubs on Friday evenings and finished off in *Angelos* for a late-night pizza. He was a frequent visitor to the house of Sean Dunbar, a councillor, and Kath Sparrow, a primary teacher, where people would congregate at the weekend, booze flow, spliffs be lit and the place fill with smoke, music, conversation and laughter. The little coterie of radicals had become his closest friends.

He was reluctant to intrude his difficulties at work into the relaxed chat before closing time, but as he finished his pint and picked up his file he said:

"Ah, well, work tomorrow, and I've got my resignation letter to write before I go to bed."

"Resignation?" said Kath her face rigid with surprise.

He told them, briefly about his interview with the Head.

"Don't be hasty," said Stan Stephen, a big, hard-boozing, red-bearded, latter-day Cornudet and full time official of UCATT, who ended most evenings in the riverside pub close by his home.

He refused to join The Labour Party, arguing it was too willing to compromise with the capitalism he hated. His work representing members who were on blacklists, sacked for petty misdemeanours, injured on building sites, some of them seriously, had taught him that management is unflinching in the defence of the employer's interest, which is always the interest of money. He was outwardly rough bluster but beneath was a gentle sensibility affronted by the cold calculation of lucre.

"I can't stay there, the man is unprofessional."

"Yeah, but you're angry," said Sean, puffing on his cigarette. "Let the dust settle and look round for another job."

"Yes," said Kath, "you don't want to lose your income. Not with Thatcher in power. Who knows how many will be on the dole in six months."

"Sit tight," said Stan, putting his empty glass on the table and picking up the next, "never resign, that's my motto. Like Clive Jenkins said, let the buggers sack you, it's more lucrative. Sean's right, you're angry. Take your time."

Andy was softened in his resolve by their concern. As he walked home alone he mulled what they'd said. It was true he was angry. Who wouldn't be? But he wasn't acting impulsively. Maybe he should think about a spell in London, which might be no bad thing, or like Steve Bancroft, who after getting his PGCE had taken a job in Wells, look for a school in some charming, pretty place away from the bitter inheritance of capitalist industrialism which scarred not only the landscape of his home but the minds of its people. After all, he'd been interviewed for a post at Newquay High School, among the last four, when they failed to appoint and would have been delighted to spend a few years by the sea in Cornwall.

At home he sat with *The Book of Laughter and Forgetting* for half an hour. Should he write the letter? He got up, pulled a sheet of A4 from his pad and standing at his kitchen table scrawled his resignation. Why should he make it neat and polite? He folded the paper three times, slipped it into a brown envelope and wrote Cooper's name; but in the morning, as he hurried his toast and took his bike from under the stairs (he'd got rid of the car when the cost of repairs was mounting close to its value), he paused a second, stared at the envelope, slid it off the table and dropped it in the bin.

The morning can always dispel the dark thoughts of the night and working on his mind while he slept, the kindness of his pals had shifted his feelings; it would be churlish not to heed their advice. They were his friends. He would look for another job and this time ensure he had Cooper's support. The culture at school was inimical but he was happy with his friends, acquaintances and fellow radicals.

Maybe they were his future. He stood on the pedals up Penwortham Hill. His anger had dissipated. This was a new day.

He didn't know this would turn out to be the biggest mistake of his life, that his instinct had been right; that had he not joined his friends in the pub and had submitted his resignation, he would have saved himself a share of agony and misery. He'd made the same mistake as when he applied for the job because his dad encouraged him: he'd denied his own most secure feeling in order not to offend someone else. He didn't know his friendships would quickly deliquesce but his job become a dead weight that would press down on and almost destroy him, nor that had he resigned and moved on, he could have had a bright and fulfilling future.

A few weeks later, when the incident had been layered over and ceased to occupy his mind, except in those quiet moments when he brought it into focus and it made his heart race with anger, Bill Coleridge came into the staff-room with a paper in his hands. It was afternoon break. The place was busy but not crowded to capacity as during the morning pause. Andy was reading *The Guardian*. Don Crawley was beside him talking to Tracey Bowe, the daughter of Ena, the bustling school bursar whose canvassing had secured her girl a temporary job as a teacher of remedial English, despite her having no teaching qualification. Don and Ena had been friends for two decades and he had known Tracey since she was a baby. As a child she'd called him Uncle Don.

"This is peculiar," said Coleridge, addressing Crawley, "Nigel Halifax's name is on the county's list of people who mustn't be employed in schools."

"Really?" said Crawley.

Andy lay the paper on his knees.

"Yes, any idea?"

"No," said Crawley, shaking his head in that exaggerated way of many of his gestures.

Coleridge moved on to talk to Keith Bird and Tim Heath. When he left, Crawley, leaning forward, called to Bird.

"Keith. Keith. I know what it'll be. Birwatching. He's had problems before about trespassing on the railway in search of finches and what not. That'll be it. He'll've been caught and got a fine."

Andy was about to comment that surely a man wouldn't be banned from teaching for such a minor offence, but thought better of it.

As far as he knew, the prohibition applied to people who were a danger to children. Maybe he was wrong. Perhaps even careless twitchers who strayed onto British Rail land in pursuit of a jay, a robin or a long-tailed tit were considered offenders too untrustworthy to teach the winds of the world or the verb second rule.

Halifax had retired the term before Andy began. He'd been back to chat to his old colleagues once or twice. He was a tall man with wisps of untended grey hair on his almost bald head, crumpled trousers that flapped round his ankles, a rapid way of speaking and eyes which seemed incapable of fixing on anything for more than a second. He slouched in the staff-room in his outdoor coat, an old, dirty-blue, zip-front affair with a hood bordered by synthetic fur, his hands in his pockets, exuding an odd self-consciousness and engaging in disjointed, staccato conversation. He'd worked in the school for more than three decades, had been a sleep-in housemaster in the fifties when the place took fee-paying boarders and was promoted to Head of German after twelve years. The pupils nicknamed him Fatkegs on account of his baggy, ill-fitting trousers. He'd taught Stu Archer and John Rutherford and other lads Andy had known. He was notorious as a *bender*, a *bummer*, a *perv*. As John Rutherford used to joke:

"He likes pocket billiards, but he's not getting his hands on my set."

Stu Archer used to quip:

"If Fatkegs asks you to bend over you'll get more than the slipper."

Andy wondered if there was more to his appearance on the list than birdwatching. He was aware of a reluctance among the old guard to mention it. One afternoon he was looking for books in the stock room when Alma Mayor came in. She was dressed in a tight, white blouse with a lifted collar, unbuttoned to her cleavage, a pencil-line skirt with a split in its rear, held by a thick, gold-coloured belt, stiletto heels on open- toed, black patent shoes and black nylons. Her blonde and silver hair was piled in a great, backcombed mass which added three inches to her height. Her eyes were heavy with mascara, her lips bright red, her fingers adorned with heavy, expensive rings and her wrists with exorbitant bracelets. As ever the heavy odour of her perfume mixed with the tinge of tobacco which was always on her filled the atmosphere.

They exchanged a few niceties and in response to his dry irony she laughed in that strenuous way which suggested her body was resistant and laughter had to be forced from her like congealed glue from a tube. He wondered if, here, just the two of them, and she trying to be complaisant might be opportune.

"What do you make of this business about Nigel Halifax?" he ventured.

She stiffened a little and her face took on a more serious aspect.

"Don says it'll be because of his birdwatching. Trespassing on the railway."

"Yes, I know. Doesn't sound convincing does it? Only I remember friends of mine who were pupils here. He had a bit of a reputation, I believe."

"I don't know about that," she said turning away.

Silence followed. She found the book she was looking for and left, pulling the door to behind her, leaving him alone among the untidy racks in the poorly illuminated cubby hole.

It wasn't long before it was in the paper. Convicted of "interfering" with young boys, as the reporter euphemistically put it, he was given two years. Andy expected there might be some discussion, but it was as if he'd never existed. Men who had worked with him for ten, fifteen, twenty years, said nothing. On the way back from the *Black Bull*, in Mike Chambers' car on the Friday lunchtime after the news reports, Andy said:

"What do you make of the Halifax business, then?"

"It'll blow over," said Chambers. "Just got to nip to the bank if you don't mind."

The absolute, tacit prohibition on mentioning the matter was stunning and appalling. He and Gerry Beckett discussed it.

"You don't need to tell me," said Gerry, "I was educated by the Christian Brothers."

Andy knew nothing about them. Gerry's enlightening and alarming stories made him realize why he had such an out-of-kilter aspect to his mind.

"You were lucky to get out with your life," he said.

"Yeah, Christian buggers, that's what I call 'em. Still, one good thing, they laid the secure foundations of my atheism."

It seemed to Andy silence was absolutely the wrong response. The man had worked in the school for decades. He'd been a housemaster, supervising dormitories of lads of eleven or twelve. He'd been in a position of responsibility with young boys and through all that time had been either an actual or potential abuser. The cancer needed cutting out. The matter should be discussed. The Head should speak to the pupils in assemblies. Silence could only let the wound fester.

He realised the defence of the school's reputation was more important than truth or justice. He understood too that many of the people who had worked with Halifax must have known. Don Crawley must have known. Were they aware, had Wellington been aware, that Fatkegs was abusing pupils and had they turned away in deference to the school's status?

Though he tried not to connect them, he couldn't keep from his mind either, Cooper's unprincipled denial of a good reference and the fact that Halifax had been promoted. Paedophilia it seemed, was no barrier to advancement, while supposed lack of deference was. The school's prestige was an empty shell. It's Greek and Latin mottos, its honours board, its pride in its sporting prowess and in the number of pupils sent to Oxbridge, were purchased at the cost of chronic corruption. Andy was convinced some of the people who worked alongside Halifax for any time must have known. The school proposed a false identity. The disease wasn't passing but fatal.

It struck him how different this was from Penwortham Secondary. No teacher there would have got away with what Halifax must have been up to. There was no status or tradition to hide behind. Established in 1954, serving the 11-plus rejects, there was no Latin motto, no honours board, no Oxbridge successes. A teacher who had made advances to boys would not only have been quickly exposed: the pupils would have hit back. Yet here, there was a conspiracy and what made it work was snobbery and advantage. In defence of those, people were prepared to conceal the most despicable crimes.

It had become Andy's habit to end his Thursday evenings in *The New Brunswick* where there was live music. The bands were amateur and some loose and unharmonious, but most could bang out a decent tune and though what they played was unsophisticated, they played it well. He relished almost any live music, even a Salvation Army band on the street would make him stop for a minute, and the crowd was drawn heavily from the streets off Manchester Road, the area where Ted Franks had lived as a boy. He'd had a few pints with Ted in the pub when he worked at F.E.D. and susceptible to nostalgia he enjoyed thinking back to those years as he stood by the bar, trying to be inconspicuous.

He walked up Fishergate Hill, through town and took Stoneygate, beside the parish church, down to the modern, ugly building whose garish lights and thumping rhythm could be seen and heard from two hundred yards. One time, at half past nine, he ran into Dave Dover coming from Church Street.

"What are you doing in this neck of the woods?"

"On my way home."

He obviously didn't want to talk.

"I'm just nipping to *The New Brunswick* for a pint. There's always a band on Thursdays."

"Well, enjoy it," said Dave as he walked on quickly with his long, vigorous stride, his hands in the pockets of his coat.

Andy paused a while and watched him go. His puzzlement came from the fact that Dave lived close to the school. Why would he be coming from Church Street? There were *The Blue Bell* and *The Lamb*. Maybe he'd just been for a pint; but alone, and this far from home? Beyond Church Street were New Hall Lane and Ribbleton Lane, poor, working-class parts of the town; not the kind of place a man like Dover would have friends or want to engage in solitary drinking.

The encounter left him bemused until a few weeks later he was in the office looking up a pupil's file. The secretaries were chatting as they worked and Cynthia Jones, Dave Dover's assistant, mentioned she was thinking of moving from New Hall Lane. He closed the filing cabinet drawer, looked over at her. She looked back.

"Do you need something, Andy?"

"No, I've found what I want, thanks Cynthia."

Cynthia he knew, was divorced. She was a friendly, obliging, down-to-earth chatty woman in her forties, not pretty or beautiful, but with the figure of a twenty-year-old, much remarked on in the usual salacious terms by some of the younger, male staff.

It was an explanation and as it was the only one which made sense, it lodged in his mind, but he made no judgement.

Nor did he when he ran into Dave Dover a second time, on a Friday evening. He ended the working week enjoying a few drinks with Sean Dunbar, Kath Sparrow and a few other Labour Party friends, including Theresa and Gene Shuttleworth. She was an English teacher in Blackpool and he, supposedly a research student at the Polythechic working on Saul Bellow, but in fact a professional drinker, who lazed around on the money she brought in, spent more in a month on booze than she did in two on food, did little around the house, and to her goading to make progress with his thesis, replied he was waiting for inspiration, intellectual work couldn't be hurried, his thesis would be ground-breaking and something so good was worth waiting for. Gene would end the night incapable. Theresa would haul him into a taxi, yank his clothes off and drag the duvet over him. She slept alone.

Usually they made a little tour of town centre pubs but occasionally they wandered out to Meadow Street, off Deepdale Road, not far from the football ground, for a last hour in *The Prince Consort*, a thoroughly working-class pub, always packed and lively, brimming with that thank-god-the-week-in-the-factory-the-shop-the-office-is-over atmosphere which makes Friday nights in working-class towns buzz and fizz and sometimes explode.

Andy was nudging his way to the bar, smiling and apologising, when in the far corner, in a suit and tie, sitting beside a man of about his own age, also smartly dressed, he spotted Dover. As on the first occasion, a little shock ran through him. What was the Head of Sixth Form in a prestigious, middle-class, well-out-of-town, Cof E school doing here? It wasn't as if Dave, like himself, was from the town, lived in it, came from working-class roots. His father had been a clergyman in the south-east and Dave had been educated at public school. How had he found his way to *The Prince Consort.*

Andy nodded. He didn't want to be churlish. He pushed through to the corner where people were squashed on the banquette seats.

81

"All right, Dave?"

They shook hands.

"This is Kev," said Dover.

Andy shook his colleague's friend's hand too and was surprised when he spoke to hear a thick, back-streets-of-Preston accent.

"I'm here with a few of my Labour Party mates," said Andy. "Can I get you a drink?"

They refused, their pints being almost full.

"Well, better get to the bar or we'll miss last orders."

The encounter floated in Andy's mind like oil on water. He wondered if Kev was a trade unionist: Dave was the local secretary of the NAS. Maybe they'd met and become friends through activism; but the idea didn't convince him. Teacher trade unionists didn't have much to do with members of the T&G or the GMB or NUPE. There had to be some other connection.

The confusion didn't clear till years later. It was Good Friday. Andy had to drive into town to fulfil a favour: he'd agreed to pick up a couple of youngsters from a night-club and get them safely home. The roads were quiet at 2.00 a.m. He was waiting at the traffic lights on the ring road, by the bus station when a man appeared from his right, crossing the road. He did a double-take. Dave Dover, heading out of town, alone. He was about to sound his horn but drew back. Dave crossed, turned right, in the direction of Meadow Street and Deepdale Road. It was too late for the pubs. Wasn't there a club on Deepdale Road, a gay bar which stayed open till all hours?

Kevin, the smart-suited, working-class bloke with the authentic speech of a Preston oik: was he Dave's *bit of rough*?

It was none of his business. What Dave did with his private life was his own affair. He said nothing and felt pity for his colleague. He had to hide what he was because the institution he worked for wouldn't accept it; and not just the institution. Dave had a wife and two children.

The conclusion seemed convincing, but it was, all the same, speculation. Andy was appalled by the thought that Dave, for years, had had to live a double life. His sympathies were with him. Yet at the same time, he experienced a stirring of resentment. If people refused to face down hypocrisy it would hold sway and the result was people like Fatkegs and the devastation of innocence. At work, Dave was in categorical agreement with the school's C of E, cut-above, very-special-place, ethos. Andy was amazed anyone could do that and at the same time be meeting male lovers in spit-and-sawdust pubs or roaming dubious streets alone at two in the morning.

He might be wrong. His conjectures were based on flimsy evidence; but it had become common knowledge he was having an affair with Cynthia Jones. None of it was any of his business. People must be free to live the private lives they choose, so long as they obey the injunction to do no harm. Nevertheless, it contributed to Andy's will to be out of the place. He wanted to work in a school where people could be open about their identities. Why shouldn't a teacher be homosexual or bi-sexual or asexual or whatever they chose to be? Why should there have to persist this sordid atmosphere of concealment and denial which made victims of the innocent and duplicity a way of life?

He kept looking for jobs. There were plenty he could have gone for if he hadn't chosen to stay close to his dad. He could have moved to London or Oxford or Bristol or Bath or Barnsley or Ipswich; somewhere he didn't know and where it would be interesting to settle in and make a new life; but his choice was made.

He cycled over to visit a couple of times a week. His dad was admitted to hospital again. Andy arrived for the start of visiting time and stayed till the end, usually the sole attendee. He pedalled home hard, through Feniscowles, down the long decline past Hoghton Tower. The doctors had run more inconclusive tests. After six days, his dad was home again. Andy began to wonder if he shouldn't offer to take him in. His house wouldn't be appropriate, but if his dad sold and they combined their resources, they could get the right kind of place; but if he did, what would happen to Mary and Sylvia's inheritance? He would have to tell his dad not to change his will, but then, the inevitable over, he would have to sell up and split his dad's portion. The complications stalled him and set him thinking: property got in the way of everything. Obviously, it would be better for his dad not to live alone, and who else did he have? He'd come into the world unwanted and was leaving it the same way. Andy knew living alone was troubling to him now his capacities were limited. It would be a good act to take him in and make him feel wanted during his last spell on earth.

He wondered if he should talk to Mary and Sylvia, yet he knew their minds were closed against his dad. Elsie had done her work well. It was up to him. He was frustrated that money, as ever, put handcuffs on doing simply what was right. On the other hand, he'd taken his job to please his dad. He knew he was proud: he, the barefoot Pongo from the roughest part of town, progeny of a wayward mother, left in the care of tottering dipsomaniacs had a son who taught French in one of the most prestigious schools in the county.

He'd made his dad proud but himself unhappy and uncomfortable. Soon there would no impulse to do the former. He needed to start making choices which would re-establish his easy-going, enjoy-the-next-hour sensibility and the first was to get a job in a more congenial school; but how much longer would he have to remain on hand for his father?

DEFEAT AND SURVIVAL

The excitement always kept her up till the early hours. Even when she'd had to be out of bed for work before six, she didn't climb the stairs till after midnight. 1945 was transformative. It had changed her inner world as well as the public arena. It was the realization of hope. In every election since, she'd hoped for the same relief, delight and appeasement of tension. Triumphalism meant nothing to her. She wanted to see no one defeated, diminished, down-downhearted. She believed results changed minds. MacMillan had to accept what Attlee had done. Heath had to work with Wilson's alterations. If people were willing to change their minds, there was no need to feel belittled and bitter. It didn't occur to her, however, that 1979 hadn't shifted her thinking an inch. On the contrary, Thatcher had reinforced her socialism. A Tory like MacMillan, though she disagreed with him, though he was a toff, though he was rich and knew nothing of what life was like for the poor, she could soften to slightly because he saw sense and built council houses. Thatcher was different. There was a viciousness in her Elsie recoiled from. Every word she spoke contained venom.

What upset her most was the defeat of Tony Benn. She was glad Shirley Williams lost in Crosby and Bill Rogers wasn't returned. She'd liked Williams. She spoke well, had been responsible for opening comprehensives and was on the side of the people at the bottom; but her betrayal of Labour she couldn't forgive. Jenkins, Williams, Owen and Rogers were to blame for Thatcher's victory and Michael Foot's humiliation. He was a better man than the four of them put together. She knew, because Andy had told her, he'd turned down promotion in Wilson's cabinet on the grounds of opposition to the Vietnam War. That was exactly the kind of action she admired. That was what would make the world a better place: people prepared to sacrifice their own narrow advantage for the wider good.

The numbers always interested her. More than fifteen million had voted against Thatcher. The country didn't want her policies. Though she despised the Alliance, she would have been prepared to see Labour join with them to keep Thatcher out. The middle-way between Tony Benn and Denis Healey was far better than Thatcher's demented determination to destroy the public sector. That she had a big ma-

85

jority on a minority of the vote appalled her. In 1951, Churchill had come back to office on fewer votes than Attlee. Her father had said it was a mistake to call the election: though they had a slim majority, Labour had done well in 1950. They'd increased their vote. Attlee should have soldiered on. It upset her terribly to see Labour's programme interrupted. It wasn't right that fewer votes could put someone in power. She knew that Wilson had done the same in 1974, but he'd called another election after a few months. Churchill had stayed in power till 1955 on fewer votes than Attlee.

She'd always thought the call for proportional representation a Liberal ploy. They were Tories in disguise and she didn't want to bring them comfort; but now she saw the case. Thatcher had won more votes than any other single party by furlongs, but the system wasn't bringing to power a government which reflected what most people wanted. She was quite willing to accept most people didn't want the socialism she believed in. She was more than ready to temper it. She could accept compromise if some of what she cherished was delivered: above all the NHS must be enhanced, people must be decently housed and schools must let all children in through the same door. Though she had no tolerance of people who thought life was an opportunity to accumulate pound notes, she could let the rich get on with it if the rest had houses, hospitals and schools.

Yet the terrible had happened. The despicable *Gang of Four* had split the Labour Party. Michael Foot had been undermined. Jim Callaghan had spoken in favour of Polaris, making the leader look a fool. A government was now in power which had an animus against the people: millions of trade unionists and public sector workers were Thatcher's enemies. What most dispirited her was that the war in the Falklands had assisted. She heard the commentators who said the polls showed people were voting on economic issues, that it was the promise of tax cuts and more money in their pockets which swayed them; but it was impossible to believe the insane war mentality hadn't shifted people.

She experienced a curious guilt. She'd brought three children into the world and wanted to guarantee their well-being. She had four grandchildren: Mary now had three sons, and Sylvia was five months pregnant. She wanted them to live well. What did she mean? She was washing her few breakfast things, alone in the kitchen, wondering how the world had arrived here. What she meant first of all was peace. Nothing was more important. She'd lived through the war. Her dad had lived through two. The insanity of the trenches had seared him though he'd been safe in Preston. Like all men of his generation, there was a disbelief at the heart of him that people could be so stupid, cruel and madly optimistic. Peace first. It was the greatest gift leaders could give to their people.

Yet here she was, the morning after the defeat of a principled man by a woman as artificial as her voice, and the lunatic mentality of war looming behind her victory. Her fears ran away with her. That tendency of the mind to anticipate what it dreads and to envisage it in the most lurid colours, brought to her imagination the demise of the NHS; having to pay to see the doctor; schools wrenched out of local authority oversight and charges introduced; people unable to feed themselves; the return of slums and overcrowding; the re-emergence of the grim atmosphere of the thirties, at least for the people at the bottom.

Nothing Thatcher said suggested she wanted to leave in the past the horrors of poverty, insecurity and division. She was retrospective. She evoked Victorian values as if the century which sent children to work in mills and saw people starve should be celebrated.

Elsie felt somehow responsible. The idea tortured her. How could it be her fault? She wouldn't have voted for Thatcher if she'd been put on the rack. Yet she was filled with pity for her children and grandchildren. What were they going to have to live through ? She'd believed there would be, for them, a society of peace, generosity and mutual beneficence but now she expected they would have to live through a period of conflict, meanness and malicious self-seeking.

It was a short walk to Sylvia's. She enjoyed the simple pleasure. On the way, she spoke to one or two locals whose names she didn't know. In Woodland Grove she'd known everyone. In Talbot Road too. She wasn't part of a community here though she'd got to know her immediate neighbours. In the bungalow attached to hers lived Mrs Chowns, a widow of seventy whose only daughter lived in Ripon. Her husband had worked in the office at the Leyland Rubber Company and having climbed slowly and not entirely painlessly to the position of accounts manager, he and his wife, proud of their achievement in owning their home, running a car and being able to pay for a holiday in Spain each summer, lined up behind the Toryism which they believed favoured people like themselves. Elsie, whose desire to be a good neighbour overcame any ideological revulsion, did her shopping when her back was bad, took scones round and offered to mow her lawn; but when Mrs Chowns insisted on expressing her admiration for Thatcher and her disdain for Trade Unions, Elsie stood her ground but swiftly withdrew to scotch a row.

On the other side were Betty and George. He'd worked for forty-nine years on the shop floor at Leyland Motors. She was overweight, diabetic and had heart problems. They were stalwarts at Leyland Methodists, down-to-earth folk whose son, Jason, was unemployed. George had hoped he would follow him into the factory. He'd earned well and had an underpinning pension; but apprenticeships had dried up. The lad trained as a car mechanic. His boss had a stroke and closed the business. He took his CV to every garage he could find but the months went by and he was at home. George shook his head:

"It's no life for young man," he said to Elsie. "Living off us. No, it's not right."

"It'll get worse wi' 'er in power."

"Aye, you're right, Elsie. But what can we do about it?"

Sylvia had Louisa ready for her little excursion with her grandma. She was a mild, affectionate child without any of those difficult traits supposed to afflict two-year-olds.

"Hello, luv," said Elsie. "Now that's a pretty dress you've got on this mornin' , isn't it chicken."

The child, whose life was bounded by three essential points of love and security: her mother, her father and her grandma, smiled and climbed on Elsie's knee. There was a playgroup in the church. Elsie took her granddaughter and sat by as she played. Afterwards, she walked her through the little town in her pushchair until she fell asleep. She favoured Worden Park, which could evoke, almost, the impression of being in the countryside. She thought back to her days as a girl when she'd walked with her friends in the Lakes. How she'd relished standing on the top of Loughrigg or Skiddaw. She regretted she hadn't made it part of her life. She should have seized it. She loved it. She was at home in a pair of boots, a bag on her back, pushing up Stickle Ghyll or Consiton. She'd let it lapse. Bert wasn't a walker. He had no feel for the countryside. He lacked the inner calm of people who can spend all day in the fresh air, completing a fifteen-mile circular and feeling they've used their time well. He was one of those get-on people who needed the town. He wanted to advance, make money, take his place in the hierarchy. What was it all for ? What did it mean if it didn't come back home, if it didn't contribute to peace and happiness?

As soon as Louisa was asleep, she turned back. Sylvia put the pram in the back room while the two of them sat in the front with a cup of tea and Elsie's fruit cake.

"How's 'e likin' it?" said Elsie.

"Fine. The work's much better. It's cleaner, you know? He was fed up of clambering under dirty floors and seeing rats and all that. And he likes aeroplanes so he's in his element really."

Barry had found himself a job with BAE at Warton. The complex wiring systems in fighter aircraft were more demanding than fitting ring mains and he was eager to learn about computer systems. The aircraft of the future would fly themselves. He wanted to be part of it. There was a great thrill when a jet took off for a test flight over the Irish Sea to hear the power, to see the magnificent push of the thing against the insuperable forces of nature and to feel you had contributed. The work was high-tech and skilled. And secret. He wasn't allowed to talk about what he did and knew. There was a sense of serious importance in that.

Elsie felt he'd made the wrong choice. She said nothing. It wasn't her place, but to Andy she remarked:

"I couldn't do it. Making weapons to kill folk. Not for a million pounds a year."

"No, you're right. We won't stop the arms trade till people refuse to use their skills to make the things. But blokes want jobs, BAE pay well, and that's the morally limiting factor."

She wasn't sure what he meant by *the morally limiting factor*. In her mind there was right and wrong and the choices were simple. She didn't know that when her own most precious interests were in question, she would sneak under the bright lights of her own admonitions without knowing it. Like everyone, she believed she was more virtuous than she was, could see the moral faults in others much more clearly than her own, and by focussing her mental attention on what she assumed about herself, missed entirely those dubious calculations and manipulations by which she sought to assert her will.

"So long as he's happy," she said. "It's a lot of travellin' though, isn't it?"

"He's a bit fed up of that. He had a scooter to start with, but in the cold and rain he was arriving soaked and frozen so he does a car share now with Craig, round the corner. But he says he'd like to move to Blackpool."

The idea was like a kick in the stomach to Elsie. She wanted to protest.

"Move to Blackpool," she wanted to exclaim, "you can't do that. I've sold up and come to Leyland to be near to you. You can't up sticks now and leave me on my own here."

But she could say nothing.

She looked into the distance, as if she could see solutions to all problems there. Her left leg began to rock, rhythmically. She sipped her tea. Was there anything in the world you could trust? She couldn't arrange her thoughts. There was a blank in her mind and it admitted terrible pain. If Sylvia moved away, she would be alone. The very idea left her isolated. She wanted to belong and where was there except family? Mary was nearly twenty miles away and busy with her trio. Elsie saw her a few times a year. She stayed while the third was born. She played the matriarch. It was wonderful to feel herself in charge of the house. She put up Ted's snap. She made tea for the boys. She hoovered, washed, ironed. In a remote corner of her mind the idea began to form that they would ask her to stay. She was so useful. The children loved her so much. There was room in the lovely, four-bedroom house Ted and his brother had built. She could sell her house, put the money in the bank and treat the children. She would be secure for the rest of her life. During the day, she would work. It would make things easy for Mary. In the evening she would sit in the warm circle of her family's affection, wanted, valued, treasured.

But the time came to leave. Mary gave her a lift home. She closed the door and was enclosed in the chilly confines of her lonely walls.

"His next project is building a plane," said Sylvia.

It didn't register.

"Eh?"

"He wants to build a plane," she stressed.

"A plane? How d'you mean?"

"Of his own," said Sylvia. "He and Craig are renting a hangar by the airfield at Squires Gate. He's going to do it bit by bit. A two-seater."

"But he can't fly."

"He's going to have lessons and get his licence."

"That'll be dear, won't it?"

"It's his money. Doesn't bother me. It'll get him from under my feet a bit. But it's a long way to Squires Gate if he's going to be fettling in his hangar every night."

"Yes. Yes, it is."

"Anyway, it's just an idea. He'll have to save up a bit first before he can start buying the materials so it'll probably be years before he gets going."

Elsie walked home disconsolate despite the kind weather. She was at a loss to understand. Her inner life and that of her children were remote from one another. She couldn't have abandoned her mother or father. Hadn't her dad come with them when Bert won the pools and they moved to Penwortham? Hadn't she looked after him till the day he died? She didn't understand. The world had changed. In her day, families lived close. It was true her brothers had visited their dad seldom. The burden fell to the daughter. Yes, it was always the women who had to take on the responsibilities which brought no reward. She had two daughters.

Sylvia and Barry might move to Blackpool. As the day wore on and the idea tore at her mind, it became ever more likely. They would move. Barry wanted to build a plane. A tiny hope leapt in her gloom: perhaps they would ask her to go; but it was quenched like a snuffed candle flame.

She was alone. Her children were happy to leave her on her own. What could she do? She loved her children and grandchildren. No one else could incite her love so unerringly. Why should she live apart from the people she loved? There was something wrong and cruel about that.

When she put herself to bed it occurred to her if she was married she wouldn't be alone. If Bert were still beside her, her grief of loneliness would be attenuated; but the idea of another man, now, at the age of sixty, was ludicrous. Her marriage had never been a success. She'd got along with him as best she could. That was all. She'd never been able to think of marriage as on the same level as her love for her family. She had always faced inwards to her mother, her father, her brothers; her marriage was a glance over her shoulder.

A calm came over her. She was alone. That was how it was. Above her head board, in a little, dark wood frame, on a card she had picked up at church was a verse:

I will lift up mine eyes unto the hills…

Her help came from the Lord. He watched over her. He loved her. One day she would be united with Him and with those she had lost. She pulled the covers round her, turned onto her side and muttered the Lord's Prayer.

One Saturday, Bert drove to Preston. He wanted to see Andy's house. He'd never been in Mary's and he didn't know Sylvia's address. He'd rolled past the big, detached house Ted had built in Newburgh village, hoping not to be spotted. What a lovely place. He parked up round the corner. What was there to lose in knocking? She could only turn him away. Or if it was Ted, he could only look blankly and make some excuse. He was used to rejection. Yet there was a hair's breadth chance they would invite him in. Mary was thirty-five. He thought of her birth, the little house in Talbot Road, his father-in-law sleeping downstairs, his ailing mother-in-law in her bed of agony, the five of them in four rooms, no bathroom, no garden. He was proud and glad Mary had this big, spacious house surrounded by grass, trees and flowers.

He started the engine. He was the outsider. He might as well still be Pongo, the unwanted, mocked boy.

Though he could still drive, getting in and out of the car was an operation. He pulled in outside the little terrace in Meath Road. Andy came down the steps and out of the gate, followed by a young woman with striking red hair. Bert felt that odd sensation compounded of shock, fear and desire which attractive women had always engendered. It mocked him. His body was a burden. He could barely control his essential movements. Yet it stirred a young man's sensations.

He opened the door.

"All right, dad?"

"Hello, Andy."

He slipped his hands beneath his right thigh and began to manoeuvre his leg. The pain made him wince. He paused for breath and to permit his weak arms to recover.

"Here," said Andy, "hold onto me."

"It's my legs," said Bert, "I can't shift 'em."

His son ducked his head in and took hold of his right leg, pulling it gently till his foot dangled two inches above the pavement.

"Christ," said Bert.

Andy held his lower leg in both hands. When his dad's feet were on the ground, he bent, put his arm under his dad's right and said:

"Come on, I'll lift you."

The young woman stepped in from the left and did the same. Bert shuffled across the pavement, hoisted first his right, then his left leg onto the step, paused for energy and to let the pain subside, repeated the measures to get onto the second step, was more or less carried by Andy and his friend into the house, flopped, exhausted into the armchair where, he had been able to choose, he would have remained till the end.

"You'll be ready for a cup o' tea, dad. Want something to eat?"

"Yes," said Bert through his pain, "if you've got something."

"Sure. This is Theresa, one of my Labour Party friends."

"Nice to meet you, Theresa."

"Yes, nice to meet you," she said, tossing her mane and standing rather awkwardly on the hearth rug. "Are you comfortable enough there? Would you like a blanket for your legs?"

"Yes, something for my legs would be nice."

She disappeared from the little, white-painted lounge, into the kitchen where Andy had gone and he heard her feet on the stairs. She was familiar enough to go up to the bedrooms. Bert had noticed her wedding-ring. Was Andy having an affair? He hoped not. Yet, what position was he in to judge? His relations with women had ended in utter failure. Theresa was a lovely young woman. Her facial features were exquisite. Her high cheek bones, big lips, arched eyebrows and huge, brown eyes made not looking impossible. How could he know what was going on? These days, marriages were falling like houses in the blitz. He wished he was a father who could offer some advice to his son, that behind him were decades of faithful successful marriage and attentive fatherhood; but it had all eluded him. Life, which was now mocking him as mercilessly as the roughnecks of Marsh Lane when he was five, had eluded him. He existed, but he had never come into life. Unreality was everywhere. Wasn't everyone waiting for their life to begin?

Though it wasn't cold, Andy had lit a fire. The smokeless fuel glowed red in the grate. Bert realised it was for him. He was glad of it. He could barely work up any animal heat. Merely sitting, he need layers and blankets not to shiver.

"This should be all right," said Theresa, laying a folded, thick, deep red blanket over his legs.

Andy brought him a small plate of wholemeal toast and honey and a pint mug of tea. He was looked after. He was cared for. It struck him that apart from the care he received at the day centre, which was provided by kindly strangers, this was the first time in maybe twenty years someone he was close to had attended to him away from home. He could live here. He could move in and be comforted. He was aware, in some small, peripheral part of his consciousness of his self-ishness; but it couldn't diminish the desire. Like a child whose exor-bitant need to be nurtured, which is nothing less than the will to live, overpowers all lesser considerations, in these last days of his life, the need to depend, to know he wasn't alone, to be able to count on someone who would always be thinking of him, was supreme.

It was agreed he would eat with them, but he didn't want to drive home in the dark. His eyes let him down. They would eat early. Theresa suggested a pasta recipe. Bert agreed. Andy had to nip out to buy the ingredients.

"What do you do for a living, Theresa?" Bert asked when she was seated opposite him.

"I'm a teacher."

"Like Andy."

"Yeah, but not in quite such a good school."

"Where d'you work?"

"Blackpool."

"What makes it less good than Andy's?"

"Oh, well. Transient population. Quite a lot of broken families, drugs, sexual abuse.."

"Crickey. It sounds terrible."

"No," she said, running the long fingers of her right-hand whose nails were painted burgundy through her hair, "it's not terrible, but it's not easy. My first job each day is to go round the cafes, flushing the girls out and getting them through the gates."

"Don't they want to learn?"

"No," she laughed. "They'd rather hang around the streets all day, smoke dope and look for boys." She paused. "Or men."

"Funny isn't it, I was forced to leave school at fourteen and I would have swum in the Ribble in February to get an education."

"Yes," she said, lifting her chin and looking towards the square, bay window, "they have it all on a plate, so they don't appreciate it and school is low-key and lacking in glamour compared to what the media offer them."

"Yes, there was no television when I was growing up."

"Oh, it's not just television. It's pop music and videos, the whole thing. It's an alternative world and they identify with it. They think they'll be glamour models. It's a kind of purchased sophistication. I don't know, it short circuits the need to put effort before achievement, but of course, lots of them end up in dull, low-paid jobs. That's how it all works. The promises are false and the boredom and hardship real."

"Surely some of them can see through it."

"Yes, well, maybe. Some of the bright girls work hard and do well, but there's no escape from the culture, is there? And the culture is rotten."

"To the core," he said, smilingly broadly. "Why don't you get out of teaching?"

"Into what?"

"I don't know. Set yourself up in something."

"I don't think I could. Teaching is what I like. I wouldn't want to set up some private business teaching English. I think everyone should get a good education, not just those who can pay."

"Oh, yes, I agree. But that's not under threat is it?"

"Not yet, but it will be. We'll copy what happens in America. There's a guy there, I can't remember his name, who has this cultural literacy theory. It's a kind of back-to-basics idea. You know, down with John Dewey, kind of thing. It's all about standard curriculum and measurement. If we imitate it, we'll measure kids to death. I think that's what'll happen. Then there'll be a call for schools to work like businesses, because business is supposed to be efficient."

Bert wondered what was wrong with measuring. Surely they had to be tested. He'd enjoyed tests because he was good. Ten out of ten for spellings gave him a boost. It was a great lift to get your work back with a high mark in a red circle.

"They have to pass exams, don't they ?"

"While exams exist, but that's not the point really. Learning shouldn't be a competition. We're obsessed with competition and control when we should think of education as discovery. Really, it's control. That's what schools are for. I have to measure how far girls' skirts are above their knees. It's insane."

He laughed. The conversation cheered him up. It was odd how talking about how bad things are made him feel better, but it did. Was it just the old truth that people like a good moan and criticising others is the best way to elevate yourself? There might be something of that in it, but listening to Theresa made him feel there was a future. There was something to hope for. Though he wouldn't be alive to experience it, the sense that young people like her and Andy would pleased him.

"Well, Andy's in a school that does well anyway," he said.

"Yes," she said with a little laugh and a jerk of her head, "and he hates it."

Her remark shocked him. Andy hadn't told him about his problems at work. Bert had assumed that because the school was prestigious, he would be flourishing and enjoying his work. Why did he hate it? The horrible thought sprang into his head that he was responsible. He'd cajoled him into applying. Why was he unhappy?

"I wasn't aware of that."

"Have I said the wrong thing?

"I don't know. Why doesn't he like it?"

"Did he tell you about his application for a job in Morecambe?"

"No."

"I'd better let it come from the horse's mouth."

"He wouldn't mind."

"Well, more or less, the Head refused him a reference."

The positive picture of his son, established in a good school, starting to make his way, collapsed like a man whose heart stops suddenly. He was stunned to find a series of images coming into his mind, a disturbing accompaniment to the discordant music of his emotions: he saw himself at school, his hands out for the strap or the ruler, in church and wary of the priest, on the troop ship that took him to Egypt, striding out of the ICI office in Manchester, being told by Elsie she wanted him to leave, sitting opposite Ken Wickham as he gave him the sack. His life was failure and imminent death, but he'd hoped his children would escape his humiliations. Denied a reference? What had he done? It must be serious.

Andy strode along Broadgate, the hint of the river in his nostrils. It was a quick walk into town if he hurried and he enjoyed the push up Fishergate Hill. He became aware of a figure on the river side of the road. He looked and saw a man disappear behind a tree: Gene Shuttleworth. Andy slowed, and when the dark, balding head of the little man in heavy black glasses peeped round the trunk, gave him a wave. Gene shrank back, as if he hadn't been seen.

Theresa had become a regular visitor at Andy's since the Saturday afternoon when they bumped into one another on Friargate as he was on his way to Halewood's book shop. There were two. One close to the ring road (which cut straight through the town centre), next to the *Black Bull*, a lively, sometimes slightly rowdy pub where he went sometimes with his Labour Party friends; and a second nearer to the Polytechic. Old man Halewood could be seen in his grey mac, stooped, his trousers flapping at his ankles, his old feet hitting the pavement with a flat step, hurrying from one to the other, books in his hands or under his arms. Two of his sons helped him run the business, but he was the expert who knew his stock, the market and his customers. He'd got to know Andy as a regular hunter of literary paperbacks and would approach him as he stood by the table packed with assorted, dog-eared, foxed and occasionally almost pristine volumes to offer a clean copy of *The Canterbury Tales* or *Silas Marner*.

It was the second shop Andy was heading for, to browse in the basement where, if you were lucky, you could find a neglected title which had lain buried or hidden for ten, fifteen, twenty years, whose price had not been updated but, with the dust blown off, was smart and would look well on his shelves, in addition to being a fascinating read. Theresa went with him. They clunked down the wooden stairs, books piled high at either side, and in the chilly cellar with its lingering odour of damp, the dulled footsteps of the passers-by audible as they crossed the grid in the pavement, shuffled between the tables and the shelves, bending and reaching for whatever looked intriguing till Andy disappeared into the recess beneath the stairs, lit by a single, unshaded bulb hanging from a twisted wire, where there were half a dozen shelves on which unsorted *Penguins*, *Pelicans*, tomes of multiple imprints, stood , lay and propped one another in their long neglect.

She followed him and as he was flicking through a copy of *Augie March*, without a word or warning, kissed him on the lips.

"You're very nice," she said.

Henceforth, his door was always open. She arrived with her cocker spaniel; company in her lonely marriage and a companion who allowed her to get out of the house and walk through Avenham Park without the awkwardness she would have experienced in promenading alone.

Andy smiled at the thought of the suspicious Gene dodging from tree to tree. What would he conclude, seeing Andy heading off on his own? How could Theresa be at his house? She'd told him the sorry story of her liaison with the impossible drunk. He was one of those regressed, babyish personalities, dependent and importunate, who conceal their lack of autonomy behind apparently adult behaviours. In Gene's case, drinking. He drank at breakfast time, in the bath, in bed, on the train, on the bus, in the park. He couldn't be separated from his bottle. This was his insignia of maturity. This was what made him a man. As if it took courage, insight, resilience, principle, endurance, self-transcendence, intelligence or effort to pour alcohol down his throat while she was at work, dealing with unruly girls, marking books, preparing lessons to earn the salary which paid for his wine, beer, whisky, vodka and gin.

She stayed with him for the sake of her fourteen-year-old daughter, born when she was sixteen, who lived half the week with her and the rest with her father in Kirkham. Theresa felt, that having been with Gene since Melissa was three, the relationship spoke of the stability she knew all young people need. Her most powerful desire, greater than her wish to provide properly for her child, was to be rid of the burden of Gene. His drinking was an insult. He wasn't married to her, though they had gone through the ceremony in the registry office, he was married to booze. He had never conquered autonomy so couldn't recognize or respect it in others. His behaviour was a way of being the centre of attention, of bringing everything back to him and his inordinate need for alcohol which was merely commonplace narcissism.

Yet, when she rebuked him with a gentle: "Is that really necessary?" as he brought to his lips his tenth pint of the evening, he turned sullen, unpleasant and potentially vicious:

"What do you know? Leave me alone. Why don't you get out of here?"

If she reminded him of it in the morning, he denied it or claimed he didn't remember.

She went on in loneliness and misery, her sojourns at Andy's the little islands of sweet repose in the bitter, surging seas of her heartbreak.

Bert sat in the living room by the fire which warmed him through as Andy and Theresa made a meal. She brought it to him on a tray: a good bowl of bean casserole with two chunks of wholemeal bread followed by apple crumble and plain yogurt and finally his pint mug of tea. To be looked after, in his state, to be warm and have pleasant company, to imagine this might be his daily experience, that his remaining time, short though he knew he it would be, could lift the desperate burden of living alone, of being able to raise the enthusiasm to make no more than a cheese sandwich for his meal, to rely on the radio and television for company. It brought inevitably to mind the good days with Elsie, the times he'd sat at the table to eat with his wife and children and the food had been prepared with care and affection. The idea bred the feeling. They had been calm, easy days. He had been at home in the world. It was true, he had experienced his moment of belonging. He didn't know that Elsie enunciated to whoever would listen that her marriage had been no more than rubbing along. He'd loved it. He loved being a husband and father. He'd loved Elsie and the children.

There was something of his mother in Andy. At her best, she was devoted and kind. He had done wrong. There was no question. He'd deceived her. All the same, his son was good to him. If only he could live here. He wanted to make the suggestion. Though this house was no good. The stairs were steep. When he needed the bathroom, he had to crawl up, Andy behind him his hands on his hips. He could sell his bungalow. It would bring twenty-five thousand. Andy's house must be worth about fifteen. Between them they could buy a big bungalow with a good garden. He would be home. He would be cared for. He wouldn't live and die in isolation and despair. He would need no more than one room. He wouldn't impose. If Andy married or if someone moved in to live with him, he wouldn't get in their way.

The relief and happiness the idea brought, made him feel he might live another twenty years. Yet he daren't propose it. It seemed desperate and selfish. When, in the conversation while he finished his tea, Andy mentioned his grandad, Bert seized the opportunity:

"Yes, I was happy for him to live with us. He insisted on the front room in Woodland Grove, you know. The best room. But I didn't mind. I've always thought the young should take care of the old. I was glad to have him."

Andy turned on the light. Dusk was beginning to gather.

"You want to get home before it's dark, dad."

"Yes. Yes, I must get going."

He had to keep himself from crying as they helped him out of the armchair. Andy held his coat while he slipped his arms in. They virtually carried him down the steps and to the car where, with great difficulty and in pain and with Andy's help he settled his feet on the pedals.

"I'll be over to see you in the next few days."

"Great. Thanks, Andy. Thanks, Theresa, nice to meet you. Hope we meet again some time."

She leant in and kissed him on his sunken cheek. Andy closed the door. The engine started. He pulled away, slowly, hesitantly. They watched till he turned left into Winckley Street.

"Oh, god, Andy," she said when they were indoors, "what will he do when he gets home?"

"He'll manage."

"Suppose he can't. Suppose he's stuck."

"The neighbours are good. They watch for him. Someone will come out and help him."

"But that's terrible. Having to rely on that. You should have gone with him, Andy."

"Yeah, maybe. But he has to get out to the day centre. If he can keep driving, that's some independence."

"Can't they pick him up in a bus or something? Don't they do that?"

"It'll come to that, I'm sure."

"Oh, Andy, it's dreadful, you can't leave him on his own."

"What can I do, Theresa? He can't live here. The stairs are impossible."

"Get a place for both of you."

"I've thought of that. My two sisters are beneficiaries of his will. If he and I buy a place together, what happens to their share when he dies?"

"You'd have to sell up."

"Think about it. I've to sell this. He's to sell his. We have to find somewhere. We might move in and he could peg out in a fortnight."

"But he might not."

"All the same, the disruption. All I can do is get to see him as often as possible and make sure he's okay."

"But he isn't okay. He's dying alone and lonely."

"I know," said Andy, standing with his back to the fire. "I know."

"It's terrible, Andy. It's terrible."

Bert arrived home just before dark. The lights were out next door.

"Damn it," he said to himself.

Dereck could be relied on. If he heard the sound of his engine, he would come to the door. He was subtle. He would step over the little border, edge round the front of the car and chat while Bert tried to extricate himself. Only if he saw he was unable to get out did he come forward and lift his legs, put his hand under his armpit and raise him. Parked at the summit of the sloping drive, Bert checked his rear-view mirror. The lights were on across the road. Maybe someone would notice. First of all, he needed to struggle.

He grabbed the edge of the car's roof and tried to haul himself so he had more room for his legs to swing. The seat was pushed back to its limit. His arm weakened and hurt and he had to let go. He was pant-ing. He waited a few minutes, checked his mirror again. Had no one seen him? He shoved both his hands under his right thigh, lifted and tried to shift it towards the door. The pain shot up his leg, suffused through his groin and abdomen. He pulled his hands out, sat back, gasping in pain his thin lips drawn across his teeth. He waited five minutes for the pain to ebb enough for him to try again. As he forced his fingers beneath his wizened thigh, the pain pulled its barbed wire through his veins.

"Oh, Christ," he said to himself.

There was nothing to do but carry on. He gritted his teeth and pulled. Sweat began to gather on his forehead, trickle down his cheeks, wet the back of his shirt. He managed to lift his leg far enough to settle his foot on the car's edge, but as he let it fall, he heard a snap and spat out a broken tooth. At the same time, he fell to the left, his el-bow hitting the handbrake and a steel bar of pain glowed white hot across his lower back. He tried to push with his left arm but it was too weak and his back too agonised.

He stayed in this position for ten minutes wondering if he would be found dead. Perhaps that would be best. If no one spotted him and he had to stay in the car overnight the cold would probably kill him. He could turn on the engine and the heater. How much petrol did he have? Maybe he should just stay as he was, leave the door open, let the cold come in and perish; but the thought of Andy roused him.

He grabbed the steering wheel with his right hand and tugged with maximum effort and in spite of the claws in his back which made him cry out. He raised himself six inches, but he didn't have the flexibility to nudge himself into the driver's seat. He relaxed his grip. His heart was pumping faster than he'd ever known. He wondered if it would hold out. Sweat ran down his rib cage. His trousers were sticking to his thighs. If he sounded the horn. He let go, tried to stretch to the centre, but could quite get there. The tips of his fingers touched the big round button but he couldn't depress it. He let out a devil's laugh.

He could never have imagined, when he was young and virile, when he could run around a football pitch for ninety minutes and hardly be tired, that his body could come to this. His body was his enemy. He was the same Bert. He was the fifteen year-old who had humped great sacks of flour for the Co-op, the eighteen-year-old who had carried small bombs in his arms for the RAF, the twenty-five-year-old who could beat everyone he knew at wrist-wrestling. His body had been his celebration. Now he was trapped in it. His front door was three feet away. Warmth, his bed, survival were yards away; but he was probably going to die, stupidly, humiliatingly in his car, on the drive.

Was there a way to die which wasn't a humiliation. People talked of dignity in old age, but only because old age was the encroachment of inevitable indignity. If there was a simple way to end his life, he would take it. If it was as easy as swallowing a pill and going to sleep, he would gladly do it. This fight to stay alive was degrading.

Yet he had passed a lovely afternoon. To die now wouldn't be so bad. Andy had looked after him. Did he love him? Could he leave the planet knowing that at the end there was one person who loved him? Yes, he believed he could. It was a miracle that his son's love for him had endured but it was true. No one had loved him as a child. He was a burden of shame to his mother. He'd believed Elsie had loved him, but her love had proven thin. Mary and Andy had loved him. Sylvia had barely known him. Andy loved him enough to give him a nice afternoon, company, conversation and a good meal. He was amazed.

Perhaps he should close the door and turn on the ignition. He couldn't reach. He gave another snorting, devil's laugh. The sweat was growing cold on his back, his belly and his legs. He was starting to shiver. How long would it take? Would he pass out in minutes or would it take hours? Would he revive. He hoped not. Let him become unconscious and know nothing of his end. He closed his eyes and let his body relax. He would strive no more. Let them find him in the morning. Let them be horrified. There was nothing he could do. His body was a lump of uselessness. Soon it would be nothing but dinner for bacteria. Burn it. Have done with it fast. He had lived. He had tried to make something of the life imposed on him. He had failed. His life was a failure in every regard. He didn't hide it from himself. He welcomed it. It was the death of illusion. Everyone was running around in search of success but every one of them would end something like this. Success. Tush. They were all failures.

He saw in a curious bright light which seemed to come from outside him, the mad futility of his society. What were they all, the successes? Money-grubbers, mirror-gazers. We were supposed to see Churchill as a great man: a bigoted toff with a drink problem descended from war-mongers and wedded to violence in spite of his jaw-jaw saw. He had admired Frank Sinatra, but what was he but a thoughtless crooner in cahoots with gangsters who thought he could act and counted his happiness in dollars. It was all wrong. Humanity was all askew, adrift. How could such a thing happen? It was enough to make every cell in your body revolt, but it was true. Humanity had made the wrong choices. His afternoon had taught him what was right: not money, not power, but love. He laughed to himself again. It sounded sentimental but it was the opposite. It was the lunatic pursuit of money and power which was soppy. They were the cissy compensations of the weak-minded. Love took real courage. He was proud his son had it and that he benefitted. Love and power, he knew, in what he thought were the last moments of his life, were sworn enemies. Why couldn't he have known that when he was twenty-one?

Whoever sought power was not to be trusted and whoever sought money was in search of power. Humanity had taken a wrong turn but it was all up for him. He was glad to be on the point of non-existence.

He heard an engine. The sound of brakes. Voices. He opened his eyes. Seconds later Dereck was leaning over him.

"My god, Bert, my god. What's happened, mate? Bloody hell. Come on, let's get you inside. Betty, give us a hand, luv. Christ, Bert, how did you get like this?"

"Knackered, Dereck," he said with a smile, "completely knackered."

He felt himself being lifted. He made no effort. Effort was a thing of the past. Dereck's arm was round his back, manipulating him towards the door; then both his arms were round his chest, pulling him free. Bert was astonished at the feeling of strength. It was as if some of his neighbour's power passed into his recalcitrant limbs; he was eighteen again; he could run a mile and be barely breathless, shift a double wardrobe single-handedly without strain. He was upright. His feet were on the tarmac.

"Can you walk into the house?" said Dereck.

Bert tried to take a step but his right leg buckled.

"I've got him, Betty, said Dereck," and in seconds, Bert felt himself raised.

He was in Dereck's arms, like a little child who has fallen asleep in the car being carried to his cot.

"Where'd you want to be, mate?"

"In the armchair."

"Sure you don't want me to put you to bed?"

"No, in the lounge."

He was lowered gently, as if by some powerful machine driven by electricity.

"Christ, your hands are frozen, Bert. Your teeth are chatterin'. I'll put't fire on, eh?"

"Yes, that's right, Dereck, put the fire on."

Betty arrived from the bedroom with a heavy, brown, patterned blanket, doubled it and laid it over him.

"You'd better make him a cup o' tea, luv," said Dereck.

"Is it all right, Bert? Can I make you a brew in your kitchen?"

"Yes, Betty, that's fine," said Bert in a voice not much more than a whisper, his head thrown back, his eyes closed.

"Do you want something to eat?"

"Toast," he said. "Toast and honey."

The two of them went into the little kitchen.

"I think you should call an ambulance," said Betty under her breath.

"Aye, I'll 'ave t'ask 'im though."

"He looks terrible, Dereck. He might be dead in't mornin'"

Dereck turned the gas fire to maximum and closed the door. Bert, a cushion inserted behind his back by Betty, ate the hot toast slowly, warmed his hands on the mug and drank in little sips.

"Do you think I should call an ambulance, Bert?" said Dereck.

"Ambulance? No. A hearse more like," and his brief devil's laugh cracked across the room.

"What about your Andy? Shall I ring him?"

"No, don't bother him. I'll call him in the morning."

"Aye. Well, I can stay with you if you like, Bert. Keep an eye on you."

"That's very good of you, Dereck," said Bert, minutely revived by the food and drink. "I can always ring you if I need to, can't I?"

"Aye, 'course you can."

Betty went home to see the children were all right, Dereck stayed for an hour.

"Sure you don't want me to stay, Bert?"

"No, I'll be fine. Thanks. You've been very good."

The room was warm in every corner. His body began to feel marginally friendly. He wondered if he could make it to the bathroom. He pulled the thick blanket aside and wriggled to the edge of the chair. Placing his feet together, flat on the carpet, he knew he wouldn't have the force to push himself upright. He turned and slid onto his knees, held onto the wide arm and by tiny degrees hoisted himself to a standing position, his legs against the chair for support. His first step made him totter. He held out his arms. His second felt more secure. He rested by the corner bureau, leaning on both hands. Opening the door, which dragged a little on the carpet took two minutes. The cold of the hallway made him shudder. He placed his palms against the wall and edged round. The bathroom was colder still. He clung to the stainless steel rail. The return journey was slightly quicker. He was glad to close the door against the unheated portion of the bunga-low. He let himself collapse onto the cushions, pulled the blanket over him. He'd made it. He'd been to the bathroom and back all on his own. He was alive, in his own house, and he could walk. He couldn't have been more pleased if he was receiving his Cup Final winner's medal from the queen.

The gorgeous heat of the room was a form of company. He thought of going to bed, but he didn't want to leave this enclosed Riviera. It was as hot as he recalled Italy or Egypt. He had survived. He wouldn't be found dead in the morning. He might live for weeks. Maybe months. To a man who has believed he will be dead in hours, the notion of months of life is like a child's anticipation of adult-hood. He fell asleep, the fire humming at high pitch, the lights on, alone.

Neither Mary nor Sylvia ever knew about their dad's ordeal on the driveway. When Andy was told, he felt guilty for not having come home with him; yet also, he was glad that Dereck and Betty had been given their chance for kindness. Now they would know how serious things were. They were good folk. He knew they would be especially vigilant. The incident had made his dad safer. Had he taken him home, they wouldn't have increased their level of attention. Now he could be slightly more assured they would look out for him. He wasn't alone.

Bert was inordinately grateful. As he was for their greater interven-tion. Dereck knocked on the door every day. Betty made him food: dishes of vegetarian cottage pie or wickedly spicey curry.

"If you're going out in the car," said Dereck, "let me know when you'll be back. I'll make sure I'm here."

They altered their arrangements and timetable for him. They were like a family. How odd it was: people he had no blood connection with were kinder to him than his grandparents, his ex-wife, even his mother.

Bert regained some ability to walk. He could get to the day centre. He had a life. He could make his breakfast, listen to the news, watch the television, read a book, converse with Dereck and the people he sat next to at the institution. Yet the terrible happened, he collapsed while trying to hoover. Dereck knocked, looked through the window, grabbed the spare key from the garage. The ambulance arrived. He was in hospital again. He loathed and dreaded it. Would he ever go home ?

The ride through Hoghton, a steady climb past the tower, the time-trialing sprints along the straights, the final slow, watch-out-for-the-psychopathic-drivers dodge through Blackburn's streets to the hospital became Andy's habit three or four times a week. At the end of the school day, he mounted, sped along the Hutton cycle track, through Howick and Penwortham, down the wind-and-rain-in-your-face hill, over the river and along Broadgate; changed from his teacher's collar-and-tie uniform as he assembled and scoffed a cheese or chicken sandwich, swigged a glass of water and set off to be early for visiting time. Dereck was often there, but no one else. It was a three-week spell. The tests revealed nothing. His dad went back home.

Friday was TES day. All the teachers who still had ambitions, were eager to scan the ads. Mike Chambers had a copy delivered. He was looking for his next move. He ought to be a Head by the time he was forty, at the latest. He needed a Deputy Headship soon.

"I'll be applying for that," he said at morning break, chomping a Garibaldi and swigging thin coffee, "it's got my name on it."

In the *Black Bull*, at lunchtime, he treated the assembled truants, which included the staff of the local primary, including the Head, a balding, rotund man of fifty, whose standard quip was: "Friday afternoon is basket work. They do the work, I throw it in the basket," to his conviction the job was his.

"Whose going to have a better record than me ? Eh? Eh? Mine's impeccable. And I interview well. I always have. It's mine. It'll have to be a good candidate who beats me," and he forked a heap of beef curry and rice into his cavernous mouth and chewed as he continued speaking, bits of masticated food flying from his lips to the table.

Andy remained moderately friendly with Chambers. He wasn't the kind of man he favoured, but life didn't throw up, in constrained contexts like work, people you would choose to spend your time with. It was a matter of getting on with people who, had your choice been entirely free, you wouldn't have spent more than two minutes talking to on the street. One evening a few teachers had been for a drink and they landed back at Chambers's bungalow. Gerry Beckett, who disdained Chambers' company had come along for the sake of getting out. There were two primary school teachers Chambers knew through playing badminton, Tracey Bowe and the curiously, cramped, stiff, pale and somewhat tormented Nancy Beech who taught maths and P.E. , lived with a houseful of cats and seemed allergic to men in their elemental identity.

As the others were crowding into a car to get home, Andy was the last to leave. He was sitting in the living-room, tucking his jeans into his socks when Chambers came through from the kitchen and stood over him. He thought it strange, but Chambers often was intrusive and clumsy.

"Going then?" he said.

Andy looked up and saw on his colleague's ugly face, a look which made it uglier. The least unprepossessing physiognomy can be beautified by a sweet expression, just as the most perfect features can be rendered repulsive by sneering, preening or vicious self-absorption. He paused a moment in his thinking. Stood up quickly, nimbly moving to the right to avoid the taller man's overbearing posture.

"What else would I be doing?" he said, raising his chin and looking Chambers in the eye.

He moved away and went to look out of his window, as if nothing had happened.

"Well," he said, his back to Andy, "better get to bed. I've books to mark before I get to school in the morning," and he began hurriedly tidying the antiseptically neat room as if to quell some unruly desire, some impulse to power and abuse.

Andy went out of the side door, jumped on his bike and, standing on the pedals, sped away. He didn't want to believe what had just happened, but there was only one interpretation. There it was. Hardly surprising when he thought it through. Still, he'd made himself clear. Chambers wouldn't try it again. He was an inadequate man, one of those people who try to fulfil through work relations and the petty, functional hierarchies on which they are based, fundamental needs which require a voluntary context. Yet, as he stowed his bike under the stairs, he did wonder how safe it was for such a man to be teaching young boys. Chambers had taken over from Halifax. Was he going to follow his nefarious path? What kind of place was he working in? Cooper abused his power. Rob Hesketh was a drunkard who during the exchange visit had spent the entire ten days marinated. Crawley was besotted with sixth-form girls and handing over thousands to the despicable Diane Clayton. Dave Dover, posing as a respectable married man, was probably a closet bi-sexual. Corruption ran through the arteries of the school. Its prestige was founded on lies. The Latin and Greek mottos, the gowns in assembly, the hymns and piety, the rugger-is-good-for-your-soul ethos, the scramble for Oxbridge places, all hid the fact of a horrible emotional crippling which led to the concealed sewer-pipe of abuse.

The only solution was to move on. He scoured the TES as diligently as the greasy-pole climbers; but he was restricted by his dad's illness. He spotted jobs in London, Bristol, Cornwall, The Dales. He needed something handy. How long would he be trapped by his decision? He could have gone to Perpignan, after all. Yet he couldn't believe his dad had much longer, and he couldn't leave. That was his fate for the time being, he had to accept it.

THE MINERS AND MUSSOLINI

Saturday afternoons brought crowds to the town. It was pleasant to be amongst them. There was no need to be part of the shopping bonanza: it was heartening to share the streets with so many, and inevitably, you would encounter someone, have a chat on Fishergate, or find a congenial pub or café. Andy would go, some weeks, to *The Continental*, at lunchtime, for pie and peas. There were always workers from the sorting office on West Cliff who'd nipped down for a sandwich and a pint. He would hand them his letters and packages and they'd always oblige. He was still sending out to magazines and getting nothing but rejections. *The Black Horse Poets*, as they'd dubbed themselves was simultaneously encouraging and dispiriting. Tom Lemon placed poems in *Ambit*, *Poetry Review, Stand*, *The Echo Room*, and had just had his first pamphlet published by *Blackstream*, a little press based in Keighley and run by the putatively bohemian Paul Flintoff who squeezed money out of Yorkshire Arts and the Arts Council, published mainly pamphlets of twenty or so poems and ran an annual competition which brought in a thousand entries at five pounds a time, which nicely supplemented what he earned from supply teaching, a job which gave him ample opportunity for his hobby of seducing teenage girls.

Andy was aware Tom's poems embraced a more acceptable, recognizable sensibility than his own. He was contestatory. Did that come from Lawrence who had said he liked to write when he felt spiteful? Was he too writing out of spite, or did he, as comfortable folk liked to say have *a chip on his shoulder*? He'd been turned down again and again by the places where Tom had appeared. He was thirty-three and for nearly two decades of dedication had no more to show than three poems in the university poetry magazine. Was he embarked on a false path? Was he a Mr Casaubon, blind to his own folly which everyone else could see as plainly as the sun?

He wished, often, the nagging need to write would disappear. Yet, the group gave him encouragement. They weren't critics in any real sense, though Andy had respect for Tom's wide reading and astute responses; but they were all he had. Will Joiner would enthuse over some of his pieces, but Andy felt him too quick to pour undisciplined sentiment over whatever appealed to him moment by moment. He too had placed poems in little magazines but he thought nothing of ringing an editor who turned down his work, or pitching up at his front door to protest his rejection.

Andy was committed to an activity he took utterly seriously, which he thought of as part of mankind's search for truth, which had engendered the plays of Aeschylus, Tolstoy's novels and Prévert's poetry but which excluded him utterly. It was a humiliating experience which pushed him in the direction of despair. He cut into his steaming meat and potato pie. The posties in the corner were laughing loudly, enjoying one another's company and their beer. The sun was warming the window and his back. He was fine here. Life was fine. He could enjoy his afternoon. Why should he worry about the poems he'd just handed over? Why not forget it? Why not leave to others what had so far brought him nothing but pain? He could go back to where he started: being an enchanted and diligent reader. What was wrong with that? Literature needed readers. Or maybe he should step back from creative writing and do what he'd thought of at nineteen: a book about Lawrence. Surely there'd be much more chance of publishing that than poetry.

For twenty minutes he was free of torment, but when he was pushing up the slope out of Avenham Park, the old feeling returned: he couldn't convince himself there wasn't something he should write. It was a matter of that *should*. The idea of *could* he might have rejected easily. There were plenty of things he could have done. He could have joined one the rock bands he'd been asked to sing for by lads at school; he could have had a crack at acting; he could have worked hard at his tennis like Stu Archer had and become a coach;but there was nothing which seemed his fate like writing. He couldn't quieten the sense that potentially he could write something original: how to move from potential to realization was the torment.

It wasn't like commonplace ambitions. If you wanted to be an accountant, a teacher, a doctor, a lawyer, a banker, even a politician, the path was evident. Martin McClintock, now Deputy Leader of the council, was making his way in power in the customary fashion: establishing the right contacts, honing a glib style, perfecting the technique of being all things to all men. He'd married Matt Ross's cousin who Andy played with in the early days in Woodland Grove. No more than a humble maths teacher eighteen months earlier, he was now reputed to be worth hundreds of thousands and had invested in

112

the new radio station established by Glyn Shrimpton, a flamboyant, narcissistic failed-actor turned estate agent. Andy despised their kind of cynical, ever-on-the-make, where's-the-next-opportunity-for-a-quick-quid mentality. He thought McClintock an excrescence in the Labour Party, a sty in its eye, a verruca on its foot, an incipient cancer in its cells. Yet the culture made it easy for such people to flourish, while finding a way to what he felt impelled to do was impossibly hard.

He went to the library where he spent an hour and a half browsing and reading, but it was disappointing. Once, he'd been able to find the complete works of Thomas Hardy, everything by Jane Austen, a full set of Thackery, the entire poems of Byron, Spenser or Abercrombie. Now, the stock was being whittled. It seemed frequency of borrowing was a greater test of importance than quality of writing or thought and that endurance was a lost value. Harold Robbins was kicking aside Henry Roth and everything cheap and transient taking the place of high-minded commitment to what would transcend time.

He sat in an armchair with a copy of *The Man Without Qualities*. Was he mistaken to believe in high-mindedness? Was it snobbish? Was it anti-democratic? Was letting the mass preference for Jackie Collins trump the minority concern for John Skelton right? Was *giving the masses what they wanted* a proper democratic principle?

As he wandered along Friargate, wondering who he might bump into and heading for Halewoods, his mind cleared a little. No, it wasn't democratic to let trash occupy most cultural space. That was to confuse incompatibilities. Democracy was a political concept and principle, not a literary-intellectual one. People should have control over their own actions. Democracy should be about spreading that responsibility. People should make the decisions which rule their own lives; but knowing the difference between good and bad literature wasn't a matter of taste. Liking Ian Fleming doesn't make him a good writer. Whether you like him or not is immaterial. Disliking Joseph Conrad doesn't make him a bad writer. He thought back to the story he'd read for O Level Literature. *The Secret Sharer* had stuck in his mind like *Odour of Chrysanthemums*. The captain, who does the right thing by doing the wrong thing, appealed to him. He searched out *Heart of Darkness*, *Lord Jim*, *Typhoon* and read *Nostromo* at university. What did it matter if all these people shopping in Preston on a

Saturday afternoon didn't like Conrad? What did it matter if they'd never heard of him? He was a supremely good writer.

The idea troubled him. There was something wrong in leaving the majority to depend purely on what took their fancy. People should inhabit a more demanding culture. Wasn't there a responsibility on those with the critical faculties to distinguish good from bad culture to establish a hierarchy of values? Wasn't it right, in a moral sense, to let people know that Raymond Chandler was a lesser writer than Jane Austen?

The doctrine of *give the masses what they want* was a renunciation of responsibility and a form of exploitation. He'd handed over his pocket money for *Beatles* records. It was a trick. They became millionaires, as did the record company executives, and the kids were left with a thin and narrow appreciation of music. The same trick was everywhere. Sell people stuff and get rich, but never ask what kind of mind is generated; and as the best way to sell people stuff is to appeal to their lowest instincts and most unsublimated impulses, the result was a culture of tat, not just in clothes and furniture and gadgets, but in the creation of the social mind.

The ideas continued to churn as he browsed in the second-hand book shop. Old man Halewood approached him.

"Now this one might be up your street."

It was a pristine paperback of *The Agony of The American Left*. Had the bibliophile attributed a left-wing mentality to him? What had he bought which might have given him away? Mostly, he'd accumulated fiction, poetry and plays. It was disturbing to think he wore his opinions so they could be read by people who hardly knew him. He flicked through.

"Anyway," said the wily dealer, "I'll leave it with you."

Andy read a few paragraphs and wondered why he'd never come across Christopher Lasch. The book had appeared in 1969. He felt ignorant. He would buy it.

He went into the basement ,which made him think of Theresa. He hardly saw her. She'd finally broken with Gene because of his drinking and taken up with an older man, an electrician who Andy knew in passing. He thought him a pleasant, easy-going bloke, but he wondered if he and Theresa were compatible. He wasn't likely to share her inclination to Mrs Gaskell. Yet maybe, after the flying-round-the-room, self-indulgent antics of her husband, a steady, unremarkable man was what she needed.

Under a heap of unattractive paperbacks, he found a copy of Priestley's *Literature and Western Man*. It jogged his mind back to his previous preoccupations. Priestley occupied a curious territory: an oppositional writer in some ways, but a comfortable one in others. He wasn't a writer of the stature of Lawrence or Conrad, but he was serious and skilled. Lawrence and Conrad were both oppositional writers. Neither offered a conformist perspective. Both troubled the assumptions of their society. Wasn't that what a writer should do? Didn't all serious intellectual or artistic work remain valuable only because of its subversive edge? Einstein was important because he overturned the prevailing view of physics;Darwin because he shattered the ignorance about how species got here; Newton because he tore up an ancient set of received ideas; Picasso because he didn't fit with the tradition of western painting; Beethoven because no one had heard a symphony like the fifth before; James Joyce because he threw the existing strictures about the novel in the bin.

What was the point of poem, a play, a novel which confirmed people in their commonplace thoughts and feelings? To write only to please an audience, to gain plaudits and money, was to deny the essence of literature. Its role was to challenge. Yet it seemed courage was being lost. He'd looked at *Hotel du Lac* because it had won the Booker. It seemed a book hardly engaged with the reality from which it emerged and the style embraced a kind of deadness. There was nothing about it of Conrad's insertion in the awful events of colonialism, or the desperate fact of terrorism, or the terrifying moral and emotional emptiness at the heart of trade; nor anything akin to Lawrence's discomfort with the facts of industrialism, the frozen sensibility of the middle classes, the moral and sensual negativism and corruption behind the display of property and respectability.

Where was today's Lawrence or Conrad?

He was appalled at the arrival of Wendy Cope whose poetry had a hint of Pam Ayres and John Cooper Clarke was obviously an attention-seeking, would-be pop star who used his sub-Betjemanesque doggerel as a vehicle. Yet, he was taken seriously. The assimilation of poetry to pop seemed dangerous and foolish, a submission to the debased notion that only what appeals to a market is of any worth.

He read Heaney, Muldoon, Roy Fisher, Alan Brownjohn, Carol Duffy in search of what had inspired him in Lawrence; but it wasn't there. Something had been lost. When had it gone and how? There seemed to be no space for rebellion, for that awkward, ill-fitting sensibility which made Lawrence or Conrad or Kafka difficult to assimilate. A suburban mentality had permeated, the kind of resignation and snobbery he detected in Larkin. The Mersey poets, who had appeared so potentially disruptive, who had been dismissed by snooty reviewers in the Sunday papers, had turned into kittens. McGough and Patten had left Liverpool and Henri was a poor man's Ginsberg, an overweight clown who hid his sleazy sexual behaviour behind the excusing slogan of free love. They were no more a threat to the existing order than Paul McCartney who recorded *Mary Had a Little Lamb* and counted his millions.

The idea came to him that whatever didn't challenge accepted views, inevitably gave comfort to them. A book which did that was worthless. Who could devote thousands of intense hours to writing something which people swallowed like apple pie and custard? The conclusion cheered him. If the choice was to write literature which caused no sleepless nights for the powerful and the conformist, or give up and grow vegetables, he'd do the latter. Yet it wasn't a case of wilful awkwardness; it was rather that what needed to be said was bound to be distasteful to those who wanted things not to change.

Was he mistaken to think literature was always driving at change? The idea defeated him for a minute or two. Perhaps it was a delusion. Did Shakespeare write for change or Chaucer or T.S.Eliot: he was a political reactionary. Yet even Eliot was pushing at what was wrong. A snippet drifted into his head: "..and nobody knows or cares who is his neighbour.." Even the royalist, conservative Eliot was writing out of a sense that things needed to change. Surely he was seeking to expose human folly, as he conceived it. A writer who wasn't doing that wasn't worth reading; and didn't exposing human folly imply a desire for a corrective? He disagreed violently with Eliot's prescription: deference to traditional authority wasn't what the world needed. Yet Eliot had kicked the poetry that preceded him into the past. His poetical radicalism sat uneasily with his political conservatism but his status depended on the former not the latter.

He left the shop reassured in his belief that literature must be in some way subversive in order to be valuable. It wasn't a matter of something factitious. It had to be genuine. Eliot was genuine in his literary subversion. No one could write like Swinburne after *The Waste Land*. Why was it he felt that subversive edge was absent? Fear was abroad thanks to Thatcher and fear diminishes people in every way. Yet the change long prefigured her elevation. The swirling, churning atmosphere of challenge he'd known as a teenager was gone. A dark period of tongue-biting sycophancy had emerged. You could walk into Waterstones and find *The Life and Loves of a She-Devil* presented as if it was the next *Secret Agent*. It was a selling ploy, but it had no critical value. Somehow the culture was slipping into this insane delusion that only what attracts big sales is worth anything. The notion of a hierarchy of values was being discarded. If people rallied to *Frankie Goes to Hollywood*, then who was to say their music was inferior to Bach? Yet it obviously was. It was insane to think otherwise.

There was a social and cultural insanity seeping through the world's veins, if insanity can be defined as separation from reality. Not to recognise that Conrad was a better and more vital writer than Fay Weldon or Mozart a superior musician to David Bowie, was to be divorced from reality. There was madness forcing its way through every institution, an entirely avoidable insanity whose purpose was to generate a confusion which would protect the rich and powerful. If people could accept, unthinkingly, that Ringo Starr deserved to be a multi-millionaire and Madonna and Arnold Schwarzenegger the centre of attention, they could accept that Richard Branson deserved to be obscenely rich too. Inequality was naturalised. The prevailing economic arrangements were normal. They were the way the world should be. There was nothing to be questioned.

It was curiously totalitarian. Beneath the noise of putative democracy, a quiet closing down of the mind was enforcing itself. What he'd taken for granted when he was fourteen, that all forms of authority must be questioned, must be required to justify themselves, was being eliminated. Now, it was taken for granted that the rich should be rich, the powerful should be powerful and by implication the poor and powerless, poor and powerless. It was an atrocious and dispiriting deadening of the human spirit and the inherent need of the human mind to be sceptical and inquiring.

He headed for the market to buy fish for his evening meal. He'd worn away the daylight browsing and thinking. He zipped his cheap, maroon jacket against the cold. The chill made him think of the summer and the week he'd spent on an Arvon writing course at Lumb Bank. The tutors were dramatists: Sam Evans who wrote for television and whose recent series *The Nurses's Prick*, had been a great success; and Adrian Shaftesbury, a fringe writer with a script currently being readied for production at the *National*, who'd had ten plays performed at *The Bush*, *The Soho Poly* and other small venues. The task had been to write a half hour play. His had gone down well. Evans had written to him, putting him in touch with people at the BBC he thought might like his work. Andy had expanded his play to an hour and a half and sent it to *The Soho Poly*. A few days earlier, he'd had a response: they liked it and wanted him to come down to a Saturday workshop.

Was this the opportunity he'd wanted? It was easy to take your desires for reality. He longed to be a writer, by which he meant not to have to teach to pay the bills, being published or performed and above all, getting some recognition, however little. It was an exciting prospect, taking the train to London to be part of day's script-in-hand readings. Maybe it would lead where he wanted; but his excitement was attended by dread. His sense that he was at odds with his society and his time discouraged the notion of easy success. He might be heading for terrible disappointment. The crucial thing was to keep expectations within limits. The idea struck him painfully. What an odd time he lived in where glib promises were everywhere but pruning your expectations was necessary.

The darkness had invaded quickly, chasing the light from the streets and the sky so the mood of night was on everything though it wasn't yet five. He walked through St George's shopping centre for the illumination and the warmth and cutting to Fishergate by *Marks and Spencer* ran into Christine Bowland who he'd met nearly a decade earlier through the catholics he was friendly with. She lived nearby, in Penwortham, and had been briefly engaged to Matt Ross's cousin, Tom Campbell, who lived two doors away from Andy in Woodland Grove. He knew she'd studied at Brunel and was based in London, but he hadn't seen or heard of her for some years. Once, in the early seventies, when he'd taken a coach from Preston to join a CND demonstration in London, they'd sat together for the weary miles through Wigan, Birmingham and Watford. They walked from Victoria coach station to Hyde Park where, on meeting a couple of her friends on the edge of the assembling crowd, she turned from him and headed off with them without any word of goodbye. It shocked him, slightly. It was an odd absence of social nicety, that common-place recognition that the politeness of greeting and parting are far from trivial but avoid offence and keep the emotions of even the most passing liaisons in balance.

It was curious how it lingered in his mind and jumped back into his consciousness now as he stopped to say hello.

She was home for the weekend. Her parents no longer lived in Pen-wortham but in a bungalow in Lostock Hall, an unprepossessing no-man's-land between Preston and Leyland. She was doing secretarial work in London while trying to organize qualification as a lawyer.

"What about you?" she said with a little cock of her head.

"Oh, just teaching. Keeps me off the streets."

She was killing time while her younger brother was in the barber's. Andy recalled him. He was much younger, probably now about fif-teen or sixteen. He was a pale, lonely looking boy. Andy had seen him riding his bike as a little kid in Blundell Lane, always alone, and with a curious, distant look on his face, as if he needed to keep peo-ple at bay, like someone might who was very sought after. He re-membered too seeing Christine with him when he was no more than four or five, holding his hand to cross busy Liverpool Road at the lights and thinking there was something odd about them; as if she wanted to advertise his presence or her care of him, as if it was somehow unusual that a sister might hold her little brother's hand and look out for him.

Once they'd exhausted the details of their mutual situations, there wasn't much left to say, without entering more dangerous territory.

"So, you're back to London tomorrow, then?"

"Yes. I have a car. My step-dad gave it to me when they got a new one."

"That's handy. What's in store for tonight?"

He assumed she'd be meeting up with old friends, maybe some of the catholic crowd she'd been part of.

"Watching telly," and she nodded to indicate the paucity of her alter-natives.

He was about to tell her he was going to see a play about the Spanish Civil War at the Polytechnic Arts Centre, but wondered if she would take it as an invitation. She might think it somewhat brutal after such a long separation as they knew one another only in passing.

"What's on? Morecambe and Wise or some such dross, I suppose?"

"I don't know. What are you doing?"

He took the inquiry as idle, It was mere conversation-making, but as she'd asked, he told her and she showed interest.

"Better than the telly, anyway," he said, swinging his little plastic bag in which was the cod loin he needed to get home to cook.

"Much better," she said, "especially sitting with your parents."

He laughed.

"Well," he said, feeling suddenly light-hearted and careless, "why don't you come along and see the play?"

She agreed and they decided on a time and place to meet.

Walking briskly home along Fishergate, down the hill and by the river, he was glad he'd have someone to go with. There'd be people there he knew. John Royce for sure, the Labour stalwart and jazz bassist whose wife had left him for the lesbian constituency secretary Andy suspected of being a charlatan and a fraud. Jean Royce, a quiet, artistic, principled woman had suffered a serious brain event shortly after the break-up, triggered, the rumour supposed, by stress and had died at only forty-five. Andy had gone for a few days holiday with John to Barmouth, one of the places he and Jean had taken their three children when they were little, to try to keep his spirits up. The poor man was devastated, utterly at a loss to understand the behaviour of the wife he'd adored for more than two decades. He talked and talked. Andy listened, nodded and smiled.

There'd be plenty of other Labour and radical folk too, but they'd just been people he ran into. He'd intended to go alone, and though it was likely he would drift off afterwards for a drink with acquaintances, to have someone beside you who was your companion for the night was different. Christine was an attractive young woman, blonde and slender and with a pleasing little face whose straight nose and pink lips had a girlish quality. Her eyes were big and green and though the left one turned slightly inwards, it somehow added to her charm. The thought of having a woman to turn up with cheered him.

Yet at the same time, there was a ripple of anxiety: she was going back to London tomorrow and in all probability, they would watch the play, have a chat, go for a drink, maybe with a few others, shake hands and not see one another again for years. There was a presumption in his mind that her life in London must be too full for her to be tugged towards him, stuck as he was in the town he thought he'd escaped a dozen years before. Yet what if something did develop? Christine Bowland. What did he know about her? Very little; but the fact of her switch-the-lights-on-and-switch-them-off engagement to Tom Campbell bothered him.

He cooked his fish with black pepper, boiled some potatoes and poured a battalion of frozen peas into a saucepan. What did he have to worry about? He was a grown up. He could handle whatever developed; but he was surprised to catch himself thinking about the state of his bedroom and wondering if he should tidy up or change the sheets.

She arrived in a rush, her hair still wet, her coat over her arm. He was balanced on a stool at the bar of *The Ship*, a pub by the polytechnic, a student haunt, though still popular with the townsfolk.

"What would you like?" he said

"I don't know if I've got my purse," she said rummaging in her big, black, leather bag.

"Don't worry. What do you fancy?"

"Where are my car keys?"she said, looking up at him. "Did I have them in my hand?"

"I don't think so."

The barman, a burly student with an agricultural beard was waiting.

"I might have dropped them. Or did I leave them in the car? Just a minute."

She began laying the contents on the bar: a brush, cosmetics, a lighter, a packet of cigarettes, two letters, an address book, a pack of cards, a comb, a woolly hat, a glove, a pair of tights.

"Oh, here they are. I was sure I'd put them in there."

"Good. What'll you have?"

"My hair is still wet," she said rubbing it with her finger ends, "I tried to dry it in the car."

"It'll dry off. Half of something?"

"Mmm. What is there?"

She inspected the pumps. She went from one end of the bar to the other and back again, as if her life depended on the choice. She propped her elbow on the bar and rested her chin in her palm. The barman's exceptionally white teeth showed through his brown beard as he forced a smile.

"Is that the only lager you've got?"

"Yes."

"I might have a wine."

"Red or white?"

"I could have a vodka."

"Vodka? Something with it?"

"What kind of gin have you got?"

"Gin? Gordon's."

"Is that all?"

"Yes."

"Mmm. I suppose I'll have a lager."

The barman drew the drink, Andy forced his fingers into the tight pocket of his cords where coins that didn't want to be spent were hiding like threatened bacteria. They took their drinks to a table in the corner.

"My hair's still wet," she said, shaking her head and pulling her fingers through the strands before plunging into her bag once more, this time in search of her cigarettes and lighter.

"Did I leave my lighter on the bar?"

"No. It's in there somewhere. You should carry a torch."

"A torch?"

"Yes, though I guess you'd have to put it in your bag so you'd never find it."

"Are you sure my lighter isn't on the bar?"

"Do you want me to have a look in there?"

"You can't look in my bag."

"Why not?"

"It's private."

"Yes, but you've just shown the lad behind the bar everything that's in there."

"Not everything."

"Ah, have you got a revolver in the depths?"

"A revolver?"

"I'll ask the barman for a light."

There was an audience of sixty for the play. Twenty of them the usual radicals Andy knew from meetings, demos, nights out or in passing. At the interval they chatted to John Royce who knew virtually everybody but nevertheless was on his own. The drama was poor, in spite of the unobjectionable politics. The condemnation of Franco and the sympathy for the republic, the criticism of Soviet manipulation and the heavy stress on the principle of the anarchists, couldn't conceal the artistic incompetence of a piece assembled with the rough, spatchcock skill need to build an orange box.

When it was over they went out into the damp night.

"Where's my coat?" said Christine.

"Have you left it inside?"

"Did I bring it? I might have left it in the pub."

"Hang on."

Andy ran indoors and came back with the long, dark blue gabardine hooked over his index finger, dangling behind him.

"Your wrap, madame."

"Good job I didn't lose that," she said. "It cost a fortune."

The Lamb and Packet sat at the end of Friargate, more or less opposite Robin House where Andy had sat in classes with Terry Kent and Amanda Ashdale. He'd nipped in often for a pie and half a bitter at lunchtime during his A Level year and occasionally he, Sean Dunbar and Kath Sparrow had spent an hour there on one of their Friday night tours. Nostalgia for his happy, productive time as student at the Harris, his friendly chats with John White and Mick Drake over a steaming meat and potato made it congenial, but on the other hand, it was one of those non-descript places without enough character to make it somewhere he liked to be.

They went there because it was handy. Most of the clientele were working folk dressed up for a night out: men in suits and tight collars, closely shaven, their shoes highly polished; blokes who spent Monday to Friday in factories, on building sites, in warehouses, driving lorries or buses, dealing with muck and having to use their muscles to pay the rent, who put on their best for a trip to the pub to sink six pints because for five days they had to wear overalls, boots, thick shirts to keep out the chill, dirty, misshapen trousers; because their hands were hard and filthy and at the end of the day they stank of oil or grease or exhaust fumes or petrol or rubble or sweat. Women who swabbed floors, polished desks, disinfected toilets, turned heavy patients in their beds, mopped up vomit, who sat at tills so long they wanted to scream, who stood by conveyor belts sorting the saleable from the rejects or performed the same limited, brainless action a thousand times a day; who served up chips, beans, pies, burgers, sausages, fried eggs, fried bread, bacon and mugs of hot sweet tea to unceremonious van drivers, warehousemen or blokes who kept planes in the air, put on their best frocks, made up their faces, slipped their nyloned feet into tight high-heels they would be glad to kick off at midnight, went to the hairdresser's in the afternoon, sprayed themselves with the most expensive perfume their husbands could afford for their anniversary, painted their nails and hoped, in some half acknowledged corner of their minds, they would be noticed, desired, admired, complimented.

Andy and Christine, university educated lefties, dressed down. It made him feel slightly out of place. He would have liked to be back in Fylde bar or the *Ring O'Bells*, surrounded by young people in jeans, sweaters, long cotton skirts, t-shirts, all the dress-as-you-like apparent carelessness of unpretentious student pretention. They had a corner more or less to themselves. She revealed more about herself.

Her father had committed suicide when she was four. He'd had psychiatric difficulties and spent a spell in Whittingham, the big "mental hospital" out of the town, towards Longridge. He threw himself out of the bedroom window. They were living in her grandmother's house, where her mother had retreated with her three youngsters (Christine was the eldest) after her husband's first breakdown.

Her mother, who never spoke of the terrible event, took a job in the council offices and became more or less an absentee. It was the grandmother who took on the principal care of the children. Christine was already a pupil at Lark Hill Convent when her father obeyed the confused impulses of his disordered mind. Things rolled along till, when she was twelve, her mother became pregnant by her *fancy man,* Billy. Out of the panic came marriage and a move to Penwortham, to a small semi in Blundell Lane the impregnator was able to put a deposit on because of the money which came to him after his first wife divorced him. She'd previously been married to a slick, cynical, any-opportunity-to-make-money-will-do trader who'd discovered that death is lucrative and made himself a few hundred thousand selling arms.

Billy had three sons, worked in a warehouse, drank copiously, admired Mussolini (his attraction to Hitler he thought it wise to play down) and was intent on getting his hands on his step-daughter's body.

It was a kind of confession, an unburdening, at once odd and flattering. He had his convoluted history too (didn't most people?) but where she was eager to make hers known, his instinct had always been to keep the shameful hidden. It still gave him difficulty to tell of his parents' divorce, not because of that tritely recognised phenomenon of children's guilt for the folly of their guardians, but because both his parents had failed to rise to life's demands, and disappointment and despair attend the inability to recognise what necessity imposes and to respond to it.

She seemed to shrink into her corner. He wondered if she regretted what she'd told him, if she felt it had been to sudden and fulsome.

"Are you a very repressed person?" she said.

He laughed.

"Thoroughly," he said. "Anyway, I'm peckish. Fancy a pizza?"

They went to *Angelo's* where he frequently sat with his Labour Party pals late on Friday night. The place was packed. They were squeezed into a corner, at either side of a tiny table where the waiter couldn't find room for the glasses and the garlic bread. Andy was glad to be in a place full of people and noise. Like peace, the silence of a deserted Lakeland fell or the depths of a forest where the sudden flight of a hawk across a path or the scurrying of a vole in the fallen leaves shocks your ears, the loud presence of others lifted the burden of isolation. To be amidst nature, in all its magnificent indifference, was to sense your unimportance; so it was amongst many others. Nothing was more depressing than obsession with the importance of your life, nothing more uplifting than escaping yourself in the contemplation of whatever was other.

At five in the morning she got out of bed and began to dress.

"Going somewhere?"

"I'll have to go home."

"Why?"

"So my mum won't know I've stayed out."

"Will she be waiting with the rolling pin?"

"I'll sneak in. She won't know what time I got back."

She was searching for something in the room where the dark was relieved by the orange glow of the street lamp.

"What've you lost?"

"My keys."

"They seem to want to get away from you."

"Did I leave them downstairs?"

"Who can say. Tell you what, wait till it's light."

"I can't. My mum'll go mad."

"You're twenty-eight. You live in London. Does she have spies?"

"Where's my bag?"

"With your keys, I guess."

"I'll go and look downstairs. If they're there, I'm off."

"Bon voyage."

"I'll come round tonight then, shall I?"

"Bring your mother."

"About half seven."

"If you can sneak out that late."

She arrived at eight. He was ironing his shirts for the week. On the board was a red and white check his mother had bought for his birthday. Christine collapsed in the armchair, her bag in her lap.

"You wear a lot of red, don't you?" she said.

"I'm a communist."

"It shows a certain lack of imagination."

He laughed.

"It shows I'm wearing clothes other people bought for me."

They went out of town, to *The Saddle* and the *Grapes at Goosnargh*. She seemed restless and on edge which he put down to the newness of things and the fact she had to go back to London in the morning, taking uncertainty with her. There was a heaviness in the atmosphere. He felt responsible. After all, she'd shared his bed. He would be serious. There was no question of opportunism; but the distance between London and Preston might be a problem. In the car, as she was about to turn on the ignition, she turned to him and raising herself in her seat, leaning towards him so she seemed physically to dominate him she said:

"Well, what's going to happen next,then?"

"Start the car, depress the clutch, put it gear, take off the handbrake, check your mirrors and off we go."

"That's not what I wanted to hear," she said and installed before the wheel set off too fast pulling on her seat belt as she drove.

At morning break there was talk of the miners' strike.

"Scargill? Loudmouth. They're going back, aren't they? He'll never win. He should never have called it in the first place," said Mike Chambers, chomping on a cereal bar, little bits of the confection flying from his mouth and collecting at the corners of his lips.

Andy, who was leaning over the low table reading the front page of *The Guardian* turned his head in Chambers' direction.

"Scargill didn't call the strike," he said.

"Eh?"

"It began in Yorkshire. Scargill wasn't present when the vote was taken. In any case, he had no power to call a strike there. It was the Yorkshire miners who decided to strike."

"He's behind it though, isn't he? He's a communist. Trouble maker. Eh?" and he turned to Tracey Bowe who was sitting beside him.

Raised in stodgy Toryism which took capitalism as much for granted as the weather, she had no political wit, but merely recycled the opinions on which she'd been weaned. Her mother, proud of the family's independent means, provided by their small holding, their chickens and her husband's steady if small income from joinery, identified with managing directors, investors, bankers, City traders, all the putative movers of the economic and financial worlds whose distant power dazzled her like an eclipse. Embarrassed by Chambers' attempt to drag her to his defence, Tracey smiled awkwardly and nodded as she might at a lunatic who told her the moon was green cheese or he was John Lennon reincarnated.

There came swiftly into Andy's head the recognition of that glib cowardice which turns for support in defence of received wisdom whenever it is challenged. Why couldn't Chambers make his own argument. He'd laid out his premise, why couldn't he defend it?

"Isn't it rather Thatcher who's behind it?"

"Eh? Pits have to close if there uneconomic. It's ridiclous." (he always pronounced the word to rhyme with Nicholas.) "Scargill wants power for himself. That's the truth. Eh?"

"The facts are the strike began at Cortonwood. There's no need to close that pit overnight. It could be wound down slowly and through natural wastage. There could have been negotiations between the NCB and the NUM, but McGregor was ordered long ago to get ready for closures. Coal stocks have been piled up. This is Thatcher looking for confrontation as revenge for what the NUM did to Heath and what the Labour Party did to her father."

"I don't think so," said Chambers lifting his chin as he always did when he wanted to dismiss any idea which didn't fit with his inherited, fixed view.

Andy went back to the paper while his colleague turned to Tracey and began talking loudly about how much marking he had to do.

Andy was about to turn to him and say "Thank your lucky stars you're not a miner," but thought better of it.

Chambers' ignorant, prejudiced opinion rankled all day. It was true *he* was prejudiced in favour of the miners, but not out of ignorance. It was a matter of the age-old principle that the burden of justification lies with authority. Miners had no authority. They were subject to it. They were forced to be reactive. It was cruel and vindictive to announce the closure of a pit without giving the workers the chance to put their case, without looking for every sensible means to avoid pain and dislocation. It wasn't as if Cortonwood was the initial closure. The papers and news were full of the idea that at the first incursion of reality, the miners had walked out to defend their high wages, fat pensions and do-nothing jobs. The fall in the price of coking coal was the excuse.

Pits were losing money. The economics of it wasn't something Andy had the time or inclination to pursue in detail. There was a simple moral matter which required no detailed economic understanding: if the pits needed to close, it should be carried out by agreement, with care, consideration and mindfulness of what sudden closure would mean for the mining communities. Andy wasn't opposed to the idea of closing pits where the coal was expensive to mine. In fact, what he knew about greenhouses gases inclined him to renewables; and who wouldn't be glad if men didn't have to do that muscle-tearing job in grim conditions?

This dispute wasn't about coal, it was about power. It wasn't about the losses at Cortonwood or anywhere else, it was about Thatcher's animus against unions, against working people, against those she viewed as failures, wreckers the "enemy within". It wasn't driven by economic need but by the twisted emotions and perverse values of a prim, priggish, Grammar School girl from Grantham whose father kept going a loveless marriage for the sake of appearances and who hid behind his mayoral chains to get his hands on the breasts and backsides of the teenage girls who worked in his shop.

This dispute was powered by the short-minded viciousness of an arch narcissist; a woman whose self-flattering identification with wealth and power was displayed in her every gesture, heard in the artificial tones of her elocution-lessons speech and evident in her confused and tendentious ideology. The technical economics was, as ever, a smokescreen. Thatcher, the putative enemy of the State, the self-appointed defender of free markets, was using every ounce of State power against the miners. The NCB was a State institution. The police force was a State institution. The courts were State institutions. There were stories of miners being stopped in their cars and told to turn back; this under a government which claimed to stand for the freedom of the individual. Thatcher, like all conservatives, didn't believe in free markets, but in the use of State power in defence of property. If a free market in labour were permitted, who would win the dispute? Tories were all for free markets in theory, but when the free market in labour threatened their interests, they became as Statist as Brezhnev. Andy would have been glad to see the dispute settled between the NCB and the NUM. Without the support of the State, McGregor was doomed.

The superficial free market doctrine of the Tories was nothing but a shield for the interests of employers. It had long ago occurred to Andy that it was in the relation between employers and employees that the essential problem lay. Work was one thing, employment another. If the temporary categories of employer and employee could be dissolved and replaced by relations of co-operation, the fundamental problems would disappear. Employment was the principal driver of inequality. Co-operative work places would equalise incomes and from that would flow greater social peace. The idea was dismissed as facile, but the truth was its rationality was as obvious as replacing the roof when it leaks. The torrent of free-market-freedom-of-the-individual-unions-are-communist-money-knows-best ideology which filled deserts of newsprint every day and sailed on radio waves as if it was as inevitable as light, was nothing but a day-and-night, strenuous denial of reason in defence of the interests of the rich and powerful; and these people claimed Adam Smith as their philosopher when Andy had read in *The Theory of Moral Sentiments* that the pursuit of personal wealth is a delusion.

Smith was right. To be deluded is to be mad. Pursuit of personal wealth is a form of madness. It is the mentality of Harpagon raised to the level of an organising, social principle. He was on his way down the stairs after the last lesson of the afternoon when it occurred to him that capitalism keeps going only because most people don't behave like capitalists: if everyone got out of bed in the morning determined to make as much money for themselves as possible, society would collapse. It was only because ninety percent of people were content with modest incomes, because they got out of bed and went to work in factories, offices, on building sites, in hairdressing salons, hospitals, shops, cafes, pubs, restaurants, railway stations, that the ten per cent could live with their insane fantasy that it was their demented addiction to money which made the system function.

He cycled home, threw off his clothes, hung up his jacket and trousers for Monday, grabbed the little holdall he'd packed before school, swigged a glass of water and headed to the railway station. The platforms were crowded. Not getting a seat meant standing for another three hours and he'd already been on his feet for four in the classroom. Being upright and not moving much brought an odd, congested feeling to his legs which made him long to get on his bike and push over Beacon Fell or up Harris End. When the engine slowed, pulling the long line of carriages to a standstill on platform four, he tried to spot the least crowded door, nipped through the huddle and stepping up after seeing five people get off, was lucky to find an empty seat in the carriage to the left.

As they pulled out, he realised he'd meant to slip *The Unbearable Lightness of Being* into his bag but had left it on his armchair. Something good to read always made the minutes evaporate. Perhaps he'd put his head back and have a snooze.

Christine met him at Euston. She took his arm and they went down to the underground. The carriages were packed. They rocked through the tunnels, changed stations, and arrived at Drayton Green. She lived in Hanwell, in what had once been a council house, bought and renovated by its owner, Wigwam, as they called him: Brian Wiggins, a local electrician who had set himself up when he finished his apprenticeship, employed four blokes, worked seven days a week and was accumulating money faster than he could spend it on greyhounds, horses, booze and drugs. There were five residents, including himself. He'd split the largest bedroom and added another. He was one of those men who can master quickly any manual skill, so laid the bricks, joined the timber, plastered the walls and fitted the gas central heating himself. Yet in spite of his manic effort to turn himself into the big, electrical entrepreneur he wanted to be, he couldn't afford the mortgage alone. It wasn't simply his addictions which defeated him, but the exorbitant price of houses.

Christine knew him through her friend Henry Stephenson, who she'd mat at Brunel, They had troubled backgrounds in common. Frustrated from his earliest years by the cold self-absorption of his mother, whose care was as perfunctory as a whore's attentions to a client, essentially sullen and self-pitying and without a glimmer of insight into his condition, he seduced a hundred girls or so during his three years at university and spoke with bottom-of-the-ocean cynicism about the boredom it engendered. It was a great source of amusement to the little crowd which gathered round him, lapsing into drunkenness and dope-induced, superficial who-gives-a-fuckism; everyone, of course, relishes cynicism when someone else is its victim.

They didn't know that those who toy with despair end up on the wrong side of it. They believed themselves the latest thing in nihilism, as if nihilism were new. Like far-gone idealists, they were searching for an absolute; they wanted to make their what-the-hell-does-it-matter hedonism the measure of all things. Mad idealists and insane cynics have in common the pursuit of an impossible absolute. All the difficulty of being human resides in learning to live with the provisional as if it's definitive. Life is a walk along a tightrope we never chose to step onto, but a loss of balance either to left or right, towards excessive zeal or exaggerated indifference, brings a plunge into the abyss.

Henry and Wigwan had drugs in common. Their evenings were befuddled by cannabis, their weekends shot into the stratosphere by cocaine. They'd met through their common, pitiful dependence. Christine had been sharing a house in Fulham, overcrowded, damp and in a bedroom too small to swing a kitten. When a bigger room in Wigmam's recently improved house (two bathrooms, a modern kitchen, reliable heating) became available at slightly lower rent, she seized it.

Wigwam wasn't around much, as he was always either working or looking for drugs. Of the other three residents, two came and went without making much contact, but the third was always there. As entangled in weed as his landlord, Colin spent most of his time in an armchair in the living room, playing chess against himself. Beside him, on the threadbare arm, was an ashtray heaped with the stubs of spliffs. As communicative as a gatepost, to Andy's greeting he responded by turning his head an inch for a second. His chess board reabsorbed him.

They went up to Christine's room. The floor was a foot deep in clothes.

"Are you allergic to wardrobes?"

She changed quickly without closing the curtains, naked for a few seconds in the light from the bedside lamp whose red shade cast a sunset glow. She took him to eat at Monty's. They went for a drink and walked home in the quickly chilling night.

The next day they got up late, ate a big breakfast and at midday headed off to the West End to see a production of *A View From The Bridge*. For Andy, the opportunity to see plays was terrific. Christine was happy to indulge him but her preference wasn't theatre. She would have preferred a football match, or to spend the afternoon drinking. Something which could offer the simulacrum of self-escape. In the evening she drove them out to the *Bull* at Barnes where they listened to Stan Tracey and Alan Skidmore. There was an audience of fifteen or so and at the interval, Skidmore came to the bar and chatted to them. These easy opportunities made Andy wish he lived in London. To have theatres and music, bookshops, poetry readings all the cultural depth missing from a little place like Preston was marvellous. Yet at the same time, London was too fast a place. It stank of money. To live in a city of this kind, you needed to carry heavy. How did teachers like him survive? They had to share houses, put up with nothing more than bedroom as their space. It was little better than being a teenager.

These weekends with Christine offered him the city's benefits without its negatives. He loved it. Away from Preston, from work, sitting in the *Old Vic*, the *Royal Court*, eating at the *Pizza on the Park*; it permitted him to bathe his feet in the waters he would have liked to plunge into. What stood in the way, above all, was money. He could lay all his pound notes in a circle and they wouldn't embrace even a little two-bedroom house like his in the least desirable parts of the city. He had his own small, petty, inviolable space but the inviolability was priceless.

They alternated. She relished the opportunity to drive home and see her mother, even if it did mean being in the presence of her despised step-father. Sunday lunch was the focus of the weekends. It occupied Mrs Thomas for the morning, once breakfast was out of the way. Billy insisted on a full plate. Anything deficient would have been less than English. Andy wondered why he didn't have a little union jack on the table. Bacon, fried egg, fried bread, two sausages, grilled tomatoes, toast, butter, jam and a pot of tea constituted what every true Englishman should consume. He'd been abroad. He'd sampled what was called a *continental breakfast*. No wonder the French gave in to Hitler without a fight. Hitler did the right thing. People who began the day with nothing but a flimsy pastry and a cup of coffee not big enough to dip your thumb in, deserved to be ruled by a more robust culture.

His belly kept him at a distance from the table. He was proud of his rotundity, believing slim men effeminate. A swollen abdomen was a sign of appetite and appetite was what defined a man. A man must eat, drink, chase women and have strong opinions. A man must swallow the world and a flat belly was a sign of weakness, like a man who couldn't take his beer. Theresa delighted in filling his stomach. In spite of the heart attack he'd suffered two years earlier and which had almost killed him; in spite of the three pills he had to take every morning to keep him alive; in spite of the doctor's warning that he should try to lose weight, take some exercise and cut down on fat; she stuffed him with beef, roast potatoes cooked in goose grease, apple pies, blackcurrant pies, gooseberry pies all lavished with lakes of double cream, lemon meringue, queen of puddings, spotted dick, rice pudding sugared to meet his babyish palate, Victoria sponge, Black Forest gateau and, inevitable ending to every bout of compulsive eating, the biscuit tin. Reached down from the top of the tall fridge-freezer, this hallowed container was kept stuffed with *Blue Ribands*, *Clubs*, *Kit-Kats*, *Trios*, *Tunnocks Tea Cakes*, *Breakaways*, *Boasters*, *Penguins*, *BNs*, *Wagon Wheels*, *Taxis* and whatever else she might toss into the supermarket trolley. The three courses over, the tall, stainless steel coffee pot settled on a mat in the table's centre, one biscuit after another would be reached for to provide the taste buds with that igniting combination of fat and sugar unknown in nature. Billy's favourite was the *Breakaway*. He contested with his son Edward, who also favoured them.

"You've had the last one, " Billy would protest.

"There'll be one left, dad, if you search," the bullied sixteen-year-old would reply.

"You'll have to buy more, Theresa," ordered Billy, "he eats 'em a dozen a day."

The step father liked to believe he was in control, but Andy had noticed he did nothing without his wife's permission and everything she commanded. He had no friends, no independent life outside the house. He never went out on his own, except maybe to fill the car with petrol. There was a curious attentiveness to Theresa in the family; as if everyone was supposed to know what she wanted all the time; as if she had no need to make her wishes or needs clear, but by some mystical process they should communicate themselves to all without the intervention of language and be attended to as urgently as a mother responds to a distressed baby. On his first few visits to the house, Andy had been struck by a curious sense of isolation. As if each member of the family were irrevocably inserted in their own reality and could establish no essential contact. There was conversation but it never connected. It seemed to him a kind of dumb show, as if there were some terrible secret everyone was aware of but which couldn't be spoken about. Of course, there was. At least as far as Christine was concerned.

Andy looked at Billy as he sat in the armchair, replete, trying to solve the *Sunday Express* prize crossword. The truth should be told and he ought to be shamed. That he'd pursued his twelve-year-old step daughter, that she had threatened to tell her mother, that he had, tritely, asked her who would be believed, filled Andy with contempt. He assumed the greedy, prejudiced bigot must know Christine had told him. He wondered if it made him afraid.

Things hadn't gone further than his attempts, because Christine had been too spikey. Confident that his wife wouldn't want to accept the truth, he nevertheless worried that if he did get his hands on the girl and she did go to her mother, there might be a terrible uproar; and Christine's bared-teeth, snarling response made him fear she would go to the police. Then there would be evidence. If he grabbed her and threw himself on her, forced her legs apart and got in her, the forensics people could find the traces. That would mean prison. He wouldn't put it past the girl. She was a leftie. Already, at twelve, she supported the Labour Party and admired Michael Foot, who was just the kind of man Billy loathed. He was supposed to be an intellectual. He hated them. He liked people who had been to the best schools and Oxbridge, people who had qualifications and letters after their name, but intellectuals he would have exterminated.

Where his step-daughter got her ideas from, he didn't know. Theresa's three children supported Harold Wilson. He disdained them, but above all Christine because in addition to being misguided she was clever. He wasn't aware that Theresa's first husband had been a fervent socialist, that their house had been used as committee rooms on election day. Theresa kept it quiet, not wanting to offend her new man and finding his borderline fascism attractive.

She'd voted for Thatcher in 1979 and 1983. She heard in her speeches what she read in *Daily Express* editorials. She liked her haughtiness, her identification with aristocratic power. In Theresa's mind, power was absolute, or non-existent. Her Catholicism had taught her that the Pope, as god's emissary, is all-knowing, all-seeing, all-powerful. In confession she felt herself shrink. She was diminished by her submission to the priest's power. She must tell him everything, while he remained hidden. Yet her submission made her rise. In a curious emotional and psychological feedback, she emerged from the dark of the church into the light of superiority. She had contact with absolute power. She was party to unquestionable truth. She was a cut above.

Andy was struck by the mental rigidity of Christine's mother and step-father. It was the contrary of his mind's essence. He'd always been attracted by contingency. Not being a scientist, he didn't know where the limits of inevitability lay, but it seemed the scientists didn't either. What seemed true was that human social life didn't follow the same rules as the rotation of the planets. At university he'd listened to the feet-in-concrete Marxists who argued that everything was inevitable before it happened. It seemed to him no better than the idea of predestination, which was akin to superstition. He'd discussed the notion of determinism with Mike Darley, who as a physicist tended to the view that everything was predictable if only we could see how. To Andy, that seemed intellectual sleight-of-hand. The idea of *hidden local variables*, as Mike called them, was just a way of wriggling out of the difficulty that the theory of determinism for predictability lacked the clinching evidence. To found a theory on the argument that if only we could see everything (Laplace's Demon was the all-seeing creature, according to Mike) then we would know the theory to be sound, was a hopeless as saying if only we could see god we would know he is there. Andy was convinced contingency was real.

"Why couldn't determinism be determinism for contingency?" he'd said.

"Well," his friend replied, laughing, "it's always been assumed determinism means predictability. That's fundamental to science."

"Maybe it's an assumption too far."

It was curious how Christine's family brought those conversations back to his mind. Billy was one of those men whose conviction he was right about everything was surpassed only by his ignorance. He was uncomfortable with democracy because he wanted certainty.

"The best leader Italy ever had," he would declare , "was Mussolini and they hung him from a lamppost."

"Upside down," said Andy, and smiled.

He didn't hate Billy in the way Christine did, but he found him a ludicrous and ugly-minded man.

"You should tell your mother," he said to her.

"What would be the point?"

"The point would be the truth. She's married to a child abuser. She should have her eyes opened."

"I don't want to do that to her. Anyway, she wouldn't believe me."

"Maybe the police would."

"Don't talk about it."

Andy thought Christine was wrong: protecting her mother's feelings required a degree of corruption, a tacit agreement with Billy's despicable behaviour. In his view, it would have been better to say what had to be said, to face the eruption but to be rid of the infection. Yet he wasn't in her position and understood how hard it was. There were conflicts and denials in his family, but nothing like this. His parents had been daft, but Billy's kind of abuse was beyond both of them.

Theresa's mother lived with them. When they married and bought the house in Blundell Lane, the old woman stayed in her terrace in Lark Hill Street, and Thomas, the younger of Christine's two brothers stayed with her; but to afford a bungalow in Lostock Hall, they needed what her house would fetch. She sold up.

Billy was glad of the move. The place was attractive and spacious. He felt he was living among the Tory-voting middle-classes. He would have preferred a community of blackshirts, but unfortunately it was denied him. His mother-in-law's money had been necessary, but he loathed her. Her presence made him feel slightly less than master. Her habits irritated him. She was always first in the kitchen in the morning and her presence riled him. Why couldn't she stay in bed and let him be waited on by his wife in peace? On occasion, when his petulance became overwhelming, he hit her. A quick cuff on the head with his palm. She dared say nothing. Christine knew and kept quiet too, her mother's precious feelings being the eggshells no one must dare crack. Andy disagreed. Someone should stand up to the strutting bully. If he'd been there when he hit the old woman, he would have twisted his arm up his back.

The blows to Nanna, as she was called, a name resonant with her status as a kind of mother-heroine, almost worshipped by her daughter, were as nothing to the beatings Edward had suffered. Now sixteen, six feet one and physically big enough to hit back, if emotionally lacking the resolve, as a boy he'd been cuffed, whacked, slapped, pushed, punched, elbowed, kneed and jabbed by the father who resented his existence. Billy would have been glad for Theresa to have an abortion, except he didn't believe in abortion. He thought of it as an insult to the man. If a man makes a woman pregnant, it's her business to see the thing through. That's nature. That's the way it was meant to be. Men went about the world trying to seduce as many women as frequently as possible. That was the right way to behave. It made a man a man. The kind of man who didn't get his hands on every female backside in reach, he considered a cissy. He'd made Theresa pregnant and he was proud of the work; but to have to bring up the son disgusted him. He enjoyed humiliating the boy who grew into the pale, alienated, lonely lad Andy had seen on his bike in Blundell Lane and recognised as troubled.

It was a curious family. The old woman was often intrusive. She had a way of finding the comment which was a jab in the ribs. One Sunday, reminiscing, she said, excitedly, pushing her face towards Christine who was sitting beside her at the laden table:

"But I was a good weaver. Four machines."

The comment illuminated her inner life. Andy stared hard at her for a moment. This was her greatest boast; it was what her life had been. The machine hadn't served her, she had served it. She'd submitted to its rhythm, dictated by the owner's wayward need for lucre, and, a slave to the boss and the shuttle, had found a petty compensation in the view of herself as a good worker; a better worker than women she stood beside for decades. It was a flimsy, pathetic, secondary selfhood built of cowardice. She ought to have rebelled against being chained to the machine; she should have scoffed at her effort paying for the boss's fancy house while she lived in a box in a street of boxes; but she'd been schooled in deference, obedience and identification with her social superiors. She admired the royals. She granted the rich superior powers. At the centre of her was fear. To attempt to rise from your knees was to risk being cut off at the thighs. She went to Mass every day and twice on Sunday. She knelt. She lowered herself. She stooped to conquer.

Later, Andy discovered she'd denied her husband sex for four decades. Her observation on the regime, frequently iterated, was:

"He was very understanding."

The family thought it amusing. Christine giggled at it; but Andy was horrified. She'd emasculated her husband. He had lived with humiliation. He ought to have told her: "You may not want sex, but I do." It was obvious to him the old woman was frigid. She'd turned her inadequacy into a source of power and he had let her. It was a terrible denial of life, but no one seemed to see it.

Andy reflected on the bizarre configuration as Mrs Thomas put the coffee pot in the middle of the table: she was the daughter of a frigid woman whose husband had been too meek to assert his needs and was now the wife of an old goat of a paedophile who admired fascists, beat his son and thought nothing of abusing an old woman.

Yet his relationship with Christine was rolling along and if she seemed still nervous he assumed it was nothing more than adjustment to newness; at least he hoped so.

A TRIBUNAL

It had become the culture that first years should be taken on a short visit to France to practise in shops, cafes and on the street what they learnt in the classroom. Rob Hesketh relished the opportunity. Anything which involved money, a bit of what he thought of as *wheeler-dealing* and booze was irresistible. He collected the dosh; changed what he needed into Francs; had his pockets stuffed with notes. They went to Boulogne, leaving from the school by coach, picking up the ferry at Dover and missing a night's sleep. Rob spent the two and a half days drunk, hungover or unconscious. When his colleagues suggested that introducing eleven year-olds to Izzarra was not the best of ideas, he swept aside their clean-underwear objections with an alcoholic gesture. At lunchtime the boys loitered, bored and idle in the streets while Rob insisted the staff sit down to a three-course meal, with pastis, white wine, red wine and liqueurs. In the evening they ate in a restaurant where he'd done a deal with the old *patron* who looked like Stefan Grappelli, served up huge heaps of *pommes frites* on silver trays which the boys devoured by grabbing handfuls and was tolerant of Hesketh's Mr Punyverse Competition which involved half naked lads standing on the table to flex their peanut-in-a-straw muscles. They spent the night in an Ibis and returned the following evening, missing another night's sleep, arriving at the school, exhausted, dishevelled and sworn to secrecy; the mantra being: "what happens on trip, stays on trip."

Andy went along with it, though he thought Rob's behaviour reckless. He declined, however, the offer to take part in the summer, three-week camping trip to the Loire valley. Hesketh had run it for eleven years. He'd found a happy welcome in a little village during a family holiday. It was *la vraie France profonde*. He had no time for Paris with its loose cosmopolitanism, its intellectuals at café tables, its demonstrations and revolutionary tradition. The folk here disliked Arabs, admired de Gaulle, believed the Algerian War justified, drank like bottomless pits and smoked like barbecues. He suggested bringing a party to the *camping municipal*. They were delighted. It would fill the *commune's* tills. The boys were welcomed by the mayor. Hesketh drank himself into a stupor every day. The local shops and cafes counted their takings. It became an institution.

On the first day of term of his sixth year in the school, an NUT member asked to speak to Andy. They were both free last period in the morning. The staffroom was empty.

"I've had a complaint from one of the boys in my form."

"Yeah? About you?"

"No, no," the other man turned to look at him, his face serious and his body taut. "About the Loire Valley trip."

"Really?"

"Mmm. Jason Nuttall, do you know him."

"I teach him. Bright lad."

"Yes. It's about Stan Buchanan."

"I see."

"What he says is, he made sexual advances to him during the trip."

"Have you told the Head?"

"No."

"You must."

"I wanted to ask your advice first."

"My advice, well no, my instruction is, tell the Head. You have to."

"What d'you think he'll do?"

"Don't worry about that. Listen, you know. That puts you in danger if you don't report it. I know. I'm in danger if I don't report it. So I'm saying to you, you have to report it. I'm going to assume you will. I'm going to cover my back by telling Regional Office. You must protect yourself. Go and see the Head."

"Right. Only, I don't want to get him sacked."

"That's out of your hands. You have been told. You must report it. Then the Head has the responsibility."

"What are his options?"

"Well, that's not for me to say. I have to protect you as one of my members, and of course the boy. Presumably his parents have told him to tell you. If you don't report it, you could lose your job, and worse."

"Okay. Okay. Thanks, Andy."

The conversation was quickly over. As with all shocks, the first response was absence of response, but as the day wore on the appalling nature of what he'd been told disturbed him more and more. Stan Buchanan was a Head of House. Cooper's only decisive act had been the replacement of the vertical year group pastoral system. He'd been educated in a private school, after all. He understood the importance of a House ethos. Buchanan who'd been Head of Third Year was transferred to Head of Sillitoe, named after one of Cooper's early twentieth century predecessors.

Andy wasn't sure of his age but he put him at about forty. An English teacher, he was a graduate of Lampeter, one of the places Andy had thought of applying to, but its size and remoteness had deterred him. What had won Buchanan his promotion was his contribution to rugby. A strong and skilled player himself, he'd been on the periphery of greatness, but was one of those who come tantalizingly close only to be consigned to amateur status. Wellington, greatly impressed by his gifts and commitment; and convinced of the *character building* power of the game, had ensured his swift rise.

Buchanan was a bachelor known for his grumpy disposition. He often seemed at odds with himself. He was one of those teachers who had his reserved place in the staff room: the far desk in the workroom was his territory. He had an in-tray in the corner, his flask of coffee beside it. It was always as neat as his impeccably combed, short, wiry blond hair. He wasn't a man Andy liked, his unpredictable prickliness making opening gambits risky. Andy sensed it would be easy to get into a row and though he had no fear of his physical bulk and strength, the professional context providing security, he didn't want the enduring ugly atmosphere a verbal spat would leave.

One lunchtime, chatting to the three of four people in the room, Andy happened to mention he was Deputy Chair of Governors in a local primary and had been involved in appointing a new Head. Buchanan looked up from his marking, uttered a curt, "No shit," and resumed ticking.

It had been Andy's view since he first met him that there was some terrible conflict twisting his emotions and it had occurred to him he might be a closet homosexual. Knowing the history of the school, his cousin having begun as a pupil in 1954; lots of lads he knew having been there for seven years in the 1960s; Stu Archer having joked often about the *bum bandits*, he was aware of its hidden-behind-the-library-shelves secret. Homosexuality lingered in the place like the odour of disinfectant in the corridors; but it couldn't be acknowledged. It was a Church of England school. It was a rugger playing school. It sent many pupils to Oxbridge. It served the middle-classes. It had to keep up appearances.

The thought that Buchanan might have to conceal his sexuality had made Andy sorry for him. It must be terrible. Yet, at the same time the vagrant thought had passed through his mind that he might have chosen the school because it was all boys. Andy was reminded of something he'd read about Auden: that when he was appointed as a teacher in some public school or other he'd written in a letter that it was "a paradise" for queers. He'd been shocked by it. The toffee-nosed, you-must-all-look-up-to-and-emulate-this culture of the private school was soaked in casual corruption. The places where most of the influential people were educated, took abuse for granted. It made him glad he'd grown up well away from it. There were advantages to being an oik.

Yet he'd never thought Buchanan might be preying on boys. The implications leeched through his mind like water filling a cellar from a cracked drain. Who knew? Buchanan and Rob Hesketh were close. Hesketh was in charge of the trip to France. Did he know what his colleague was up to? How many people knew and kept quiet for the sake of the school's reputation? What was that reputation ? It was a silken flag flying over a sewer. It was legerdemain to divert everyone's eyes from the despicable exploitation of the innocent. It was a culture which permitted the satisfaction of the most degraded desires by people placed in authority by society's respectable agencies.

The sudden, horrifying but enlightening thought came to him that Buchanan's abuse wasn't peripheral; it wasn't an exception; it was the way the official culture functioned. Sexual abuse was as essential to the culture as employment. Society was founded on exploitation and its denial. In such an atmosphere, the healthy satisfaction of instincts was impossible. All relationships were sullied by the essential corruption. Society in its entirety couldn't face the truth of its exploitative nature and that dishonesty spread through all relations liked spilled treacle across a table.

It brought to mind Marx's view of the exploitative relation of capital and labour, whether capital was in private or State hands; but Marx was wrong: he believed capitalism a necessary phase in a teleological progress. Andy thought that deterministic tosh. Capitalism was no more inevitable than the internal combustion engine. It was the product of agency and choice. It wasn't a necessary stage, it was a mistake.

Exploitation of any kind was a mistake, which was why people had to hide it. There was a ceaseless effort to mystify. Propaganda was at work every second to deny the fundamental fact that to use others for your ends is inadmissible, even if they consent. There were those morally insane people in the Paedophile Information Exchange who argued that children could initiate and consent to sex with adults. No consent is acceptable where there is a gross imbalance of power, Wasn't the same true in the economic sphere? People, so the glib argument went, consented to work forty or fifty hours in lousy condition for not enough to pay the mortgage and feed their kids. What kind of consent is it when the choice is: accept the conditions or starve? Why couldn't the employee require consent from the employer? Why couldn't the employee draw up the contract, put it before the employer and require them to sign?

Power and exploitation were like energy and matter.

Where power ruled, love was driven out and where love was expelled, exploitation flourished. Societies organised around power were loveless. People compensated by retreat to extreme forms of intimacy or subjectivity; but it didn't work. The drive for power pursued them into the most private moments in the bedroom, haunted their most concealed thoughts. The instrument of power was money. All powerful people were wealthy and all wealthy people had power. Not until the power of money was broken could love lift its face from the mud and humanise social relations.

He was part of the culture. He was an employee in this corrupt place. Cooper liked to call it "this very special place". He would have liked to walk out. He wondered if he should go to see him, but he hadn't received the complaint. It had to be reported by the boy's form tutor. He hoped there would be quick action. Buchanan would be suspended. The investigation would get under way. The stinking stables could be cleared of their rotting filth.

He informed Regional Office. They told him he was safe. He'd done the right thing.

He waited. Nothing happened.

Could the boy have lied? It was inconceivable. Andy had an urgent desire to talk to him, which had to be fought down. He would have liked to say:

"I know about your complaint, Jason. You should tell your parents to go to the police."

It was one of those clear, October mornings when there is almost a frost first thing. Jason was in Andy's classroom at quarter past nine. A self-contained, polite, hard-working boy, he arrived among the early cohort of five who preceded the noisy, let's-sabotage-Lang's-lesson, gang of cynics who made a point of coming in after the bell, threw their bags across the room and spent their time drawing attention to themselves like narcissistic pop stars or Hollywood actors.

"All right, Jason?"

"Yes, sir," said the boy taking his books and pencil case form his bag.

"Bit nippy today, eh?"

"Yes, sir."

"Come on your bike?"

"Yes, sir."

"Me too. Forgot me gloves. My fingers were icicles."

"It *was* cold, sir."

"D'you live far?"

"Penwortham, sir."

"Not too bad then. What's on your timetable today, then?"

"Maths, sir. P.E.. Geography. English."

"Who takes you for English, Jason?" said Andy, though he knew.

"Mr Buchanan," said the boy, his eyes lowered.

"Ah, I bet he's always sweet-tempered, eh?"

The boy looked up at him, a question in his eyes. Andy fixed him steadily.

"He's all right, sir," said the boy, looking down again.

"Is he?"

"I suppose so, sir."

"Good. Take care of yourself, Jason."

The room had filled suddenly. A pair of the disruptive crew crashed through the door like Laurel and Hardy on speed, threw their bags towards an empty desk, shouting as if across an Alpine valley.

"Morning Kyle, morning Shaun. I see you've had ecstasy on your cornflakes again."

In the last minutes of the lesson, Andy made appointments for the parent's evening. Mrs and Mrs Nuttall, 7.10.

He remembered them. He stood up and shook their hands. The father was a broad, dark, quiet man who looked like he might have been an athlete. He wore a sombre suit and a collar and tie beneath one of those expensive overcoats which descend below the knee. His wife was a slender, smiling, pretty woman who had the appointment sheet in her hands and apologised for being slightly late.

"Don't worry. It never functions like clockwork, thank goodness."

She gave a little laugh as she sat on the blue, plastic chair. Her husband posed himself in a slow, stately manner and laid his joined hands on his lap.

It was an untroubled interview. Jason was a clever, diligent lad whose work was always neat and correct. He was one of those pupils so easy to teach it was self-pitying to call it work. Andy would have been glad to get him up to scratch in French for no reward, other than the pleasure of doing it. Sending parents away happy was a great uplift; but when he'd finished talking about French, he said:

"And how are things in general at school? Jason all right?"

The father bridled almost imperceptibly and Mrs Nuttall, with a charming smile, turned to him and then back to Andy.

"Yes, yes. I think so. He's happy and coming along well. Isn't he?"

The father nodded and said nothing. Andy looked him in the eyes. His almost black eyes stared back unflinchingly, betraying no emotion. His face was set in blank seriousness.

"That's good," said Andy. "He's not only bright and conscientious, he's a very pleasant character."

"Oh, thank you," said Mrs Nuttall, wriggling a little, smiling and folding the sheet in her hands.

Her husband stood up and reached out his hand. Andy got up and shook it.

"Thank you," said the father without a glimmer of emotion, turned and walked away.

"Thanks," said his wife, straightening the chair. "Thanks very much, Mr Lang."

"My pleasure."

Andy rode home in the dark, alternating the blowing on his cold fingers. He went at a leisurely pace because it was harder to think intensively if he was racing at full speed. Were Mr and Mrs Nuttall protecting the school's reputation? He wouldn't have done so if the penalty had been perdition. What a curious position he was in: his girlfriend, now his fiancé, had been subjected to the predations of a gutter-values step-father at the age of twelve and he was working in a school which harboured child abusers. He'd never imagined this kind of vicious, degraded behaviour would enter his life. Christine refused to expose her step-father out of a desire to protect her mother's feeling, and it seemed the Nuttalls drew back from throwing the grenade out of respect for the school's standing. In both cases, nothing serious had happened. It was no more than an attempt. Yet the attempt was enough to humiliate and to leave an irreparable diminution of trust.

He'd been in the school much longer than he intended. Cooper had stood in his way. Yet he must get out. He must find a healthier atmosphere. He wondered if his colleague had done what he told him. Was Cooper informed and keeping it quiet? Was he too protecting status before innocence? He wished he had a way of exposing the matter, but if the Nuttalls weren't willing to press, what could he do?

He tried to imagine himself in Jason's position. What would he have done if a teacher had made advances? He would have told his mother and she would have acted. There was no doubt. She would have had no respect for the school's status and no fear of raising her voice. For all her faults, his mother had a core of principle and courage he loved and admired. He knew, had he been in Jason's position, she would have protected him.

Too tired to cook and dispirited at the thought of his limited culinary skills which would grant him the usual steaming plate of spaghetti bolognaise or shepherd's pie, he parked his bike outside the Taylor

Street chip shop. There was a queue of four. The two blokes in front of him had been drinking. One of them, six feet four, bulky, with the typical expanded waist of the northern boozy man turned to look at him as he counted his change in his big, thick hand. His eyes rested on the badge Andy had pinned to his coat.

"Fight racism," he read. "Not many people round here dare wear a badge like that."

Andy was about to say:

"And what have I got to be afraid of?"

but thought better of antagonising. He merely remained impassive and looked his interlocutor in the eyes.

At home, unwrapping the hot package and tipping its clinging contents on a plate, he wondered if he'd been in danger. He recalled the time in the mid-seventies, the National Front on the rise and two of its councillors elected in Blackburn, he'd distributed Anti-Nazi League leaflets outside Preston North End's ground. He'd covered the Spion Kop and Dave Warburton the Town End. Dave was a shop steward at the GEC factory on Strand Road, a radical from a Catholic family steeped in Irish republicanism who had led his members out on strike several times and subscribed to the possibility of a worker's movement vigorous and enlightened enough to take over workplaces and transform the economy to co-operative forms of production. He would later be sacked, take the company to tribunal, win his little compensation which would provide the deposit on a big town house, sign up for a TOPS course in computing and keep his nose clean; but for the time being, he was bent on fundamental social change.

Handing out the flyers alone, they were swamped. When a gang of skinheads arrived, Andy moved closer to the police horses. He'd been in danger of a beating that evening but the giant in the chip shop was probably just taunting him.

He ate his fish chips and peas in the chilly house. He couldn't be bothered with the fuss of lighting the fire. His weariness, the petty incident, the thought of Jason Nuttall and Stan Buchanan dragged his feeling down. He was about to embark on a new venture. He and Christine were getting married the next month. They'd decided in principle, Andy glad of the end of his extended bachelorhood, a fact which had puzzled and defeated him. As a teenager, he'd imagined he would be married at twenty-one or two, a father soon after, that by now his children would be on the verge of secondary school. He still didn't understand why it hadn't happened. He'd expected it would; that it would happen rather than he would have to make it happen. There was a social expectation and a cultural drive which should ensure it; but something had changed. He searched in himself for the fault but finally ended in emptiness and despair. The inadequacy was elsewhere.

Stu Archer had married at twenty-three, Matt Ross at the same age, Blackie at twenty-five. Surely that pointed to some flaw in himself; but he rejected the idea. Matt's marriage had lasted a scant couple of years, Carol had run aground as quickly. There was a social change taking place which was transforming intimate relations. He couldn't see it clearly but it was to do with an extreme form of individualism which implied a fear of dependence. What was love without dependence? Its essence was the recognition that your well-being, in all respects, depends on someone else, on their care and kindness. Yet in the current climate those things sounded almost sentimental. It was the saw-blade out-of-my-wayism of Thatcher which ruled, as if each of us is not simply individual but utterly self-sufficing; a delusion he believed could bring only social breakdown and collective misery.

Still, he was getting married. One afternoon, just before Easter, when he and Christine had spent the afternoon in town and she was about to go to her mother's for tea, she said:

"Is it okay if I tell my mum we're getting married?"

"Of course," he said, assuming she meant in principle.

When she arrived back at his house at seven thirty, she was brimming with arrangements: she and her mother thought October would be best; they'd made a list of possible venues for the reception; her mother would ring round; they would have to book the registry office the following week; she wanted a vintage car; her dress would be antique; her best friend from university would be her witness; who would be his best man?

Slightly taken aback by this rush to settle matters without consulting him, he had the odd feeling that he might be about to become an unwelcome guest at his own wedding; but he'd agreed in principle. Why delay? He raised his pint as they sat in the *Fox and Grapes*.

"We should move into a house of our own," she said, "rather than stay in yours."

"I agree. We'll look for one."

She took his arm.

"Where, do you think?"

"Question of what we can afford. There are some decent houses off Broadgate. Connaught Road, Balderstone Road. We could afford those."

"Okay. Somewhere we can make nice."

"Yeah. We'll find something."

Andy was trying to get a tape recorder to work in Don Crawley's teaching room. It was an old *Grundig* which had always been reliable but which now wouldn't produce anything but the moaning of a cow in labour. Alma Mayor came in, one of her long, expensive cigarettes between her fingers. She loitered by the language lab console, useless now that the cubicles and their machines were waiting to be removed, the great experiment having turned into a depressing failure; adolescent boys, unsurprisingly, having taken the opportunity to record obscenities, snap the tapes, whizz them one way and then the other and generally turn what were supposed to be avant-garde means of accelerating their foreign language skills into a circus of broken devices, disorder and laziness.

"You don't mind if I smoke do you?" she said. "It calms my nerves."

"Just had a bad class?"

"Oh, no. I can cope with them. It's Don who's driving me insane."

"What's the matter now?"

"Diane's getting married."

"Oh, her. Who's the unfortunate man?"

"An American millionaire."

Andy laughed.

"Poor old, Don. He can't compete with that."

"He's distraught. He was crying like a baby in the stock room at eight o'clock this morning."

"You should see the Head."

"It wouldn't do any good. Anyway, he knows. Jim Hunter has told him. Tim Heath has told him. He doesn't want to face it."

"But it's a professional matter. If you're having to play confidante to Don's pre-adolescent psyche, that's something the Head needs to intervene over."

"Since when has the Head been professional?"

"Sure."

"I've just seen him heading out of the back gate with his dog."

"Yes, it's a nice little fiefdom he has, isn't it?"

"I'm going to resign."

"I don't think you should do that."

"Oh, I can't bear it. Everyday. Blow by blow. He shows me the letters she sends him. It's pitiful."

"Well, at least now she's found her gold mine, Don won't be handing out money like an alms house."

"Don't you believe it."

"You're joking."

"He's just paid for her and her parents to have a fortnight in Spain."

"He's lost his mind."

"He's lost a lot of money."

"It must be thousands."

"Tens of thousands I should think."

"God. Surely the marriage will put an end to it."

"I don't know. He can't think straight when it comes to her."

"Did he imagine his money would buy her?"

"Oh, yes. He proposed."

"What a charming young woman she is."

"He's invited to the wedding."

"Will he go?"

"He says so. I've told him to stay away."

"Maybe he'll protest when just cause is invoked. Perhaps he'll shout from the back pew: 'Yes, I know a reason. She's had all my bloody money."

Alma laughed in the odd, tense way she had, as if she was being shaken from within by some force she was trying to resist. She stubbed her cigarette out in the metal bin, opened the windows and swung the door to and fro.

"Is there a class in here next period?"

"No. Nothing to worry about."

She took a small, silver canister of room spray from her black, leather bag and filled the air with its artificial scent.

"Go easy, Alma. I think I prefer the nicotine."

"Better go and mark some books," she said, trying to laugh again. "Don't say anything will you?"

"Not a word. I might send her a wedding present though. Do you know where I can get hold of a hand grenade?"

She trembled with the effort of amusement, picked her bag and clicked out on her tall, thin heels.

Andy unplugged the machine, searched the console drawer for a luggage label, scrawled *Hors Service*, tied it to the handle, and set the thing on its end by the front wall. He sat behind the console looking out at the trees in the garden of the neighbouring house. It was a peaceful, pleasant scene, almost enough to make him feel the world was well. Yet what a place he worked in. It was supposed to be professional. He let his mind explore Don's character. How odd it was he could be a Cambridge graduate in French, Head of Department in a school the middle classes would kill to their kids into, yet his inner life was as chaotic as neglected kitchen drawer.

This was a man who had studied French literature: Rabelais, Mme de Lafayette, Racine, Corneille, Moliere, Marguerite de Navarre, Madame de Sevigny, Diderot, Rousseau, Beaumarchais, Balzac, Stendhal, Madame de Staël, Flaubert, Anatole France, Marguerite Duras, Simone de Beauvoir, Annie Arnoux; yet none of it, apparently, had touched him emotionally. He was intellectually developed, but emotionally regressed. How could that happen? How could a man get to fifty and be as callow as a thirteen year-old?

The old idea came back to him, one he'd run through his head thousands of times: the culture had no care for maturity. What it required was conformity. In that regard, immaturity was an advantage. Don Crawley might represent an extreme, but he was legion. Everyone was asked to make a categorical agreement with the system. In childhood, the work was done by the education system. In return for putative rewards of exam passes, places at university, lucrative jobs, status, power, children were required to abdicate their ecstasy. The phrase from Mallarmé, a poet he had generally little time for, came back to him. What did it mean? Giving up your freedom, renouncing your autonomy, ceasing to live, in the belief that at some time in the future your life would be returned to you.

The one thing you were not allowed to learn at school was how to be free. The renunciation of autonomy, necessary for success in the system, could never be rectified by the potential rewards. They were secondary and compensatory. Society was populated by ghosts, men and women who had lost touch with themselves, who had been required to suppress, repress, deny, block, curtail, head-off, dispel, mangle, destroy their most elemental impulses in order to be given team-points, gold stars, certificates, prizes, none of which, any more than the fat salaries, fancy titles and arbitrary powers of the jobs they would take in adulthood, could restore what they had wiped out. Hence the manic pursuit of the compensations. An entire society lost to itself, unaware that its compulsive rush after money, fame, power, sensation was the inevitable outcome of its insistence on absolute adherence to its own distorted priorities and demented standards.

The kids he taught said school was boring. They were right. It was meant to be. Children couldn't be allowed to find life interesting or they might reject dull work. They couldn't be permitted to conquer autonomy or they might refuse to obey their boss. They couldn't be encouraged to think for themselves or they might decide they'd rather work three days a week and not have a car than try to keep up with the folk next door. It was a circle of madness. It had produced Don. He had obeyed. He had been a model pupil. He'd received the team points and the gold stars, the place at Cambridge and the job in the prestigious school; but he was a baby. A manipulative, cynical, desiccated young woman had used her sexuality to squeeze money from him and he was so out of touch with himself he'd fallen for it.

He was a highly educated man but he was as stupid as a man could be.

Something similar, though more sinister was true of Stan Buchanan. He was educated, respectable. admired for his contribution to rugby. Yet, incapable of fulfilling his emotional and sexual needs in a responsible, adult way, he preyed on fourteen-year-olds.

It occurred to Andy, in a way it had never quite done before, that this wasn't peripheral. This was the culture. Immaturity, emotional regression, sexual abuse these were characteristic of the culture. They were what society was founded on.

The following Sunday he visited his mother. He was tempted to tell her, but he didn't want to ignite her worry. As usual she talked at him, her leg rocking, her eyes glazing, in a descent into that near madness which was the outcome of her self-denial, isolation and making resentment and bitterness her close companions. He interrupted her.

"What did you make of Kinnock at the Conference?"

"Eh?"

"Did you hear his speech?"

"Yes, I did. It was good. I think he's right, if there's bullying going on, you have to stand up to it."

"You do, but it's really about accepting democracy. Those Marxist derived political positions, the Communist Party, the Socialist Workers, all of them, they're lost in a fantasy of historical certainty. They're not really interested in freedom, they want control. They believe they know the future, which is a crazy belief."

"You think so? Well, I don't know, but if you're in't Labour Party you have to accept its rules. That's what I think. And giving people redundancy notices, that's not how a Labour council should behave. That's people's lives."

"Hatton doesn't care about that. He cares about himself. Just watch. He'll get some lucrative, in-the-public-eye position. People like him always do. He's a fantasist who's read a hundred pages of Karl Marx in English and thinks he knows all there is to know about human beings. The far-left is populated by these pseudo-intellectuals and crass manipulators. I once heard a Socialist Worker bloke stand up in a meeting and tell us all the revolution was coming and a lot of people were going to be killed, but it would be okay because it would allow his lot to come to power. That's just psychopathic. It drives people to the Tories."

"A lot of people going to be killed? That's silly talk."

"It's what you get when people think they know the truth and the truth gives them the right to control. You know, the Tories have been handed a gift by the tosh about dictatorship of the proletariat…"

"The what?"

"It's in Marx. It's rubbish. A stupid and glib phrase, but it appeals to people who want power. It's a deeply conservative impulse. The whole notion of predictability is conservative. If people are free, you can't predict what they'll choose or control their behaviour. Freedom is what matters. Let people make their own choices about their lives. But everyone in power fears that: bosses, politicians. They all want life to be neat and ordered. If people are to be free, there has to be some degree of disorder."

"I don't know about that. Disorder? What d'you mean?"

"Not violence or mass crime or anything. Just that if people have real choice they won't necessarily do what's convenient for big business or big politics."

"Aye, well, I'm all for freedom. For't th'ordinary folk. Let 'em think and act for themselves. I'm all for that."

He was glad he'd raised her from her stupor. She could always be brought back to lucidity by talking about politics. The events at work had made him realize how lucky he'd been in his mother. She'd made mistakes but she'd seen clearly that children shouldn't be driven to conformity; she'd stood like an oak against that shabby deal in which you surrender your independence, in fact your selfhood, for a salary, a house in the suburbs, a bigger car than your neighbours, a colour t.v., a fridge, holidays abroad. She'd allowed him his freedom as a child and he loved her for it. It had taken courage.

The tragedy of her life was that she was a woman in a society which denied women the fullness of their being. She'd had no education, no opportunities. Yet not only had her gender condemned her, she was born into poverty too. Poor, female and denied, she'd found her way to a position of principle. She was a tragic heroine, but she was a heroine. She had never flinched in putting love before power. What had dragged her down was the failure of her marriage, her inability to find a way to a new life. She'd been a fool, but heroines are often foolish. What granted her grandeur was that poor and powerless she refused to comply. She'd created a space within the culture in which all its values could be challenged.

Andy knew what was true for him wasn't for Sylvia. She hadn't benefitted from the freedom he'd known. His mother's fear had made her cling. She lacked insight. Yet he knew, had someone told her, had a wise voice explained to her, she would have changed her behaviour. She would have flinched from anything that would damage her children, if only she could have seen what damage she did.

He tugged on the brakes as he flew down Pear Tree Brow. There was no doubt his mother's was a tragic life. Yet society had been the architect of her heartbreak. The economic system had consigned her to poverty; the education system had denied her learning; a culture of male power and abuse made equality in intimacy impossible. Andy was starting to realize how deep and wide that abuse spread. He was thirty-four, about to get married, flashing home on his bike, in essence still the careless, I-know-where-my-dinner's-coming-from boy his mother had allowed him to be. She was in the final quarter of her life, but the Craxtons were long-lived. Her fell-walking uncle had died three weeks before his hundredth birthday. Maybe she would enjoy another thirty years. He hoped so, as he hoped he could help to make them happy.

Rob Green agreed to be Andy's best man. They went for a few drinks the night before.

"Oh, you dickhead," said Rob, "putting me through this."

"You'll be fine. Have another."

Andy had asked him partly out of remorse over Sue Border, but principally because he'd been a good friend. It was almost a decade since they'd left university. He didn't know they would lose touch, that the messy business of living would separate them and years later he would discover he knew nothing of Rob's life.

In the morning, Rob needed further liquid courage. They went to a neglected, ill-frequented pub on Avenham Lane where Rob downed two, smoked three cigarettes and uttered over and over:

"You dickhead. How am I going to get through this?"

The registry office ceremony was brief and unfussy. Christine had expressed disgust at the thought that her step-father would give her away. To sit with him in the car on the way from her mother's, tense all the way that he might put his hand on her thigh or try to touch her breast, to have to take his arm as they stepped down and walk with him into the square, unprepossessing building, filled her with horror. That little trial over and her stiff silence in the car enough to deter him, the day was to enjoy.

Her London friends had booked into the Bartle Hall hotel for the Friday night. Henry had brought a generous supply of cannabis and cocaine. Mrs Thomas had no idea that behind the three-thousand-quid respectability, the antique little blue car, the equally ancient wedding dress, her new more-than -she-could-afford suit, hat, gloves and coat, the lavish meal and the three-tiered cake topped with the little sugar bride-and-groom figurines, her daughter's pals were locked in Henry's room, snorting like pigs, puffing like dragons, descending into a sordid, brain-befuddled self-abandonment which was the best response they could find to the serious business of embarking on married life with its long, burdensome responsibilities, its difficulties and necessary restraints.

But Elsie Lang was not so naïve.

There was something odd which troubled her. The meal over, the hotel at their disposal, people walking in the gardens, chatting in the bar or the lounge, she noticed that all Christine's London friends had disappeared. That was no way to behave. Wedding guests were there to lift the couple into their new life. The requirement was to talk to people, to make the acquaintance of people you'd never seen before and might never see again. Where had they all gone? She suspected they disdained the ceremony. She noticed one of them, a brisk young man in a white shirt and black waistcoat, gallop up the main staircase a bottle of champagne in his hands. Were they drinking, as a party, in one of the rooms? That was no way to behave.

It disturbed her, but not as much as the presence of her ex-husband. She knew Bert was ill but she was shocked when she said to Sylvia:

"Who's that man with the walking stick?" as they assembled for photographs.

"That's my dad, mother."

"Heaven help us."

When she felt he wouldn't notice she stared at him and little by little she was able to see the features of the man she'd been married to. He was wizened, the quick vigour which had made him so charming when he was young, replaced by the slow, painful movements of a living corpse. His cheeks were sunken. She felt she was looking at a skull with eyes. His thin lips were pulled down at the corners. His clothes hung on him as on hangers. She wouldn't have been surprised if he'd closed his eyes and died right there, in the armchair.

Her pity almost made her approach and talk to him, but her pride held her back. All the same it was terrible to see him so reduced. He couldn't have long to live. She was glad Andy had invited him. It embarrassed her, but he was in the last weeks of his life. Let him enjoy his son's wedding. Ted sat by him and chatted though Mary and Sylvia avoided him. She almost wanted to go to them and say:

"Speak to him. He's your father. You may never see him again."

She herself would have liked to say:

"Eh, Bert, I don't like to see you in this state. What have you done to yourself?"

She was convinced if she been looking after him he would be healthy. It was poor food which had brought him low. She experienced, for the first time since she'd kicked him out, a nostalgia for her married life. There'd been good times. If only he'd been an honest man. Discreetly she dabbed a tear.

Towards five, Andy went up to the bridal suite for respite. It was a big, square room with a capacious four-poster and a bay window looking over the grounds. He wondered where Christine had got to. No doubt locked away with Henry and his tribe. The door opened. He turned to see her stagger in.

"I'm going to take this dress off," she slurred.

"Uncomfortable?"

"Yes. Kind of."

She moved round the bed and sat on a chair to unfasten her shoes, but when she leant forward, slid ungraciously to the floor and couldn't get up. He lifted her.

"Maybe you should lie down for half an hour."

"What?"

"Perhaps you should rest for a bit."

"Rest? This is my wedding day. Take these shoes off will you."

She lifted her foot. He unfasted the strap of the left then the right. She got to her feet and took hold of the bedpost to keep stable.

"Unhook this bloody thing."

The dress loosened in the back she struggled out of it, opened her green, leather suitcase began tossing clothes right and left which Andy gathered, folded and placed on the chair.

"Where are my black trousers? Did I forget to bring them? Oh, god."

He went and sat in the window seat while she rummaged, stood up, staggered, pulled on jeans and blouse and searched for shoes. When, finally she found some and managed to get her feet into them, she turned to him with a wave.

"I'm off."

"Okay."

"See you later."

"Don't fall downstairs."

"What're you talking about."

She yanked the heavy door. It didn't move. She tried again.

"Turn the handle clockwise," he said.

"Clockwise?"

She managed and disappeared.

In the evening came the inevitable disco. John Redford and his girl-friend arrived. Andy was delighted to see him. It was touching he would make the trip from Essex simply for the end of the celebrations. Mark Hiscock turned up and most of Andy's Labour Party mates. The hotel served chips and pies. It was midnight before people began to drift away.

He and Christine went up to the bridal suite when all the guests had gone. Henry and a few of the London crowd followed.

"Enjoy your nuptials," shouted Henry as he headed for his room.

Andy turned to face him. He was drunk and stoned.

Christine collapsed across the bed.

"I'm exhausted," she muttered. "Get me some water."

He pulled her clothes off and manipulated her under the duvet. By the time he came back from the en-suite, she was asleep.

They had to interrupt their honeymoon. The blue skies brought chilly days to the Lakes. They had a little cottage in Outgate where they could lay a fire at five, go out to eat and come back at nine to cosiness. They tried the *Harvest* vegetarian in Ambleside and *Quince and Medlar* in Wordsworth's birthplace. Quiet and calm, they sank into one another's company, climbed Loughrigg and Stickle Ghyll, sat in the *Outgate Inn*, warmed up and went home tired and satisfied.

On the Wednesday they were up at six, drove to Blackburn, picked up Andy's dad and took the motorway to Manchester. Andy's palms were damp on the steering wheel. He kept to the inside lane and a steady sixty. A lorry hung on his bumper. He nipped into the middle, accelerated, slipped back to the left, but when the cars he'd put between himself and the juggernaut raced ahead, the monster appeared again, three feet from his hatchback. He knew the statistics: motorways were safer than the little, twisting, treacle-dark-at-night roads of the Lakes; but he wished he was setting off to walk round Derwentwater or Consiton, away from the insanity of homicidal truckers.

Christine had told Bert he was eligible for benefit because of his immobility and his needs. She'd helped him fill in the application and when it was rejected had pursued the appeal. When the date fell in the middle of the week after their wedding, Bert shrugged but she insisted. He couldn't go alone. She would represent him.

There were three men on the panel. Also present, sitting to the side, was a social worker, a man of fifty, balding, with big, black glasses, a paunch, dressed in ill-matching and neglected jacket, trousers, shirt and tie; one of those diligent, idealistic public servants who come into their professions young, hoping to do good, and persevere for thirty-five years, in spite of bureaucracy, underfunding and political ill-will.

The test was: *unable or virtually unable to walk*. Bert had to shuffle from one side of the room to the other. One of the panel's doctors, a slim man with greying black hair, gold glasses, a smart, black suit and a crisp white shirt held by gold cuff-links , shook his head and turned down the corners of his thin lips. He had one of those sharp, spare faces which speak of strict adherence and lack of easy sympathy. Andy watched him as he wrote on his pad with his black fountain pen.

Christine had to put the case. She'd prepared well and citing the regulations in detail enumerated, one by one, the ways in which Bert met the requirements. The man in the black suit kept shaking his head. When she'd summed up, the social worker was allowed to speak. He said it was appalling that Mr Lang had been dragged to the hearing; that he should have had the benefit months ago; that it was obvious it existed for precisely cases like his.

Bert had to undergo an examination. He was asked to strip to the waist and lie on the bed in the corner. The doctors inspected and prodded.

"Look at this," said the one in the black suit, in his Scottish accent, and pointed to a twitch in the muscles in the Bert's upper arm when he stimulated the nerves lower down.

The three physicians drew aside and muttered. Bert lay, emaciated, pale, still and silent. They stood beside the bed again. The Scot asked Bert to raise his legs, bend them at the knees. He had to take off his shoes and socks and push his toes against the pressure of the medic's hand. Sombre suit shook his head as the three took their seats behind the desk.

There came an adjournment during which Bert, Andy and Christine sat in an adjacent room. The social worker came in, looking shame-faced.

"I'm sorry you've had to go through this, Mr Lang. Your claim should never have been refused. I hope they'll make the right decision. I think they will. Your daughter-in-law did an excellent job."

It was true. Christine was a skilled advocate who had a thorough grasp of the legislation and a jurisprudential mind. She was quick to grasp the details of a case and to spot the weaknesses in the other side's position; and she had a commitment to justice, a sense that the law, properly enshrined and applied, is a powerful weapon in defence of the weak and vulnerable. Behind her advocacy was a philosophical conviction that in democratic societies, the law will be bound to offer protection to those most adversely struck by ill-luck, disease, lack of opportunity or the simple, inevitable working of an economic system rigged in favour of the fortunate. Welfare law was her passion. She believed that diligently and intelligently used in combination with a political movement for change and resolute pressure groups, it could be transforming. She wanted her life's work to be advocating for society's casualties.

When they were called back, the Scottish doctor was first to put his case: it was clear Mr Lang could walk. He'd walked across the room, and back. The rules were clear: unable or virtually unable to walk. Mr Lang's progress was slow and painful, but he had seen nothing to convince him that in spite of the laboured nature of his gait, he couldn't walk quarter of a mile.

The other two took a different view. The Chair, who appeared seventy at least, white-haired and dignified, softly spoken and with a careful clear enunciation put their case: Mr Lang could walk, but with such difficulty it fell under the definition of *virtually unable*.

The award was granted, and backdated. Bert would receive two thousand pounds and then the weekly allowance.

Bert treated his son and daughter-in-law to tea in the *Music Rooms* in Blackburn. They took him home and made sure he was comfortable. He waved from his chair by the window as they got into the car. He was overcome by their goodness. All his life he'd met cruelty, ignorance, self-seeking, egotism, opportunism, narrow-minded self-serving, greed, prejudice, snobbery, indifference; but they'd put themselves out for him. They'd even given up a day of their honeymoon. He was going to get two thousand quid. That was something; and the regular payment would help. He could pay for a taxi to the day centre; but for how long? He was dying. He might not wake up in the morning. For months he'd hoped there might be an improvement or the sawbones would find what was wrong, prescribe a drug and he'd be able to walk normally again and would put on weight. Those fantasies couldn't persist. There was only decline. Part of him hoped it would be fast, another that he could hang on for years. In spite of the pain, disability and restriction, there were still fine moments. He'd relished Andy's wedding and today, once the tribunal was over, had been marvellous.

He was glad Andy had found a good wife. Christine seemed to him a wonderful young woman, principled and willing to put herself out for others. If only he could live with them. He tried to fight off the thought. It was selfish. He'd had his life. He'd made his mistakes.

Why should they take him in? They should be thinking about having children. He was a useless old bag of bones fit for the knacker's yard.

The nothingness of death had a curiously telescoping effect on his nostalgia. The details of his experience congealed into homogenous chunks. In no more than a few seconds he could run the film of his life through his head. It was appalling. He couldn't look back on a life well lived. He'd struggled to survive in a culture trying to destroy him. His life had never begun. He'd established provisional arrangements with existence and nothing more. He accused himself of foolishness and cowardice, but something Andy had said to him came back into his consciousness: "Everything's wrong in our culture. It's founded on exploitation and abuse. The rest is excuse-making."

It was the kind of cheeky defiance which heartened him. Was the failure of his life his own fault? Had he asked to be born to a wayward, hopeless mother who abandoned him before he was in school? Was it his choice to be brought up by drunken grandparents? A child has needs and it's the moral duty of adults to respond. What chance had he when all his needs had been denied or ignored? He was the bastard boy who was shame and guilt to his mother, a sin to the Catholic Church, a burden to society (until he was need to fight Hitler), a runt, a reject, a problem. He tried to fight his way through, but now, when he might have no more than days to think about it, he realised you can't do for yourself what can only be done by others.

He'd tried to be *a self-made man*. The concept was absurd. No man makes himself, in any way, without others. It was nothing but an empty slogan, a piece of propaganda to blind people to the truth that everything we are is a product of our life together. It was the kind of idea Ken Wickham would like. Something to make his greed and egotism look like a matter of principle. There were no self-made men. There was a society organised around self-seeking hypocrisy and he'd tried to find his place in it. Hopeless. Andy was right, the only thing worth doing was to change it.

Yet his life hadn't been wasted. Andy was his son. Mary and Sylvia were his daughters. It was a little miracle. Mary and Sylvia were married. They had children. They were good mothers. At least he assumed they were. Andy was a teacher. He'd married an intelligent woman who was devoting her working life to helping people in difficulty. He might have made a mess of his own life but he'd brought children into the world who wouldn't repeat his mistakes. There was a future and his children would help build it.

Of his two other children, he knew nothing. He'd been an idiot, even with Laura Bruzzese. She was desperate and he'd helped her but it had ruined him. In any case, it was dishonest to pass off making her pregnant as altruism: he found her irresistible. He'd done it for his own satisfaction. He didn't resent her. She'd got what she wanted. No doubt her marriage had been a success; but he'd burdened himself. He had a secret which destroyed him. Stupidly, because he should have confessed to Elsie. No doubt she would have rejected him, but why? Only because of society's ludicrous, twisted values. She had her head filled with ideas of sin and saintliness which stopped her from living. She was a good woman. He knew her in the depths of her being. She was kind and generous and strong; but what could she do against the manipulation of her mind by power?

The good core of his life was his marriage to Elsie and their parenting of three children. Yet he had the feeling his chance of happiness had always been doomed. Laura had easily tempted him. Many men would have resisted. He'd treated making her pregnant as an opportunity. Idiot. He hadn't seen the enormity of his action.

He struggled to put himself to bed. The sheets were cold and he shivered. The bungalow was utterly quiet and dark. He heard a noise. He lay still and listened. Again. It seemed to be coming from the side path. He reached out and switched on the bedside lamp. Another sound. Then silence. He listened for half an hour, switched off the light and turned on his side. His feet were still cold. Had someone kept an eye? Did they know he was vulnerable? What would he do if he heard someone breaking in through the side door or the bathroom window? Once he would have leapt out of bed and confronted a burglar with nothing but his fists. Now, he couldn't have fought off a five-year-old.

If only he could live with Andy and Christine.

TWENTY-FOUR THOUSAND

They found a house in Connaught Road: a terrace with four bed-rooms, a front door onto the street and a back yard. It was occupied by a young couple with a baby. The woman had been in same year as Christine at Lark Hill. When they looked round, she said:

"Dave has done all the work himself. You don't want to buy this place. He's a bodger."

Andy was somewhat alarmed by the comment but Christine played it down:

"She was joking. Did you see that lovely fireplace in the big bed-room. I could work on that and make it a real feature."

It needed a rewire. Sylvia mentioned it to Barry and he offered to do the work, with Andy as his labourer. They moved in early December and Andy spent the two-week holiday following Barry's instructions. He was a quick, energetic worker, strong and accomplished. He could pull up floorboards with a crowbar which left Andy straining as the nails refused to squeak. He chiselled out for a back box in twenty minutes. Andy was at it for two hours. He could strip wire to perfection with a flick of the side cutters. Andy cut through the cable and Barry had to rescue him by tugging on the exposed end to drag a bit more length through.

Barry's superior practical intelligence made Andy sharply aware of the daft distinction between academic-literary-scientific cleverness and his brother-in-law's astuteness. He understood the physics of electricity in a way Andy didn't, but even if he'd book-learned that, he would never have had the instinctive, there's-a-way-round-everything thinking which came so easily to Barry. He was a linguist and Barry wasn't, but the notion that being able to read Baudelaire was superior to being able to solve the myriad problems that arose in rewiring a house, was just snobbery. They were equally intelligent, but in different ways.

In the spring, Christine was pregnant. Shortly after it was confirmed, Andy spotted a vacancy at The Lakes School, Windermere. It was a Scale One post but a sideways move was better than no move and the idea of bringing his children up in the Lakes appealed.

"Yes," said Christine, "if you want to. Don't know what I'd do about the CPE, but I'd work something out."

"We need to look into that first, I guess."

"No, it'll be okay, even if I have to travel to Preston."

"Surely you'd be able to do it at Lancaster, or maybe somewhere in Kendal?"

"Yeah, there'll be a way."

He took the precaution of discussing it fully with Cooper.

"Do you think they'll look negatively on a sideways move?"

"Not necessarily."

"And you're happy to support me."

"Yes, of course."

Andy assumed he'd get an interview, partly from arrogance, partly from experience. After his PGCE, he'd been interviewed for every application and been told more than once his profile was very strong. Given a decent reference, he should be sure of being called and competing against three of four, he fancied his chances. The date of the interviews passed. A letter arrived. They thanked him for his interest. They'd appointed a Miss Juliet Turnbull. He reasoned it must have been an impressive field. Windermere, after all, who wouldn't want to teach there? Maybe he no longer looked so good on paper. Into his sixth year in the same school. Perhaps he looked sluggish and unambitious. The little vision he'd elaborated of a potential life in one of the most beautiful parts of Britain, starting with a house in Kendal, which would be all they could afford, but maybe, in time, moving to Ambleside or Grasmere; his kids enjoying the benefits a small primary where everybody knows everybody, and moving on to the Lakes School, was consumed in his moment of disappointment. He had to carry on where he was and keep looking; but when again would there be such a pleasant opportunity?

It was quickly forgotten in the bustle towards birth; but six months after the failure he was in Cooper's study for a union matter. The conversation concluded, as Andy got up, Cooper said:

"By the way, did you ever hear from that school in the Lakes?"

"Yes, they wrote to say they'd appointed."

"Ah. Only they did take up your reference, but as it was after the final date for giving notice, I told them I wasn't willing to release you."

Andy stood and looked at him. He was sorting papers on his desk and refused to meet his eyes. Andy had the sense of being cornered, outwitted. What could he say? Cooper was the Head. He had the power. He had the right. Yet it was outrageous. He left.

Was Cooper lying? How could Andy ever know? Maybe the request did arrive after the final date, but maybe not. Why had he said "the school in the Lakes"? He knew well enough which school it was. Was he trying to pretend he couldn't remember, to play the matter down? Why had he waited sixth months to make the revelation? Why didn't he call him in the day the request arrived and say what he was going to do? Had he done so, Andy would have protested. He would have appealed to the union. If necessary, he would have complained to the Chief Education Officer. The delay made it impossible. Why had he told him at all? Had he said nothing, Andy would never have known. Was it a deliberate humiliation? Did he want to rub his nose in it?

The more Andy thought about it, the more he realised he could never know. Cooper had used his power cleverly. Yet one thing was undeniable: to make such a decision and not to tell the person involved till months later was despicable. It was unprofessional. This was the second time Cooper had prevented him. Did he have an animus against him? Had he taken a decision to block him? Were all Andy's ideas of moving on hopeless?

Curiously, he began to accuse himself: perhaps a sideways move was foolish; maybe the Lakes School was the wrong place for him; why hadn't he realised the timetable for interviews would overrun the final date for resignations? Yet, at a certain point, he rebelled. He'd applied for a job. He'd done nothing wrong. The dates were beyond his control. Cooper had said he would support him but he'd broken his legs. There should be some remedy. The awareness there wasn't, that power had had its way, that he'd been outmanoeuvred. enraged him.

His mind ran to speculation. Did Cooper believe he should be kept away from a place like The Lakes School? Did his public school, Oxbridge snobbery make him see Andy as an oik who should teach oiks? Was there an element of jealousy? After all, didn't Cooper have a house in the Lakes? Wouldn't he have liked to teach there too?

He could confirm nothing, though he suspected much.

Our alignment between our view of ourselves and the outside world, meaning other people, has to be constantly adjusted. Andy had no difficulty with that. He'd hoped and expected to be out of his first teaching post quickly. Maybe the expectation was too dream-like; but when he reflected, he thought not. Had Cooper supported him, he could well have been in his second post after six terms. Now, he was six years in and as fixed as a concrete fence post. He'd soon be a father. Christine had her legal ambitions to pursue. It was going to be harder in the coming six years to move on. The thought of being in the same post for another six years crushed him. He wouldn't let it happen. He'd find a job, any job, to get away; but the dreadful thought insinuated itself , creeping into his mind like sewer water into a cellar, that Cooper had taken a decision: he was going to prevent his progress. How could he know? Yet if it were true, it would define his life. How could that be right, that a man might make a choice about another man, say nothing, and quietly ruin him. He couldn't believe that the ostensibly liberal Cooper with his frequently reiterated confidence in his staff as autonomous professionals, was secretly conniving at his frustration.

Yet the more he pondered, the more he began to suspect. Perhaps the man's liberalism was a pose; maybe he understood the best way to wield power is to convince those in your sway you have no interest in it. There was a discrepancy between the way Cooper presented himself and the facts: what was liberal about denying him a reference and refusing to release him on a petty technicality? What was liberal about doing so and keeping it quiet for six months?

One Wednesday afternoon he took his mug of tea into the staffroom and sat next to its sole occupant, Matt Mann, the Head of Maths. He wasn't particularly friendly with him. Matt was an ambitious Cambridge graduate, a mathematical brain-box who had secured his promotion by the age of twenty-seven. To be Head of a big department in a prestigious school before thirty encouraged a realistic expectation of moving on to Deputy Headship in his mid or late thirties. He was single and a member of the ATL because he was broadly opposed to strike action. Andy felt they didn't have much in common, but he chatted to him now and again and over recent months had detected a disaffection which made him more congenial.

"All right, Matt?"

"No."

Andy looked at him. The big man kept his eyes on *The Times*.

"What's up?"

"That idiot."

"Which idiot?"

"Cooper."

"Oh, the idiot in chief. What's he done."

Matt shook his head.

"Bad as that, eh?"

"Bloody idiot."

"Anything the unions could help with?"

"No. I don't think so." He lay the paper on the narrow wooden table marked with mug rings. "What do you think? Can the unions do anything about him refusing to support me for a promotion?"

"Possibly. He has a duty of care and part of his job is to look after staff development. You could contact your local official."

"You think so?"

"Well, if it were one of my members I'd want to know the reasons and if they didn't sound kosher, I'd inform Regional Office, though appointments and promotions are a touchy area."

The mathematician sat up straight.

"I suppose I could try."

"You could. Is this recent?"

"Today."

"Today?"

"I've just come out of his office."

"Really?"

Matt faced him. Andy smiled, hoping he would open up.

"Deputy Headship. He won't support me because it involves some pastoral responsibility and he says I haven't had any. He claims I'm weak on pastoral matters. My strength is departmental."

"I see."

"What do you think?"

"I think it's an excuse."

"So do I."

"Is he denying you a reference altogether?"

"No, he says he'll have to include a reservation."

"He did the same to me."

"When?"

"In my second year here."

"What did you apply for?"

"Second in department. They took up my references but he scuppered me."

"Bastard."

"I guess you need to look for other jobs, ones that require your subject expertise, then he'll have no excuse."

"Yeah, maybe I'll try for adviser posts."

"Good idea."

The conversation deepened Andy's suspicions. Cooper was the Head. He had the right to make his judgements. Maybe Matt was lacking in pastoral skills. Yet wouldn't the liberal thing be to write the best possible reference and let the interview panel make up its mind? To act in a way which ensured Matt wouldn't get an interview seemed vindictive. Why should Cooper have something against him? He was in command of his subject, a good teacher, punctilious in marking and record-keeping. There was something odd about it, especially when Cooper had been so lax in other way. The Head of Geography retired. The only other Geography teacher was promoted without the post being advertised, without interview. It didn't fit together.

Did Cooper have some need to assert his power? Did he feel that the reverse side of his apparent liberalism needed to be on show now and again to keep the staff guessing? Why had he picked on Matt? Was he jealous of his rapid ascent?

Over the next few months, Andy talked weekly to his colleague about his applications. He tried for two more Deputy Headships. Cooper included reservations in both references. He found an advisor vacancy. Cooper thought him unfitted for the role. Matt became ever more enraged, tense and bitter, till he was signed off with stress. Andy was stunned. How did this serve anyone's interest.

Five weeks before the Easter holiday his dad was taken into hospital again. Andy was able to use Christine's car for some of his visits, but he missed the bike ride and as often as he could, even after an ex-hausting day at work, he pedalled through Avenham Park, down London Road and enjoyed pushing up the long, slow climb past Hoghton Tower.

His father had deteriorated badly and was aware of it. Andy could see that he wasn't only afraid of death, humiliated by his physical condition, but also terrified of dying alone. He brought home his soiled dressing gown and laundered it, only to have to slip it in a plastic bag the next time. The doctors were no nearer a diagnosis. The deep vein thrombosis which had been the source of the pain in his leg wasn't what was killing him. There was something else, but they couldn't identify it. After a week, they decided to try abdominal surgery.

"These blood thinners I'm on," he said, "I'm gonna bleed like a stuck pig."

"I'm sure they'll know how to handle that," said Andy.

His dad looked away. There was little left of him. He probably weighed no more than seven stone. His cheeks were so hollow the tendons were plainly visible. The skin hung from his arms once well-shapen and strong. He was sixty-three. Andy had no doubt this was his last stay in hospital. The doctors were down to speculation and desperate interventions. Andy looked at him and saw the power of biology. Oddly, the power of life. The processes which were wiping him out were irresistible. It felt like cruelty to see his dad so reduced, but there was no cruelty in biology. There was no intention. It was mere process. Life required that individuals must die. Birth was no easy matter nor, usually, was death. Leaving the world was as wrenching and stunning as entering it. Pity, he thought, his dad couldn't just sleep and not wake up. Pity he had to suffer physical and mental anguish to be done with life.

He saw him young and vibrant, when he, as a boy, had loved and admired and wanted to be like him. They were walking along Woodland Grove, to the shops on Liverpool Road. His dad was repairing the door on the big, blue, wooden cupboard in the breakfast room and needed some hinges. They were going to Gardener's, the little hardware shop on the corner of Crookings Lane, with its sideline in sweets and ice-cream where Andy had run every Saturday morning his half crown in his hand for gob-stoppers, sherbet, *Penny Arrows*, aniseed balls, *Black Jacks*, *Fruit Salads*, *Spangles*, *Refreshers*, all those teeth-bathing, sugar indulgences which had filled his mouth with amalgam. His dad was striding briskly as he always did and Andy was trotting to keep up. He was very proud of his dad's strong stride. He looked at his legs in the off-white trousers and the chunky, pale green, v-neck sweater whose sleeves were pulled up to his elbows and knew when he was a man he would dress like his dad and step out in his manly, confident way.

Then they were climbing the black, muddy slope in Church Woods. He was seven or eight. He'd been there with John Rutherford and Barry James who lived nearby in Priory Crescent and whose dad was a bank manager. His mother had blamed Andy when her son came home with filthy knees and caked shoes. Barry was one of those boys who was supposed to do well in everything for the sake of his parents. Andy liked him, but he didn't like his parents and stayed away from his house.

"Where've you been to get in that state?" said Andy's mother, wiping her hands on the little, white towel by the kitchen sink.

"Church Woods," Andy said. "It's dead good."

His dad came to see if it was safe and together they climbed. Andy in front. He remembered looking back and seeing his dad's smiling face and being glad they were together and that his dad liked what he was doing and encouraged him.

That was the time before the rift, the time when he took his parents as they were, with all their virtues and their faults, knowing how to read them and to get the best out of them, knowing that his dad would be funny, mocking and ironic and his mother, as immune to irony as a lizard to sunstroke. Then there was the great blank when his father became a stranger. He wondered how much it had hurt him. How it had contributed to the decline in his health.

One evening, Dereck arrived while he was there.

"I'll not stop long," he said.

"Stay as long as you like," said Andy.

He was keeping Bert's garden tidy.

"I did the front lawn today, Bert. It looks grand."

"Thanks for that, Dereck. I'll see you right when I'm home."

"You bloody well won't."

When they left together, taking slowly the stairs which gave off an odour of disinfectant, Dereck said:

"Are they any nearer?"

"No, they're at a loss, Dereck."

"Aye? And what's this operation for then?"

"I dunno. Because they can't think of anything else I suppose. Part of me wants to tell him not to have it."

"You may be right."

"I have a feeling they're almost experimenting now."

"That's terrible."

"Well, maybe they hope they will find something, but on the other hand I think curiosity is part of it. I just fear the anaesthetic will kill him."

"Surely they wouldn't do it if they thought so."

"They've told him there's a risk."

"Bloody hell."

"I know."

"And if he recovers, will he come home?"

They stopped at the exit.

"I don't think he'll be home again, Dereck."

"It's a bloody shame. Aye, it is. He's been a good neighbour. He's put up wi' my kids and they're a pair o' bloody tearaways."

They shook hands.

The operation left him weakened, unable to get out of bed, disorientated for a few days. A phone call came at seven one evening telling Andy he needed to get to the hospital quickly. He had to ring Mary and Sylvia. They both turned up, Mary alone, Sylvia with Barry. Christine came with Andy. Bert was being given regular diamorphine. Immediately after, he was calm, his eyes staring into the distance, his body relaxed; but when the time for the next dose was approaching, he was wracked, agitated, calling again and again for the bed-pan and muttering in his pitching delirium, "Knackered, absolutely knackered." They stayed till two, when the nurse told them he was stable.

Sylvia had known so little of her father he was a stranger to her. She couldn't recall living with him. Andy knew she didn't feel connected to the dying man and couldn't feel any grief for his passing. She was sorry for him as she would have been for anyone in his state, but she wasn't losing a father. Mary was. Though she'd distanced herself from him emotionally under her mother's insistence, she'd loved him for fourteen years, and, as a little girl, with that innocent, boundless affection which can never be recovered in adult relationships. She had her husband and children. Her affection and commitment were anchored; but Andy could see she couldn't hold back the memories of when she'd delighted in being picked up by him, by sitting on his knee with a book, by being taken to hear the Hallé at the Public Hall, her father's first, his pride, the lovely, clever, self-possessed girl he had such hopes for.

When the diamorphine was administered Bert's pain became a distant memory. It didn't disappear but it was so remote it caused him no agony. The experience of his body was almost a pleasure. His children were there. His three children. Three of his children. They were there because he was dying. The thought upset him. In spite of his failing faculties he could still be emotionally upturned. How long since he'd seen Mary? He'd never visited her house. Her children didn't know him. It was good of her to come. He mouthed his thanks and his voice came from elsewhere. It was good of her but he'd needed her while he was alive. Why couldn't she have been a daughter to him after his divorce from Elsie? He'd missed so much. He'd missed life. He'd failed.

174

Yet in his separated-from-his-body state he entered a brief spell of lucidity. When the pain was as its worst, till he felt it was impossible to bear any more and wondered why his body didn't simply shut down, he couldn't think. His mind flitted from image to image without coherence. It was a mad cascade of tormenting dream-visions which made his mental anguish as great as his physical. The effect of the drug plugged their source. He had some capacity to order his ideas. It came to him that the meaning of his life didn't end with his life. Andy was here. He might live another forty years and so long as he lived, he carried the memory of his father. He was going to be a father and his children might in turn have children. If they were born twenty-five years hence and lived seventy-five years then his memory might be alive in a century. What would be preserved in memory? He hoped it would be the good. Did Andy know about Laura? Probably Elsie had told him everything. No doubt he knew that somewhere he had two half-brothers.

Bert regretted bringing children into the world so carelessly. The three by him now were the good work of his life. Better than anything. Nothing was more important than parenting. It was the greatest opportunity life offered. He'd wanted to make money, to run his own business, to own a big, comfortable house; he'd coveted pretty women and fine clothes; but here when life was dispensing with him, he realised he'd granted too high a value to trivialities. People run after what they imagine will fulfil them but life asserts itself. It's accepting what life demands that is the great fulfilment and the essence of life is reproduction. The love of a parent for a child is creation's greatest accomplishment. If only he'd known that when he was twenty.

He thought of Slick Sticks. He was dead and Bert hadn't been able to get to his funeral. They found him slumped on his sofa, half-dressed, an extinguished fag stuck to his dry lips, his trousers soaked in spilt beer. Bert had loved the old fool. Life had evaded him. He'd spent six decades dodging, propping himself on booze and dangerous, unstable women. How could a man be on earth so long and never even begin to live?

Who would remember Slick Sticks, and if they did, what good would they recall? The meaning of a life lived on through generations. There was some of Bert in Mary, Andy and Sylvia. Not only genetically but experientially. Something of how he had lived would be transmitted. So it was. Down the ages, some small influence of the good and the bad he had done. The meaning of a life.

He'd never known his father. He had no ancestry. On his mother's side, he knew of nothing further back than his grandfather. The poor have no genealogy. The rich can trace their forbears through centuries. The royal family, like all aristocrats, knew who their pre-medieval progenitors were. Class determined the very meaning of your existence. He'd been born without a history, like all the poor. He'd made his own biography. It was tragic but there was good in it. If his life had meaning it was these three of his children. He believed they were good people. His life had been a terrible mess born of poverty, drink, degradation, false ambition, the cheat of the money system, yet, he'd done some good. There was something which deserved to live on, and that was all the could be meant by immortality.

His children said goodbye to him shortly after the painkiller coursed through his veins. Would he see them again? What did it matter? He closed his eyes. He wanted to sleep and never wake.

Barry drove Sylvia home.

"It's very sad," she said as they sped along Blackpool Road, "but I hardly know him. I don't feel like I'm losing someone."

"Well, that's not your fault, luv. You're doing the right thing. You can't do any more."

Mary drove home alone. She had two fathers: the one before the divorce and the one after. The first, she'd adored and cherished. The second was a stranger. She knew all the details. Her mother had made sure of that. She wished she didn't. What was Laura Bruzzese to do with her? She'd taken her mother's side because she felt she must. Her mother had been wronged. How would she have reacted if she'd learnt that Ted, before she knew him, had fathered a child? Would she have divorced him? She wouldn't. She would have absorbed the little shock and said:

"That's in the past, let it stay there."

There began the stirring of resentment against her mother which she quickly staunched. There was nothing to be gained by running through her head how things might have been if her mother had stayed calm and kept the family together. She would have loved for the chasm never to have opened. She'd hated being the only girl she knew whose parents were divorced. She'd had to gird all her self-possession and fight away self-pity and anger to stop herself falling into inconsolable grief; but she'd come through. She had four children. She relished her life as a mother. She was active and respected in the village. What her parents had done was their affair.

She parked in the unlit lane round the corner from her house and wiped the tears on her handkerchief. By the internal light, she inspected her face in the rear-view mirror. She didn't want Ted to know she was upset. She sat alone and quiet for ten minutes. If only she could have helped her dad. She would have been glad to have him in her home. No one, let alone the father she'd loved, should die lonely.

The following afternoon, Bert had other visitors. Like any junkie he needed his fix. The steady rising of pain, the incursion of the bright, sharp sensations he was powerless against so his shrunken frame seemed nothing but a generator of agony, made him try to see the clock to work out how long he had to endure. He screwed his eyes but couldn't make out the figures. He wasn't expecting a day-time visit. Andy would arrive in the evening. Maybe Mary and Sylvia, if the doctors were alarmed, perhaps Dereck. He turned to look at the couple. A woman. A big dark woman. A tall, broad, younger man. He sank back on the pillow and closed his eyes. The woman spoke but her voice sounded as if it had passed through water. He was overcome by the need for a bedpan. He reached for the red button. The woman pressed it and spoke. A nurse arrived and set the screen. He could produce nothing in spite of the sense of urgency.

He lay flat, exhausted, all pain, wanting to be out of life, to be rid of suffering. Death was keeping him waiting. It felt like a punishment. Who was chastising him? The woman spoke. He turned his head.

"Hello, Bert," she said, "it's Laura. This is my son. I've brought you some flowers and some grapes."

Laura? He closed his eyes. He saw his grandfather in his unwashed vest, sitting in the chair on the cold floor of the little house in Marsh Lane, his feet bare, his head hung, his white hair like a flash of sunshine in the gloom; a priest holding the leather strap, looking down at him, imposing and distant, the cold authority of the punitive church; a table set for Sunday tea in a neat, clean room, Tom Craxton opposite him, taciturn and kind, Elsie fussing to bring the bread and butter and tea-cups; a bar in Cairo, four airmen at a table outside in the crushing heat, young men glad of one another's company in spite of the war and being far from home, happy because they were young and, with luck their lives were ahead of them; a road, the broken white line in the middle and the bonnet in front of him, driving on his own, at ease on his way to another easy-to-please customer; Ken Wickham waving to him from an ocean-going yacht sinking in a calm sea while the partying crew paid no heed; the body of Slick Sticks in its coffin, a fag in his mouth, a glass in his hand and a woman whose lips were smeared with bright-red lipstick weeping; a beach, Mary running to the sea holding Andy by the hand, his brother-in-law's Eddie's boys climbing on the rocks and Elsie slim and pretty beside him in her swimsuit; a woman on a bed, a dark, sumptuous woman, inviting and willing.

Laura?

He tried to raise himself a little and to look at them.

"Thanks," he whispered.

"That's all right, Bert. This is my son. Do you remember him?"

He sank back into the pillow. He was beyond thinking. Images cascaded through his brain in hypnogogic confusion. He heard the woman speak again but he couldn't move.

Andy got a call at five in the morning. He needed to get to the hospital quickly. When he arrived, the screen was in place. A male nurse, small, dark, broad and young approached him.

"I'm sorry," he said.

Andy nodded.

"I'm sorry."

"He's gone?"

"Yes."

The little nurse stood between Andy and the bed.

"Can I see him?"

"Are you sure you want to?"

Andy stared. What could he mean? It was his father.

"Yes."

"Okay. If you follow me. Just for a second. Okay?"

"Yes, okay."

The man turned his wide back and went quickly behind the screen. Andy followed. The covers were pulled up to his dad's chin. His head was thrown back, his mouth wide open, stretched in agony. It was almost a skull he was looking at. The nurse turned and tried to hurry him out.

"Okay?"

"Just a minute."

"Okay, Mr Lang. Okay. Shall we go?"

Andy stared at the face which was barely human. It might have been the head of some ape killed in a fierce battle with some predator. There was nothing in the features which expressed his dad's person-ality, unless that meant only unbearable suffering.

"Okay, Mr Lang."

The nurse took him by the upper arm and guided him beyond the screen. He wanted to pull away, to go back and look. He could have stood and looked for an hour. It had been a vicious end. There had been no peace, no moment before death when he could relax. At once a doctor appeared, his white coat unbuttoned, a stethoscope around his neck. He extended his hands like the Pope in blessing. He was about Andy's age, taller, with neatly brushed, sandy hair. He shook his head.

"I'm so sorry," he said, "I'm so sorry."

He directed Andy into a little ante-room.

"We couldn't get to the bottom of it," he said. "There'll be a post-mortem. Pneumonia will probably be on the death certificate. We'll have to see what the post-mortem finds."

Andy shook his hand. As he emerged into the still chill air of morn-ing, he was thinking of the little nurse who wanted him not to see his dad. Did he think the shock would be too much? Didn't he know that not to see him would have been worse?

Mary and Sylvia wouldn't see him. He was the only one. Apart from the medical professionals who saw a corpse as a corpse, no one had seen him after his horrible fight with death. Andy was glad he had, though the image was branded into his brain and made his heart beat

179

heavily. Why couldn't he have had a peaceful death? At least that. Life had been cruel to him to the very last second: born illegitimate, abused, abandoned, impoverished; from such inauspicious beginnings that he had made himself a man of some principle, who defied all prejudice and smiled on all forms of justice, freedom and equality, wasn't bad. What could he have made of his life with a little help, a little love, a little kindness?

Andy had to take his will and papers to his dad's solicitor. He was a man in his mid-forties in a smart, black suit, stiff white collar and impossibly shiny shoes, one of those where's-the-lucrative-niche-for-me people who defeated Andy's spirit. He was friendly and expressed his condolences as he gave the papers a cursory look, before switching to a personal tone and recounting a few anecdotes. The final one, which amused him greatly, was about a gathering at Bert's bungalow. There were nibbles and wine and a little huddle of business folk and professionals. By ten o'clock, he was starting to feel a bit chilly and slipped his jacket on.

"It's cooling off in here, Bert," he said.

"Yes," the host replied, "the heating goes off at nine."

The solicitor rocked with amusement and shook his head. Andy, slightly affronted, stiffened and stared. He would have liked to say: "Yes, that's the effect of growing up in poverty; and in any case, though he was comfortable he was never well-off. Not as well-off as you for example."

He would get his probate clerk on the job quickly. Probate clerk? So he wasn't going to do the work himself. Once again, Andy was moved to say something spikey:

"Well, if the work's going to be done by a clerk, I guess we'll be billed for a clerk's time?"

He restrained himself, but as the professional was patting the papers neat and chivvying the interview to a close he said:

"One thing. Somewhere in there is the agreement my dad struck with Ken Wickham. He was owed four thousand. I wanted to take action but he wouldn't let me. I want Wickham pursued for that money."

"Yes, okay, I'll have a look and see if…"

"No, no. I won't accept any question about it. Wickham had four thousand of my dad's money and paid back virtually nothing. He must be made to pay. There is an agreement. I've seen it. Wickham signed it."

"Right. Right," the solicitor became more serious. "I'll ensure we do everything we can to get the money."

They shook hands.

On the train home, Andy thought about the solicitor's little story. It was true his dad could be parsimonious. He never left a light burning in an unoccupied room. He clung to money like a man to a life-belt. He was mocked for it by the people he tried to live amongst. The poverty of his early years, the deprivations of war and the years following, and the terrible insecurity of his bed-on-the-floor-and-a-cold-tap family, made him cautious and sent him to money as a substitute for affection.

He tried to make his way. He'd worked for ICI. He'd run his own little business. He'd worked hard to make Wickham's company thrive. He'd always wanted to believe there was a place for him. He'd never been able to arrive at a dismissal of his culture; but in the solicitor's laughter was the measure of his mistake.

There was no place for him. There was no place for anyone. There was only a chaos of competing interests. To an extent, the system held. Not that people could live, that they could fulfil the potential of their selfhood. They could survive, make money, gain power or status, but living was impossible; even for the most successful, for success was assessed in false terms. The system held; but at its bottom edge, it failed disastrously. People were condemned to poverty, humiliation, the impossibility of a way out; because in a money system only money guarantees you can't descend to animality. Had his dad been able to strike out and build a life for himself; could he have staked out a few acres of land, hewed stone, felled timber, raised livestock, grown crops, he could have made a good life; but in the money system, without money you can't do anything. Everything is owned. There is title. All you can do is sell yourself. It is a system of prostitution. Everyone, every day, must make a whore's bargain to be able to eat.

His dad had tried to make an agreement with this system. That was his tragedy. His life was tragic through no fault of his own. The sexual hypocrisy which made his mother wayward and his father (whoever he was) opportunistic was in place before he was born. The economic system which ensured his poverty was nothing to do with him. He arrived in it, new-born, innocent and abused. That was the money system: it abused all innocence.

The only chance of life was to face down the system. He looked out of the window as the train pulled into Preston. The back yards of the terraced houses were drab. Face down the system. It was all many people could do to pay the rent or the mortgage and get by. Millions of lives, over before they had begun. That was the collective tragedy. People were born in to a system established long before they were conceived. It grabbed them as they emerged from the vagina, shook them by the back of the neck, plunged them in the cold water of the money system and shocked them into conformity. Ghosts. The world was populated by ghosts. Phantoms at a distance from their humanity because in order to sell yourself to live it had to be denied. He had decided to face down the system, but what chance did he have? He was stuck in a school where he didn't want to work because of the machinations of a sly Headmaster. He was about to become a father. He had a mortgage to pay. The money system was an alligator which had sprung from its submerged hiding and had his balls in its teeth.

The tragedy was collective and only collectively could it be overcome. His sensibility was individual and unique. How to fit the two together? In spite of its near impossibility, it must be tried. The alternative was acceptance and acceptance was living death.

Bert's body was burnt at Blackburn crematorium and his ashes scattered in the garden of remembrance. Sylvia and Barry were there. Mary came alone because Ted was working. Dereck and Betty turned up as did two of his Satsangi friends. A tall, stooping man with a little R.A.F. type moustache introduced himself: he was one of Bert's old colleagues from ICI. His name was vaguely reminiscent to Andy. There was no after-the-ceremony collation. Andy, Mary, Barry and Sylvia went to Bert's bungalow to begin sorting his belongings. Mary, ever anticipatory and efficient had brought luggage labels which she attached to the furniture with the name of whoever wanted each item.

The books came to Andy. Barry and Sylvia wanted a little, three-legged table and some of the ornaments. Mary asked if she could have a few small things: a framed painting of a Lakeland scene; a figurine of a ballerina; a graceful glass vase. Everything else would have to be disposed of. Andy had the gold watch with the thick band his dad had always worn. As they were leaving, Dereck appeared in his path.

"All right, Andy?"

"Yeah. Thanks for coming, Dereck."

"That's all right. I'll miss him. He were a good neighbour. Aye, he was."

"I'd like you to have this, Dereck."

Andy took the watch from his pocket and held it out on his palm.

"For me?"

"Yes."

"No, I couldn't take that, Andy."

"I'm sure he would've liked you to have it. He spoke very highly of you and Betty."

"Aye," the neighbour took the heavy timepiece and weighed and examined it as he shook his head. "That's very good of you, Andy. His watch. No," he said, holding it out as if he was being offered stolen goods in the pub, "I couldn't take it, Andy. It's an expensive item."

"The value doesn't matter."

"No, I can't. Aye, it's good of you. He were a damned good neighbour. It's a bloody shame it is. I couldn't take it, Andy. It must be worth a pretty penny."

"It's not the money. Have it. Something to remind you of him."

Dereck retracted his arm and inspected the face closely.

"It's a good 'un. He liked good things. Aye, it's a bobby dazzler. No, I can't Andy. Thanks. I can't."

He held it at arm's length once more. Andy reluctantly took it from him and slipped it in his pocket. He was sorry Dereck wouldn't accept it. He had no intention of selling it. He would keep it for the rest of his life and maybe his children would keep it. He would have liked Dereck to have it so that a little bit of his father would be always in Dereck's house. He understood why he didn't want it. He didn't want to appear venal. He didn't want Andy to think he might flog it for the few hundred quid it could be worth.

The bungalow sold quickly. The solicitor gathered in the assets. Shortly after the start of the academic year, Andy got a call: counsel's advice was the debt could be retrieved; did Andy want him to press on? A few days later, Ken Wickham was on the phone.

"Hello, Andy my friend. So sorry to hear about your father. A great pal of mine. Yes, I admired him enormously. Better at his job than anyone I've ever known. So sorry I couldn't get to his funeral. When you're in business, you know…Now this matter of the money, Andy. You know me, I'm not the kind of man who doesn't pay his debts.."

"Well, pay it then."

"I will, Andy, my friend. I will. Of course I will. You know me, I'm a man of my word. Now don't you think, between friends, we can do without all this legal nonsense…?"

"No, I don't. Just send the cheque to the solicitor and it's done."

"That's right, Andy. You're practical. Like your father. I can hear him in your voice. That's just what he would have said. Now, all I need is a bit of time…"

"You've had years."

"That's right, Andy. Your father was a reasonable man. He understood how things work in business. There's a cycle. Cash-flow changes. That's all it is. Business, Andy. Nothing personal…"

"It's personal to me. You've had four thousand quid of my dad's money and I'm having it back."

"Of course you are, Andy. If I were in your position I'd say the same. Of course I would. But you and I, we're men of the world. Your father was a man of the world. We know the pros and cons. I'll give you the money. That's my promise. That's my promise to you, Andy. Now, am I the kind of man who breaks his promise?"

"You made a binding agreement and you reneged on it. It's with the solicitor. You want to talk to someone, talk to him."

"Solictors, Andy. You know what they're like. You and I we're…"

Andy hung up.

"Who was that?" said Christine.

"Wickham."

"Oh, him."

184

"Unctuous git."

He went into the long, narrow kitchen that looked out on their little yard. Did Wickham really think he was going to trust him? He was one of those men who seemed to have no sense of the existence of other minds; as if his mind filled the entire universe and others were mere appendages, toys to be manipulated. It was disturbing to talk to such a man. It made Andy think of Mike Chambers who had the same kind of inability to know the boundaries of his identity. They were deeply flawed people. His thoughts ran on quickly: were they flawed by nature or culture? Surely both. It could never be only one or the other. Yet what kind of universe was it that could contain such flaws? His pregnant wife was in the next room. In a few months, they would be responsible for a young life. How could he guarantee his child's well-being in a world of Ken Wickhams?

All the same, the fact he could recognize Wickham's despicable character was a source of hope. What did he mean by his despicable character? What did he mean by thinking of Mike Chambers as essentially obnoxious? Wasn't it that there was something normative from which they deviated? Nobody advertised themselves as venal, manipulative, sly, untrustworthy, selfish, purblind, vicious. Even Hitler had to hide behind putatively high-minded motives. Everybody did? Why? Because it was an expectation that people would be kind, thoughtful, generous, caring. Why? Because we were wired for it. It guaranteed our survival. As Shakespeare said: *"There's no fault in nature but the mind/ They only are deformed who are unkind."* Everybody liked kindness, modesty, warmth and the ability to recognise the needs of others. Yet society was organised around alternative impulses. He was dragged back to Rousseau, but he didn't think he was right. People weren't born free, they were born social. Society could recognize or deny the need for empathy. Ours did the latter. Why? Money. That's what made Wickham such a slug.

When the probate was settled, they got twenty-four thousand each. Not a bad little stash. Take into account that he bought Woodland Grove too and he could be said to be worth the other side of a hundred grand. For a boy who began life without shoes to go to school in, a decent pile in 1986. For Andy and Christine, it came just at the right moment. They received the cheque three weeks before the baby was due. For a time at least, they would be free of that last-week-of-the-month squeeze when they had less than fifty in the bank, no petrol in the car, the shopping to do, and the washing machine had coughed and died, or the iron sent out a last, desperate, malicious spurt of steam before starting to smoulder.

Twenty-four thousand quid. Andy held the Woolwich account book in his hand and looked at the figures, written in black ink. It was vastly more than he'd ever had. His bank statement had never shown over fifteen hundred and if he had savings of five he thought he was doing well. Twenty-four thousand quid. What could he do with it? It was his dad's money. Though it was now in his name, he didn't feel he owned it. What would his dad have done with it? He'd have set up a little enterprise: a café or a restaurant. Why not? He had no skill with food, but running a café didn't require cordon bleu subtlety. This was enough to get him out of teaching. He could be selfish and say to Christine:

"Look, I'll probably never have a windfall like this again. I'm going to use it to set up a little café with a bookshop on the side."

He slipped the book in his inside pocket and headed along Fisher-gate. He couldn't do it. There was a child on the way. Christine wanted to qualify. The responsible thing was to move to a better house and keep a reserve to help them through till she was earning. Maybe then he'd be able to change tack.

That night he dreamed he was in his dad's bungalow. Pound notes were floating from the ceiling. His dad was in the chair, his leg raised. He was shaking his head as Andy explained why he couldn't open a café. They were in the packed cellar at the *Minotaur* a rock band playing. He was behind the counter. People were queueing out of the door. He opened the till. It was packed with notes which float-ed into the air as he tried helplessly to catch them. He was in Cooper's study, writing his notice on a ten pound note.

The loss of his father and the arrival of the money clashed painfully. He wished there'd been no inheritance; then the grief of loss would have been unsullied. As it was, there was celebration in the mourn-ing. His dad was gone. He had twenty-four thousand quid. He couldn't deny having the money was pleasant. Yet the association of the uplift from the lucre with the devastation of the disappearance of the dad he'd lived with and loved for eleven years, left a vague sense of disgust. Lucre. It always brought disgust in the end. It corrupted every relationship. He recalled, when he'd made his first visit to the solicitor, he'd been asked whether there was likely to be any dispute in the family over the inheritance. The idea had shocked him. How despicable it was that people could rub their hands with glee at the thought of death if there was a little bundle of dosh to be had. Yet that was lucre. He wished he didn't need the money, that he could afford to give it to Amnesty International or CND. He was slightly sickened by the thought that he could profit from death.

Elsie Lang reflected that the only husband she'd had was gone. She stayed away from his funeral, but asked Andy about it. Who was there? What kind of service was it? He wasn't religious. He couldn't expect a Christian send off after the way he'd lived. She tried to summon up a sense of loss, but there was nothing. To Sylvia she said:

"Sixteen years and three children. You don't forget that. He were my husband after all. I can't help feeling it. No, I can't."

Her daughter saw through the performance but in her sympathetic, practical way offered her comfort all the same.

It was from Sylvia she learned of the inheritance. Twenty-four thousand each. Seventy-two thousand in total. Had she still been married to him, it would have come to her. Of course, there wouldn't have been a house to sell but on the other hand he'd probably have saved more. She'd say that for him, he was good with money. He wasn't wasteful. He didn't drink or smoke or gamble. He spent silly money on records and books, but she'd say that for him, he was prudent. He could save. Mind you, he probably learned a lot from his father-in-law. His own family were no good. They were a mess. He couldn't be blamed for that. No, he didn't have a good start, but he should have behaved right. One partner. That's what it said in the Bible. You've got to live right if you want eternal life. He was damned. He'd be burning in the fires of hell now. She didn't wish it on him, but that's the way it was. There had to be hell or there could be no heaven. At least she wouldn't have to meet him in the afterlife. God would see to that. He would have a place reserved for her, beside her mother, her father, her grandparents, her aunts. She'd lived as the Bible said and she must have her reward. Those who didn't must be damned. Aye. He would be going through the torments of hell now and would do so for eternity. Amen.

All the same, the thought of the money came back to her. Seventy-two thousand. It might have been more. It would have come her way. She could have treated her grandchildren. She did anyway, but with that kind of money in the bank she could have paid for holidays and meals out and they would have loved her all the more for it. Oh, what a fool he was. How much grief he'd caused her and now, how much money she'd lost. She had her small savings. There was eight hundred pounds in the Nationwide. She put a bit away each month. She was frugal. She cut her own hair. She never went out. She hadn't been to the cinema for twenty years. He sole indulgence was to climb on a coach with the other ladies from the Women's Fellowship and visit Skipton or Keswick or York or Chester. It was two or three times a year. She saved up. But seventy-two thousand. Dear heaven, if only she'd had a good husband.

Bert was dead at sixty-three. She recalled the day she'd met him. He was charming, almost handsome, and gave off an appealing sense of energy and love of life. His face seemed to smile. He was different from her father's taciturn lugubriousness. How could she have known then, or later, on their wedding day or during the years in Talbot Road or Woodland Grove that he would die at what she thought of as prematurely? Oh, he'd have lived longer if she'd been cooking for him. Good food could keep a man alive for years. He'd neglected himself like all bachelors do. They fall into lazy ways. There's nothing like a wife for making a man live long.

He was gone. She couldn't mourn him, yet it felt as if part of her had been removed. He was part of her past. Times were better then, in spite of everything, even the war. People looked out for one another. They talked behind one another's backs, but you could rely on them if you needed help. She sat in her chair, the television illuminated; but she wasn't watching it. She was staring out of the window at the bungalows opposite but she wasn't seeing them either. She was watching the film of her girlhood. How she loved that carefree, inno-cent child she'd been. How she regretted what her life had become. How could she, who had once been surrounded by people she loved, who never knew an instant's loneliness, have arrived at her condition of isolation? It almost made her nostalgic for her life with Bert. She was lapsing into that hypnogogic state which came so easily and she saw herself dusting the back room at Woodland Grove while he sat on the sofa with the paper. When she'd lifted all the ornaments and wiped the wooden mantlepiece, she dusted his head. He gave a little laugh and went on reading. It was a moment of happy, light-hearted intimacy. She loved him then.

STUPEFACTION

In September 1992, Andy began teaching a little selection of Zola's *Contes Choisis* to his lower-sixth class. He followed his standard procedure and gave them a week to read the first story: no more than ten pages. The following week he began:

"Okay. What's the gist of this first story?"

They sat with their arms folded, or upright, defiant, resistant and silent.

"Have you all read it?"

No one responded.

"Joanna, have you read it?"

She shook her head.

"What about you, James?"

"Nope."

"Anybody?"

He paced from one side of the room to the other.

"Okay. It's obvious you haven't read it. Why not?"

"It's too hard," said Melissa, a tall, dark girl sitting on the front row.

She'd come to the sixth-form from Westholme, the private girls' school in Blackburn with an array of splendid GCSEs and was hailed as highly intelligent.

"Did you give it a go?"

"Yes."

"How far did you get?"

"A paragraph."

"Maybe you should have persevered."

She lowered her eyes, pressed her lips together and bridled as if he'd suggested she dance naked on the desk.

"What about you, Paul. How much did you manage?"

"First line."

The rest of them smirked, wriggled and shuffled. Andy nodded as he paced.

"Okay. I get the picture. This is what we'll do. For next Monday, Paul you can read page one, Melissa page two, Joanna page three… and each of you will explain to the class what you've read. Does that sound reasonable?"

They sat silent and unmoved.

He'd completed twelve years. In the early days, once he got sixth-form classes, in spite of Don Crawley guarding them like a child its teddy bear, he would hand out copies of *Le Misanthrope* or *La Gloire de Mon Père* and tell the students they had three weeks to get to grips. Using an English translation was fine, but by the end of the three weeks he would expect them to know the plot, the characters and to have a rude idea of what the work was about. He knew that was no longer possible. If he'd asked these students to read a play by Molière, they would have accused him of abuse.

This, though, was something different.

His expectation became that they would fail to read the pages. They'd make the same case: it was too hard. He'd encountered the objection in his *General Studies* classes when he'd handed out news-paper articles a thousand words long and students had protested that there were "too many words". The course book he was required to use for A Level, *Nous les Français*, was bitty and undemanding. Previously he'd used *Horizons*, which had good, long pieces the students had to work over. Now everything had to be short, attention-span demolishing. It seemed that expecting students to deal with text, with writing, with language, without the titillation of childish images, was too much for their poor, little brains.

He was perfectly aware that the culture was becoming more visual, that language was being elbowed out and the requirement to read hard and long becoming outdated; but something else was going on. As he turned it over in his head again and again before the next class, the answer came to him: OFSTED.

Its creation had put at the heart of the educational culture the notion that the profession was riddled with incompetence, but more importantly, that pupils and students were customers. It wasn't only his lower-sixth class which was behaving as if they were in *McDonald's*. All his classes were beginning to exhibit the same combination of I-know-my-rights, teach-me-if-you-can, I'm-not-doing-that-it's-boring recalcitrance and celebration of ignorance. When one of his Year Nine pupils had pushed the textbook away like rotten meat saying: "French is boring," Andy had responded:

"Listen, when you've asked 'Do you want fries with that?' for the five hundredth time in a day, you'll understand what boring is."

The boy, relishing his dismissal of learning had met his gaze and said:

"I'd rather work in McDonald's than be a French teacher."

Andy tried to tell himself it was the comment of a callow boy, He'd grow up. It wasn't to be taken too seriously; but there was a spreading sense of dread beneath his rationalization. The boy really did believe the culture represented by McDonald's was preferable to that of school. Pupils were expecting to ask for certificates like they asked for a *Happy Meal*. They were hatching the lunatic idea that they had a right to good grades just as they had a right to Big Mac and chips if they had the grubby coins in their wet palms; and behind them were their parents.

It was OFSTED which had turned the culture. Previously, parents had accepted the school's regime. Now they challenged it at every opportunity.Teachers were game. The season had begun. Every parent with a grudge, every know-nothing who wanted to challenge the skill and knowledge of professionals, reached for their shotgun.

When Andy asked his students to summarize their pages, they responded as he'd expected: they hadn't read them. It was too hard.

"Okay," he said. "With all due respect, you've signed up for this. This is A Level French. You are required to read these stories. How do you suggest we do it, if you're not prepared to make an effort?"

"You should translate them," declared Melissa.

"Sorry?"

"You're the teacher. It's your job. You can't expect us to do that. You should do it."

"But I've pointed you in the direction of the English translations. It's perfectly all right for you to use them. Surely with the translation beside you, you can manage to make sense of a page each."

"Why should we get the translations?" said Melissa, who seemed to have appointed herself spokesperson.

"Sorry?"

"Why should we do it? It's your job. You should do it."

"I can't learn for you," he said.

He paused, leant on his desk and surveyed them. Their opposition was palpable.

"So what you'd like me to do is translate this hundred and sixty page book, in class, line by line."

"Yes," said Melissa.

The rest nodded.

He was about to put his case: it would be as boring as counting grains of sand in the desert. The better way was to move to the discussion of the stories as quickly as possible, because that's where all the interesting questions of character and moral dilemmas would arise. It was a waste of time to use the lessons to translate. In any case, the work had been done. Some of the existing translations weren't good, but that was no reason to throw yourself into a patch of nettles; but he realised he was facing something irrational. There was no blame to be heaped on the students: they were responding to what the culture was telling them, mediated by their parents. They'd accepted the falsehood that learning is no different from buying a washing machine or fish and chips. It's a product. A commodity. Their parents paid their taxes. The school was required to hand over the education. The ideology, originated by the government and cast into the waterfall of education officers, advisors, headteachers until it doused the poor teacher in the classroom in freezing water, destroyed the notion of education as a relationship. It was a transaction. The closer it came to being a cash transaction the better. These students now felt themselves entitled. The idea of being challenged, of education existing in the space between teacher and learner was dead. They wanted to be served. It wasn't spoon-feeding. They wanted the bottle in their mouths. They wanted to do no more than suck.

He sat down, opened the book and began translating.

Week upon week he did the same. His only joy was in his expertise. He could work at the renderings and make them more vigorous than some of the limp translations he'd looked at; but it was an utterly stupid use of his and their time. The students diligently copied his version into their French text in pencil. The first story complete, he sent them away with a question about its characters. They came back having done nothing. It was too hard. He should tell them. So he told them, though it disgusted him.

What was under way was a thoroughgoing corruption of education. It was deliberate and malicious. Major was one of those Tories who peddled the lie of the wilful destruction of the grammar schools by Harold Wilson; that it had done more harm to Britain than the Luft-waffe; that comprehensive education was a rank failure; that most teachers were closet Marxists pushing *trendy* pedagogical theories; that the Black Papers were unsullied truth and the existence of schools which admitted all pupils, regardless of background or puta-tive ability, a social and moral catastrophe.

The truth was the first comprehensive was opened in Anglesey, hard-ly a breeding-ground of Trotskyists; the Grammar/Secondary system couldn't endure because middle-class parents wouldn't wear it: they paid their taxes and their rates and saw their children sent to over-crowded, under-funded schools with a narrow curriculum where five O-levels were as difficult to reach as Andromeda. They were using their votes to get justice for their kids. The system, never intended by Rab Butler to set up a snobbish opposition between Grammars and Secondaries, had descended into a form of apartheid. The middle-classes paid a fortune for private tuition to get their progeny through the 11-plus; were horrified at the idea of their precious social climb-ers having to be schooled alongside the children of bus drivers or school cleaners; paid for places in private schools if they didn't make it; but the ones who couldn't afford to saw clearly they were being let down. They were convinced by the comprehensive system. It gave everyone a chance. It was better than their offspring being branded failures at eleven.

Major, in his twisted view, his support for a system founded on the delusions that people are born with a chunk of IQ which is unamena-ble to education; that the size of the chunk can be reliably measured; that those with a big chunk should be sent to well-funded schools with highly qualified teachers and a broad curriculum while those with a lesser should be consigned to poorly-funded schools to be taught in corridors and denied Chemistry if they study French, be-cause to try to educate the congenitally stupid was a waste of money, was willing to drive a diseased commercial principle through the arteries of the system as an act of petulant revenge against his political rivals.

The Tories were commercialising education and the result would be Kafkaesque. It was bound to be, because it was founded on fundamental falsehoods. Andy heard Woodhead on the radio reiterating his egregious claim that fifteen thousand teachers should be sacked. The assault on teachers was the first battle in the war to destroy the comprehensive system. The clue to Woodhead was simple: he had narrowly missed being sacked for inappropriate relations with a pupil. He had had to beg for his job. Like all guilty people he was accusing others of his fault. It was the classic strategy of fascism and Woodhead was distinctly fascistic.

What was coming was control. The excuse would be doing the best for the children. Too many were failing. The system must be improved. Motherhood and apple pie are always the pretexts for viciousness and destruction. Andy could see his days as an autonomous professional were doomed. There would be clipboard box-tickers in his classroom. He would be reduced to the level of an operative. Everything would be controlled from the centre and any deviance from orthodoxy punished. In such a system, he would be Gregor Samsa.

Major was a thoroughly detestable man. Anyone who believed in the deluded, corrupt dogma of Cyril Burt, who thought measuring children at eleven through tests a six-year-old could see were as reliable as a baby's bowels, labelling eighty percent of them failures and treating them as such, was no better than a fascist. You might as well send children to different schools on the basis of eye-colour, hair-colour or the size of their feet. In essence it was no different from claiming people with black skins are inferior.

What stunned Andy was his colleagues' compliance. The introduction of the National Curriculum had seemed to him an obvious wrenching of independence from the classroom teacher.

"It's Napoleonic," he said to Luke Mallory, the genial Head of Physics in the staffroom at morning break.

"It's just an attempt to raise standards," said the scientist.

"That's what they have to pass it off as, Luke. They can't say what they're about is grabbing power, that they want to prevent us teaching in ways we've worked out for ourselves because they're lost in a paranoid fantasy of schools populated by kaftan-sporting, dope-smoking refugees from Katmandu with copies of Ivan Illich in their pockets. They have to find some reasonable-seeming excuse for their bid for control."

"Well, they're the government. They have the right to control."

"In a democracy? They're supposed to be implementing the will of the people. Where's the clamour for teaching to be reduced to a pro-duction-line function?"

"We have to do it, anyway. We can't say no."

"Why not?"

"We have contracts. We have to do what the employer asks."

"Really? If they asked us to pin yellow stars on Jewish kids, would you do it?"

"That's an exaggeration."

"It's hyperbole, but it makes the point. We're employees not slaves. They buy your work not your mind. You know there's no need for a National Curriculum."

"I wouldn't introduce it, I agree. But it's not that bad. We have to give it a try."

"It's the first tug on the crowbar, Luke. Just wait and see. They'll rip the heart out of teaching and people will be running for the door."

"I don't think so."

Andy thought of Luke as one of the more liberal, amenable members of staff. He was a greasy-pole climber like almost everyone, but that could be taken for granted. People like himself who believed in flat-tening the hierarchies and running schools democratically were as rare as roses in December. He'd always thought the physicist willing to listen to alternative arguments and at least a little resilient to what was handed down.

That his colleagues offered no resistance and seemed barely aware of what was happening, assuming, it seemed to him, that authority must be benign and therefore the National Curriculum and OFSTED genu-inely products of a beneficent desire to help pupils, astonished him. They seemed to have little appreciation of the nature of power, tak-ing its smiling, public face for the truth of its character.

What added to his disillusion and increasing sense of the closing in of a malicious will to supervise, oversee, spy, check up on, measure, pigeon-hole, entrap, enclose, box in, browbeat, intimidate, diminish, overburden, frighten and humiliate, was that Don Crawley had retired at the end of the previous academic year and been replaced by a nobody-could-be-more-compliant-than-me young woman who saw herself as an educational whizz-kid and *would* have pinned yellow stars on Jews if the Head had told her to and there was promotion in it.

He applied for the post. When Cooper had asked him to take over General Studies a few years before, he'd said:

"Of course, I don't expect you to stick with it till the end of your career. I appreciate you may want to relinquish the burden in a few years ,and in any case, you'll probably have responsibility for French by then."

What could that have meant other than that Cooper was intending to offer him Head of French when Don retired? Yet he advertised the post nationally. Andy suspected at once. He wondered if he shouldn't apply. That might be better than being rejected. What stopped him was being a father of two young girls. Christine was working as an articled clerk, still trying to find a place on the Law Society finals course. Her employer took advantage and paid her the minimum. His salary kept the family afloat. Had he been single, or childless, he would have listened to his suspicions and avoided the chance of humiliation.

He thought it through again and again. It was customary for internal candidates to be given an interview. He was confident he could handle himself well. He anticipated the negatives: he'd been teaching twelve years, why was this his first application for departmental promotion? Why hadn't he pushed for more responsibility? He knew he could deal with those.

He completed the form and wrote his covering letter. What should he do about referees? It was the protocol that your Head gave you a reference. The other obvious source was Don Crawley. He decided to leave the spaces blank.

On the Friday morning before the interviews the following Tuesday, he took a small, manilla envelope from his pigeon-hole, unfolded the single white sheet and read:

Dear Andrew,

I'm afraid I'm unable to offer you an interview for the French post. The other candidates have more experience than you. I know you will be disappointed but please don't feel slighted.

Merrick Cooper.

He was shocked beyond expectation. He had a Year 10 class to teach first thing. He told them to get on with some homework or amuse themselves. He had something to attend to. He sat in the store room. His heart beat with anger and humiliation. He cursed himself for having applied. He'd made himself vulnerable. His instinct was to leave. He could walk downstairs, collect his bag, take what belonged to him from his locker, get in his car and drive away never to return. That was the only commensurate response. Yet he had two kids and a mortgage, not to mention Christine's wayward behaviour with credit cards.

He thought back to his inheritance. Twenty-four thousand. They'd moved to a bigger, better house with a garden in Ashton, paid the kids' nursery fees, bought a second-hand *Nissan*, had a holiday in Brittany, and they still needed what remained to get by month by month. Fuck it. He should have used the money to work for himself. He was trapped. His dad had given him a way out. A small gap in the fence. He'd made the wrong choice. He was screwed.

What was Cooper's motivation? Andy knew he was panicking about the coming regime: OFSTED wasn't going to be complaisant to his insouciant attitude to his job. No doubt he thought Andy a risk. No doubt he needed a puppy dog which would sit at the inspectors' command. Was that the whole of it, or did he have an active animus? It was impossible to know. The essence of power was opacity.

He contacted the NUT. They were reluctant to intervene: appointments and promotions were sacrosanct. He thought the response pusillanimous. He paid his subs. He'd been school rep for twelve years. All he was asking was for the union to put on a bit of pressure. Cooper had a duty of care. He was supposed to look after his staff's development. Andy pestered the local and regional officials. They sympathised; yes, Heads were often unfair; yes, it looked as though he'd been badly treated; but they did nothing.

He was tempted to throw away his card and save his money. Christine commented that if he'd paid a retainer to an employment lawyer he'd have some help.

The following Wednesday, Dave Dover caught up with him on the corridor.

"Are you free?"

"Yeah."

"Come on."

They ducked into the Committee Room. Dover had been part of the panel which chose the candidates for interview.

"He's erratic," he said, "you never know which way he's going to jump."

Andy was surprised at how upset he felt. It was good of Dave to reassure him. He obviously thought he might take it very badly and do something silly. The only silly thing Andy would have contemplated was walking out. He'd let himself be trapped and undermined. Cooper had used his power in a raw and self-defensive way he hadn't expected.

"What reasons did he give?"

"None, to speak of. He's terrified of OFSTED. He wants everything to look obedient."

"I hear Colin Pennington is being interviewed."

"Yes."

"He's never taught A Level."

Dover gave a cynical little laugh.

"That's politics. He has no chance, but Cooper needs to keep sweet with the Head of his school."

"Why?"

"Oh, they've been in dispute. Something to do with finance. Cooper thinks he's got something on him."

"Really?"

Dover nodded and smiled.

"I believe the woman they've appointed hasn't taught A Level either."

"That's right."

Andy shook his head.

"How can he get away with that?"

"Who's going to stop him? He rules by divine right."

"Anyway," said Andy, "I'll let Christine earn the money. Her prospects are much better than mine."

As soon as the words were out, he realised how empty they were; how he was battling upwards. He was forty-one. There would be no further opportunity here. If he applied for a promotion elsewhere, Cooper was sure to include in the reference that he'd turned him down. He had nineteen years to retirement. Cooper, who liked to pose as the easy-going, I-let-my-staff-get-on-with-it liberal, had revealed his claws. If his own interests were threatened, he would destroy whoever he needed to.

One of the things Andy gleaned from his talk with Dover was that the shortlisting meeting took place on the Thursday. A doubt appeared in his mind. He checked Cooper's note. It bore Wednesday's date. Then he overheard a conversation between Cuthbert Norris, the nearing-retirement History teacher whose younger wife who taught French in a Catholic school in Wigan had been interviewed, and Tim Heath.

"I went to see the Head," Cuthbert said, " and told him she only had a B.ed. Would that stand in her way, I asked him."

"I see," said Heath, casting a glance Andy's way.

So Chris Pennington, who Andy had met on various courses, had been interviewed though he wasn't a serious candidate; Hilda Murphy had been appointed though she'd never taught an A Level lesson; and Cuthbert Norris had canvassed for his wife. The process could have been organised by the Mafia.

It went through Andy's head that if he took what he knew to the Chief Education Officer, the appointment would be annulled. Canvassing was strictly forbidden. Nor were Heads at liberty to offer interviews as part of their machinations regarding local jockeying for influence. For sure he could force a re-advertisement, but the cost would be real rancour. He knew the staff wouldn't be on his side. They closed ranks if the institution was challenged. He would be utterly alone. He might secure the promotion. Cooper might be disciplined, but he would come to school every day and face the inspissated hostility of his colleagues.

When he challenged Cooper about the date on his note, he squirmed, smiled and said he'd had a long day, he was tired, it was a simple mistake. Maybe he was telling the truth. He asked why he'd been denied an interview. Cooper pointed out he hadn't indicated his referees on the application form.

Andy snorted.

"But you're one of them, Don Crawley is the other. It would be absurd for me to put your name on the form wouldn't it?"

Cooper's clinching argument, enunciated in his best public-school tones was:

"You have neither been given nor have you assumed responsibility."

"That's not true, I've had responsibility for General Studies for two years."

"Yes, Dave Dover speaks very highly of your work in that regard."

"That doesn't make sense."

Cooper leant forward over his polished desk and narrowed his eyes in the ridiculous way he did when he intended to look inscrutable.

"That's pastoral responsibility, this is departmental."

The vacuous, excuse-making dishonesty of the formulation disgusted Andy to silence. What was the point in talking to a man who was willing to be so mendacious? There was no sense in conversation with power, for conversation implies equality. Power must deny conversation. It must replace it by diktat, sermons, diatribes, rants, speeches, briefings, press conferences, all the plethora of means by which messages can be delivered but not responded to. Power could almost be defined as the annulment of conversation.

Andy explored the possibility of a grievance, but the local NUT official emphasised the difficulty and the bad feeling it would engender. Christine rolled her lawyer's eyes.

"You should do it," she insisted. "You need a remedy."

What was for the best? One thing Andy knew: his resolve to resign ten years earlier should have stayed firm. Not doing so was the worst decision of his life.

Cuthbert Norris was in the staff workroom. It was lunchtime and Andy, unusually, had stayed. One of his A Level students who was trying for Oxbridge had handed him an essay on Flaubert at registration and as he was teaching her last thing in the afternoon, he decided to get it marked. Normally, he left the site at lunchtime. He'd got into the habit during the dispute in the early eighties. Union members were asked to withdraw goodwill and as lunchtime wasn't paid time, activities and duties were best avoided by not being around. He'd got into the habit of driving into town and having a coffee and a squint at *The Guardian* in *Brucciani's*. It occurred to him one day, when he was free after morning break, that if he left school at the start of period three, he didn't have to be back in his classroom for two hours. That was easily long enough for a leisurely absence during the middle of the day. He found it wonderfully therapeutic. It broke the day up beautifully. On a morning when he was free after two periods, he checked the cover sheet eagerly. To be in his car at eleven thirty, ensconced at a table in the congenial café by quarter to twelve and not needing to set off till one fifteen, remined him of his time in France when schools and shops took a two hour break, the restaurants and streets filled up and the middle of the day seemed like a brief holiday.

The days when he could get out felt much shorter. Above all, he felt he was reclaiming his life, or at least a small portion of it. If he was free last thing in the afternoon, he did the same . It lifted his mood. If he was going to be stuck in the place for another nineteen years, he would reduce his working days to the minimum. He worked out that most weeks he could do what was needed in thirty-five hours. What was the sense in doing more? The ambitious flaunted their effort, signed up for every course, nestled close to advisers. They were shinning the greasy pole. He was stuck down a manhole whose cast-iron cover had closed over his head, sickened by the stench of shit.

He was sitting opposite Cuthbert who was laboriously working through one of the three sets of books on his desk. He was one of those teachers who marked too meticulously for his or the pupils' good. Andy marked selectively: if a class had done an exercise on the perfect tense, that's what he corrected. Other mistakes he ignored. He told them. That way he could mark fast and they got focus on what they were supposed to learn. Cuthbert treated marking almost as a penance. He might have been St Anthony, punishing himself lunchtime upon lunchtime filling books with red ink which would mostly be ignored. He might have been ordered by the priest:

"Father, I have sinned…"

"Five hail Marys and three sets of Year nine books, my son."

Mike Chambers was the same. The idea of being efficient in marking or preparation he thought a crime. Work must be a burden, an imposition, it must weigh, restrict, hamper, spavin, prevent joy, freedom and mischief. Andy lifted his head, as if he was thinking over what he had read, and examined Cuthbert. Yes, he and Chambers were brothers in their submission to whatever the employer imposed. Chambers had told Andy that as a child he'd been forced to sit with his books while he could hear other kids playing football in their gardens. On summer evenings he'd been sent to bed before the light began to fade and lay listening to the cries of the boys and girls who were allowed to play till eight.

Work for these men was a proof of obedience, a plea for worth; under no circumstances were they going to be seen dispatching it quickly, enjoying it and heading out of school carefree and in good spirits to enjoy their evenings or weekends. Their back must bend. They must be loaded like asses. Chambers would hold forth in the staff room:

"I was marking till midnight last night. Sixth-form essays. Eh? Eh? They take some marking. There are staff in this school who never take a book home. Eh ? I was at it all day yesterday. That's conscientiousness. Eh? Eh?"

Andy couldn't bear to hear him. He was such a sloppy bucket of self-pitying, self-aggrandizing blather. He was tempted to say:

"Sixth form essays? I can mark twenty an hour. If you've taught them well and set the right question, the marking is swift," but he knew the sycophant would probably go running to Head with tales of his negligence.

He felt sorry for Cuthbert. He had behaved badly. He had canvassed for his wife, sucked up to the Head in the hope of advantage; but if Andy reported it, he would be devastated. He would be disciplined. Teachers knew what was allowed. Andy wondered if he was being too soft. Cuthbert's action had helped secure his humiliation. Maybe he should be less like Hamlet and make oppression bitter; but did he really want to fill the region kites with this slave's offal? It was unpleasant to look at him, to think he had sat in the Head's study, obsequious, deferential, stooping in the hope of conquering. He could destroy him. He had the means. As he had the means to destroy Cooper. Measure for measure. Haste still pays haste. Like doth quit like. Yet, to have a giant's strength didn't mean you had to use it like a giant. Both Cuthbert and Cooper had demeaned themselves. He had just applied for a job and been turned down. There was no shame in his action, but much in theirs. Somewhere, in spite of their rationalisations, they must know it.

He resolved not to use what he knew. He could absorb what had happened. What does not destroy me makes me stronger. Yet at the same time he knew it would take much of his mental resources to cope with his broiling sense of injustice. And there was Hilda Murphy.

She'd applied for a job and got it. No blame lay with her. Andy was determined to get along with her; but she was quickly drawn into Chambers's orbit and lacking the ability to challenge anyone above her in the petty hierarchy, conformist, fearful of authority, obedient, fawning before the power that could lift her or her cast her down, she became his poodle, adopted his perspective and was duteous to his vices.

Cooper expected her to sit with him while he ate his lunch. She didn't dare refuse, though the sight of him stuffing his chicken salad sandwich into his mouth as he talked, bits of lettuce sticking to his chin and crumbs and damp morsels of half chewed meat flying from his lips and landing on the table, the floor or his colleagues almost made her vomit. Two minutes before the bell, he sent her to collect his register and she complied, as if she were a pupil, as if his power over her were absolute. He sat, spreading himself like a pasha, till she returned, dutifully handing him the black folder.

When he took over as Head of Department, Cooper instituted lunchtime meetings. They wouldn't have to stay at the end of the day. Would Andy agree? To be free of having to stay till five, Andy was willing, but at the first meeting which began five minutes after the bell, as they sat around the two pushed-together tables he held forth for fifty minutes about himself: he was going through a dark patch; not sleeping well; his irritable bowel syndrome had revived (Andy was tempted to throw in "I see your irritating bastard syndrome isn't much better either"); it was a big responsibility he'd assumed; he was tossing and turning all night thinking of this meeting; he would get through it but he depended on them; his team; are you with me, team? Not until two minutes before the end of the lunchbreak did he ask if anyone else had anything to add. They were so browbeaten by his domination they wanted to escape.

The department was now Chambers, Andy, Hilda and Maggie Brough, a part-time Germanist who filled in with a bit of lower years French. Andy and Maggie took the stairs together.

"Charming use of an hour," he said.

"Driving me mad."

"Yeah?"

" On my back before I put my bag on the floor in the morning."

"Oh, it's his bowels."

"He was in my front room for three hours on Saturday night."

"Uninvited?"

"More or less. He rang and said there was something urgent he had to tell me. Could he come round. I said okay. He arrived at eight and stayed till eleven."

"I bet your husband loved that."

"He would have thumped him if I hadn't stopped him."

"Not worth the trouble."

When the next lunchtime meeting arrived, Andy didn't turn up. Chambers came into his room as he class was queuing.

"Did you know there was meeting today?"

"I did."

"Why weren't you there?"

"I had other things to do."

"But you agreed."

"Yes, that's a voluntary agreement."

"I would have been very angry," said Chambers, pulling himself to his full height, "if one of the pupils had behaved like that."

Andy stared at him. Did he really think he could assimilate his status to that of the pupils? His dismay provided a more penetrating insight into Chambers's inner world than his customary recognition of his preposterous adherence to authority and his insistent need to bolster a flimsy sense of self. He tilted into madness. He might have been one of those poor souls who populated asylums in nineteenth century France declaring themselves Napoleon. His idea of his power exceeded the real limits. He was an employee. Any authority he had was granted by the school governors and the local authority. It was minimal and set within strict procedures. He had no right to suggest his colleagues and the pupils were on the same level. Yet his need for control tipped him beyond the acceptance of his actual, petty, rule-bound status into a fantasy of omnipotence.

His comment was so outrageous, there was no responding to it short of a colossal row.

"I've got to let my class in," said Andy.

The following Friday afternoon he was about to begin his last lesson when Chambers rushed in as if there were a fire or the four-minute warning had been sounded.

"Are you going to be one of the team?" he said, marching towards the teacher's desk.

"What?"

"You're being obstructionist and uncooperative."

"Can you get out of my classroom, please?"

"I'll have to report you to the Head if you don't start following instructions."

The pupils, delighted at the beginning of a bout between two teachers, had fallen silent and stood by their desks, their eyes wide, waiting for the first punch to be thrown.

"Do you imagine this is a professional way to behave?"

"Eh? I'm the Head of Department. Things have to be done my way."

"Can you get out of my room, please. Sit down, lads and get your books out. Come on," he clapped his hands, "sit down, let's get started."

Over the weekend he expected to calm down, but on Monday morning he was still too furious to contemplate what he might do if

206

Chambers came at him again. If he broke the bounds of professional restraint, he could be disciplined or sacked. What were the chances Chambers would pull back? He needed to set some space between them, to send the man a message which would force him to click out of his fantasy of absolute power. He decided to take the day off, but reflecting on going back the next day he decided he needed some support.

"I'm going to the doctor," he said to Christine. "I'm going to tell her the stress is too much. If I can get myself signed off for a week, that might make the idiot think."

"Good idea."

The G.P., a smiling, Indian woman listened to his tale nodding rhythmically.

"Oh dear," she said "all too common a story."

"Yeah."

"You wouldn't believe how many teachers come to me complaining of stress and nine times out of ten it's because of bullying management."

She gave him a note for a fortnight. He had no intention of taking two weeks off. There was nothing wrong with him. He simply needed to be away from Chambers and to make him think. This was a better way of doing it than getting into a row and risking saying something that would remove his livelihood. He made contact with the union again to explore the chance of a grievance; but the response was the same: a bitter, difficult business; better to try to smooth things over. The odficer was full of sympathy, but devoid of action. Smooth things over? That was like asking the Palestinians to smooth things over with the Zionists. Power. It was ugly and it drove people mad. Acton was nearly right. Power does corrupt but more importantly it induces insanity, if insanity is remoteness from reality.

Andy spent a pleasant week reading and fettling. On the Wednesday, his kids in nursery, he got out his bike and cycled to Dunsop Bridge, sat in the *Hark to Bounty* for an hour and was home for two. Without employment, life was remarkably pleasant.

On Saturday lunchtime he and Christine arrived unannounced at her mother's. The children were at a birthday party nearby so Christine had suggested they beguile the hours to their collection there. Andy would rather have gone to café or for a walk but it was a short time and, as ever, Christine was keen to be near her mother. She was in her eternal kitchen preparing eggs, bacon, sausages, grilled tomatoes, fried bread, fried mushrooms, the place full of the odour of fat and cooking meat which Andy found slightly nauseating. It was a different odour from Sunday lunch which was usually a thick meld of chicken fat, lamb or beef with the almost school dinner background of boiled cabbage. Sunday lunch was the enforced routine. They were invited every week, which was rather like being invited to tea with Stalin. Theresa cooked and her family must assemble. The pale and vague Edward emerged from his room where he seemed to spend long hours playing computer games. Andy who had viewed the Sinclair ZX80 with disdain and thought the ridiculous green screen ping-pong games he'd seen, entertainment for monkeys of below average intelligence, was mystified and appalled by the long hours of isolation the boy spent in his crypt.

He would try to engage him in conversation but he had a curious inability to engage with objective reality; it was hard to tempt him onto some broad ground where conversation could flow.

Sometimes, Thomas would be there, up from Oxford where he was trying to make his way as a technical illustrator, and on occasion Sam, the brother closest in age to Christine who worked as a printer in Barnoldswick where he lived with his half West-Indian, half Italian wife, Astrid. Andy wondered how Billy adjusted his admiration for Mussolini to having a black daughter-in-law. Maybe Sam being his stepson he was able, mentally, to establish a distance between Astrid and the inner world of his rank, ignorant prejudice.

The kitchen was on the side of the bungalow. Directly opposite was Theresa and Billy's bedroom with its neighbouring, spacious *en suite*. The hallway was topped by a high ceiling. To the left were the dark, wooden storm doors and beyond them the little, oblong, tiled porch and the PVC outer door Theresa had insisted on, to blend in with the neighbours. To the right, was a matching pair of doors leading to the big lounge which ran from one side of the building to the other and whose ceiling was an acute pitch of attractive, polished timber. Beyond were two more bedrooms and the bathroom.

"How de do?" said Theresa, wiping her hands on a tea towel.

Christine sat at the oval, polished table.

"Do you want a cup of tea?" said her mother.

"Yes, I'll have one."

"Do you want one, Andy?"

"That'd be lovely. I'll just nip to the bathroom."

"All right. Billy and Olive are in the lounge."

Olive was an old workmate of Theresa, one of the few visitors to the house. It struck Andy that as well as hardly anyone coming to the house, Billy never went out alone. He had no independent social life. No friends. Nor did people come to visit him, except family. It was oddly isolated. Theresa seemed to sink into a queer self-absorption in her kitchen, as if the rest of the world didn't exist. Cooking became, almost, a substitute for life. A ritual. He wondered if it was derived from Catholicism, if the odours of the kitchen were reminiscent of burning incense and the closing off a replication of the dark secrets of the confessional and the virgin's denial of reality.

He went through to the lounge. It was empty. He hesitated a moment, opened the door onto the little hallway leading to the bathroom and heard at once a hurried noise from the bedroom to his right. The door was slightly ajar and through it he glimpsed Olive pulling on her skirt. He paused. She turned to the bed. He could see no more than a section of the footboard. She bent and spoke in a whisper. He heard Billy's curt reply:

"Shut the door."

She turned to come towards him, he nipped quickly into the bath-room. When he emerged, Olive was sitting prim in an armchair, as if butter wouldn't melt up her arse while Billy was on the sofa, his glasses on his nose, a pen in his hand and a crossword puzzle maga-zine on his knee.

"Oh, hello," said Andy, "Christine's mum said you were here. I must have missed you."

"Yes," said Olive looking at him through her spectacles with her typ-ical what-a-good-girl-am-I smile on her lipstick-pink mouth, "we just nipped out to have a look at the garden."

"I see. What's growing in the greenhouse?"

"Mmmm?" she said.

"Tomatoes," said Billy. "Not much else."

"Of course. Well, I think there's a brew waiting for me."

Theresa served up the great plates of late breakfast. Billy, his girth pressed against the lip of the table, doused his food in H.P. , grabbed slice upon slice of white, buttered bread and crammed his capacious gob with the hot, greasy fare. Olive tried to appear ladylike, as if she were auditioning for a part in the school production of *Sense and Sensibility*. She cut tiny nibbles of bacon or sausage, dabbed her mouth on the napkin after every prissy forkful and laid her knife and fork on the table as she chewed, as if she were to be given marks for etiquette.

Andy, sipping his tea as he leaned against the door jamb was tempted to say:

"Yes, sex always give me an appetite too, mate. But not you, eh, Olive?"

Theresa sat between her husband and her best friend as if she belonged absolutely, as if here her well-being were guaranteed. Looking at her, Andy was moved to pity, depression and laughter. Her naivety was all-embracing. She was married to a greedy bigot who had tried to seduce her daughter when she was no more than twelve and was now shoving his wayward dick in a woman who posed as her pal while she turned bacon in the frying pan, watched sausages under the grill, cracked eggs into lard in the belief that love and admiration would attend her efforts. It was pitiful.

The old woman, who had been napping in her room, appeared, smiling in her odd, childish, slightly ingratiating way. Theresa poured her a cup of tea.

"Sit down here, mum."

Nanna perched on a stool beside Olive who stretched her made-up face into a queer grimace that was the simulacrum of a smile, as if the old woman were a congenital idiot to be pitied and condescended to.

"What's the matter with, Andy?" said the matriarch. "He looks miserable."

She turned to view him.

"Is it bein' so cheery as keeps you goin'?" she said.

It was one of her small armoury of intrusive remarks, poisoned little barbs she fired off at will, retreating quickly behind her cultivated demeanour of pseudo-innocence, as if oblivious to the wounds she inflicted. Andy wasn't going to deploy his irony or sarcasm against an old, uneducated woman in her own house. He clicked from his reverie and went to the sink to rinse his cup. In an instant she was next to him. She pushed her little weight against him, grabbed the mug from his hand and swung the curved , chrome snout towards her. He stood for a moment, dismayed at her aggressive rudeness, resisting her feeble effort to shoulder him aside; but realising she wasn't going to desist, went back to his station by the door.

The silly, unpleasant incident remined him of her empty boast about her skill as a weaver. Clearly, she had a proprietary relationship to the sink. It was her territory. She must control the washing-up. He'd seen Billy do it after Sunday lunch, but his mother-in-law was always hovering. How odd that the idea of him rinsing his cup under the tap could drive her to such torment she had to get up from her cup of tea and try to shove him aside. What a collapsing sense of self she must harbour for it to need to be propped by being the dictator of the washing-up. Where did it come from, this sense of a perished inner life? He didn't know enough about her to start to piece it together, but his mind was drawn to her fundamentalist Catholicism and vacuous admiration of the royals. The Queen and the Pope were the powers onto which she projected her own potency and from which she drew some meagre sustenance for her starved selfhood.

The mug washed, wiped and shelved, she took her place again. Andy surveyed the table: a paedophile fascist; a perfidious, underhand seducer of her friend's husband who took communion every Sunday; a naïve wife who thought her blustering spouse whose risible bravado was the reverse side of his childish inability to suffer frustration, a fine, strong, bold man; and an octogenarian tyrant of the kitchen taps. Christine sat amongst them as if they were the average family of the year. What a strange family he'd married into. All families were strange. It was a strange institution; passing itself off as the haven of love and security but harbouring abuse, violence, control and struggles for power that put eighteenth century Europe in the shade.

The horrible thought occurred to him that his own family might turn out corrupt or blighted by alienation and conflict; but his children were yet unblemished affectionate little girls and he couldn't believe it.

"Come on," he said. "Time to collect the girls."

That morning he'd had an acceptance from a little magazine. He'd sent them nine poems, in the usual mood of near-despair, wondering if he was a fool to waste the postage; but surprisingly all nine had been accepted. It was a typical, back-bedroom, stapled-spine, five-hundred-print-run affair called *Herbert Truzinski's Back*, edited out of Halifax by the lugubrious poet Kevin Healey, but it had featured poems by Armitage before he became the boy wonder and went flying round the poetic firmament in his super-poet suit, and published work by ambitious folk who were nibbling at the edges of literary fame like Lavinia Greenlaw or Maura Dooley.

It was his first acceptance since his three poems appeared in the university magazine more than twenty years earlier. It was hard to suppress expectation. If Healey liked his work, maybe he could publish a dozen poems or so a year in his mag; and that might give him enough purchase to sneak in to other nobody-takes-any-notice-of-this publications. Perhaps he'd then be able to persuade some subsidised publisher to do a pamphlet. Maybe Paul Flintoff who had brought out a book of thirty poems by Will Joiner called *Love Song of The Yorkshire Moors*. There was a slim chance of moving on to a full collection, though the big publishers were out of the question. They were looking for products not poets.

The *Black Horse Poets* had folded some years earlier. Tom Lemon had got a promotion and moved to Kent. Andy was sorry. He could have been an enduring friend and he was a pleasant character who kept the mood in the group away from self-indulgence. Mike Flowers was still around and had managed a Gregory Award, but Paul McCaffrey had gone back to his native Liverpool and Claire Southworth given up on the dispiriting round of typing up, sending out, getting rejected, typing up, sending out, getting rejected again. Andy had fallen out with Will Joiner.

He stayed in touch with him as the group collapsed. Will moved into a council flat in a high-rise in Preston with his wife Janet, a small, slender, charming woman who worked as a hairdresser while Will sat at home, smoking joints, drinking beer and writing poems he hoped would make him rich and famous. One Saturday evening, when he was still single, Andy went to eat with them. Will was well stoked with dope and booze when he arrived at seven and by the time he was ready to leave at eleven was almost incapable of lifting his glass to his lips or rolling the next spliff.

"I'll give you a lift," he said, pushing himself up from the tattered armchair.

"No, no," said Andy. "It's a mile. I can walk it in ten minutes."

But Will insisted.

"Listen," said Andy as they went down the cold, concrete steps, "you get stopped you'll lose your licence. I can walk. I like to walk."

"Hey, man. Why walk when you can ride?"

He had a blue *Robin Reliant*. The bodywork was heavily patched, great streaks of white, sanded filler scarring the dirty paint. The passenger seat was torn and losing its stuffing. Will turned the key. The engine strained like an old man with clogged arteries on a hill. He tried again.

"I'll walk, Will."

"No, man. She'll start. She's just a bit cold. She's like a woman. Needs warming up,man," and he laughed in that knowing, salacious way he had, as if nothing was ever remote from sex and seduction.

When he finally got the engine chugging, its rhythm was uneven and the little vehicle rocked as the timing misfired. Will spun out of the car park and taking the roundabout in front of the polytechnic, carouseled, ending up on the pavement facing the way he'd come.

"Wow man, that was something else," he said.

"Good job there were no pedestrians."

"Always look on the positive side, man."

It was queer how Will's brain seemed to be frozen in optimism, like a body trapped by molten lava or a statue carved in marble. He had just lost control of his unstable three-wheeler, it had mounted the pavement, Andy's mind had gone blank for a few seconds; they had come to a standstill a yard from the wall of the *Lamb and Packet*. The nose of the car could have been buried in it. If some unwary, late-night drunk, staggering home to his unhappy house with seven pints of *Matthew Brown* swilling around his stomach had been lurching round the corner, he might have had his bowels turned to mincemeat. Yet, to Will, it was fun. There was no room in his mind for self-criticism or regret. He was as drunk as a one-night-in-six-months-onshore sailor and as stoned as rock guitarist on tour, yet he exhibited not the least sign of remorse of responsibility.

The remainder of the journey was a swerving, near-miss, bouncing, jolting game of chance with death or serious injury.

It was some weeks later, when Andy was away for the weekend cycling with a group of pupils in the Lake District, that Will asked if he could stay in his house: things were going badly with Janet; she was talking about moving out to live at her brother's. Having spent an evening in their flat, Andy felt it would churlish to refuse. He would be back at about four on Sunday; could Will be gone by then?; he'd be tired and would need a shower, to cook and get things ready for Monday morning. That would be fine. Will needed a bed for Friday and Saturday. He'd be gone well before four on Sunday. Andy granted him use of the second bedroom in which there was a single bed.

When he arrived home, drenched, cold, hungry and exhausted, he heard at once the unmistakable sounds of love-making. He stowed his bike under the stairs, the yard being too insecure and stood at the bottom of his steep stairs. The unchained little gasps of the woman's pleasure filled the stairwell and the rhythmic thumping of the bed banged like a call-to-arms drum.

"Will," he shouted. "Will. I'm back. Time to go."

The activity stopped.

"Okay, Andy. Be with you in a minute, man."

"Yeah. Come on, Will. I've just cycled home. I'm drenched. I need to get in the bath."

"Sure, man. Coming down in no time."

The sudden gasps and screams restarted. Which bed were they in? Andy went quietly half way up his stairs. His bedroom. The double bed. He was tempted to walk in. Yet the woman couldn't be blamed. It would be wrong to embarrass her, if it was possible to embarrass a woman he'd never met who was filling his house with the sound of her illicit pleasure at four on a Sunday afternoon.

He went down to the kitchen, took the little towel which hung on the back of the door and dried his hair, put some water in the kettle and a slice of bread under the grill. When he'd eaten his toast and drunk his tea, they were still at it. She was no sprinter. She was a girl for marathons. He went to the stairs again:

"Will. Come on, time for you to go now."

There was no reply. At length the sexual noise subsided. He heard movement. He was chilled and thought he was going to have to get the fire going, a rigmarole of lighters, kindle, and the long wait for the smokeless fuel to start glowing he hated. Someone was running water in the bathroom. He called up:

"Hey, I need to get under the shower."

"Yeah, man."

It was twenty minutes before Will appeared, smiling, shaking his wet lengths of black hair, a spliff in his fingers.

"Whoo," he said. "How was your weekend, man?"

"It was okay. Okay. Where's your friend?"

"She's just having a soak."

Andy was staggered. He stared at will for a second.

"Can you tell her to get out of the bathroom now, Will? I need a shower."

"Hey, cool it, man. The lady's just freshening up."

"What's her name?"

"Lucy. Lucy in the sky with diamonds," and he laughed that gruff, inward, self-indulgent laugh which Andy had once thought fairly appealing but now found disgusting.

He went to the stairs.

"Lucy?"

"Yes?"

"Hello. I'm Andy. This is my house. I need the bathroom. Can you get out of there now, please?"

"Back off, man," said Will. "Give the girl some space."

"Were you in the double bed?"

"Yeah. Great bed."

"You were supposed to use the small bedroom."

"Can't ask the lady to sleep in a single bed, man."

Andy made himself another slice.

"You got any cheese?" said Will searching the fridge.

"Oh, excuse me," said Andy, "haven't had the time to do the shopping today."

"That's okay, man," said Will, apparently null to the sarcasm.

When he heard the bath draining, Andy went up. He was about to dodge into the second bedroom to take off his clothes and find a towel, when the girl emerged, naked. She was about eighteen, small and white skinned, with a jungle of dark hair, small, tight breasts and a thick pubic triangle.

"Hi," she said, smiling at him as she rubbed her head with one of his hand towels. "I was looking for a bath sheet. This was all I could find."

She cocked her head to the left, leaned against the door frame, and balancing her lower leg on her big toe, swung her right knee outwards as she looked into his eyes.

"My apologies," he said as he went into the smaller room and closed the door behind him.

He nipped into the bathroom and locked the door. Stood under the hot shower and determined to stay there until they left. After half an hour, Will shouted:

"Hey, we're going to find some food man. Could you lend us a fiver?"

"No," Andy called, turning off the water, "I haven't got a penny in the house."

Yet it wasn't this which caused the permanent breach but an evening when John Royce had invited people for a curry, Will got wind of it and turned up. John, as ever, laid out the food and plates in his little kitchen. The guests helped themselves before going to sit in his pleasant back or front rooms whose walls bore paintings and framed posters and where the shelves of books and records gave off the atmosphere of unpretentious cultural interests.

Towards the end of the evening, Andy found himself in the back room with John, Will and a woman he'd never met and whose name he hadn't gleaned. Will had commandeered the stereo and was playing a David Bowie album someone had brought along. John Royce was a jazz fan who could listen to serious music, but had no taste for rock or pop. Andy disliked Bowie. The music was ordinary and the rest was flummery.

"Wow, man," said Will, stroking his long hair away from his face and drawing on the inevitable joint, "what a genius."

It was the kind of remark Andy usually ignored. People comparing *The Beatles* to Mozart. It was as daft as comparing Max Bygraves to Borodin. Why not accept *The Beatles* for what they were? Half-way competent musicians with a talent for easy melody who put together factitious songs to make money. They weren't serious artists and to think of them in that way was daft. He had the same view of Bowie. You couldn't put him in the same category as Bach or Shostakovich, and why bother? They were real artists, he was an entertainer. The attempt to insinuate entertainment into art infuriated him, but it was so prevalent in the culture resisting it was like trying to breath under water. But it was late, he was tired and Will's ludicrously exaggerated assessment of the singer stirred his sarcasm.

"I think Bach's reputation is secure," he said.

"What, man?"

"I don't think Mr Bowie is about to dislodge Bach as the great genius of western music."

"Hey, millions of people love Bowie, man. He's much more popular than Bach."

"Hitler was popular. Popularity is no test of value."

"Hitler? What're you talking about man?"

"Bowie is popular but of little value. He's an entertainer like Lulu or Alma Cogan. That he has pretentions to being an artist makes no difference. He isn't Boulez or Stravinsky and never will be. He's interested in fame and money not truth."

"You're crazy, man," said Will.

He leaned forward in his chair. His expression had changed from the usual beatific, life-is-beautiful, hey-man-pass-the-joint, what-a-wonderful-person-I-am inanity to a grim seriousness that threatened violence.

"No," said Andy, "it's the culture that's insane. It refuses to accept proper boundaries. Bach worked out equal temperament, Bowie writes three chord ditties. There's no comparison."

"You saying millions of people are wrong, man?"

"Of course I am. Millions of people are wrong about most things."

"You're dangerous, man."

Will was looking so ready for a fight Andy got up and thanked John. He laid his hand on his shoulder.

"Great food. Really enjoyed it. See you soon."

He shook hands with the woman and left as Will sank back in his chair, closing his eyes and puffing on his joint as he sank into his deluded nirvana of identification with the supposed genius of a spatchcock pop star.

It was a short walk from Osborne Street to Meath Road but long enough to stimulate thought. Will was a Kerouac fan. A great lover of the Beats. When Andy had asked him if he had any politics, he'd replied:

"Yeah, man. The Wobblies"

Andy had let the comment pass. It seemed to encapsulate Will's distance from reality. What had the Wobblies to do with Britain in 1983? He examined his response to Will's view of Bowie. Was he exaggerating? Was it neurotic of him to feel the remark was wildly wrong? No. There was a mad denial of truth abroad. Its purpose was to confuse, beffudle and stupefy because stupefied people can't resist power and manipulation. It wasn't trivial to recognize the difference between Bach and Bowie. To fail to do so was the first step on the path to disaster and madness. Which, he was convinced, was exactly where the culture was heading.

Fifteen thousand teachers should be sacked, according to the Head of OFSTED. It was one of those typical cases of the guilty accusing the innocent. People who knew Woodhead at the time claimed he'd wanted to establish a *ménage à trois* with his young lover and his wife. He'd been an advocate of progressive education and, like all recanters, had swung violently to the opposite extreme. He was a fan of Lawrence. The latter made Andy laugh out loud.

Did the fool think bedding a seventeen-year-old pupil was in keeping with Lawrence's ethos? No doubt. What was he but a cynical seducer, one of the legion of men who abuse their authority to satisfy their lust, like Nigel Halifax? Lawrence was pushing for an ideal of erotic love. He would have scoffed at Woodhead's low behaviour. The girl was seventeen. She was over the age of consent. If she was daft enough to have an affair with a sleazy manipulator like Woodhead, that was her business. Andy wasn't prissy about the matter. But it stank of corruption. Expecting his wife to accept a threesome was despicable. Andy wasn't prissy about that either. If his wife wanted it, that was her business; but for him to try to force it on her was the action of a cockroach.

All this was nothing but the plain fare of sexual relations. Dickins seducing his secretary, Don Crawley being led by the foreskin by Diane Clayton, Dave Dover having it off with Cynthia Jones while the kids were reciting French verbs or looking up logarithms. It was the sexual chaos of the immature and unprincipled. Yet Andy had no right to feel above it. It had grabbed him by the ankles and pulled him into the mud and cow dung.

What was different was that this man had been given the job of inspecting the nation's schools. A teacher who lacked the discipline to keep his dick in his pants was claiming fifteen thousand people were incompetent and should be dismissed. He'd been elevated by Major. Maybe his mind had been turned by thinking too much about Edwina Currie's cunt. Major, posing as a respectable, married man, a man who was more passionate about double-entry bookkeeping than fellatio had appointed to a high, powerful office, a slug who had betrayed the trust placed in him by seducing a girl he was supposed to be teaching. Shakespeare and Chaucer by day, shagging at night. It seemed to Andy a perfect metaphor for the pus of corruption which dripped from every principal institution.

Things were taking a bad turn with the school's budget. Cooper sat in front of them in staff meetings, his knees dutifully clenched, leaning forward over his notes and speaking in a voice so low the people at the far end had to ask him to raise the volume.

"I'm sorry," he said, "I'll repeat that if you didn't understand it."

Jack Halton, the three-year-old- suit, down to earth maths teacher who made the request was livid.

"The cheeky fucking bastard," he said when the room had almost cleared. "I'm going to see him."

"So you should," said Tim Heath.

Cooper's strategy was to bamboozle. He would whip through a set of figures no one could possibly understand or retain; reassure the staff by saying they should get on with their teaching while he looked after the finances; but everyone knew the money-chasing-pupils regime was madness and, one way or another, disaster was on the way.

Every year, Mike Chambers took a ski trip. He tried to pass it off as a great responsibility and contribution. In fact, it was a free holiday. He thought himself an expert. Ungainly and unathletic, he was a modestly competent badminton player, had thrown himself around in goalmouths pretending to be a keeper and was nothing but a typical tourist skier. The stories of his control and stinginess were recycled like tin cans. He kept the purse. If the other staff wanted a beer or a hot-dog, they had to ask, like children pestering mummy for an ice-cream. The tale circulated of them being in the hotel *après ski*, tired, thirsty and hungry. Chris Bikerstaffe asked for a second beer:

"No," said Chambers. "One's enough. We'll be eating soon, you can have a drink with your meal."

The furious P.E. teacher had to go out into the snow to save himself grabbing Chambers by the lapels or foul-mouthing him.

Andy was glad when he was away, though Hilda Murphy had become his spy. Sycophantic as a Vatican underdog, she was given her instructions. Andy was perfectly aware he needed to be as canny with her as with her boss. The pair of them could have been lifted straight out of Kafka or Joe Orton. There was a *petit drame* during Chambers' absence when Vanessa Broughton, a girl in the lower sixth, in a panic over her coming mock exams, complained to Dave Dover that Andy hadn't covered the syllabus: they were studying selected poems by Prévert and had read only thirteen of the seventy. Broughton had an elder brother who had gone through the school, achieved four A grades at A Level and was now studying medicine at Oxford. Her parents, typical, middle-class, educational snobs, who considered their children's success in the system a proof of their own biological superiority, expected the same of their daughter. She was predicted a B in French.

Dave Dover sat behind his desk in the corner of his out-of-the way office. As Andy took his seat he was tempted to say:

"You could fit a single bed in here, Dave. Bit better than the floor."

Andy explained there was no requirement to read everything. The specification said "candidates will be expected to show familiarity with a selection of the poems". They'd covered thirteen. By the end of the year, they'd have done thirty. That was easily enough. Dover was reasonable and friendly. It was usual. Every year, as the mocks approached, this happened. Panicking pupils always tried to blame the member of staff. He shifted the conversation to genial, personal matters: how were Andy's kids; how was his wife getting on in her job.

Andy was sympathetic to Dover. He was liberal and would have been much more tolerant had he not worked in a school trying to maintain a false view of itself. He was relieved by his reaction. Yet he knew he'd spoken to Murphy and he wondered how Chambers would react when he got back from his frolic in the snow.

"I believe there was a bit of a kerfuffle while I was away," said the Germanist, in his shirt sleeves, in Andy's room as he waited for a class to arrive.

"Chaos in a coalbox."

"Can you come to a meeting in my room at break?"

"What for?"

"We just need to chat it over. Myself, you and Hilda."

"At break?"

"Yes. It'll only take a few minutes."

"Break is short."

"It won't take long. My room. Soon as the bell goes."

He left.

Andy was tempted not to turn up. He cursed the pusillanimous, arse-licking Murphy. Why didn't she just keep her mouth shut? Why didn't she smile at him and say:

"Everything ran like a newly-serviced boiler. We didn't notice you weren't here."

She was a Catholic, schooled in obedience to authority to the extreme that she would have prostrated herself before a washing-pole had it been given a title. He despised her almost more than Chambers. She had the opportunity to resist him. She was Head of French. She could create a space for herself and defend it; but she never did. Whatever he told her to do, she did it. Had he been given the French post, he would have stood up to Chambers, told him that what he did regarding German was his business but in French, things would be done differently. That, of course, was why he didn't get an interview. The system was a scam. People weren't promoted for competence but for deference. You had to have the mentality of a slave to advance. Society was held together by fawning, submission and domination; and it dared to call itself democratic. It was in a flat-out funk about people having control over their own lives.

When he walked into Chambers' room, the two of them were behind his desk. A chair was facing them.

"Sit down, please," said Chambers.

Andy was on the verge of saying:

"Haven't you forgotten your wig?"

They looked grave as they consulted their papers.

"Now, if we can begin," said Chambers. "It seems there was a complaint against you by a sixth-former. Is that right?"

Andy didn't know whether to laugh out loud, tell him to fuck off or simply walk out. Did he imagine he had the right to establish an inquiry? Didn't he know there was a procedure? Didn't he know as a Head of Department he had no right to conduct disciplinary investigations?

"You know perfectly well it is," he said.

"Hilda tells me," he went on, his tone as distant and severe as a law lord handing down a death sentence, "that the sixth-form students have multiple complaints about your teaching…"

"Students?"

"That's right, isn't it, Hilda."

The prim assistant, who would have administered a lethal injection had he ordered her, pursed her lips, gave a curious little shudder, picked a few hairs off her dull, brown jacket and held them away from her to drop them on the floor, as if they were infectious, alien bodies, as she nodded.

"The students have multiple complaints…"

"Multiple complaints haven't been conveyed to me."

"They have multiple complaints, don't they, Hilda?"

She wriggled her thin shoulders in that odd self-conscious way she had, as if she was always performing, always being watched, always trying to please some supervising eye.

"Yes," she said, not looking up from her papers.

"You haven't covered the syllabus properly, you come to lessons unprepared, you mark books while they complete work.."

"What's wrong with that?"

"What?"

"Marking books while they work."

"Marking should never be done during lesson time."

"Why not?"

"Because it's bad practice, isn't it, Hilda?"

"Yes," she said, "OFSTED would fail a lesson for it."

Andy was tempted to say:

"Fuck OFSTED, it's run by a paedophile. If he was doing now what he did in the sixties, he'd be imprisoned."

"You see," said Chambers, as if he'd had proven some impossibly difficult theory, "it's bad practice. OFSTED says so."

"Well, I don't," said Andy. "I say what am I supposed to do for twenty minutes while they're translating or answering questions? It's perfectly rational to make use of the time."

"You should be teaching all the time."

"What?"

"That's what lesson time is for, isn't that right, Hilda?"

The lapdog nodded like one of those mutts people dangle in their cars.

"Are you saying the sixth formers should never complete any written work during a lesson?"

"No, but if they do you should be teaching. You should go round the class and look at their work. Correct as they go."

"I thought you said marking shouldn't be during lessons."

"Correcting their work while they're doing it can be done in lessons."

"That's marking, isn't it?"

"It's assessment for learning."

"Okay," said Andy. "Marking."

"One time you came into a lesson, tossed the text book on the desk and said, 'Well, what shall we do today.'

Andy laughed.

"It's no laughing matter," said Chambers.

"Yes, it is. It's hilarious."

"You're supposed to prepare your lessons."

"You think I hadn't?

"That's what the students say, isn't it Hilda?"

Her head nodded as if she had a key in her back.

"And you take that seriously?"

"It's our responsibility as managers…"

"I was joking. I knew perfectly well what I was going to do in that lesson. I always do. I was creating an atmosphere of ease and spontaneity. They fall for it because they're seventeen. You're a bit older."

"We have to take student complaints seriously.."

"Which students."

"All the sixth formers."

"All of them?"

"Yes, that's right, isn't it, Hilda ?"

Andy noticed a reservation in her response, a nervous little twitch of her head and a furtive glance in Chambers' direction. Scenting his opportunity he said:

"Both lower and upper?"

"Yes, that's right, isn't it, Hilda? And there's a letter of complaint coming from an upper sixth parent, isn't there, Hilda?"

Andy watched her closely. She stiffened. A little blush appeared on her pale cheeks. She looked sideways at Chambers with wide eyes and gave the merest hint of a nod. He knew at once Chambers was lying. He stood up.

"You two do what you've got to do. I'm going for a cup of tea before I lose my break altogether."

That afternoon he taught both groups. He abandoned teaching and asked them to come clean. What complaints did they have? Whose parents were intending to send a letter of complaint? The upper sixth students were bemused. Letter of complaint? In the evening, Andy wrote an account of the morning's meeting and a request that Dave Dover investigate the claims. In particular the threat of a letter of parental complaint. He put it in Dover's pigeon-hole and waited.

The next morning Hilda greeted him on the language corridor as if he were her greatest friend, or a long-lost relative returned from Tierra del Fuego or the jungles of Papua New Guinea. He was almost sickened by it. Dave Dover, ever concerned for the reputation of the school and the stability of its hierarchy, played the matter down. When Andy went to see him three weeks later, he said he'd looked into it. There was no evidence of students being disgruntled nor any sign of pending parental complaints.

"Does Mike Chambers understand that?"

"Yes."

Once again, Andy knew he had perfectly good grounds for a grievance. Chambers had made up the parental complaint. It was bullying, dishonest and unprofessional. It seemed to Andy if he pressed his case, he would be sure to win. Justice was on his side. Yet he knew the governing body would be more concerned with protecting the school than justice. No doubt the committee would be composed of two dribbling vicars and local J.P..They were no more likely to find against their own management than the police to admit to giving people a kicking in the cells. Corruption was everywhere. There was no space to live away from it. The system thrived on it like bacteria on rotting flesh.

He'd come into teaching out of high-minded idealism, yet what had he found? Cooper, a manipulative, lazy, public-school prig who had effectively barred his way and condemned him to humiliation; Chambers, one of those inadequate people who use the workplace to try to fulfil needs they are incapable of satisfying elsewhere; Don Crawley who had an emotional age of twelve and was played for his money by a girl no better than a whore; Hilda Murphy whose mentality was so marinated in obedience she had no more autonomy than an alarm-clock.

It was a dismal picture. And he was married with two young kids. He had to put his daughters first, as every responsible parent must, and that made it impossible simply to walk away. He sat in the staffroom during last period in the afternoon on a dull day. He had to collect his daughters from nursery, take them home, get them something to eat, look after them till Christine finished. Her work absorbed her time and energy. The care of the children and the house fell to him. He found great comfort in looking after his children well, but it didn't dispel the gloom of work. Teaching French was as pleasant as ever, but the context was insane. Was he being metaphorical? No, society really was mad.

Chambers for example. He identified with authority as if his needs would be guaranteed by punctilious obedience. Yet the more he complied, the more his inner life was destroyed; which was exactly what society wanted. People had to be turned in duteous, frightened, compliant, conformist, sycophantic, fawning, servants of the system, or in other words, money. The whole crazy arrangement was powered by the desire of a few to enrich themselves. For their sake, or rather the sake of their money, the inner lives of millions must be turned into deserts of loneliness. No one was real. Society was composed of ghosts; people who had never conquered autonomy, who knew themselves about as well as they knew the surface of Pluto. Lawrence was right; the middle classes were emotionally curtailed, and it was their feelings which governed. It was nothing short of a vision of hell.

He left early, drove into town, parked up on Winckley Square and went for a walk through Avenham Park. Passing the shelter at the

226

foot on the sloping entrance, he was reminded of Carol, and taking the path by the river he thought of Maggie Swift. Maggie was in love with him when he was twelve. Had he treated her badly? Should he have ignored his emotional unease and stuck with her? But it would have been wrong. The strong feeling wasn't there. Maybe it would have emerged. How could he know? It was there with Janice Eaves who turned out to be a perfidious *allumeuse*. His feelings had betrayed him. As they had with Jane Bentnick who was as unstable as a blind woman on a bicycle.

Was it his fault there been so much heartache and anguish? He'd come to girls innocently, full of guileless affection and expectation of honesty and seriousness; and what had he found: ambivalence, lying, cheating, insults, humiliation. Was it that he'd chosen badly? No, it was the culture. The mad imposition of the injunction of no sex before marriage which his parents' generation had effected; the demand on young people of an impossibly high standard of ideals in erotic love; the middle-class horror of premature pregnancy on the one hand and daughters choosing a boy with no prospects on the other; the adherence to respectability before happiness; the obsession with property which would have seen most parents glad if their daughter married a millionaire brute rather than a kindly oik; all this made the potentially sweet simplicity of love between teenagers impossible. Society evinced disgust at the idea. Pass your exams. Get a job. Make money. Get a mortgage. Get a car. Have holidays abroad. Buy a washing machine and a fridge. Be the first to have a colour telly. Love? Forget it. And forgotten it was. Society was a loveless machine for making money.

He'd known it, emotionally, early. Long before he could think things through. He and Wheels knew it when they were thirteen. They were disillusioned. Oddly, he realised it was disillusion which made him happy. It set him free. He had none of the ambitions society tried to force on him. Nor did Wheels. The distance of disillusion was the ground of reality. Why had he ever abandoned it? The hard work to get to university wasn't the cause. He didn't regret that at all, Nor the years at Lancaster. He'd loved university because it too granted distance. You could spend your day reading Prévost while people were slaving in offices, banks, schools, shops, on building sites, buses, trains, all in the service of the greed of a few babyish egos. It was marvellously irrelevant to the workaday concerns of the culture.

He ought to have found a job in a university or trained to work in the theatre, or something where imagination wasn't treated as an ailment. School had the imagination of a slug. Reward depended on having a dead imagination. The slightest deviance from what was thought of as the norm was magnified into a threat to existence itself. Rigor mortis of the imagination, paralysis of the intellect, emotional regression and moral idiocy where the qualifications needed to do well.

He realised he had let his disillusion slip. He'd moved an inch towards agreement with the system and the system had destroyed him. He had to play the role of teacher. He couldn't give his disillusion full rein and stay in the job. Such was the trap. Unless Christine could earn enough to let him get out, he was a phoney. He no more believed in the education system than he believed in Father Christmas.

He wondered what Wheels was doing now. He recalled running into him some time after they'd left school when he was working for the *Midland Bank*. They wanted him to take exams and dangled the supposedly irresistible carrot of higher pay. But Wheels was no donkey.

"Fuck that," he said. "They can stick their exams. I can manage on what I earn."

There was none of that among his colleagues . They would have strangled one another for an extra grand a year. He laughed at the idea, but it was true. Psychological murder was how the system worked. No one dared put other people's interest on a level with their own. The Christian injunction was mocked every day, in this most Christian of schools. No one loved their neighbour. Neighbours are rivals. Your neighbour gets more money, you get less. Your neighbour gets more status, you feel diminished. Your neighbour gets more power, you feel threatened. Everybody secretly wished for bad things to happen to others, so they wouldn't happen to them. Everybody was secretly plotting their neighbour's downfall. Everybody was metaphorically slipping poison into their neighbour's tea. The fantasy in every head was solipsism. The world is me and only me. Reality begins and ends with the limits of my ego.

The disillusion he'd shared with Wheels, and to a degree with Duddy, was an escape from that ruinous fantasy. They liked one another. In fact, they loved one another. Duddy had saved his life. A small act of kindness from Duddy's point of view, an unpayable debt from Andy's. They genuinely did value one another more than money, or success, or exam passes, or property or respectability. Did you have to be utterly disillusioned to be able to do that? Yes, you did. The system was a rotten cheat. Invest your feelings in it and it turned you into a lunatic. It robbed you of contact with yourself, of reality. Only the disillusioned are real.

Cooper was one of those people who believe in the system. How he squared his Christianity with an economic system founded on greed which left millions in poverty, Andy couldn't work out. Yet he seemed to think the two were as compatible as bread and cheese. It was too easy to say it was hypocrisy. It was, but Cooper genuinely did think supporting big business and its mad hierarchies was the way to fulfil the Christian promise of humility, equality and love. It wasn't a matter of hypocritical ideas. It was an emotional adjustment. Cooper was an overgrown obedient schoolboy naively accepting the masters' promises of great rewards for boredom, tedium and submission. It was as if the universe was a great public school. It couldn't be founded on lies. It had to be true. It was no better than a child clinging to a belief in the tooth fairy.

His faith in the system was so complete, purblind and arrogant, he imagined he could run the school into hundreds of thousands of debt and the County would do nothing. This was his *very special place* after all. It had tradition. It was always in the top hundred maintained schools in the league tables. They wouldn't dare move against him. But they did.

When the debt reached half a million, they sent in the auditors and the advisers. There would have to be job losses. The bureaucrats shook their heads: he should have been reducing his staff through natural wastage for years. He hadn't because he assumed the County would inflict the pain on lesser schools. There were plenty of places which taught the lower classes where the results were dismal. They would go after them. They should go after them. That was the natural order. Cooper had been raised to believe it. People like him, educated in public schools and at Oxbridge, people with accounts at merchant banks and portfolios of investments in tobacco, oil, mining and pharmaceuticals, didn't get it in the neck. Though he hardly knew it, Cooper believed there was an intimate relation between property and virtue. He'd absorbed the old excuse for piracy, colonialism, imperialism, the slave trade, child labour, racism, the degradation of women, that property is a proof of election. God looks down and sees how much you have in the bank and his list of the virtuous begins with the richest.

He was Head of a school which served the middle-classes. There was money and influence among the parents. The County would save money by sacking teachers in ex-secondary moderns in Burnley; they would go after Ribbleton Hall which served some of the poorest pupils in Preston, drawn from the sprawling, unappealing council estates. They would inflict suffering on comps in Leyland and Bacup. But they would stay their hand when it came to his elite institution. It was only half a million, after all. What was that to Lancashire County Council?

It was taxpayers' money.

Seven jobs would have to go. Out of a staff of fifty-five it was a big loss. The worst was there had to be a process. From his appointment, Cooper had run the school as his fiefdom. The governors were in his pocket. The staff were taken in by his apparently liberal regime. He did what he liked. Now, there had to be consultation. The unions had rights. There was employment law. The idea made his lip curl. He would employ his usual sleight-of-hand and get his own way.

The County made him an offer.

He could go with his dignity intact. They'd enhance his pension. The idea made him livid. Everyone would know. It would be failure. Humiliation. He would be got rid of. Pushed out. Some younger man (he couldn't imagine it being a woman) would be brought in to sort out what they thought of as a mess. He wouldn't have it. He would go when he was ready. No one would push him out. They weren't going to save money on his post. The staff would be culled but he would come out unscathed.

Andy rang the Regional Office . A sniffling officer was brought to the phone. He explained and she said she'd send the documentation. Two days later a booklet arrived explaining redundancy. He looked at it in dismay and rang the local association secretary. She recognised the seriousness and made things move.

He had to meet with her, a Regional Officer and the union's local number cruncher. They had lunch in the *Anchor Inn*, a cavernous, somewhat depressing pub a few hundreds yards from the school. The number cruncher was retired maths teacher from East Lancs, a bubbly bloke whose conversation was simultaneously self-referential and self-excusing. He pushed his grey, dry hair from over his ears as he forked a chunk of microwaved steak and ale pie and laughed at his own comment. The Regional Officer had already extracted the accounts for the last seven years from Cooper.

"Does he pay rent on his house?" he said to Andy

"No idea."

"What about the swimming pool? It seems to be hired to various groups, but there's no revenue."

"Beats me."

"Have you never talked to him about the school budget?"

"He doesn't talk to anyone about the school budget. He probably keeps it secret from himself. Getting to talk to him is like getting into Albania."

The Regional Officer was about forty-five, dark, with a face pockmarked from acne. He wore expensive glasses and the kind of suit Andy would have expected to see on a cabinet minister. He talked to the number cruncher about how things would progress. Andy was out of his depth. This was his union but these people were insiders. He was just the mug who'd been school rep for a decade and a half.

When the half hour meeting ended he walked back to school feeling inadequate and excluded. The Regional Officer was *au fait* with employment law, the number cruncher bamboozled him with talk of ratios, percentages, funding streams and accounting procedures, and the local secretary was astute about how to handle the consultation. He'd expected to meet them as equals but they'd left him feeling like an ignorant neophyte.

The teacher governor was Bernard Bray, the long-serving CDT teacher and Tony Bennett fan who'd invited the singer to his daughter's wedding. He got a signed, framed shot in response which he proudly showed to the staff-room. He picked up on Cooper's suggestion that selection should go by attendance. Andy was stunned that a member of staff elected to the Governing Body to speak for the teachers was willing to see people lined up for execution because they'd been ill. The longest recent absentee was Bel Bridges who'd fallen downstairs and broken her leg.

Andy went to see Cooper. It took four attempts.

"I wanted to mention the idea of absence as the main criterion for selection."

"Yes," said Cooper with a smile, as if they were arranging a Sunday picnic or talking about where they should hang the bunting for the school fete, "it seems a good idea."

"I don't think so. If it were used for any of my members, we'd be claiming unfair selection."

Cooper looked suddenly woeful, his face taking on the pulling-down-to-the-floor expression it often had.

"Why would you do that?"

"Because it plainly is unfair. Bel Bridges isn't one of my members, but she's been absent for six weeks. The idea she should head the list for redundancy is without justification."

"I don't see why."

"A tribunal would. Selection criteria have to be fair. She broke her leg. Why should she lose her job for that?"

"We don't need to talk about tribunals. This school has nothing to do with things like that."

Andy was turned to concrete. Cooper surveyed him as a lord might look at a recalcitrant vassal. There was no point going any further.

"Okay. That's all I wanted to say."

Cooper looked down at his papers. Andy left.

Did he really believe that his "special place" was beyond the law? Did he imagine he could behave like a highwayman or a wild west gunslinger? He was the Head. Didn't he know how the process worked? Hadn't he taken advice? Could he really be so far-gone in his conviction that any institution he was part of was granted special dispensation that he thought there was no remedy if he made Bel Bridges the first candidate for redundancy, regardless of anything but her absence?

At the first consultation meeting, Andy discovered Cooper did think he was no more subject to the law than Bonnie and Clyde.

They met in the Committee Room. There were two advisers. Two vicars from the governing body plus Bernard Bray. The NASUWT executive member for Lancashire. Andy's team of himself, the local secretary, the Regional Officer and the number cruncher, and finally Cooper and the secretary to the governors who kept the rest waiting for ten minutes. Cooper was stiff and grey. He began with a fluttering welcome before presenting his plan. The secretary intervened the moment he stopped speaking:

"Mr Cooper has made clear how he intends to go about making the redundancies so I suggest we move straight to a vote on his proposal.."

"Just a minute Chair," said Dave Vickers, the Regional Officer, " I believe we have the teacher governor in the room."

The secretary nodded.

"Nothing can be decided prior to the consultation, so as a member of staff the teacher governor is as subject to selection as anyone else. How can he therefore be part of the deliberations. Isn't that a clear conflict of interests?"

There was an iceberg silence, broken by one of the vicars, a bald, big-bellied man with a voice as thin as his waist was swollen.

"I think that's a decision for the person concerned to make himself," he said.

"I don't," said Vickers, "but if the meeting is happy with that, we'll go along with it."

There were nods of assent. The NASUWT man kept still and mum.

"In that case," said the secretary, "if we can move to a vote.."

"One moment," said the number cruncher, "it's customary to permit questions."

The secretary turned to Cooper. He gave a little jig of his head.

"Very well," she said, "if you've got a question."

"I've got a long list," said the number cruncher with a laugh, "but to start with, you've just told us you intend to make seven point five posts redundant. The County is asking for only seven."

Cooper turned his mouth down at the corners, looked over his glasses and said:

"It's only point five."

"I'm requesting an adjournment," said Vickers. "It's obvious the posts to be lost have already been decided. There has to be consultation. This is a legal requirement. An adjournment of half an hour, please Chair."

The dismayed secretary looked to the advisers. They both nodded.

"Well, it seems that's in order. So we'll reconvene in half an hour."

Cooper, his secretary, the two vicars and Bernard Bray left. At once, Vickers addressed the advisers.

"If I was sitting in a room with you, fighting for a member who had made as big a mess of running her department as this Head has of running this school, you'd be asking for dismissal wouldn't you?"

"Yes, we would," said the first adviser, a little, mousey dapper man with greying sideburns and a fixed smile, as if he knew some secret denied to the rest of humanity.

"Well," said Vickers, "If one of my members is selected for redundancy, I'll be going to the Chief Education Officer and asking for him to go. None of my members is to blame for this and none of them is going to pay the price."

The second adviser leaned forward. He was a tall, gaunt man, with huge hands and a face mountaineers might have considered a challenge.

"I suppose we should go and tell him that?"

"It might be an idea."

The two advisers stood up, one so tall he might have had a lightning rod running down his spine, the other small enough to pack into a suitcase. As they made for the door, the NASUWT officer, who up till then had behaved as if he were on a Trappist retreat, said:

"We wish to be associated with Mr Vickers' comments."

There was nothing to do but chat and wait. When Cooper returned, he looked as though he'd been sentenced to hang. The secretary asked for silence.

"Of course," said Cooper, " having spoken to the advisers, I'm quite willing to modify my plan. We don't want to force anyone out of their job. We shall think again about how we can redeploy, though that will involve people teaching outside their specialism…"

"Perhaps, Chair," said Vickers, " the school rep might have something to say about that."

The secretary looked at Andy as if he was eating a pork pie in a Synagogue.

"The staff would much rather teach beyond their specialisms than see compulsory redundancies," he said.

Cooper took up his thread, but Vickers interrupted:

"I think we need to adjourn,Chair. There's nothing further this meeting can do till the Head has produced a new plan. But if I can just make one thing clear, if any of my members is forced out of their job, we will be asking for the Head to lose his."

"I wish to be associated with that remark," piped up the NASUWT man.

Cooper flushed as if he'd been caught naked on the cricket square. The meeting dissolved.

It wasn't long before an audit of staff skills was underway, Cooper's original plan which had earmarked departments and specified numbers was in the bin, and offers were being made to people over fifty-five.

The meeting was a revelation for Andy, not only because of the effectiveness of the union, or more precisely, Dave Vickers, who used his powers with a bit of chutzpah while the NASUWT man behaved like a boy caught pinching gob stoppers from the tuck shop; but more because of Cooper's utterly pathetic performance. Did he imagine he was going to get a rubber stamp? Did he think the legal necessity of consultation was beneath his dignity? Did he think, because he was educated at public school and Oxford, the laws to give employees some say in how redundancies are handled had nothing to do with him? Yet what pervaded Andy's thinking was that if he was woeful in this context, wasn't he probably the same in most? He'd been the Head for nearly two decades. He'd bamboozled everyone into thinking he was in control. He was the Calvin Coolidge of the school. Maybe that's why he'd made himself the invisible Headteacher. Maybe the reason securing an audience with him was like getting your fingers on the crown jewels. He'd behaved in a boyish, silly way, as if he had some absolute right to control. He'd decided who would go. Legal consultation? Tush. A bagatelle. He would sweep it aside. In the meeting, he'd been made to look foolish, ill-prepared, a non-swimmer in armbands tossed into Atlantic breakers. He'd been humiliated by an oik, educated in a we-take-everyone comp, who got himself a degree, moved from teaching to the union and bustled his way to Regional Officer. It had been a contest of arrogance, presumption and tradition against democratic, egalitarian irreverence and Cooper had been trounced.

Seven staff took redundancy, but no one was forced out. What appalled Andy was that Cooper kept his job. He spread it among the staff that Cooper had been made an offer but refused to go. They remained supportive. He was amazed at their continued faith in him despite the disaster he'd led them to. Departments like his, which had lost a teacher, were now going to struggle with obese classes, impossible sets, disaffected pupils, crammed timetables while Cooper would close his office door, switch on the red light and go home for lunch five minutes before the bell.

Going up to his room at the end of a wet lunchtime, Andy heard the row halfway up the stairs and thought he knew what he was going to encounter; but when he swung open the red door he was met by Bill McFarlane, the Deputy Head who'd been in post for five years. Behind him was chaos. Pupils were running up and down the corridor. Books were being thrown from classrooms. The floor was splattered with discarded sandwiches, squashed oranges, apple cores, puddles of sticky drink. McFarlane shook his head.

"The sooner I can get out of this job, the better."

He passed through the door Andy held open for him and trotted down the stairs, his back cast-iron straight as ever, as if he'd been raised by a sergeant-major. Andy's teaching room was a Year 11 form room. On wet lunchtimes they were allowed in. They'd opened the cupboard where the collections of French literature were kept. Copies of *Germinal, Madame Bovary, Le Misanthrope, Les Illusions Perdues, Une Vie, La Peste,* their covers ripped off or the book torn in half were on the floor, on desks, on top of cupboards. The *Harraps* dictionary he'd used for years was now a hundred tatters marked with footprints. On the whiteboard, in permanent marker, was a crude dick and balls and the witty observation, *Lang is a cunt.* A dozen boys in a state of high excitement sprawled on the desks, stood on the radiators or were swinging on the flimsy metal chairs, intent on snapping their legs.

"What a bunch of champions," said Andy. "Out you go."

"We're allowed in," a lad, red in the face from his orgy of destruction challenged.

"Well, I'm telling you to get out."

"That's not fair," objected another boy.

"Complain to the United Nations," said Andy. "Now get out or I'll be in the office phoning your parents."

"We haven't done anything," said the florid-faced boy.

"The books tore themselves, did they?"

"You can't prove it," said another boy.

"French is shit anyway," said his mate.

"I'll count to ten and whoever is still here comes with me to the Head's office."

"He doesn't care," said the lad with the burning cheeks.

"He will do if I bring him up here."

Slowly, reluctantly, foul-mouthing under their breath, they filed out. Andy began clearing. He reached between the filing cabinet and the cupboard for a splayed book and found behind it sandwiches, fruit, a spilled yogurt. This was John Major's work. This was what you got when the Head of Ofsted told the country teachers were incompetent. This was the inevitable outcome of the cynical abandonment of the public sector by politicians driven by the mad ideology of the free market. As if such a thing existed. As if such a thing ever could. There was no more a free market than there were Easter bunnies delivering chocolate eggs. There was the power of the State used in the defence of property. That's how the economic system worked and always had. Its core was the relation of employer to employee and in that, the State made sure the employer had two dicks and the employees no balls. It was so simple a five-year-old could get it. The rich had to be protected. The powerful had to be made more powerful. And the rest got it in the neck, especially those at the bottom. What was free about that? He wasn't even free to come to school without a tie. The market? Just a place where stuff is bought and sold. When it came to people selling their labour, where was the freedom? Why couldn't he present his contract to the County? These are the hours I'll work, this is what you'll pay me, these will be my holidays, my sick pay, my pension. Contracts were imposed by employers. Where did the right to do that come from? The State. He didn't live in a free market but in a society rigged in favour of money where the State for centuries had murdered, tortured, imprisoned, impoverished, starved and brutalised the poor and anyone who dared threaten lucre. Thatcher, Major and their ilk raged against the State only when it gave the common folk schools , hospitals, pensions, a bit of leeway, a bit of security, a bit of chance for fun, choice and relaxation. The State that punished the poor and tied trade unionists in barbed wire, they delighted in.

Andy believed in neither business nor the State. He believed the common folk should run their own lives and to do that they had to escape from employment. Let people cooperate in making and providing. Let them meet on grounds of equality. The rest was propaganda.

The atmosphere in teaching had become grisly. Chambers was retreating more and more into the fantasy of omnipotence which compensated for his feeble sense of identity. Hilda Murphy became more sycophantic every day. Andy was only surprised he didn't ask her to wipe his arse. He had to get out.

Without kids, he would have handed in his notice with a skip; but the responsibility of children outweighed all others. He had no intrinsic moral duty to the education system, to Lancashire County Council, to the State, to the school; but he did to his daughters. He was still writing but had long let go of the idea it could make him money. Paul Flintoff had brought out two pamphlets of his poetry. Andy drove to Yorkshire one Sunday morning to pick up copies of the second: *The Optimist's Depression*. Flintoff lived in a stone terrace. They sat in the kitchen where he was in the middle of his late breakfast. There was a crusty, unsliced white loaf in the middle of the table, a serrated knife, fluffy crumbs, an opened jar of cheap strawberry jam and a pat of butter with its wrapper folded back. Flintoff was a small, wiry man who'd once been energetic. He liked to think of himself as a bit tough. He wore jeans, a t-shirt and a denim jacket, which reminded Andy of the sixties. On the table was a box of seventy copies of the pamphlet. Andy had agreed to buy them at half the cover price.

"So will you make money on it, Paul?" he said as he sipped the stewed tea the publisher had poured from the aluminium pot.

"I don't make money on anything," said the little man. "I get a grant from Yorkshire Arts. It's a matter of what I can squeeze out of 'em."

"Yeah."

Andy wanted to know what he was going to do to sell his book. He was taking his stack of the three hundred copies. What was Flintoff going to do with the remaining two hundred and thirty?

"What about review copies?" he said.

"Sure. I can send out a few. I mean, I usually do. You know, *Ambit*, one or two other places."

"What kind of response do you get?"

"Depends. Lots of my publications have been reviewed. I do okay. But the big places aren't interested in small press poetry. I mean, you can't get the *TLS* to look at anything."

"Yeah. What kind of money do you get from Yorkshire Arts?"

"Last year, four thousand. Then I ran the competition. That brings in more."

"Really?"

"Oh, yeah," said Flintoff, lighting a cigarette, "I got fifteen hundred entries for the last one."

"Fifteen hundred?"

"Yeah, more people enter competitions than read poetry."

Andy was trying to recall the entry fee.

"That's a good entry. What was it, five quid a shot?"

"Yeah. I had to pay Campbell to judge it, and the three winners get their pamphlet published. Three hundred print run, but I persuaded them to buy half each, so I made about five grand."

"Not bad."

"No, keeps the thing ticking over."

Andy remembered Flintoff had told him the cost of producing a book was usually a quarter of its cover price. His pamphlet was selling for £3.95. Three hundred copies must have cost about three hundred quid. He was buying seventy at two quid a time. If Flintoff sold another forty he was home and dry. But there was the grant to think about.

239

" Do you get the grant as an overall sum or is it per book?"

"Both. Kind of. I have to pitch each book. Estimate the cost and they give me a percentage."

"I see. How much?"

"Varies. On your kind of book, fifty."

Andy nodded and drank his tea as he did the sums. A hundred and fifty from Yorkshire Arts, and hundred and forty from him. He was ten quid short of breaking even. Not much need to do a great deal to shift the books.

"Get into many shops?"

"Alternative places. A few. *Compendium. Grassroots*. Yeah, I can get a few on the shelves. The big one was the anthology of Asian female poetry."

"That did well, did it?"

"Yorkshire Arts asked me how much I wanted."

"Blank cheque, eh?"

"More or less. Ticks the boxes."

"What did you ask for?"

"Ten grand."

"Wow. Did you get it?"

"Every penny, and the book sold out. I'm doing a reprint."

"I'm amazed it sold so well."

"Get reviewed everywhere. Even the *TLS*. We had a big launch in London. Sold a hundred copies."

There was a ring. Flintoff went to the door and came back with a man of about thirty, dressed in an old anorak and baggy jeans. He was pale and thin.

"This is my son, Tom. Tom, this is Andy Lang, one of my poets."

Andy shook the son's cold hand.

"Better be going anyway, Paul. Long drive back."

"Yeah. Thanks for coming over. Good luck selling the book."

"Oh, I won't sell them," said Andy. "I'll give them away. I don't have any illusions about being a commercial writer."

The journey gave Andy plenty of time to think. He ran the figures through his head. Flintoff was doing okay. If he offloaded copies on all his writers, he could turn a little profit every year and do virtually nothing but act as a conduit between the writer and the printer. Andy could have taken his poems directly to the printer. Involving the third party was a guarantee of a degree of objectivity. Yet he couldn't believe in Flintoff as a judge of literature. He was better than the average person, of course, who couldn't tell the difference between Shakespeare and the verse in a Valentine's card, but he was a chancer, a literary wheeler-dealer. Four grand from the Arts people became four grand in his back pocket by printing the books and getting the authors to buy enough of them to close his losses. He'd asked Andy to take a hundred.

It was pretty dismal. Poets in their youth begin in gladness, he thought. There was a big discrepancy between his high-minded beginning at seventeen seeing literature as the pursuit of truth, and Flintoff's little scam. It wasn't much else. He shouldn't be churlish: the man had brought out his books. But he almost wanted to toss them in the bin. Writing was a thoroughly dispiriting business. Publishers and agents were money-grubbers. Somehow, good literature got through. But there was no robust literary culture. He was involved in a hole-and-corner, back-bedroom, tiny-print-run culture ignored by very nearly a hundred per cent of the population. Three hundred copies for an adult population of thirty million. If even one per cent had some real interest in literature, he might expect sales of a few thousand. Literature was of no more interest to the general populace than quantum mechanics.

He'd had a bit of luck in the theatre though. The ninety-minute script he'd submitted to the *Soho Poly* got him invited to workshops. His play was performed in a script-in-hand reading and went on to a one-off production at the *Riverside Studios* as part of a festival of new work. The phone rang. Directors from *The Young Vic*, *The Bolton Octagon* had been given his name. Did he have a script? He banged out half a dozen two act plays and passed them on, but the promise always fizzled.

Sarah Bentham was the *Soho's* script advisor. Her son was the same age as Andy's elder. They chatted about kids' matters when he went down for readings or workshops. She was a sympathetic young woman, sharp about drama, but with little of the out-of-my-way egotism of people trying to make their way in the arts. She liked his plays and put his fourth under the nose of the artistic director, Melanie Duckworth.

"Don't think if she turns it down it's not a good play. She doesn't choose on intrinsic merit. It's a matter of what she wants to do. If she favours it she will, if not she won't."

She didn't. But Sarah encouraged him. It usually takes about eight years, she said, from the first script to a full production. He was doing okay. She'd stick by him. He'd get all his scripts done in rehearsed readings. A full production would come. She'd ensure it.

He sent her his next. Six months and there was no response. He penned a little note to jog her. The reply stunned him: her son had been hit by a virus which went to his liver and killed him. She wasn't working for the theatre anymore, but she'd speak to the new adviser and ensure his plays got readings. He wrote back an apology for pestering and commiserated as best he could.

When he contacted the new script man, he was told he'd never heard his name, had none of his scripts and in any case, the weekend workshops and readings had been cancelled.

He went on submitting scripts to subsidised theatres, but it often took six or eight months for the rejection to arrive. He was getting nowhere.

Where did he want to get? He had an almost overwhelming desire to give up writing. It brought little but rejection, being ignored and humiliation. Yet the desire was only almost overwhelming. Had it been totally irresistible, he would have renounced it there and then. The trouble was the infinitesimally small residue of commitment and hope. To give it up felt like irresponsibility. In spite of his failure, he couldn't relinquish the idea that he was a writer. There was something he could say which had never been said quite his way before. It seemed a renunciation of his identity to give up. All the same, the longing to have done with it was enormous.

Always he came back to the idea of writers who had struggled for years. Lawrence had seen *The Rainbow* lack a publisher and had died without his plays being performed. Kafka was virtually unknown when he perished. He should just keep going and hope. But it was terrible. He wouldn't wish being a writer on anyone. There were the successes of course. Armitage was everywhere as was Duffy. Ian

McEwan had managed an early, easy start. David Hare was thriving and Ayckbourn ran his own theatre where dozens of his plays had been performed. Maybe he just lacked talent. Perhaps he was a writer, but a bad or mediocre one. Wasn't it crazy to judge your own work? Didn't it drive you towards the lunacy of Gerry Beckett? Wasn't he on the verge of declaring: "James Joyce? Oh. I'm a much better writer than him."

All the same, he found Ayckbourn dull and predictable and his dialogue cast in a flat, middle-class register. He agreed with Alan Bennett' view of his own work that "occasionally it strays into literature". There was too much melodrama in Pinter's menace, Stoppard was a cute writer with little to say, Beckett was marred by superciliousness for all his exquisite use of language and dark humour. Perhaps all that made him a critic. Maybe he should write a book about Lawrence or Flaubert or Kundera.

He was acutely aware of his inability to compromise. He could imitate the kind of work the publishers favoured. Maybe he should write a novel in the manner of Margaret Drabble. The idea made him laugh and wince. He had to stick to his own vision and that, he knew, meant work which offended or bemused. There was no point writing with an eye on the market. If he wanted money, he'd be better becoming an estate agent. The whole point of writing was finding your way to that remote point in your own consciousness; a territory your everyday consciousness couldn't reach; a place you had to trek to through inner blizzards of disbelief and wonder; where you could find the means to express what surprised and even appalled you but which you knew had to be said. Anything else was dilettantism.

The story came back to him of Kafka meeting someone on the street who mentioned *Metamorphosis.* Kafka shook his head and said: "That was a terrible thing." That seemed right. Writing was about getting at the terrible things. It wasn't entertainment, whose purpose was to distract, to make life appear less demanding. It entertained at a different level. *Lear* was riveting, but it wasn't written to send you home feeling cheerful. *Oedipus Rex* was fascinating, but it didn't leave you at ease with yourself.

He thought back to himself at seventeen, in his mother's house, typing up his first poems on the old *Remington*. He'd believed then, in his bottomless naivety, that the world would welcome him. He knew his poems weren't first-rate, but they held together. Surely editors would want to encourage a young writer. Wouldn't they see potential and want it developed? Wouldn't there be an open, warm reception? What he didn't know was that the literary world is a telephone box a thousand people are trying to squeeze into, a postage stamp a hundred people are trying to stand on. Behind it all lay money. The curse of his culture. There ought to be enough outlets for all competent literature. It shouldn't be a competition for money and status. But everything in the culture was. He had no idea of the lives of literary agents, almost all of them in London, living in big houses in Blackheath or Mayfair, wanting millions in the bank, coveting contact with the wealthy and famous. He had no conception of the venality of publishers, the disdain amongst the employees of the big houses for hard-up provincials, the greed for money and the urgent need for distance from those who didn't have it.

He had no idea then, but he did now.

He arrived home, stowed the box of books in his back-bedroom study and went into the garden where his daughters were playing with the girls from next door.

THE LOVELESS GENERATION

At seventy-six, Elsie Lang suffered a heart-attack. It began with a slight pain in her left arm. Her chest felt tight. She was hot and cold. She began to sweat and vomit. She telephoned her son. He was eating spaghetti bolognaise with Christine and the girls. He told his mother to sit down. He'd be there in fifteen minutes. He grabbed the car keys. As soon as he was driving he cursed himself. He should have called an ambulance. He should have told her to take aspirin. There was nothing to do but get there as quickly as he could. The dreadful thought crept into his imagination that he might find her dead. His grandad had gone quickly. At seventy-eight. But he was a smoker and diabetic. His mother had never smoked. Were genes more powerful than bad habits?

What was he going to do when he arrived? Should he call an ambulance immediately? The speed limit sent him crazy, but he kept his foot off the accelerator.

The side door of the little bungalow was unlocked. It was one of those cheap, plastic things; part of unit with window to its right. Badly fitted, the entire installation wobbled when the door was closed and a damp patch had appeared on the anaglypta. He shut it behind him and went through to the living room where his mother was sitting in her armchair, facing the window.

"How you feeling?"

"Not too bad."

"Have you taken some aspirin?"

"Haven't got any. I've some paracetamol in the bathroom…"

She was about to get up.

"No, no. Don't get up. Paracetamol is no good. I'll call an ambulance."

"I don't think I need an ambulance," she said.

He didn't want to say he thought she'd suffered a heart attack. He wanted to keep her calm.

"No? What do you think it is?"

"I don't know. I were hot and cold, then I were sweatin' like a pig and being sick. It's passed off a bit now."

Should he ask her about pain in the chest or her arm? Would that alarm her? If he was right, any sudden anxiety might be disastrous.

"Look, to be on the safe side, I'll call an ambulance."

"You could ring't surgery."

"It's eight o'clock."

"Aye, but there's a number for out of hours. They're very good. I'll get it."

"No, let me."

"It's all right," she said, getting to her feet. "It's in't drawer in me dressing table."

She went through to the bedroom. He watched her. She seemed to move quite well and showed no signs of chest pain. Maybe his two-and-two-together diagnosis was wrong. She returned with a slip of paper.

"Sit down. Take it easy."

He went to the phone in the hallway. The G.P. answered.

"I'm ringing about my mother, Elsie Lang, who is one of your pa-tients. She seventy-six. I'm her son. She's called me because she feels pretty ill. Hot and cold, severe sweating, vomiting…"

"Any chest pain?"

"I think so."

"Call an ambulance."

"I suggested that, but she…."

"Call an ambulance. I can't come to see her. If you think it's serious you must call an ambulance at once."

As he dialled 999, Andy realised he'd allowed himself, like so many times before, to be influenced away from what his instincts told him but his mother's insistence. More bluntly, her awkwardness. It was obvious she needed an ambulance. Why hadn't he called one from home? He'd wasted half an hour. It could be here by now. They could be giving her oxygen. He needed to be direct.

"My mother has had a heart attack. She's seventy-six."

The ambulance arrived fifteen minutes later. There was a male and a female paramedic. They asked her a few questions, gathered her medications, gave her oxygen and put her in a wheelchair. Andy followed the ambulance after calling Sylvia. The young, Chinese doctor was quick to judge it a heart attack.

"We can't say for sure till the results of the blood test come back, but I think so."

She was put on a drip in the cubicle. Sylvia and Barry arrived. After an hour she moved to the ward. They had to wait outside. It was the early hours before the sister spoke to them.

"She's very poorly. She's had a severe heart attack. If she comes through the next twenty-four hours, she'll be all right. But it'll take a bit of time to get her back on her feet."

There was no point staying. They weren't allowed to be by her bed. Barry took the day off work to be with Sylvia and so they could turn up for afternoon visiting. Andy went into work, distracted and exhausted.

"Can you come to an after-school meeting tomorrow, about National Curriculum levels?" said Mike Chambers.

"No. My mother's in hospital."

"I'm sorry." He paused. "But we need to get it done. What about Thursday?"

Andy would have liked to say: "For fuck's sake, go and stick your levels up your arse. My mother's had a heart attack. She'll be in hospital for a couple of weeks. I won't be going to any fucking meetings."

"No. Forget it for the next couple of weeks."

"We can't wait that long. It's a statutory requirement."

"Then do it without me."

It took ten days before she was ready to go home. She was prescribed beta-blockers, aspirin and under-the-tongue nitro-glycerine. Her distress manifested itself in attempts at control. Andy, Sylvia, Barry and Ted were visiting the night before her discharge.

"Move that chair. Andrew, move that chair over here."

He put the chair where she wanted it.

"Did you get me milk?"

"No," said Andy, "I'll do it when I leave. I'll make sure everything you'll need is in the house."

"Only he won't know, will he? T'milkman. Once you've cancelled, he won't know I'm home tomorrow will 'e? I shall need some milk. Skimmed. It has to be skimmed. I'm on a strict diet now. And porridge. There is some. In that big cupboard in't kitchen. There might not be much...."

"No there isn't," he said. "I'll get a box of Scott's. Don't worry."

"Did you turn't water back on? I don't want to turn't tap and nowt comes out...."

Andy had ignored her instruction to turn off the water at the mains. He nipped in every day after visiting.

She was taken home by ambulance. Sylvia followed. Andy arrived in the evening. They left at ten. She had everything she needed, except company.

Maybe loneliness had made her ill. He wished he could welcome her into his home, but there was hardly room and Christine wouldn't have agreed. If anyone's mother was to live with them, it would have been hers; and Andy knew there couldn't have been an atmosphere which would have made his mother happy. Had Mary still been alive it might have been different. Had Mary not died of breast cancer, more or less everything would have been different. He wondered if the loss had contributed to his mother's physical deterioration.

It was dreadful to drive home leaving his mother alone. It was dreadful but what else could he do? She was a lonely old woman deprived of adult love. She loved her children and her grandchildren, but she had no companion. It struck him she never had. How many times had he heard her say that she and his dad "got on; that was t'best you could say; we got on, more or less." What was wrong with getting on? It was better than being lonely. He was glad to get on with people. Most of his relationships had been about getting on. There was nothing perfect about any of them. Why should there be? Why should the wild, exorbitant ideal of romantic love be a reality? It was a childish wish for an absolute correspondence between your desires and the world beyond them, as if there was no need for a buffer, for a filter, for that chirpy, ironic, make-the-best-of-things, life-is-what-it-is-not-what-we'd-like-it-to-be acceptance which permitted the most pleasant feelings to flourish by not pushing them to extremes.

The following Saturday he arranged to devote the day to her. By ten o'clock he was sitting on the sofa facing the chimney breast where the gas fire was burning at its lowest. As usual there was no conversation. Her odd, convoluted, winding, impossible to follow monologues made his mind shut down. There came silence. She offered to make a cup of tea. He did it. At twelve she went into the kitchen to put a chicken breast in the oven. She would have a bit of boiled potato and some broccoli. She offered to cook for him. He declined. He could nip out for something if he was hungry. By two, when she'd eaten and was ready for a nap she said:

"There's no need to stay. I'll be all right."

It was true. She would. She followed the physician's advice as strictly as a nun the Pope's encyclicals. She ate no red meat, no biscuits, no cake, no eggs; she used only skimmed milk; she ate an apple and an orange every day, whether she wanted to or not. Every meal included fresh vegetables. She renounced entirely her beloved cheeses. Her walking regime began with the length of the path. She paced from her side door to the gate and back two or three times a day for the first week. In the second she ventured twenty yards down the pavement till, by small degrees she could manage the mile to *Tesco*. At first, she caught the bus back but in time she walked with a bag in either hand. She tried to keep them light. Sylvia came once a week with potatoes, carrots, parsnips, cabbage, broccoli, leeks, celery, turnip, cauliflower. She wouldn't permit Andy to bring them; he refused to accept any money.

Her recovery was remarkable. The doctor was delighted. She suffered no chest pain, no discomfort in her left arm. She lost a stone and a half. She was able to do the housework, bake her exquisite scones and take them to the church coffee bar in airtight tins, work for a couple of hours serving drinks and cakes, get home and make herself a good hot meal, without any discomfort; though she invariably fell asleep in the chair as she tried to watch the evening news. Yet she began to divest herself of life. She gathered ornaments from her mantelpiece, chest of drawers and window ledges, wrapped them in newspaper, packed them in carrier bags and handed them to Sylvia or Andy.

He brought them home and unwrapped them. There were three blue Wedgwood, heart-shaped dishes, decorated with white vines. Why had she passed them on? Did she think her life was over? Little by little most of the small luxuries which had adorned her bungalow were given away. Andy wanted to say to her: "Wait till your dead. You may live another twenty years. Don't hand over all these things that make you home nice." He knew he was wasting his time.

Elsie did think her life was over. In spite of feeling better once she'd lost weight than she did before her illness, she was convinced she wouldn't last long. The doctors were good. Their advice had made a big difference. She felt well. She could walk a few miles and glow afterwards. There were days when she felt tired, but she'd known those before the heart attack. She wondered if she'd avoided cheese and cakes and red meat years earlier she could have. Her mind always returned to fate. If god had decided it was her time, there was nothing she could do. If she'd had a heart attack, it was god's will. He had decided her life must come to an end. She must accept it. She was well now, but she'd been close to death. There was no point resisting what god wanted. He'd saved her. He'd allowed the doctors to do their work and bring her back to well-being. But it couldn't be long. Why would he send her a sign if he wanted her to live. She wouldn't see ninety-nine like her uncle. She might not even make seventy-eight like her father. It was right to get ready for death. Giving away her plaques, pictures, candle-sticks, photographs was a way of preparing for the next life. They would be useless there. She would be with god, her mother, her father, her lost relations and friends and most of all her beloved daughter.

Had she known she would live another thirteen years, she would have behaved differently. She was convinced death would arrive any day. She hoped it would be painless. She didn't want the discomfort of the heart attack again. Maybe god would let her fall asleep in her chair one evening and would take her soul to heaven without her body having to suffer. However it came, it couldn't be far away. Her heart had been badly damaged. The drugs were effective, but something would go wrong. She would soon be gone from the life which had caused her so much pain and confusion. She would be gone to glory.

For many years, she'd lived in the past. Once the years behind outnumber those ahead, it's almost impossible not to. Nothing is quite so ludicrous as people of seventy behaving as if they're twenty; as if the great adventures of life are to come. Ghoulish, face-lifted Americans, prancing around in leotards at seventy-five, only reinforce the sense of their lives being behind them. The refusal to age is a rejection of life. It is the strategy of those whose lives have never begun.

There was nothing to look forward to. If she turned her thoughts to the future, it was to think of her children and grandchildren. She wanted a better world for them. She still raged inwardly against the cruelty of her culture. She despised war and big business and injustice. For them she wanted a world of peace and co-operation. Yet whatever the world would be, and too often she feared it would be worse than the world she'd known, it wasn't for her. Her world was gone. It existed in her memories and they were her comfort.

She sat in her armchair looking out of the window and let her mind take her back to Marchand Street and Talbot Road. It was a good house, number sixty-six. Small but well built. The front window, though it gave directly onto the street, had leaded lights. So did the porch door. She was proud of them. They were a sign of the good taste which was important to her. Her family might be poor but they had the right values. They worked hard, kept things clean and disdained vulgarity.

Her dad was in his shirtsleeves in the front room, smoking his pipe and reading *The Daily Herald*. She liked to play at his feet. Her toys were few and simple. The whip and top didn't work well on the rug, but on the bare boards she could make it whizz.

"Look, daddy."

He turned from his paper.

"Aye, champion."

That was enough. It was all she could get from him but she didn't need more. Her mother was the talker, She could talk the hind legs off a donkey, as the adults said. She wondered if a donkey's legs would fall off if you talked to it too much. She listened to her mum who talked and talked and often had things to say which sounded important. Her dad said hardly anything, but when he did it seemed more important than what her mum said. She liked him being quiet. He was there. He was always there. She knew he would always be there. He didn't need to say anything.

The church was full. She was with her mother. Her brothers didn't come. She worried they would end in hell. The men's voices boomed when they said the Lord's Prayer. She loved the hymns. It was so lovely to sing with all the people:

"Father hear the prayer we offer

Not for ease that prayer shall be...."

No, she didn't want ease. Her dad didn't have ease and her mum worked very hard. Was that living courageously? She thought so. It was good to be brave and proud. She was brave and proud. She would never be like those people who let themselves go. She heard her mum condemn the men who were always in the pub. Wasting their money on booze. Leaving their children, to make fools of themselves by letting the beer talk. She heard her criticize people who didn't keep their front step clean. No one in Talbot Road was so poor they couldn't keep things decent. Elsie knew there was a kind of shame in being poor, but her mum and dad rose above it. They wasted nothing. They were good strong people in spite of their poverty. She put her hymn book on the pile as they left and took her mother's hand. They walked along Marsh Lane together. The sun was out and she skipped with happiness, even as they passed the pub.

Her dad came home with blood on his shirt. Her mum had to cut it off his shoulders. She bathed the wounds and made pads to sit under his jacket. He'd been taken on at the docks and might get another day's work. All day he'd carried timber on his shoulders. She stood and watched and wondered at the strangeness. She didn't want her dad to go to work if he came home injured. The docks were a funny place. She'd never been there. Henry said ships came from all over the world, from places she'd never heard of, and thousands of men had to unload them. She wondered why ships had to come from far away but she liked the idea of the sea. She would like to travel on a ship, across the seas to the places Henry spoke of.

Her dad said it was all mad. The world was going mad and it would end in war. Another war. Like the one before she was born. Her brothers would have to fight. What would happen to her? She looked at herself in the oval mirror set into the oak mantlepiece in the front room. She was a pretty girl. Everyone said so. She got a valentine. One of the boys in her class told her she was the prettiest girl he'd seen. She began to take care of her hair. In her best clothes for church she looked fine. She felt like a lady. You could be a lady even if you were poor. It was a matter of the way you behaved. She bought lipstick and nylons. There were no boys she thought handsome. There were good lads, but they didn't make her feel like she thought she ought to. She went into town on her own and men on Fishergate gave her looks. Jimmy was married. When would she get married? Who would it be? Marriage could mean all kinds of things. She might marry a man of any kind. She might marry a man of a superior kind who would work in an office and drive a car. She worried she was thinking selfishly, but boys liked her. She could take her pick.

She knew of Bert Lang. Her mum said they were a wild family. His mother was wild and her sister. His grandfather was a boozer. They were people to stay away from. When she met him for the first time she thought her mum might be wrong. He had a nice smile. He was smart. She knew he'd been called Pongo. But he was clean and his hair was combed. He smiled at her and his voice was warm and deep. It wasn't Christian to judge. It wasn't his fault if his mother was wild and his grandad always in the pub. He was quick and decisive in his movements. But the war was starting. He was signing up for the RAF. All the boys were going away. They might never come back. Her brothers might never come back. There shouldn't be war. Her dad said it was all about money. It was always about money. It was evil that people would kill one another for money.

Cars passed along St Anne's Road but she didn't notice. Her leg rocked, rocked. Her surroundings became dim. She had no connection to the world as it was. It had left her behind. Andy had offered to buy her a computer and show her how to use it, but she had no desire to master one. He said she'd be able to send e-mails, to keep in touch easily with all the family and her friends. She had a telephone, and anyway, if people could send her messages by computer, maybe they'd be less likely to visit. She liked people in the flesh. She liked to see their faces and hear their voices.

Mary was helping her in the kitchen. She was attentive, neat and happy having something to do. Elsie showed her how to use the rolling pin to stretch the pastry. Her daughter handled the big, wooden roller in her small hands. Her fingers were long, like Elsie's mother's. She sprinkled a dust of flour from the blue paper bag and rolled on, forgetting herself. How happy she'd been then. Her two young children always with her. Mary not yet in school. Even Bert, who annoyed and frustrated her because of his desire to get on, his failure, as she saw it, to find happiness in what was at hand, was a sweet presence. She was convinced she had no favourite among her children. Yet the three years when Mary had been her only child had established a special bond. She was a good child. Elsie pondered it. Was it because she was a Christian? Was it because she was taken to church? But Henry had been taken to church and no one could say he was good. He wasn't bad, but he didn't have the blithe, even temperament and concern for the feelings of others Mary showed. Was it born into her? How could that happen? Was it the holy spirit? Did it come from her family? Was it something inherited from her father?

She was at a loss. She didn't know how inheritance worked. She had a sense, vague and culled from she didn't know where, that everyone was born the same. Yet that couldn't be true. She wasn't like Henry. He wasn't like Jimmy. Were they born different or made different? The ideas were too confusing: she ran to the simplicity of her faith. We were as the good Lord made us. He'd made Mary a pleasant, willing, caring child. She never gave Elsie a moment's trouble.

Her head lolled. She fell asleep and dreamed of throwing Bert out on the street. She locked the door against him. She was safe with her family. There was a new house. Money was floating in through the windows and down the chimney. The vicar asked her where it had all come from. The police appeared. She sat on the sofa as they wrote in their notebooks. She was holding Mary's hand as they walked to school. A letter arrived. Her daughter was expelled. All the other girls were laughing at her. Elsie was scrubbing a school corridor. The walls were smeared with excrement. Andy came into the house carrying a big silver cup and his tennis racquet. She told him there was no room for it and sent him to give it back.

When she woke she experienced, as usual, a few seconds confusion. She didn't know the day, the time, where she was. There was a curious liberty in that blank, along with panic. She looked at the clock. Had she eaten? It was time to make something. It was Tuesday. She must bake some scones for tomorrow.

Andy Lang too was thinking about the past. He'd become a teacher partly out of subversive intent. He'd read, like many of his contemporaries, *Teaching as a Subversive Activity*. It didn't convince him, in all its arguments, but its drift was appealing. As were John Holt., Ivan Illich and A.S. Neill. That the education system was a means of control, that's its hidden curriculum was more important than its overt, was taken for granted by most of his contemporaries at university. They talked long into the night of how the system should be changed: let children learn what interests them. Let education be a thread pupils follow wherever it may lead. Let the idea of pupils as vessels to be filled with content which was to be poured out in exam rooms be consigned to the past. He and Rob Brown had talked over and over about the stupidity of exams. Peter Greig had published an essay calling for exams to be scrapped.

What had happened to all that? It had evaporated like a puddle in the sun. He was stunned how quickly and thoroughly the culture had transformed. His colleagues were buried beneath the OFSTED dung heap. No one dared think beyond league tables, national curriculum levels, the next inspection. Everybody, more or less, knew it was wrong, but hardly anyone resisted. He didn't hear people in the staffroom praising OFSTED or rhapsodising about having to complete a database of levels. They complained. They moaned. They despaired. They went along with it.

He was formed in a time when going along with it was in question. The protests about Vietnam, the events in Paris in 1968, trade unions trooping in and out of Downing Street, the beginning of the collapse of deference, the atmosphere which rejected the dim assimilation of received ideas, had left him convinced the future lay with greater equality, democracy and the spread of responsibility to the ordinary people.

It had all turned sour. What he was part of was hilarious and tragic. Hundreds of thousands of educated adults, many very experienced, were complying every day with what they knew to be senseless, stupid, wasteful, ignorant, because they feared for their jobs. He'd watched as David Blunkett threw two thousand quid in the gutter and defied teachers not to get on their hands and knees and scramble for it. They did. He believed they should have refused to apply. They should have torn up the forms. If the entire profession had refused to have anything to do with it, Blunkett would have been left looking daft. But lucre had too much lure. People were prepared to crawl for it. They would demean themselves for it. They would prostitute themselves for it. It was a sickening spectacle.

"It was simply a way of the government giving us a pay increase," said Colin Black, one of his NUT colleagues who he met at a reps' day. "They had to justify it to the public, so they introduced the threshold. It makes it look like they're getting their pound of flesh."

"You think they won't?" said Andy.

"Not if we fight."

Andy threw back his head and laughed. Colin looked up sharply from his plate of beef curry.

"We didn't need to fight," said Andy leaning over the table, his eyebrows raised, "all we had to do was tear up the forms."

"You can't expect people to give up the chance of two thousand quid," said Colin.

"Why not?"

"It's what people work for."

"Then how do you expect them to fight?"

"Case by case. When they turn people down, we'll fight it."

"You roll over, you debase yourself for a bit of lucre, you accept their argument that all you work for is money, and then you talk about fighting. No one filled in that form saying, "I hope everyone else gets the money." They all did it saying: "I hope I get it. What happens to anyone else is none of my business." It's like the lottery. No one buys a ticket hoping their neighbour will win. Lucre sets people against one another. That's what they've done. There won't be a fight that'll overturn this. There'll be the opposite. This is performance pay writ large. Before long teachers will be in Heads' offices being told why they don't deserve a pay rise."

Colin shook his head vigorously. He was a small, bald man who wore thick glasses. One of those working-class kids who'd been kicked upstairs by the 11-plus, he was Head of Maths in a big comprehensive, a long-standing union and Labour Party activist.

"That will never happen. The union will never allow it."

"The union is its members, Colin, and they won't stop it."

"They will with the right leadership."

"No, they won't. They'll do what the common folk always do: submit."

"That's a defeatist attitude."

"I'm not a defeatist, Colin. I refused to apply to go through the threshold because it's demeaning. I do my job and then I have to prove that I'm doing my job and if some bureaucrat judges I'm not, I don't get a pay rise? It's straight out of Kafka."

Colin looked up again, puzzled.

"There have to be standards."

"Now you're talking like a boss."

"The union has never been opposed to national standards and inspections."

"That's not what it's about, Colin. It's power. Control. It's the vicious revenge of John Major and the rest of the Tory Party for the success of comprehensive schools. It's irrational. Genuinely mad. They'd rather destroy the education system than admit comprehensive education is an improvement."

"We won't let them do that."

"Whose we?"

"The union."

"You know what's wrong with unions, Colin?"

The little man pushed his glasses up his nose and met Andy's eyes. His plate was empty. He drank from his glass of water.

"What?"

"They entrench the relationship between employer and employee."

"They try to improve that relationship."

"There we are, let's improve our relationship, says the angler to the worm," said Andy, remembering Brecht.

"There'll always be employers."

"Five hundred years ago people said there'll always be vassals."

"We have to keep fighting. One battle at a time."

"The members aren't fighting, Colin. The people I work with aren't fighting the system, they're trying to get on in it. How many teachers voted for Thatcher? How many bus drivers and postmen and school cleaners? That's not fighting, it's being cowed. The system is always in crisis and its always the common folk who have to suffer. Have you noticed?"

"You're right. But it isn't always in crisis and we've made gains. You can't do everything at once."

"No, but you can do one thing: refuse to submit."

"That's what the union's for."

"I wish it was. Look how the rich behave. When the stock market booms or unemployment is low they congratulate themselves on their fine system. But when the bust comes and millions are on the dole, do they admit their system is a bag of shite? No, they blame the common folk. They cut spending on the NHS, schools, social care, local councils. They say the people have to tighten their belts. They punish the common folk, and what do the common folk do? They vote for their own punishment. There isn't an ounce of rationality in it. People blame themselves and kiss the feet of their oppressors. You should read Kafka, Colin."

"Who's Kafka?"

"A Czech novelist who understood that when a system punishes people, they feel guilty."

"I don't feel guilty."

"Why should you, you're Head of Maths."

Colin bridled and Andy realised he'd gone too far. The mathematician got up, his plate in his hands.

"I'm going to look at the desserts."

Andy finished his vegetarian chilli and went outside. The hotel had extensive gardens and a centre where people bought compost, hanging baskets and bedding plants. He wandered the paths, his hands in his pockets. He hadn't intended to insult Colin personally, but it was true that if you were going to make the arguments that mattered, people were going to be offended. Into his head came the eighteenth century thinkers he'd read at university. Diderot and Beaumarchais and Voltaire were offensive to the church, the nobility and the aristocracy. The offence to the clergy was also an offence to the lowly folk who put their faith in it. The revolution hadn't been effected by the peasants sunk in superstition who thought the priest was in direct contact with god. It was a small group of educated Parisians, angry at their exclusion from decision making which brought down the *ancient regime*. The intellectuals and artists who helped ferment the uprising had to be offensive.

It was impossible to make the argument against the prevailing arrangements without offending people; maybe the majority. He'd offended Colin by suggesting he'd compromised with what he claimed to oppose. But it was true. Andy had tried to do the same. He'd sought promotion for money and status in a system of money and status he despised. Such was the trap.

There had to come a point at which you made the choice. It wasn't accidental that Andy had been thwarted. Cooper recognised his sensibility. A conformist who would have worn red underpants if the State or the church had ordered him, he shuddered at Andy' sensibility. Agreement must be total or not at all. Andy was a known atheist and leftie. That was enough to jar Cooper's nerves into opposition.

Beneath the rhetoric of democracy was a steel hand gripping your balls. For women it was worse. Beneath the rhetoric of democracy was the imminent threat of sexual assault and the ceaseless demeaning of female identity to tits, cunts and arses. The rhetoric of democracy was a fraud because identity was against it. People were slaves. For democracy to flourish, they had to cease to be afraid of their employers. It was the relation between employee and employer which was the core of the problem. Till that was reformed out of existence, democracy was a joke.

The following Sunday he visited his mother. It was duteous rather than pleasurable. He would have liked to spend a few happy, affectionate hours with her, talking about nothing; but she was unavailable. As ever she began her rambling monologue while he sat and pretended to listen. What had destroyed her capacity for ordinary communication? What had driven her to this insanity of word-spilling without connection? He marvelled in horror at how denatured she'd become.

This was his mother who he'd loved intensely as a little boy but never been able to reach. That odd perception he'd had as a child of life having been postponed, the thought that people were playing parts in some mad drama which must surely soon be exposed as a joke, came to him once more. He realised that was how his child's brain had dealt with the artificiality of his culture. It was all artificial. There was nothing genuine about it. It was a culture founded on the denial of what it means to be human. How could it be that humankind had the capacity to destroy its own nature? Our nature is cultural. We evolved to live in social groups, so all our capacities need a social trigger, like language. This gave us the capacity to go wrong, and we did. We denied our nature in the pursuit of the conquest of the planet for the purpose of amassing wealth. We had become rich ghosts.

There was no reason why material abundance had to entail the destruction of the best in our natures; that simple capacity for love; life organised around nurture; but our brains were not of our making and we'd elaborated a culture which ignited ingrained negative reactions. His mother was tormented by a sense of inferiority. She was divided against herself by a sense of guilt. Why? Because the culture told her she was inferior. She was born poor. The culture's message was that poverty was a fault. It was an inborn weakness. The poor were inferior by nature. That's why they were poor. The Tory Party was organised around the belief that the rich were superior by divine right. The Labour Party tried to help the poor but humiliated them by paternalism. To be born poor was to carry the indelible mark of inferiority. How could his mother have fought beyond it? She was given no chance. She was doubly inferior because she was poor and a woman. Her sense of inferiority wasn't some individual, psychological fault; it was the definition the culture imposed.

He knew the experience himself. Having failed the 11-plus he was deemed inferior by the grammar school girls and boys and their parents. Of course, Stu Archer and his other mates at the grammar had to acknowledge his skill with language. He outstripped some of them in French. They had to make an exception. He shouldn't have been sent to the secondary. Yet he knew that, all the same, they could never quite accept him as an equal. The superstition lingered that the system must be right. He must have some inborn inadequacy.

He'd had chances his mother had never known. He was male. He'd known the lush years after they moved to Penwortham when they lived in a lovely house and his did was earning well with ICI. He'd been to university and discovered he could hold his own with professors. He was cocky, no respecter of place and willing to stand his ground. Yet all the same, the system, in the personage of Cooper had done him down. Cooper with his pubic school and Oxbridge prejudices, his tight-gutted nervousness, his liability to be spooked by the least hint of non-conformism, his Anglican obedience and his witless faith in institutions had trapped him, corralled him, as if he was a wild colt which needed taming.

There was a quirk in the human brain: grant anyone an advantage, however small, and it set off some weird cascade of neurons which engendered an exorbitant sense of superiority. Pay a man fifty pence a week more than his neighbour and in the unexplored recesses of consciousness was formed, without conscious effort, the idea that the tiny distinction implied an unbridgeable gulf of superiority and inferiority. Give a woman three square yards of garden when her neighbour had nothing but a concrete yard, and some automatic process clicked in which elaborated a self-congratulating, high-handed mentality which convinced her she was a chosen creature and her lowly neighbour must be kept in her place.

Where did it come from?

He puzzled over it as his mother's voice continued in the background and her leg rocked with the regularity of a steam-driven piston:

"And er, and er..Well, we know what she's like. I said. I said to Ethel, crafty as a cartload o' monkeys that one. Mind you, she's no better. God 'elp us. She's wipin't surface in't kitchen at coffee bar and I says to her, I says: 'Ethel, dear 'eaven. What you usin' there? There's food to be prepared on that surface. You're just spreadin't bacteria around. Look at that. Put it in't bin. You'ave to disinfect it, wash it down. You'll not kill't bacteria that way. Dear 'eaven we'll 'ave folk goin' down wi' food poisonin'. Then where shall we be?' Well, you might as well talk to that wall….."

It seemed to him it must be some hangover from the time when any potential advantage needed to be responded to strongly. Had natural selection wired in an exaggerated response to any perceived superiority because it might be vital for survival? Was the human brain equipped with a mechanism which meant that the slightest favour made people arrogant, conceited, arbitrary? He wondered. Maybe in the conditions in which our biological ancestors evolved, it worked. People lived in small groups. There were virtually no hierarchies. There was no economic surplus. If a man could shoot an arrow better than the rest of his tribe or a woman find edible roots and tubers far more effectively, perhaps their sense of being special was shared; maybe it belonged to the whole tribe and brought benefit to everyone. But in our kind of culture, where people were divided from one another by money, property, class, opportunity, it became deadly. It became snobbery, racism, greed, arbitrary power, State tyranny, the assumed right of the few to exploit and denigrate the many; the whole miserable charade in which people concealed their heartbreak behind their privet hedges, their shiny cars, their double glazing and conservatories. Such was the dismal destination humanity had arrived at by failing to understand itself.

He was surprised at himself. Did he really believe humanity had cut off its own legs? Yes. Here was his poor mother, descended into near lunacy. He was here. Her son. He loved her still. Yet connection was impossible. She wasn't half-mad because of any innate failing, but because her culture had driven her mad. Her humanity had been denied. She'd been formed by a culture which instilled a sense of inferiority and guilt. Religion had terrified her as a little child. God was watching her. He read her thoughts. It was impossible to be autonomous. There was no territory where her selfhood could take root. Her mind was controlled from without. She had to police every thought for fear god would condemn her for it, as she had to be constantly, painfully aware of her poverty and its stigma.

It was her society which had divided her from herself. She ought to have grown with love and care. She ought to have known equality. She ought to have lived without crippling fear, guilt and humiliation. Life was one ought after another.

Sitting close by while she lapsed into her confused, eddying, unstructured word-spewing made him anxious. What was missing was an inner filter, a capacity to hold and organise her own thoughts and feelings. Of course it was missing. She'd been brought up to believe it was evil. Autonomy was sinful. Your mind belonged to god, which meant to the church and the school and the State. All she could manage of real selfhood was a desperate fighting upwards whose result was a brittle self-righteousness. A phrase came back to him from Jules Henry: *culture invades and infests the mind like an obsession.* Yes, when culture is at odds with our nature. Were human beings the only creatures who could do this? Apparently. We alone have evolved to be cultural to the degree that we can build a culture which destroys us.

It made him wonder about himself. His life had been untroubled before his parents' divorce. He recalled it as paradisal. He loved his family. Nothing serious ever troubled him. Yet he was aware of a fundamental anxiety. As he tried to focus all his mental energy, it occurred to him its source was his inability to establish a warm relation with his mother. For the first time he realised he had no memory of ever sitting on her knee, being cuddled, being read to. He couldn't recall her ever tousling his hair, kissing him on the cheek or forehead, telling him he was a good boy. He was shocked to think he'd never thought of it before.

He had memories of sitting on Mary's knee. If an image of her when he was a little boy was lodged in his mind, it was of her smiling at him, being kind and gentle with him, of his mere presence pleasing her. That broad, sweet and at the same time excited smile of Mary had been so important to him as a child. He recalled his dad reading to him. He could see himself nestled close to him on the sofa, his dad's arm around him, the big book with bright pictures on his knee. But there was no memory of physical closeness to his mother. She'd avoided it, as if an affectionate cuddle was intrusive.

He understood, by a supreme effort of concentration, that this was the source of an anxiety he could never eliminate. What little boy could fail to be cuddled by his mother and not have a lacuna at the core of his being? It was like a scar from a serious wound. He would always have it, yet it didn't bleed anymore.

There was no remedy. It would require another life to set things right. To dissolve and be reborn in different circumstances was the only way what had been wrong could be rectified. Wasn't that the source of his mother's fantasy of life after death? By believing in a renewal of life beyond life, she could live with the devastation of her selfhood her culture had inflicted. He asked himself if her damage wasn't partly self-inflicted. She'd made bad decisions. Very bad decisions. Everybody does. But it wasn't those which had ruined her. It was the context in which they were made, and for that she bore no responsibility. She'd been born into a poor family in 1922. Poor because her culture was organised around the greed of the rich. Her father had left school at twelve. Work was poorly paid and in the thirties, almost impossible to get. She'd been taken to church, sent to the school. There was punishment if you dared to speak. You could barely live without being punished. Born thirty years later, like him, she would have grown in different conditions. She would have had the chance of an education. She would have been a different person.

In different circumstances, he would have been a different person, as would everyone he knew. What was true of him was true, more or less, of all his friends, all the kids he'd grown up with. When he thought of Wheels, Duddy, Marek, Blackie, Matt Ross, Rob Brown, wasn't it true that their parents too exhibited a degree of cold distance? Wasn't this a social phenomenon? The warmth of physical affection was viewed as dangerous. What was important was for your kids to get on in the world, and what good was love for that? They were, in a sense, the loveless generation. Their parents housed and fed and looked after them, but there was a barrier. Love was conditional. It depended on doing well at school, adjusting to what was needed to succeed. Love was a kind of bribery.

The idea made him laugh to himself. Was he exaggerating? Were his ideas running headlong because there was no interlocutor to rein them? Maybe, but it was essentially true. Parents used coercion of one kind of another to make children conform. That had been the experience of everyone he knew. Oddly, his mother had been generous in that regard. She never exerted pressure to try to stop him growing his hair long or wearing Cuban heels. All the same, her hope was that he would be like her; that the centre of his life would be Methodism. It was true of all his friends and acquaintances: their parents were obeying a social injunction to ration love in order to drive their children to success; and what did success mean? Money. When everything else was stripped away, there was lucre. The motto of his culture might be: lucre before love.

Society imposed its needs and the individual brain responded. He really believed it was the brain. Most of what went on in his head was unconscious. Not in the Freudian sense of a sump where unwanted content was dumped, but the much simpler sense that our brains are wired by our biological inheritance and whirl away performing tasks we aren't aware of. We create our culture out of what biology has given, but as part of that is a need to be cultural, we create ourselves. It was inescapably paradoxical and complex, but it meant we could, over and over, mistake the cultural for the given. It was what he heard all around him: it was human nature to want money. There was a pecking order prescribed by god. Men should be breadwinners and women homemakers. Mind was what culture created from what biology had endowed and the collective mind of his society was sunk in illusion to the point of near-insanity.

Money was a drug. It was a shape-shifter. It fascinated and seduced. It represented all capacities. It reduced everything to its level. It was the universal whore and his culture had its head up her skirt. It intervened in every relationship. It was in the lovers' kiss, the bride's wedding vows, the parent's bed-time tucking in. There was no cranny it didn't occupy. It struck him as if he'd never realised it, though he'd turned it over in his head many times, that there was terrible contest between love and power abroad. The objective sign of power was money. Without money, there was no power. No one without money was powerful. The pursuit of money was a power struggle and love and power were sworn enemies.

His mind was cast back to Janice Eaves, Carol, Jane. Love and power. Weren't they more interested in the latter. He found a curious connection between love and politics which amused him: Janice, Carol and Jane came from Tory backgrounds. They were adjusted to existing circumstances. No one who put love before power could accept a system founded on money. Had they been real lovers, then like him they would have disdained their culture. He pushed the idea away because it seemed outlandish. Was he suggesting the whole culture was loveless? Surely there was a private realm where people could escape the culture's grip. Surely even a sunk-in-the-miasma Tory like Jane Bentnick could find an oasis of release, the capacity to escape herself, to find absorption in a life other than her own.

Yet when he rejected his original, shocking idea and was able to see it as if it came from elsewhere, it didn't seem too beyond-the-solar-system. Most marriages were more to do with property than affection. He thought back to Woodland Grove. Were the neighbours passionate, gentle lovers? Was there a pervading atmosphere of love? No, snobbery hung in the air like the stench from a sewage works and had a black family moved in, teeth would have been gnashed to powder. Most people were more proud of their house and car than of their spouse and children, and should the latter go astray, should a teenage girl find herself with an unbidden swelling belly, there was anguish and disowning. Where was the love in that?

Power drove out love like a virus chased away health. He'd gone through life wanting affection to be its guide. The love-in-friendship he'd felt for his mates, the erotic commitment to girl-friends was at odds with the culture's demands. To love was to be vulnerable, to cease to be on the *qui-vive*, to forget to treat everyone as a rival. The pursuit of money-power demanded ceaseless vigilance, constant self-supervision, relentless effort to stay ahead of the next man or woman. It was bound to turn off those parts of the brain which needed to light up for love. The culture's intent was to produce people whose central interest was money-power. Had it been to produce people whose central interest was affection, things would have felt very different.

How strange. He wondered how people would respond if they were asked: What is more important to you, love or money? His guess was people would choose love. Yet a more difficult question might tease out the truth: If you fell in love with a pauper, would it bother you? The poor made inadequate love objects. The poor were shunned. Most people, he speculated, fooled themselves. They were more attracted by money-power than human qualities, hence the women who handed their hotel keys to film stars and rock guitarists. The culture was awash with sentimentality. Sugary pop songs were poured into people's ears like poison into Hamlet's father's. All you need is love, sang some of the richest men in the world. This was the unhealthy water bubbling up from a blocked drain. It was only because love was so rare its simulacrum was sung about in order to fulfil pop stars' desire for money-power.

What held it together? Why was the culture able to do this? Who mediated the culture? Why wasn't it easy to overturn its lunatic assumptions? It made him think of his childish naivety. The time when he was a boy and believed everyone was a person of goodwill. It was only a matter of making them aware of the misguidedness of their ideas, and they would change. What a fool. But what a charming fool. Who would you want for a friend, someone who trusts in the essential good will of humanity, or a suspicious, wary misanthrope? Had he become the latter? No, but he knew goodwill didn't flow through people's veins like streams down mountains. Money-power turned it to venom. A passing incident drifted into consciousness: he was chatting to Vic Tetley-Mitchell, an English teacher, during a morning break. Tetley-Mitchell had trained in drama and was intending to mount a production of *Oh What A Lovely War*. Andy said he was interested and would give a hand, if he liked. His colleague became suddenly slightly aloof. A fortnight later Cooper an-

266

nounced in the staff meeting that Tetley-Mitchell was being promoted, having assumed responsibility for the school play. At once Andy understood the aloofness.

The culture was held together by its own false assumptions. Yet how had humanity taken such a wrong turn? Who, given the choice, would turn away from love, warmth and affection for the sake of lucre? Officially the culture believed in love. Love your neighbour as yourself. Another empty sentimentality. The reality was force. Violence was at the heart of it. The capacity for violence had evolved to ensure survival. Killing bison or woolly mammoths took some force. Everything that evolved is imperfect. Killing for meat was nature's solution in tough conditions. The tragedy was killing could be turned inward.

His mother was still talking. He hadn't absorbed what she'd said for some minutes.

"Eh?"

"Sorry?" he said.

"D'you want a cup o' tea?"

She was about to push herself to her feet.

"No," he said, getting up, "stay there, mum. I'll do it."

"I'm not helpless," she said."

"No, but I'm a fully grown, fit adult. You shouldn't be running after me."

"There's no cake. I can't eat it. I've not even any scones left. I took 'em all t't coffee bar."

She would have got up and waited on him. It was her expression of love. Always, it had taken these indirect forms. He wondered, as he added the drop of milk she permitted herself to her tea, why? Why couldn't he give her hug before he left? There was no doubt her love was no less deeply felt for being obliquely expressed, but it was enormously sad.

He placed her green mug on the little round mat decorated with roses on the low, dark-wood mantelpiece above her gas fire. He knew there was a terrible loneliness in her. It had been there when he was a little boy. It puzzled him. He knew the undemonstrative taciturnity of his grandfather had something to with it, but his mother's relations with his grandmother were hidden. He'd never known her. He'd never seen her move, or read her facial expressions or tone of voice. What had gone on between them? Had it instilled some visceral fear of physical signs of affection?

She was coming to the end of her life and he wished he could make her last years sweet. He was no different from that little boy who had lingered an hour in the gift shop trying to find something pleasing for her birthday. All his life he'd wanted to dissolve what seemed to him the knot of tangled feeling in her, to set free the lovely, warm woman he knew she could be. The tragedy was he could never reach her. She was forever, in some vital part of herself, cut off. He blamed her culture for it. The culture of money-power. It was his enemy because of what it had done to his mother and he would fight it ceaselessly.

She was talking again. She mentioned her brother Eddie.

"Ah, have you seen him recently?"

"Yes, they came round't'other Friday. They only stayed an hour but it were very nice."

The thought of uncle Eddie took him back to Talbot Road. He liked his joiner uncle. He was gentle and kind. He was glad he'd been to visit. She virtually never saw her brother Henry and Jimmy was long dead of lung cancer. There was a time when these people populated his inner landscape. He loved them all. His dad had got on well with Eddie and very much liked his boys. His mind went back to Marsh Lane. His father was a tragic figure too and for the same reason as his mother. What chance had he, born into poverty and drink in a dirt-and-scuffle part of the town? Yet his mother and father had found one another. For a time, for maybe quite a long time, there must have been love between them, however distorted its expression, however beneath what in better circumstances it might have been. Two tragic people ruined by money-power. Their lives were insignificant. They were the nobodies who made up the workforce, that were conscripted, the forgotten people whose names appeared in no annals, the fodder of history, the undifferentiated masses. But they were his parents. They were people he'd loved with all the exorbitant, unlimited love of a child for its mother and father. There were no statues to people like them, however virtuous they might be, however exemplary their lives. The rewards went to those who served money-power.

His father was dead, but he remembered him. He talked to his daughters about him. When his mother died, he would remember her and so would his children. They would talk to their own children about her and in that way her life would live on for decades. Even longer, perhaps, because he knew about his great, great grandfather, dead long before he was born. The meaning of a life didn't end with that life. He could rescue his parents from absolute obscurity, ensure that the layering over of history didn't wipe out completely what they had been.

Tragic people, but people whose lives could have been complete and healthy in every respect, had there been a culture to welcome and nurture them, rather than exploit, degrade and punish. He could keep their memory alive; but he could do more than merely talk to his children and hope they would talk to theirs. He was a writer. He was still struggling. Every opportunity seemed to be still-born. Yet he wouldn't give up. It was impossible to see a way through, but he must commit himself to what he was in control of. Publishing, reviews, the circus of literary prizes; all those were in other people's hands. What he could control was the writing. He must work and work and be tough enough to do without recognition. The work was everything. In his writing, somehow, he must rescue his mother and father.

He penned a few poems. He got half way through a play script. He didn't know it would take him years to get where he needed to be. He had no idea he would be an old man himself before the conception would become clear in his mind and he would open his laptop, sit with it on his knee and begin:

The shabby little terrace shared a wall with the mill so the drumming rattle of the looms was always slightly audible…….

www.ingramcontent.com/pod-product-compliance
Lightning Source LLC
Chambersburg PA
CBHW052024020726
47501CB00004B/1222